PACE

PACE

by

K.M. Halpern

Epsilon Books

ISBN-13 (Paperback): 978-1-945671-04-3

ISBN-13 (Hardcover): 978-1-945671-05-0

ISBN-13 (Kindle Ed.): 978-1-945671-06-7

Library of Congress Control Number: 2018910948

Published by Epsilon Books

Printed in the United States of America

Cover Art and Design by Jeff Brown

DISCLAIMER: This is a work of fiction. If it weren't, we all would have much bigger problems than worrying about who wrote what about whom. Nonetheless, since it seems obligatory to state the obvious, any resemblance of characters in this work to real individuals, living or deceased, is purely coincidental.

CHAPTER 1

Day 6 — Glasgow, Scotland

Elise Broderick was a pragmatic woman. At 41, she had been through plenty of scares and had read of many more. She remembered when people thought some crazy American would take the cold war hot. Then there were the disease scares — mad cow and SARS and avian flu and resistant Mumps. Inevitably, a vaccine was found or the anticipated pandemic just petered out. There had been one stretch in the late 20-teens when the BBC decided to mimic America, and every drizzle was Superstorm this or Deathcyclone that. With all the terrorists and epidemics and natural disasters, it was a wonder that anybody survived an average day. But she somehow had muddled through quite a few.

Of course, the best trick was to keep the telly off. But Elise needed it. Her strategy was to treat everything like a BBC drama. The news turned out to be less threatening when you knew that things would work out a few episodes down the line. Under the new government, the BBC newscasters had returned to their traditional stoic understatement, even as American TV kept reaching new fever pitches of hysteria. Elise suspected she would not have done well in America; there didn't seem any way to tune out the noise. But here, she could pretend. Except for the internet.

It may just have been Elise's imagination, but the time between new doomsday rumors seemed to be shrinking. When she was young, the memes had been light-hearted: a bunny saying something rude, a farting cartoon character. But at some point, they had taken a dark turn. There was a pedophile stalking your kids, some deadly batch of drugs, a food that would kill you. The world was back to death, disease, and destruction. And it just went downhill from there. The internet hadn't grown up, it just seemed to be stuck as a sullenly nihilist teenager.

Elise would have liked to believe there were people behind this, some cabal which decided to push a dark agenda; perhaps those crazy news people had metastasized to the internet. But deep down she suspected it was nothing that complicated. Maybe this just was where *every* medium ended up. The people who spoke loudest were the craziest, and all the sane people just changed the channel, leaving a vertiginous suet of bile. It's what people want, what people are. Whatever the reason, there wasn't anything cute or cuddly about internet rumors anymore. Unless you hid in some quiet, sane corner of the web, everything was gloom and doom. And there seemed to be fewer and fewer quiet, sane corners of the web.

However, even by internet standards, all sorts of crazy rumors had been gaining real momentum lately. Worse, Elise was hearing them reiterated by ordinarily sensible neighbors, the sort of people who probably didn't even know how to use the internet. So much for isolation. The rumors didn't seem to contain much concrete information, but their abundance and consistency pointed to a real underlying cause. 'Chatter' in intelligence parlance, Elise recalled from some TV documentary. You had to listen to the chatter. She listened to chatter every day in her shop, and had yet to spot any intelligence. Or meet any. She had a laugh at this. Indeed.

In the present case, however, there were other signs something was afoot. The government had ordered a media blackout regarding whatever was happening nearby. Of course, the internet was beyond anybody's control and wasn't really 'media'. They couldn't shut it off without causing much bigger problems. As everybody knew from that debacle a while back, attempting to censor sites just wasn't feasible.

As was typical, there had been no official announcement

beyond the blackout itself. The British telecoms would comply with the ban, but it was empty lip-service at best. Everybody knew you could just route around them. There were plenty of other sources, but none of those sources seemed to be saying anything meaningful. Of course, just because there was a media blackout didn't mean anybody knew anything worth blacking out. Rumors and conspiracy theories ran amok; they were the currency of the internet, after all. But there was nothing consistent. Usually all the chatter was *about* something. Here they didn't even know what there was to talk about.

In the meantime, ordinary programming and news continued in all other regards. There was no alien invasion or nuclear war or massive disaster. Whatever was going on was local. From what Elise gleaned, something had happened — either an outbreak of some disease or a reactor meltdown (did they even have them in this area?) or something like that. Maybe some crazed militia was having a standoff with the police. That sort of thing mostly happened in America, but who knew. No doubt the blackout had been intended to avoid panic and rumor-mongering, but it had precisely the opposite effect. Sometimes, not knowing was worse than any possible knowing. She wondered whether this really were true.

Elise had grown up in the outer suburbs of Glasgow and, like many of her friends, never married. She was, according to statistics continually cited by the current government, part of the proximal cause of population decline. Or, she was until recently. She just had passed the age when having a first child became a very risky proposition, even if one managed to conceive. No, they now would have to rely on other sensibly disillusioned youth to make up their statistic. Elise had no doubt that she now contributed to some other citable social ill. She had no regrets on either account.

Children never had appealed in her youth, and she decided that if she had an epiphany later in life she simply would adopt. Elise was grateful that the notion of spinster didn't really exist any more. She wasn't some lonely old lady, knitting whilst dreaming of the prince who never came, the subject of a Beatles elegy. She owned a shop, had friends, even the occasional boyfriend. Hers was a deliberate choice based on economics, lifestyle, and the state of the British educational system. Even if she had a child, it would have been too difficult to raise him (or her, it could have been a her, but she always imagined a boy for some reason) the way she intended. There were too many constraints, rules, mandates governing every aspect of motherhood.

Perhaps if rich she would have considered it, but Elise simply couldn't imagine sending the kid to State School, where he'd get crapped on for speaking well and probably end up a chav or worse. Elise wasn't a snob, she was of humble origin. But she *did* value education and comport, things that the present system did not. The result of this and many other concerns was that she remained childless. The fact that she never found the right guy probably contributed as well, but less than one would suspect. She had early realized that there was no 'right' guy, that the right guy was a myth foisted on you, a romantic fairy tale well-intended, but which invariably led one astray. There were no right guys or good jobs. You lived, you worked, and if you were lucky you had a little something you cared about that wouldn't break your heart. And this was precisely how it had worked out for her. Shop, no kid.

There were benefits to being a successful shop owner, one of which was that she had the opportunity to converse with many people. Better still, hers was a flower shop, so she interacted with people from all walks of life. And most, but not all, were happy when they came in. The flowers were imbued with optimism, for that night or beyond. Even when the occasion was sorrowful, the flowers could evoke a bittersweet sentiment, a recollection or nostalgia. It was romantic to imagine that the scent of beauty opened hearts, unlocked feelings, elevated and ennobled. Elise had studied botany and knew this to be nothing more than a neurological response to certain olfactory triggers, but the existence of a clinical explanation didn't matter. There remained romance in beauty, whether easily explicable or poetic enigma.

The rumors Elise heard formed an enigma, but not a poetic one. She had no children to worry about, and her family mostly seemed to have congregated around Aberdeen and Edinburgh over the years. Nobody really stayed in Glasgow forever, unless they happened to own a shop there. Edinburgh was by far the more beautiful city, and Elise acknowledged this every time her parents urged her to move there. Which was pretty much every time she saw them. Once they had given up on grandchildren, they turned their attention to *her*. Surely, she would be a good daughter and move to Edinburgh, they needed her nearby in case something happened, they weren't young anymore, and so on. She was only a two-hour bus ride away, but apparently that wasn't good enough. They wanted her *there*, with them. Perhaps they did have that old-fashioned view of her as a spinster.

Even if the shop hadn't kept her there, Elise had no intention of moving to Edinburgh. Her friends were in Glasgow, her life was in Glasgow, and her parents weren't in Glasgow. For all its charms, Edinburgh was too ... she couldn't say provincial, it *was* the seat of government. No, it just was too small, too touristy. Edinburgh was fun to visit, but Elise would get bored there. For all its many flaws, flaws which everyone everywhere liked to harp on, Glasgow was a real city. It had what she needed. If you are not going to create life, you need to surround yourself with it. And this was what she had done. She could find dozens of places to sip wine at 10 PM. She could go out to new restaurants all the time and never run out. And most importantly, she had a circle of friends. People like her, not 70-year-olds. She wouldn't say she loved Glasgow, but it was the only city in Scotland for her. Well, the only city in Scotland, period. Maybe she would move to London one day, if she could afford it. That's what her sister had done, minus the affording it.

To Elise, disease sounded like the scariest scenario, and the most plausible. Maybe somebody brought something horrid back from a third world country, or even Iceland — she'd seen a movie like that once. Whatever the disease, Elise suspected it had been brought by immigrants. Like most people, she had nothing against immigrants in the abstract, only in the concrete. She wanted to help people find better lives, offer refuge to refugees, be a good Christian and person. The problem always arose when you stepped back from the general notion of helping your fellow man and saw just whom you were helping.

The refugee influxes from various Middle Eastern wars had brought their share of problems. Elise didn't fear, as did many, that the cultural integrity of Scotland would be swept away. It had been swept away a half-dozen times since the Romans first invaded. She just didn't like the poverty and dirtiness and crime. It felt to her that Scotland was being punished for being kind-hearted, for letting in large numbers of refugees. Before they seceded from the UK, Scotland had been bound to adhere to its parsimonious quotas. The UK had adopted a policy of stymieing almost all immigration, and Elise always had felt this to be mean-spirited. But Scotland's secession had freed them to do as they saw fit. By agreement, the borders between the two countries had been kept open; however, the UK (for it had retained that name) would only allow real Scottish citizens to cross freely. This was a consequence of Scotland's generosity.

When the UK and most of the EU refused the refugees, and the US made its usual noises but did little, Scotland opened its doors to over 100,000 of them — a sizable fraction of its own population. There was plenty of space, but not plenty of jobs, and it remained a controversial decision even within the ruling SNP. Elise respected it, though she strongly disagreed with the mandatory integration policies. Why could nothing ever be accomplished in reasonable measure? Once the immigrants were absorbed, all sorts of anti-discrimination policies had been put into place — as if the very people who had voted to harbor the refugees were incapable of treating them well unless ordered to. This created tension, and resulted in the deterioration of large parts of Glasgow. Elise felt that Scotland had been a sucker, doing what needed to be done when nobody else was willing, and being punished for it. It certainly wasn't the fault of the immigrants, if anything it was the bigots in Whitehall and Brussels who were to blame. At least that was what she would have liked herself to believe.

Elise tried to keep an open mind, but could not help wondering what else was arriving with all these people, first from the Middle East, then from Africa. Unlike the politicians, she wasn't particularly worried about terrorists; there hadn't been a major attack for many years. Like most of her countrymen, she viewed them as vague bogeymen conjured by the government to suit its needs. But the immigrants could have brought *other* things, unintentional things. Things they didn't worry about back home, were long immune to, but which were deadly to their new neighbors. Wasn't that how the Bubonic plague started? Could that sort of thing still happen these days? You'd think with global commerce it wouldn't, but perhaps it was a function of sheer volume.

A customer came in, and Elise put aside such thoughts. It was Hew, an elderly pensioner who frequented her shop. She guessed he found solace in keeping fresh flowers around him. Or maybe he just was lonely. He smiled and squeaked in his usual unsteady voice, "the usual, Janice, please." She never understood why he insisted on calling her Janice. He knew her name. Maybe he was a bit senile. Maybe everyone was Janice to him. She wondered if it was the name of his wife or some lost love. To be successful, a shop owner must be able to deal with all sorts, never take umbrage, rarely judge.

Hew's usual was the "summer bouquet special", a variety of flowers that looked nice but didn't offer much scent, truth be told.

"Of course," Elise smiled, noting, "I'm afraid I'm going to have to go heavy on the Heather this time, all this nonsense up North has stopped our supplies."

"All this nonsense?" Hew asked in a quiet voice, peering at her sternly.

She never had noticed his sharp nose and piercing eyes. He must have been rather imposing when young. She could imagine him in a proper suit, managing a business meeting. Well, she supposed, *anybody* could look impressive if you tidied them up enough. She smiled disarmingly, another important tool of the shopkeeper.

Elise wasn't the type to say something simply to be agreeable, but she *had* learned to avoid arguments. It was an important trick, and involved only a smile, a raised eyebrow, and some silence. Not the fabled British awkward silence, but just enough to let the dust settle. This time, however, she was distracted and failed to follow that cardinal rule. Besides, he was a harmless old man who probably had a crush on her. His name wasn't really Hew, that's just how he introduced himself when they first met. He probably meant it as a joke, a play on her rapid-fire greeting: "How may I help you?" But for some reason, they had stuck with it. She asked his name once, his real name, and he had given it. What was it? Craig, she seemed to recall, or something like that. Arcraigsle, that was it. A proper Scottish name. Well, if she was Janine, he could be Hew.

"You know," she waved broadly in the direction of the

North, or at the linen shop across the street depending how one interpreted it.

"Ah, *that* nonsense," he laughed, almost a cackle, but quickly devolved into coughing.

"I'm sorry, do you have anybody up there?" Elise asked, suddenly concerned that she had been insensitive.

"Up North?" Hew asked with an appraising look.

"Yes. I just thought you may have been worried about somebody up there." She leaned in and grinned coyly. "I didn't mean to give offense."

Hew waved dismissively with surprising energy. "Don't be ridiculous. How could you give offense? To give offense you have to take offense first. Otherwise how would you have any to give?"

She couldn't argue with that, and laughed. "I suppose so."

"Up North," he grumbled, ignoring this acknowledgment. Suddenly he gave her a suspicious look. "Why would I have anyone up *North*?"

Elise felt horrible, and said nothing.

"Not for a long time," Hew mused distractedly. Suddenly he smiled at Elise and took her hand. "You're a nice lass, Janine."

She patiently extricated her hand. "Thank you." Did anybody really say "lass" anymore? Elise had learned some Scots in school, but it sounded so archaic outside the classroom.

Hew gave her a worried look and leaned in. "Listen, Janine. I've been around long enough to know a few things. Sometimes things that start small get big. They don't stop, no matter how much you want them to, no matter how much it hurts."

Elise didn't say anything, and waited for him to continue. Best thing with these old guys was to let them get it off their chest. Nod and accept their advice, even if it seems trite or makes no sense whatsoever. What was it they used to say? Ah, yes, the 'usages of age'. He was exercising his prerogative, the usages of age.

"It's always the thing you don't think of that gets you. When you're in a bar fight, it's not the big guy in front of you that takes you out. It's the little guy who clocks you from behind."

Somehow, she couldn't imagine him in a bar fight.

"And it's worse than that. The big guy is straightforward. He would just hit you until you went down. Then he's the winner, king of the hill. You're nothing more to him. But the guy behind you … he'll hit you with that beer bottle. Then he'll kick you in the face, gouge your eyes out, keep kicking you until your face is a mush of blood and gore and you don't have teeth. He'll leave you a cripple in a hospice."

Maybe indulging these old guys was the wrong approach. Things had taken a morbid turn. Elise could understand why, of course. At his age, Hew desperately wanted to seem dangerous and mysterious and knowledgeable. Anything other than old and helpless. But more importantly, this was how the world must look to him. A bunch of people getting their teeth kicked out. Maybe the little guy was a metaphor for time, or something.

Elise felt a bit uneasy and tried to dispel the tension, teasing, "Well, I don't see you getting into bar fights. Too much the gentleman, you are."

"It's nice of you to say so." He smiled, and leaned in with a conspiratorial air. "I was the one who came from behind."

Well, this chat had taken an ugly turn. Janine expected this sort of blather from the drunks who came in late at night to get flowers for that gal who tossed them out. They'd usually start sweetly plastered, but sometimes they'd end up playing out scenarios where she didn't take the flowers or had some other guy over.

Elise had heard all sorts of threats and plans. In those cases you had to use discretion. She only had called the police twice over the years, once when the guy seemed to be on something more than alcohol (probably PCP, she guessed) and once when she'd spotted a dual-cut blade in the man's belt. A dual-cut blade was a nasty bit of work: two razors strapped together, with a small gap. It was designed to leave a thin bit of skin between gashes, almost impossible to mend, guaranteeing a nasty scar for life. The football hooligans used them a lot in the old days, but they were pretty rare now. That guy clearly was planning some unpleasantness.

A cop later told her he was some sort of petty gang-member from down South. Elise worried for a while that he'd be back, but apparently he was killed a few weeks later in a brawl. Those two were exceptions, however. All the other times, she figured it just was a drunken rant. They'd have half of Glasgow in jail if they arrested every drunk who said something stupid. That's what they did in America, maybe England too, but not here.

In this case, Elise wasn't worried for herself or anyone else. But she didn't like the tenor of the conversation. She also was concerned about letting this frail old man get too worked up. She replied soothingly, "there, there, I'm sure that all sorts of nasty things happen, so it's best to avoid fights altogether." This was a mistake.

Hew looked at her sharply. "Don't patronize me, young miss." But he quickly softened. "It's just that I know about these things."

Yep, she thought, every old man knows about everything. Most of the young guys she dated seemed to think they did too, so maybe it wasn't just age.

"Like what's going on up North?" she asked curiously.

He looked around for a second to make sure nobody was listening, and then leaned in. "You'd do well to head out before the rush. I've seen things — back in the wars, and other places. Things can get ugly in a hurry, especially in the cities." After a moment, he added thoughtfully, "Of course, countryside has its own problems," before looking up earnestly and taking her hands again. "Best head out before things get hairy. It won't be long. It never is."

Once again, she gently released her hand, this time on the pretext of wrapping some flowers. Conversing while working was second nature to Elise, and she had been cutting, arranging, and wrapping the whole time. She handed Hew the completed bouquet. "That will be 11.95, if you please". The first few hundred times she had used that phrase, back when she apprenticed at another florist across town, it felt so awkward. It sounded odd and distant, and she almost hoped a customer would respond that, no, they didn't please. So far, it hadn't happened.

Hew raised an eyebrow. "Price went down?"

"No, I was short of flowers, so you get a discount."

Nonetheless he gave her the usual 13.95, carefully counting out the change. Sometimes when there were other customers behind him, she found this process infuriatingly slow. But today they were alone.

"So are you going anywhere yourself, Craig?" Elise wasn't sure why she used his real name all of a sudden.

He looked at her. "At my age? Where would I go?"

She laughed. "And where would *I* go? I've got a shop and friends here. I have a life here."

He raised an eyebrow. "No, you have a life *here*," he poked at her heart, though it seemed suspiciously close to her left breast. "Take it while you still do."

As he left, she raised the money in her hand and called out, "Thank you, Craig."

He turned with a concerned look. "Remember what I said — it always gets worse. Never better, always worse. Run before it's too late. You can come back if I'm wrong."

On his way out he whispered, "Goodbye, Elise."

The riots started that night.

CHAPTER 2

Day 843 — Near Denver, Colorado, 1 AM

There was something about a crisp night in the mountains. This place once had been awash in light and life, a destination. *The* destination for skiing, snowboarding, and a host of activities. Night after night, a nonstop queue of cars would sit here, waiting to get through the bottleneck, lights glimmering, an occasional honk muffled by the snow. Now, all was dark.

In two hours a luminous wedge of moon would permeate that calm, lending an eerie, almost necrotic sheen to the landscape. But that too only would last a few hours before the sun washed it away. To Dwight's mind, this was the most dangerous time, when the heart thinks it's day but the mind knows it to be night, with all its attendant dangers. One thing he had learned hiking and hunting was not to trust the moon, a deceptive patroness. She may illuminate a path, but her light offered no warmth, no hope. One could freeze to death beneath a full moon as easily as beneath the stars. And shadows were distorted, things were not what they seemed.

There was some truth to a universal lunacy. It was moonlight that made you listen for something to fear. The distant cry of a baby or the barely audible growl of something that shouldn't be there, all the nightmares unlearned as adults. Nights like this had spawned those German fairy tales, and their ancient counterparts in languages unwritten or lost to time. They all were the same. *It* was coming to get you as you shivered, defenseless in the woods.

Dwight laughed. This was true. It *was* coming to get him. And it was implacable and murderous and far worse than any of those tales. But he knew where it was, or at least where it would come from. As he peered into the woods and the

13

wreckage of what had once been a highway of romance, he realized that this made all the difference. He still was afraid of what was out there, that it was coming for him right now. But mostly he was afraid that he didn't really know *what* it was. Nobody did. Dwight shook himself off, along with his melancholy, zipped up, and headed back to the cabin. He made his way in the dark to the bunk and almost tripped over his rifle. That was foolish; he had forgotten it when he went to take a piss. Not that it would have mattered. What was coming wouldn't arrive for a while, and nothing could stop it. The rifle was to deal with what may come first, driven in terror before it. As he got into bed, Dwight glanced at the barely visible forms on the only other two occupied bunks. At least here he wouldn't die alone.

CHAPTER 3

Robert Halifax clutched a satchel of papers. He would much rather have his tablet, but all electronics had been banned. There were certain downsides to cameras on every piece of consumer gear, and one of them was security. He understood the need, but was annoyed nonetheless. Robert had been given a mere two hours notice, and had squandered most of it trying to get the drivers for his old printer working. The rest he had spent frantically trying to print everything that conceivably could be useful.

Support teams like SQ7 never were invited to anything meaningful; they just provided certain useful data. Robert never had met anybody from the Joint Command, much less been privy to a session. From the atmosphere when he arrived, he could tell this was no ordinary meeting. After a thorough search and scan, he was ushered into a small room where two women and a man in suits were seated at a cheap plastic folding table. They looked bored. They looked like lawyers. The left one thumbed through some papers until she found a sheet.

"John Durnier?" she asked unenthusiastically.

"Um, no, Robert Halifax," he answered, inexplicably embarrassed that he wasn't John Durnier. Had he been invited by mistake? The woman flipped through some more pages, and then drew one forth. She perused it quickly, and gave a brief, forced smile but offered no apology for the mix-up. Without ceremony, she launched into a drab recitation.

"In addition to the ordinary responsibilities attendant to a security classification of AC3, you temporarily and solely for the purpose and duration of this meeting will be granted and accept all responsibilities of AC8 clearance."

The sentence didn't even make grammatical sense. Robert was a bit of a stickler for language, and legalese always annoyed him. English had been his minor in college, though nobody really seemed to care around here. The government had its own magical jargon. It made sense to somebody somewhere he was sure, but not to him or anybody he ever had met. It dispensed with articles, repurposed verbs, deployed and rendered and mitigated, among other travesties. The military did to language what a military is supposed to do: destroy. And this was the best of both worlds, a military lawyer.

Robert made his best effort not to mentally correct the woman as he listened to a lengthy recital of his responsibilities. They appeared to be the same responsibilities associated with an AC3 clearance, but couched in stronger words and with more injunctions not to mess up.

When she had finished, the woman rotated a clipboard toward him and pushed it across the table. A pen was attached to the table by a chain. Just like a doctor's office Robert thought, and couldn't help but smile. Apparently, he could be trusted with the nation's secrets but not with a pen.

"Is something funny?" the middle lawyer asked, raising his head. He looked like he had been reading a document while his colleague delivered her monologue, but he very well could have been asleep.

"Sorry, not funny," Robert responded apologetically, eyeing the pen. The lawyer glared at him for a few seconds, then shot a meaningful glance at the woman who had lectured him, before returning to reading and/or sleeping.

The first lawyer looked at Robert sympathetically and suddenly reached across the table, covering the pen with her hand before he could pick it up.

"Listen, this may all seem dumb to one of you tech hipsters, but I'll put it in simple words. You're going in there. You fuck up, you die. Got it?"

She smiled and leaned back, releasing the pen. Robert looked at the form. It only had one paragraph and a slot for his signature.

"This doesn't say all the stuff you just went through," he objected.

"Doesn't have to," the middle lawyer chimed in without looking up from his document.

Robert guessed that he was the boss. The two women who flanked him weren't particularly good-looking and something about them seemed less elegant, though the one on the right clearly paid more mind to her appearance. Or maybe she just was thinner. The man, on the other hand, had a very classy looking suit and watch and seemed well-groomed.

"Just sign it," the left lawyer sighed, "we've got to get through twenty more of you."

"And what if I don't?" he asked, putting the pen down defiantly. Or at least what he thought of as defiantly. Robert was not cut out for defiantly. He knew this, and everybody he met knew this.

"We find some nerd who doesn't want to end up homeless and unemployable within the week," the right-most lawyer offered sweetly. Her voice definitely was that of the archetypal television lawyer-bitch.

Robert knew there was no point in refusing; he already had signed so many nondisclosures and codes of conduct and heaven knew what else that they could prosecute him just for breathing the wrong way if they wanted to. But he felt he shouldn't just do as they asked without getting something in return. Even if he really wouldn't be giving them anything they didn't already have, it should be more of a negotiation, a give and take. As if anything with the government could be.

"What is this about anyway?" he asked as he pushed the signed form back to the left lawyer. He tried to sound as casually interested as possible, a client chatting with equals, but it came off as squeaky and diffident.

The left lawyer ignored him and banged on the door. The same soldier who had ushered Robert into the room now escorted him out. They proceeded down a hall until they reached a large pair of worn oak doors. Before entering them, Robert was passed off to one Captain Raymond.

The Captain wasn't discourteous, but had the type of intensely engaging personality that invariably puts people on edge. His unblinking stare bothered Robert, who looked down and to the right. He had read somewhere that this was considered submissive behavior in the animal kingdom, and wanted to kicked himself for it. But he didn't get the sense that the Captain derived any satisfaction from successfully dominating him. In fact, the man didn't even seem aware of it.

"So they've explained it to you clearly?" the Captain asked in a surprisingly mellow voice.

"Um what? I still don't know what this is about."

The Captain clarified unhelpfully, "your security obligations."

"Yeah, everything is secret, and nothing leaves this room." Robert tried to make it sound like a joke, but was worried it may have come across as sarcastic. The Captain didn't notice.

"That's right. You've never been in a meeting like this, so I'll explain protocol. You'll sit in a group behind your division head."

"I've never met...," Robert began. "I'm just in SQ7," he stuttered in explanation.

The Captain adapted to this news without missing a beat. "That's Doug Harving, his seat will be tagged. Look for his name plate, and then sit in one of the six box seats behind his. There will be a TCD at your station."

"TCD?"

"Text Communication Device. Do you text on your phone?"

"Um, yeah." Robert seemed puzzled.

"Same thing. Except you only can respond, not initiate communication. You are not to speak."

"Why not just keep us on call in the office, like usual?"

The Captain ignored the question and continued. "In the unlikely event that it is deemed expedient to engage you directly, you will be addressed verbally. Do not stand. Use the microphone at your station. It has a single button to allow you to speak. Do not use this unless asked to directly."

He explained all this matter-of-factly, and there didn't seem to be anything condescending in his tone. Robert wondered if he gave the same speech to everyone, regardless of importance.

Captain Raymond paused. "Do you understand?"

Robert nodded.

"Ok, in you go." The Captain swiped a card and punched something in the keypad. The pair of heavy oak doors swung open, revealing a large and oddly shaped room. The space was very dark, and it took a few moments for Robert to realize that the walls, ceiling, and floor were covered in some sort of black material.

The room was arranged much like two facing conference halls, each with rising rows of seats. In the central pit and running almost its entire length there was an oval table with seats around it. A briefing packet and empty glass had been placed at each station, along with a microphone and an electronic console of some sort.

Three rows of long thin desks with seats rose on both long sides of the oval, with a few steps between levels at each of two aisles between the tables. The whole gave the impression of a fancy auditorium or performance space. Behind certain stations at the oval table, the outer seats were partitioned by cubicle walls into clusters of six.

There was something disturbingly formal about the whole arrangement, and Robert experienced a rising sense of dread.

He wasn't ready for this sort of thing. Why couldn't they just let him work quietly from his cubicle? Nothing good could come of this. At best he would be a wall flower, at worst he'd make a staggering fool of himself. No, at worst he'd "mess up and die." Had that been hyperbole?

The Captain patted him on the back, pointed to a seat cluster behind one particular station, and whispered, "Good luck," as Robert walked in and the doors closed. It only occurred to him afterward that Captain Raymond had conducted the entire interview without referring to any notes.

Robert felt a knot in his stomach as he entered, but made his way to the designated cluster. He paused momentarily to look at his boss's station. Was this all that separated him from the head of the division? Six feet, perhaps seven, and a slightly better seat. It made him wonder what exactly he was aspiring to.

But these were thoughts for another day, and he put them aside before choosing the outermost seat in his cluster. He did this partly from a general desire to avoid drawing attention to himself, but mostly from a fear that the other seats were meant for important people. What if he sat down and was told to move, while everyone laughed at his presumption?

Over the next half hour, a motley assortment of support staff trickled in and behaved much as Robert had. A number of the clusters sported more than one person, and one even filled up; however, Robert's remained empty but for himself. He did not recognize anyone else in the room.

Things would get awkward soon if everybody else was conversing while he sat conspicuously alone. To a different personality, serving as the sole support for the head of a department would have been a golden opportunity. He would have the chance to visibly shine in front of senior officials, perhaps even engage in a little informal chit-chat with them.

But to Robert it was a nightmare. He had no idea how to talk to anybody more senior than himself, and Doug Harving was *six levels* more senior. Heck, he probably had close to three thousand people under him. Why did he pick Robert? There was something that smacked of vanity in this question; he probably didn't even know who Robert was. Why had his secretary's secretary accidentally picked him? Yes, that had to be it. He was there due to somebody's screwup.

Robert felt a sense of relief. The imposing surroundings aside, there was far less pressure if he was some assistant's blunder than the handpicked choice of the department head himself. He could just see Doug Harving, whatever he looked like, slowly shaking his head as he left the meeting. "But he seemed so smart from his reports." No, he'd probably just wonder who on Earth Robert was.

Suddenly Robert panicked. What if he *was* in the wrong cluster? What if this was reserved for the big shots. It would have been reassuring to have a fellow peon to confirm and commiserate with. That was why Robert never sat in the front row at talks. What if the speaker gave thanks to somebody great who was meant to be sitting there and pointed at Robert to stand up and receive credit for not being himself.

The room was filling up, and the volume level had risen significantly. Many of the support staff were chattering busily amongst themselves, no doubt sharing uninformed gossip. What *was* this about, Robert wondered. Well, they all would find out soon enough. It probably would turn out to be something really boring. If there was one thing Robert had learned about the government, it was that it liked to make mountains out of molehills. And everything really is a molehill.

A few official looking attendants adjusted the materials on the central table. They then proceeded to fiddle with some equipment at a podium at its head. Robert wasn't sure how he could have missed the podium, it was the centerpiece of the room. Then he realized that it had not been there when he came in, or maybe it had been hidden by the dark. The lights seemed brighter now, though the room absorbed most of it. What was the point of illuminating a place made of shadow, he wondered?

The attendants acted like AV staff or caterers, but wore military uniforms. From what Robert could see, they all had a rank of Captain or higher. None of the occupants of the main table had arrived yet. After pondering the statistical chances of this for a moment, it occurred to Robert that they all would enter right before the meeting started. Either they were in some other room socializing, or their time was deemed too valuable to waste waiting around. Clearly, his wasn't.

Robert remembered when he had started, six years earlier. He was right out of college, and his first boss had been Larry Wollenby. British, short, plump, and unapologetically rude Larry Wollenby. Larry liked to stare at employees until they were uncomfortable. Sort of like Captain Raymond, but in a sinister way. If you asked him a question, he just would look at you as if you were the most contemptible insect that ever crawled the earth.

"How, but how could you ask something so stupid and yet still biologically function?" his eyes would wonder.

As unpleasant as it was at the time, this never had a lasting effect on Robert. His ego was invested in other things, things that wouldn't make sense to a man like Wollenby. He simply was too oblivious to allow a sociopath to get to him.

And in retrospect, Larry *was* a sociopath. Probably the first Robert ever had known. The irony — as all the interns used to joke while complaining about Larry over drinks — was that his parents both were shrinks. 'No straighter path to crazy than to have two shrinks as parents'. He forgot which intern had said this, they all were fungible in his memory. At the time, Robert had shuddered and doubted he even could stomach a single psychologist parent.

This would have inspired a degree of sympathy for Wollenby, if he hadn't been such an asshole. One time, Larry dumped a particularly nasty piece of busywork in Robert's lap. It was something that was easy to automate, but Wollenby insisted that he do it by hand.

Naturally, Robert protested, "wouldn't it be a better use of my time to script this?"

Larry had smiled and put his hand on Robert's shoulder. "But, Robert, your time isn't worth anything."

For some reason, that had stuck with him. It didn't *bother* him, just felt profound in a perversely cathartic way. He wondered what had happened to Larry. Hadn't he moved back to London at some point? Robert couldn't remember.

The doors opened and a group of people filed in and took their seats at the table. Robert smirked with satisfaction; just as he suspected, they all had been schmoozing prior to the meeting.

Most of the newcomers were older and had a distinguished aura, or perhaps just an air of command. They were followed by a tall woman in an immaculately tailored pant suit, and finally by two soldiers who closed the doors and stood guard by them.

The woman wore her hair in an elegant ponytail, and clearly was Asian. When she walked to the podium, Robert realized that she actually was not very tall. She must have seemed that way because she was slender with heels and because everybody else was sitting. He could not determine her age, but suspected she was in her early fifties. Suddenly he realized who she must be.

Lillian R. Tao was the Director of ORAD, the Office of Research on Anomalous Discharge. The latter was the official term employed by the U.S. government for the Front. It derived from one of the first proposed theories concerning the nature of that phenomenon, a theory which quickly had been debunked.

A Harvard physicist named Mary Delphi had written a

book claiming that a variant of dark matter could account for the Front through a supersymmetric process she termed 'anomalous discharge'. It turned out that Delphi was better at writing fiction than doing credible research. The book was a winner, the theory was not.

Her prior reputation in the community had been mixed at best. However, she was one of that small cadre of popular physicists who assiduously court media attention and ingratiate themselves with the government. As a consequence, they took her theory seriously long after everyone of repute had laughed it away. The result was the title of a department, quite a bit of grant money for Mary, and innumerable copies of a coffee-table book that nobody read.

Robert wondered how Tao, herself a former physicist — and from what he had heard, quite a solid one — felt to have the name of a crackpot theory on her stationary. The minute she began speaking, he realized she couldn't care less. She was all business, one of those people who clearly does not waste a single thought on extraneous matters. Robert always admired such people, though he didn't imagine he would like to be one himself. It just takes too much energy to filter the noise.

Tao skipped any formalities, welcomes, introductions, or their ilk. She launched right into the matter as if picking up a conversation mid-sentence. Fortunately, she also decided to include a bit of background. Robert wondered if this was for people like himself or for the military types.

The flow of information had been under very tight control for almost half a year now. He knew this because he was part of the internet disinformation campaign. Within the United States, the internet had remained fully functional. Unlike television or other centrally-controlled means of information dissemination, mere martial law wouldn't effect the desired level of restriction.

Robert caught himself as he realized with disgust that he was lapsing into govvy-speak, even in his thoughts. In his profession, it was a never-ending battle to keep from degenerating into a jargon-spouting zombie. That was the worst fate imaginable for somebody like Robert, at least other than the ones which involved physical torture, psychological torture, or sitting in meetings.

The point was that you couldn't prosecute or take control of the internet. And you couldn't shut it down without sparking the very panic you sought to avoid. So the government left the internet in place, along with all its superficial trappings.

A great deal of energy was directed toward the interception of information, but people can detect intrusion or revision. There were a surprising number of people who spent a surprising amount of time squatting in their little corner of the internet waiting for something to happen. Robert likened them to a redneck sitting on the porch of his trailer waiting for the 'gubment to come and mess with him.

So without massive efforts to control or arrest individuals, the government could not manage the flow of information. The old U.S.S.R., Romania,... now *they* knew how to control information. He wondered how they would have dealt with the internet. It stymied even China and the most oppressive Arab dictatorships. But the U.S. just couldn't do what was necessary. Well, it could — the Supreme Court had ruled that it could in People vs Myers, the first major post-Front test of freedom of speech. Executing Myers just had created more problems, and the press had been clamoring about it ever since.

Without exponentially increasing the incarceration and execution rate there wasn't a viable solution, and the government didn't have the resources to fight both the Front and its own people. This is where Robert's group came in. If you can't beat them, join them. His job was to introduce absurd rumors and drive them to the top of the search engines' listings.

It was basic information theory — if you can't reduce

the signal strength, increase the noise until it drowns out everything else. It was creative and fun. He got to pretend to be a complete nutjob, say the most ridiculous things, and make people believe them. Sometimes Robert even injected bits of truth (or as little as he knew of it), but distorted. These often were the most effective rumors, generating the greatest confusion.

Once, when he was bitter about how mathematically inept most people were, he tried to make the propaganda educational. One video proposed that if you learned calculus, you could discover your own date of death. Technically, this almost was true — though it was geometry, not calculus, and assumed you didn't move at all. He created a video in which a bikini-clad model explained the calculations involved. But even with bouncing boobs, nobody wanted to learn math. The project flopped so badly that he had been reprimanded. But, missteps aside, the job was pretty interesting and Robert was quite good at it.

At first he had a little trouble with the Orwellian element. Most people in his division didn't seem to be bothered by it at all, and that disturbed him more than anything else. A few had initial qualms but quickly became institutionalized. Robert had a more elegant solution to the moral dilemma.

The government was working to fight an extinction-level threat. It wasn't simply pursuing power for its own sake. And while there might be people who would take advantage, this wasn't an overreaction to a small attack or a flimsy excuse to roll back civil liberties. Everyone was going to die if they didn't solve this. Everyone.

In the face of extinction, a society no longer has the luxury of philosophical disquisition, the leisure to indulge in moral debates over the abstract nature of justice. And so far, the government had done pretty well at keeping people safe from one another. There wasn't widespread or organized civil disorder, nor was there mass repression.

Robert's attention returned to Tao. He realized that in his reverie he had missed some of her explanation, and almost panicked. What if she called on him? Then he realized that she just was describing the Front pattern. He already knew this.

"... and per previous calculations, the Front was believed to move at a constant surface speed of 0.2 miles per hour."

Was believed? God, Robert hated bad grammar. At least she was calling it 'the Front'. He hated the acronym AD, it sounded like Jesus was involved. Not that there weren't plenty of people who believed that Jesus *was* involved. In the course of his work, Robert had become intimately familiar with every form of idiocy regarding the Front.

"As you know, there was much confusion immediately following Z-Day. The existence and behavior of the Front were unknown at that time, and it wasn't long before the primary European data centers went offline. The Trans-Atlantic connection remained functional for a short period, but succumbed to marginal degradation after a mere six days."

Robert loved that term. Marginal Degradation. It referred to all the bad stuff that happened when the Front moved through the carapace of civilization. Cities burning, reactors melting down, uncontrolled chemical dumps. Robert liked the other term less: "Implemented Degradation."

That meant somebody was jealous or angry — jealous or angry enough to want to see you die before the Front got to you. Before *they* went. Basically, it meant they nuked you. And why the hell not? There was nothing to lose. It wasn't even clear if it was immoral. After all, you were going to die anyway. They just saved time the trouble. Fortunately, for all the talk and worry about it, there had been no Implemented Degradation. Yet. Robert had the uneasy feeling that if there was, the U.S. would be the one doing it. Wasn't that what they said during the Cold War — if there was a first strike, it would come from the U.S.

"That rate of 0.2 mph has changed only marginally over time since Z-Day. There has been much speculation on the nature and cause of these fluctuations. We now have statistically significant evidence that the speed has increased slightly."

There was a gasp and then silence. A light went on over Leslie Bromind's station. He asked "What is the increase?"

"It has increased by 0.0001 mph per week."

Leslie laughed dismissively. "You had me worried. I think we can handle that." There was some uneasy chuckling.

Lilly smiled wanly. "Hang on to that worry. It gets worse." She paused and looked around the table. "Much, much worse."

CHAPTER 4

Day 7 — Glasgow, Scotland

Elise stood on the sidewalk, sobbing quietly. Last night's screams of rage and pain were eerily absent from the streets, and the red spots which had punctuated the city were replaced by wafting smoke from gently smoldering remains. In the placid drizzle, it smelled like the morning after a campfire. She'd loved that smell as a child. Thank god the city was built of brick and stone, otherwise it could have burnt to the ground. But when Elise looked at her shop, she decided there was nothing to thank god for.

The city had turned on itself. But it did not feel that way, could not feel that way. It was more personal. For each victim, it had turned on them, specifically, intentionally, and personally. Elise had grown up here, loved the city, known many people. She had been a part of it, and it had been a not insubstantial part of her.

Along with her shop, that bond had been destroyed. She wondered if this was how it felt to be betrayed by a friend or lover. To have all your assumptions upended, and realize that permanence isn't so permanent, that the one you trusted and depended on is neither trustworthy nor dependable. For a moment she felt fortunate that this never had happened to her. Then she realized that now it had, and things never could be the same.

It had taken a lifetime, but Elise finally saw what her betrothed really was like. And it wasn't the immigrants; she couldn't just blame some outsiders. These were Glaswegians, tried and untrue. She even had recognized some from her own neighborhood, some who had been to her shop, some with whom she had exchanged greetings and friendly words.

It hadn't just been hooligans or kids in hoodies. A few were well-dressed, and they too laughed and drank and pointed as her store burned, as if it were a beach bonfire and they all were having a merry old time.

The signs of unrest had begun around 5 PM. Nothing extreme, just a sense of tension and some distant sirens. The street was crowded with people returning home from work. What Elise had noticed was the unusual quiet. Ordinarily the evening bustle was rather noisy, and a steady stream of customers stopped by her shop on the way home.

But today there was nobody. It was as if their team had lost and everybody was minding their own private grief. No, even then there would have been a few drunks cursing or shouting unintelligibly. Something had happened, and they were digesting it.

She had seen this before, a few years back when there was the terrorist bombing of Flight 104 from London. England had been the real target, but almost everybody on the plane was Scottish. She remembered the silence, a seething anger that had gripped the city. What was there to talk about? Everybody knew what had happened. Gossip would serve no purpose but to diminish the memory of the dead.

She never could tell if the anger was at the crazies who bombed the plane or at England for dragging them into this mess with their inane foreign policy. That very foreign policy had been a large part of why Scotland seceded in the first place. But no, this was a different sort of silence. It felt like a silence born of fear, not anger or sadness.

By 5:30, there were small groups of people running down the street outside the shop, as well as a few unsettling sounds from afar. But there still were plenty of professional-looking individuals walking by. Perhaps they walked a little more quickly than usual, but without any obvious sense of panic or peril. That made sense; this was one of the more upscale avenues in Glasgow.

If there were groups of kids looking for trouble, they probably just would pass through on their way to areas with more pubs and fewer police. Then again, Elise hadn't seen any police at all this evening. She decided to close shop for the day; there didn't seem to be any business anyway. Proceeding in her usual unhurried manner, she tried to figure out what to do with the evening. If there *was* trouble, it probably would be better to sleep in the shop than risk the walk home.

Her condo was well-situated, but it was about three quarters of a mile away and she wasn't certain what was happening in between, or whether all the kids in hoodies had a particular destination in mind. She remembered reading about "flash mobs" that were coordinated via the internet and appeared out of nowhere. That seemed the preferable scenario; it was aimless gangs of kids which most worried her, they could be real trouble.

Nonetheless, Elise decided it was better to weather it out at home. Truth be told, her desire for a shower outweighed any real considerations of risk or security. Being stranded at the store during a crisis may have been exciting, even festive, when she was twenty. But at forty-one she needed two things: a shower and sleep. Not that blackouts or lockdowns or major storms were frequent occurrences; she could remember only three times she had slept at the store over the past fourteen years.

Elise was confident that as long as there were many people on the street the walk home would be safe. Well, at least as long as there were many *reputable-looking* people. She almost laughed at the absurdity of this, that she would be safe if there was one other person in a suit nearby. Somehow that person would defend her against the horde of murderous thugs with his tie and umbrella, like in a bad 60's show. It was light, not yuppies, that would keep her safe. Despite all the modern technology, crime still seemed to favor the night.

Elise hastened to finish the end-of-day chores. It was summer, and the sun would be up for a while, but she really wanted to get home sooner rather than later. She would feel much safer in her fourth floor condo than exposed to the street. Then again, nobody would be there to help her if somebody *did* go to the trouble of climbing those four stories. *Exposed to the street?* What was she forgetting?

Suddenly, Elise heard the sound of glass shattering down the block. *Shit.* Pulling down the metal grill was the *first* thing she should have done when there was a hint of trouble. There was some high-pitched laughter accompanied by more shattered glass, still a block away. Elise put down the receipts she was filing and quickly walked toward the front of the store.

Fortunately, she was only halfway there when when the display window exploded. Somebody had thrown a rock. She saw him outside, pointing and laughing. Sure enough, it was a kid in a hoodie. He had another rock in his hand. Elise ran for the back door without even bothering to close the register. There was no second crash or thunk; he must not have bothered throwing it. Perhaps all the glass was broken already.

The rear door opened onto a cobblestone alley between streets, and Elise ran down it as quickly as her heels would let her. She felt too slow; they easily could trap her in the alley and do whatever they wanted to her. Through her panic, she remembered that she had left the store keys inside. She began to turn around, but glimpsed a shadow at the other end of the alley and kept running.

When she reached the end of the alley, Elise stopped and peered out cautiously before sprinting onto the side street. She fully expected to be set upon by a gang of thugs lying in wait, or for hands to grab her from behind at the very moment she thought herself safe. They would drag her back into the alley, and do all manner of horrible things to her.

Nothing happened. The side street was quiet except for two people walking by. Elise turned left and walked up to the main street, taking care not to be seen by whoever was throwing stones. The avenue looked just as it had from inside the shop: groups of kids running by, and a few normal people as well. The one who had vandalized her store was nowhere to be seen. Nobody seemed to notice her, nobody seemed to care.

Elise was too shaken to walk home directly, so she went into the sandwich shop across the street. Customers were entering and leaving, so it felt like a safe bet. Surely nobody would risk attacking a store filled with witnesses. These weren't terrorists, just kids. So why did Elise feel terrorized?

And why was this shop doing a brisk business while her own had been devoid of customers? This bothered her more than the rock through the window, for some reason. Then again, maybe there was no call for flowers today. There *always* was call for flowers, she felt like shouting. Elise sighed. That sounded like some awful advertising slogan.

Most customers were buying takeout and, when she finally got her tea and biscuit, Elise had no trouble finding an open table. In fact, she even found one from which she could keep an eye on the shop. That probably wasn't a bad idea. She would be safe here, and could wait for the police. Surely, they would be here soon. She looked at her watch: it was 5:50 PM.

The police still hadn't shown up by 6:30, so Elise tried calling them. The line was busy. She wondered why there didn't seem to be a single cop on the street. At least there had been no further vandalism. Probably just one bad apple. That didn't make it any better, of course; she groaned thinking of the insurance hassle and downtime and lost business. But this sort of nonsense was par for the course for a shopkeeper, she supposed. At least she had gone fourteen years without being robbed or vandalized. The increasingly elusive bright side.

Elise barely registered the flickering out of the corner of her eye, but some shouting on the street caught her attention. She hadn't noticed before, but the general noise level had grown quite loud. She also could make out screams, though whether of laughter or something worse she could not tell. Were there more raucous kids outside?

Elise lifted her head from the tea and saw smoke issuing from the front of her store. There was a glow within, as if from a burglar with a red flashlight. It took a few moments for her to register what actually was happening. Elise ran outside and screamed, but nobody could hear her above the din. People were pointing and laughing.

She looked around anxiously for some clue to the culprit. No other store was on fire, and nobody had a Molotov cocktail or anything obvious in their hands. Maybe that only happened in the movies anyway. Elise wanted to grab people and shake them and ask who had done this thing. But then she reconsidered. Her store had been attacked twice. Maybe *she* was the target.

Once again she looked around anxiously, but nobody even seemed to notice her. Better not to draw attention to herself; she would go back to sipping tea and watching and hoping that the police showed up. When she returned, somebody had taken her seat in the cafe. There was nothing for it. Elise began the long walk home.

CHAPTER 5

Day 843 — Near Denver, Colorado, 6 PM

Dwight shivered a little as he leaned into his rifle and surveyed the road ahead through the scope. The cold wasn't new to him. He had grown up not far from here, but he always had his own gear. A Gore-Tex shell with a down jacket, two light synthetic layers (Bioprene and Lavitex were his favorites), and some proper mittens. Not that you could shoot wearing mittens, but usually the adrenaline carried you through that bit. Adrenaline and some quality neoprene liners.

But there weren't mittens or liners or goggles here. Instead his eye was glued to freezing metal, staring at the reticle of a government issue scope. That was another thing which irked him. He'd grown up around guns. Some were better, some worse, but he'd never seen such crap as the Guard foisted on them.

He envied the Staties; at least they could use proper State-issued weaponry. And if there was one State which equipped its troopers well, it was Colorado. It's not that the feds didn't have good gear; they had all sorts of amazing equipment at their disposal. The Guard simply was at the bottom of the pecking order.

They always got the worst garbage imaginable, the stuff nobody else would take. They got called up for the worst jobs, the domestic crises nobody else wanted to touch. And they got no respect. Everybody viewed them as kids who wanted free money for college, or people too wimpy to join the Army. Federal mall cops, basically.

Of course, nobody told him this when he was recruited. They'd just waved glossies with all sorts of promises of glory and money and fun. The recruiters failed to mention that there were a million paths to military service and it made all the difference in the world which you took. Join one way and you'd serve your country, join another and you'd serve dinner to the officers who *had* asked the right questions before signing up. Still, the Guard was a lot more than it used to be. Over the years prior to Z-day, they had gone from a last line of defense to an effective army of their own. That was more than could be said of the Reserve.

Since the second Gulf war, nobody had any illusions about ROTC. Everyone knew that it was pretty much tantamount to joining the military for life, minus any social recognition for doing so. You still were viewed as having tried to wiggle your way out, as having been drafted against your will.

That image probably wasn't helped by all the complaints of disrupted lives and third and fourth tours and post-traumatic syndrome during the Gulf war. Soldiers weren't supposed to whine, but Dwight hardly could blame a bunch of kids who just wanted an education and instead found they had signed a deal with the devil. Then again, you had to be pretty naive to think that anything came free. Especially anything from the government.

The lesson clearly had been learned, and ROTC recruitment dropped considerably in the years which followed. But the same wasn't true of the Guard. The old rule of one weekend a month, two weeks a summer had endured until quite recently. Even after Z-day, the training only increased slightly.

Dwight assumed this was for the same reason there hadn't been a draft, though he wasn't sure what that reason was. At first he thought they just were trying to preserve the American way of life, freedom, and so on. But when had that really mattered to anyone in power? Perhaps the regular army had proved sufficient so far. There had been two major sets of national riots, yet the Guard hadn't been called up until now. This had to be really bad.

A rustling caught Dwight's attention and he looked up from his scope alertly. After a few moments, he relaxed again. It's not like there wouldn't be any warning. They weren't up against an organized army with snipers and skirmishers, just a bunch of desperate people. Of course, if those desperate people were anything like some of the folks Dwight grew up with, it could get pretty bad.

Most of the people he knew loved guns because they were part of life out here. Dwight had lived in Denver proper for a few years, but hailed from a rural area Southwest of it. Many of his formative years had been spent on his uncle's small ranch there, and guns just were part and parcel of everyday life.

Like most people in the area, Dwight had mixed feelings about the anti-gun lobby. He imagined they mostly were people from places like New York City. Not any more, he reflected, though with a tinge of sadness rather than satisfaction. He had understood them to some extent, these gunphobes. To them guns were things bad guys used in crimes, just like in the movies. Or weapons that crazies used to shoot up schools, just like on the news.

But to Dwight they were as much a part of the ordinary fabric of existence as cars. Come to think of it, he supposed people would react the same way to cars if the media reported every automobile accident. He always laughed when some news show complained that the latest lunatic owned five guns, and they listed all sorts of scary sounding names like the AQ140 0.223 tactical assault rifle with calibrated lethal response laser scope. All that meaningless marketing crap that companies used to sell guns to one demographic was coming back to bite them with another.

Dwight owned fifteen firearms. When his anti-gun friends expressed dismay at this, he'd joke that he only had two hands. It seemed an obvious point to him, but they rarely laughed. If there was one thing liberals were good at, in his experience, it was taking themselves way too seriously. After all, nobody ever claimed that a man was five times as likely to drive drunk because he had five cars. Then again, the type of rich asshole who had five cars probably *was*.

The whole gun debate was something Dwight never understood. If the Democrats had just let up on gun control, they'd have garnered so many more votes. Heck, *he* would have voted Democrat every time, along with many of his gun-toting friends. It was the condescending attitude that upset him most. None of them had ever shot a gun, let alone owned one. How could they know anything about them? Ah the redneck's dilemma, he laughed to himself.

But it was no laughing matter. There had been a Republican president when Z-day hit. And look at things now. Not that it ultimately made much difference, of course, he chuckled to himself bitterly. Even the very best of presidents couldn't have done much. And, sadly, Margaret Larisse was far from the best of presidents.

"Something funny?" A large hand clapped him on the back.

Dwight looked up without flinching or tensing in the least. "How many times have I told you not to do that?"

As always, Dwight kept his finger off the trigger until the very last moment. It was good gun-safety, especially when there were guys like this around. Unfortunately, the "guy like this" was Brad Pry, his friend of twenty-odd years. Brad was precisely the type of guy he hoped wouldn't be coming up the hill. The type who sat around itching for the 'gubment to come and try something. The type who eagerly furnished liberals with every gun-crazed-moron stereotype they could ask for, lent credence to every anti-gun argument they could find time to muster.

Dwight always had considered it an odd way to look at the world. He could think of many good reasons to have a gun, but having one solely so it couldn't be taken away seemed rather pointless and sad. After all, the government never *did* come for those guys. Why would it? They just sat around waiting for it to come; they were harmless.

These days, most of the government's efforts seemed to be aimed at keeping *them* from coming to *it*. The real kicker was that despite all the 2nd amendment hysteria over the years, in the end the government never tried to take away anybody's weapons. Even when martial law had been declared and there were the tightest controls on everything else. It just didn't care. When push came to shove, it used the same military-grade weaponry whether you owned a gun or not. With the same effect.

Not to mention that, like himself, Brad now *was* that 'gubment, or at least its armed representative. Perversely, if they *had* sent anybody to come for the people like Brad, it probably would have been him and Brad.

"Shouldn't you be at your station?" Dwight asked testily when Brad continued to stand, hovering over him.

Hover, hover, hover. Finally he looked up in irritation. Brad was smiling, and had two cans of Coors in his hands. Dwight shook his head slowly. "Well, why didn't you say so, asshole."

There wasn't going to be any action tonight. And who *didn't* need a cold Coors on a freezing December night? He looked around warily, flipped on the safety with his thumb, and stood up. Normally the safety would have remained on until Dwight was ready to fire, but he specifically had been ordered to keep it off, 'just in case'.

"Ordered". Now, that was a strange sounding word. Sure, Dwight had spent the odd weekend training over the years, but nobody took the orders seriously. It was more like a club meeting or a summer camp, and the sergeant was an avuncular coach. This was different. He was given "orders", and expected to obey them. He had become the type of guy who was "ordered" to do things. It never had sunk in what this meant.

He was in the army now in the only way that mattered: he was a grunt who had to do what he was told.

"Where's Mull?" he asked before making a move for the beer.

"He's off at the shitter," Brad laughed. "Or so he says." This was accompanied by an obscene gesture of the hand.

"I didn't think he even had one," Dwight chuckled.

Brad was the archetype of a redneck, straight out of central casting, replete with unkempt beard, gut, and crass mouth. He would have worn the requisite flannel shirt too, if not for that pesky military dress code. Instead, they all had to don the same cheesy government issue uniforms. Who the hell used cotton anymore?

The irony of the situation wasn't lost on Dwight. Brad and his friends spent most of their civilian lives pretending to be military bad-asses, wearing fatigues and army boots and Ka-Bars. But the minute the real military issued them that same equipment, there was nonstop complaining. At least Dwight was consistent; he had thought the stuff was crap back then, and he thought it was crap now.

Dwight reached for the beer, popped the tab, and took a swig. "I do believe this constitutes treason." He raised the can and clinked it against Brad's. There were a few seconds of beer-swilling silence before Dwight spoke again.

"I'll repeat my question, though. Shouldn't you be at your station? I mean, Mull's not going to spend *all* night jerking off."

"Don't be so sure," Brad countered, performing a new extended pantomime. Dwight gave him an impatient look and Brad drew the show to a close in slow motion.

Dwight looked down at his beer as if noticing it for the first time. "Where did you get these anyway?" It suddenly occurred to him that they shouldn't be drinking these. Not because it was wrong, but because the beers shouldn't exist. Even when he was a civilian, they had been in short supply.

Brad offered a toothy grin. "I've got my ways. Never ask the Pryster how he does his thing." He saluted Dwight with his beer.

"You snuck them on the truck?"

"Yep. Well, not exactly. Remember Sergeant Cope? He let me take them. Real nice fellow. He's the one that let me post with you." Brad sipped his beer.

"Yeah, I was kind of shocked by that. I thought they all were hardasses like..." Dwight gestured with his thumb toward the outhouse.

"Nah, well, *he's* NTA. The guys at Alamosa were a great bunch. You didn't really get to know them, but I was there for three days before you came. You'll never meet a better bunch of guys."

"Sounds like I missed quite a party," Dwight responded dryly and took a swig of his beer.

"They had been deciding where to post me, but when you showed up I asked outright and they just went with it. Even gave me this six-pack for the road."

"Six-pack?"

"Not all of it made it to the end of the road," Brad smiled, "or the start. This," he raised his can, "my friend, is the last of the cheer."

They had finished their beers. Nobody probably would care, but you never could tell with these stick-up-the-ass NTA guys. They both crinkled their cans and threw them as far into the woods as they could.

"Well, it chilled me pretty good," Dwight griped. But then he added earnestly, looking at Brad, "Thanks, buddy. It's been a while since I had one. And for the record, I'm glad you're here."

"Well, since you mentioned it..." Brad, got down and sat close to Dwight. "I'm here all right," he grinned toothily.

Dwight raised his eyebrow.

Brad slapped him on the back. "Dickless decided we all

should stay in the same tower until the rest arrive." He leaned in. "Frankly, I think he got tired of dragging his sorry ass back and forth to keep tabs on us."

"Great," groaned Dwight as Brad reached around the outside of the door and retrieved the rifle he had stowed there. Dwight's jaw dropped in disbelief. "You left it *there*? What if somebody took it?"

"C'mon, who's gonna take it?" Brad smirked, "we both know this is just a big circle jerk. Nobody's coming."

"Dickless may be."

"Dickless is here," a voice announced dryly. Mull was looking down at them with his usual long-suffering expression. He turned to Brad. "And I'm glad you think so. You're on night watch."

Dwight remembered the words from the briefing the previous morning. Mull's words. The first time anybody had explained anything since he had been activated a week earlier. *Think about the sort of people who will make it this far. Think about what really will be coming up that hill.* Despite himself, he was glad that Brad was at his side.

CHAPTER 6

Day 266 — International Space Station

Captain Alex Konarski gazed through the porthole window at the blue mass below. It looked the same as it had for the last nine years. When first informed of the Front, he had half-expected to see a pestilential wall of grey or a glowing force field or some other tell-tale sign. Instead there was nothing, just the same globe that always was there. The same boring old globe.

Konarski remembered the precise time it had taken for her charms to expire. Six months, twelve days. It was the same for every newcomer to the ISS; at first, they gawked at the beauty of Earth and couldn't shut up about it. Then they did. Konarski always waited a discrete period after each arrival before asking how long it had taken.

Nobody seemed to remember the point at which things changed, they just woke up one day and the magic was gone. How like marriage, he'd laugh, slapping them on the back. By now the joke was well-worn. Of course, it wasn't just the Earth itself. When somebody new arrived, they acted like a hyperactive puppy, bouncing with delight at each new experience, or perhaps ricocheting was a better choice of word up here.

Once the excitement died down, they discovered it was a job like any other, except that home was a tiny bunk a few feet from where you worked. The tourists had it right: get in and out before the novelty wore off. The ISS basically was a submarine posting with a better view and better toilets.

Earth became something to occasionally note out the corner of one's eye. Yep, still there. Being so high up almost bred contempt for the tiny ball and its billions of people. This had been less of a problem in the old days, when the ISS sounded like the inside of a factory. But since the upgrade, things were so quiet that one could not help but feel aloof. Aloof was invented for this place. As a general rule, it was hard to hold in high regard any place toward which you flushed your excrement. Well, not quite *toward*.

There was a fun problem in orbital mechanics that Konarski used to stump newbies with. Of course, Alex had learned it in high school, but his colleagues — particularly the Americans — seemed to have spent their formative years doing anything but studying. For some reason, America believed it was better to send jocks into orbit than scientists. Worse even, it made a distinction between the two. Nerds are nerds and jocks are jocks and never the twain shall meet. It was a view that Konarski and most of the older generation of Eastern Europeans found bewildering. But that was the way it was.

So, Alex and his friends gave the newbies the infamous "orbit" problem. If you are working outside the ISS and fling a wrench toward Earth what will happen? Invariably, the response was to the effect that "well, duh, it will fall to Earth." With carefully practiced condescension, Alex then would inform them that this is not correct. The wrench will rebound and hit the pitcher. It was one of the many vagaries of orbital dynamics, unintuitive but fairly obvious on close reflection.

The victim would argue, debate, complain, declare it an impossibility. Alex patiently would explain the mathematics. It was no mistake. Only after the victim had labored for days over a calculation that any kid should be able to do would they — sometimes — get the answer.

For some reason the first question they asked after accepting the result always was, "How do you flush the toilets?"

"Very carefully," Alex would answer.

Then everybody had a drink and a good laugh. Yes, shit would fall to earth just as it always had and always would.

The spectrometer indicated that there was some sort of

smog developing over Rome. Alex wondered if this would be a repeat of Paris. There had been sporadic fires for weeks after the Front hit that city. Some were attributable to the usual suspects: car crashes as people fled or died, overloads and short-circuits, the chaos of large numbers of people fleeing, probably even arson, not to mention the ordinary incidence of fires in a major city, now with nobody to nip them in the bud. Mostly, though, it just was the unattended failure of humanity's mechanized residue.

The Front couldn't eradicate every trace of our existence, but perhaps it would smile gleefully as our detritus burned itself out. Those last embers likely would outlast us, a brief epitaph. Of course, the smaller fires weren't visible from the station, and Alex only could surmise their existence from the occasional flare up.

The same had occurred everywhere else the Front passed. In most cases there had been a small glow for a day or so and then just the quenching smoke from a spent fire. On the other hand, there was a thick haze over parts of Germany since fires had spread through the coal mines. These probably would burn for years to come, occasionally erupting from the ground without warning. There was no need to speculate on *that*; Konarski's own grandfather had perished this way many years ago. The mines had been killing people long before there was any Front. But the occasional fireworks aside, cities inside the Zone were cold and dead.

The ISS orbited the Earth approximately once every ninety minutes. This meant that close observation of any given area was limited to a few minutes, after which they must wait until the next pass. During the time between passes, the Front would expand a little over a quarter mile. Nothing remarkable had happened during the hundred passes it took for the Front to traverse Paris. And it wasn't for another twenty or so that the trouble started.

Trouble? Something about the word struck him as callous. It seemed irreverent to call a fire "trouble", while ignoring the millions of deaths which surely preceded it. Well, the "event", then. Once it started, the event was evident within a few passes. Alex had noticed something wrong fairly quickly. Instead of a series of small and short-lived flare ups, the blaze simply had grown and grown.

At first he suspected the meltdown of some unadvertised nuclear reactor. But there was no indication of enhanced radiation levels. Of course, it was hard to tell for sure through the smoke plume. By that point it looked like there was a small hurricane over Paris, a hurricane that occasionally flashed red. It really was quite beautiful from his vantage point, but he shuddered to think what it would be like within that mile-high vortex of flame.

It had not ceased for seven days. Some meteorologist explained the effect early on. It was called a firestorm, when countless small fires merge into a monster that generates its own weather, commands its own destiny. It was a good thing there was nobody left for it to kill, though Alex was unsure what effect the fountain of ash would have on the rest of Europe.

In theory there probably were operational video feeds on the ground, but the Central European power grid had failed two months earlier. It had shown surprisingly little resilience, and shrouded most of Europe in darkness. Of course, the relevant machinery lay within the Zone and repairs were impossible.

Konarski wondered how many millions had died prematurely because some engineering firm cut corners years ago. It probably was Ukrainian, that firm. Alex never trusted the Ukrainians. Whatever the cause, the result was that there was no power. And by the time Paris was hit any battery-driven units were long dead. Other than some satellites and the occasional drone, he and his crew were the only ones to see what was happening.

The Paris conflagration eventually had withered and died out, of course. What was of interest now was Rome. The ISS had been asked to keep an eye on the regions within the Zone, gleaning valuable information to help others prepare or, if one were fool enough to hope, understand and dispel the Front altogether. However, the real action always surrounded the Front itself. Especially when it hit a densely-developed area, even if now deserted. But it wasn't just orders or morbid curiosity that compelled Alex to watch. Where evident, the destruction could be aesthetically beautiful.

Safely beyond the reach of the Front, Alex could watch the end of a world. How many people would have the opportunity to do so? There was a certain pride in knowing he would be among the last, perhaps even *the* last. Once everyone had perished, the crew of the ISS would be alone for a while, left to contemplate the silence. Then their supplies would run out, and they too would die.

Based on the current consumption rate of his six person crew, Alex estimated they could survive for another six years — two years past the Front's anticipated circumvallation of Earth. Of course, he doubted the process would be an orderly one. Four of the crew members (himself included) came from military backgrounds, one was a woman, and three different countries were represented. Even at the best of times, there was a simmering competitiveness.

Konarski assumed that he would be the first casualty. No other scenario made sense, other than something random in the heat of passion — and such things didn't require the Front. No, barring any insanity, he would go first. He was the leader and also happened to be bedding the only woman. Who else would somebody bother killing? Of course, with *this* woman, he shuddered to think what would happen to the murderer. Of course, *she* was the one most likely to kill him in the first place.

Obviously, they hadn't screened for mental health in the Chinese space program. In fact, he guessed that any screening they *did* do was just lip-service to be allowed to join the ISS. But Ying was stunning and endlessly hilarious to talk to, and Alex had nothing to lose.

If the Front hadn't come along, he would have faced compulsory retirement the following year. Then he would have had the privilege of returning to good old Poland, a living anachronism in a country that shunned any sign of its past. Alex gave it about a year before the bottle would have taken him. Who the fuck wanted to grow old in today's world? The Front was the best thing that ever happened, as far as he was concerned. It made him special.

Alex would try to protect Ying for as long as he could, but he knew how things would unfold. Perhaps it would be best to kill her first, before anyone got to him. Or maybe he just should suicide the whole crew. It would be the easiest thing in the world, all he really had to do was stop trying to keep everyone alive. Or he actively could space the place and kill everyone at once, a grand ceremonial gesture. But that would be boring.

Besides, part of him wanted to see who *would* be the last man standing. The whole of humanity in one man. The one to turn out the lights, not first but final hand. Humanity would end the way it began, with one man killing another. After all, everybody always was talking about returning to your roots. Alex just was sad they no longer had a gun on board. That *really* would have made things interesting.

These were distant considerations, however; worth planning for, but hardly imminent. At the moment the world remained very much alive, and was counting on them for critical information. Alex wondered if it would be better to be the last man alive or the man who saved the world.

"The savior, you dumb fuck," part of him screamed. "Nobody will be around to care if you're the last one alive." Of course, Poland already was gone. There was no home for him, even the one he wouldn't have wanted. Maybe he was the last Pole. But how would he change a light bulb?

For some reason, a series of bad Pollack jokes popped into Konarski's head. There was a time when he would have taken great offense at such jokes, jumped to his country's defense, maybe even thrown a few obligatory punches. But not now, not after what Poland had become over the last decade, and especially not after how they had behaved toward the end. They could go fuck themselves. And now they had. Or somebody bigger and badder had fucked them, just like had happened through most of their history.

Still, he felt a certain pride. Maybe he would be the start of a new, prouder race of Poles. No, that was just the sort of talk that had made him sick of his country, the reason he was commanding ISS under a Russian flag. Besides, there probably still were plenty of Poles around the world. He wasn't alone. Yet.

If Alex watched Rome's demise closely, he couldn't be accused of exultation or cruel delight. He had watched his home city of Warsaw perish just three days earlier. Of course, it was nearly empty by the time the Front reached it. But he had listened to the broadcasts, the chatter, and he was ashamed of the conduct of his countrymen. They had acted just like the self-absorbed Western pigs he detested.

Ying understood. She was Chinese. When *they* left their old and infirm behind it would be from calculated expedience, not blind selfish panic. The decision would be institutional, not individual. The throng would push and perish and each would look to their own interest, but none would bear the individual moral responsibility. *That* would be absorbed by the State. What else was the State for?

But it turned out that his compatriots no longer thought this way. They had become soft since the fall of communism, soft and scared. When the moment came, they didn't stand proud and sink with the ship. They scrambled over one another like a bunch of terrified mice, making a horrid mess and spitting on the morals of their homeland and a thousand years of national dignity just to buy a few more precious moments of lives clearly not worth living. They disgusted him. He would die the last true Pole.

In the meantime, he would carry on — his duty now to the species. Part of him felt that if *his* world had perished, so too should all the others. He harbored a certain resentment when he imagined some American scientists discovering the answer just in time to save their own country. It would be *his* data that accomplished this. What right had they to save themselves using *his* data, when his own people had perished. Yet still he sent it. Data that perhaps would one day allow another world to grow from the ashes of his. Maybe this was a sign that there *had* been some small progress over the thousands of years, that he was first and foremost human.

Alex's thoughts were interrupted by a soft voice.

"We're almost over Rome," Ying whispered, breathing gently into his ear.

"C'mon, I have to record this," he protested in half-genuine exasperation.

"That's ok, we'll just catch the next pass," she shot back from behind him.

Alex heard some shuffling and felt something strange on his shoulder. What was Ying doing now? He had to focus, dammit. She was the funnest, craziest woman he had known, but sometimes he just wished he could lock her outside the station for a few hours. Yeah, he'd probably ask her to marry him at some point. Maybe soon. After all, living with somebody on the ISS was ten times more difficult than being married. Alex shook his shoulder free of her grip. It would have to wait.

Then he noticed that she wasn't touching him. She was on the other side of the room, pointing at him with her mouth open. Why was there no sound? Then he was screaming, then he couldn't scream anymore. Before things grew dark, he saw Ying's decaying flesh. She still was pointing, almost like a mannequin. His last thought was how disgusting Ying had become, and that he soon would be the same.

CHAPTER 7

Day 7 — Glasgow, Scotland

As she sifted through the rubble the morning after the riot, Elise was in a daze. Did people always act like this? Why hadn't she? Had she been living amidst another species her entire life, fooled by their similar appearance? Maybe she was the same, but didn't have the opportunity or motive. Maybe she was the posh, the upper class, the kulak. The one who had a little more, the one who needed to be dragged down into the muck. Chaos is, after all, the ultimate form of democracy.

What hurt most was that they hadn't even waited, the bastards. She could have understood if hers was one of the last stores hit. If the city had said, 'you've been a good friend to us, a good neighbor, and we won't harm you until there is nobody else left, until we have no choice in our madness.' Or if some had defended her place — the police, the neighborhood, the other shopkeepers. If they had stood in front with their arms spread and declared, 'not Elise, we will vouch for her.'

But no, hers was one of the first stores destroyed. Bricks through the glass, interior gutted, building set on fire. Nobody had tried to stop them, nobody had even tried to talk them down. Whoever "they" were. Elise had been there, and still had no idea. She hadn't seen who set the fire, barely glimpsed the first brick thrower. Then again, if she hadn't been willing to stand in front of her shop to protect it, how could she expect others to? She wondered if this was how the jews had felt in Germany. Or the pakis in last decade's riots. But Elise wasn't a jew, a paki, a foreigner. She was a Glaswegian, born and raised.

It was as if the city had said, 'We've always hated you, despised you, wanted to see you burn. And now you will.' Where were the police, she had wondered? Surely all the looters would be caught and punished; didn't they know this after the London riots? But she suspected they wouldn't be. Or if they were, it wouldn't be by the police. In the last 24 hours she had not seen a single policeman, not even the beat cops who regularly passed her shop, sometimes popping in to chat a bit. As she wondered this, Elise slowly dialed emergency services. She only got a busy signal. Eventually, a recorded message came on and informed her in a chirpy voice that all operators were busy and to please call back later. Just as it had the last 28 times.

Elise returned to digging through the rubble for something salvageable, a memento, a sign that her shop had been there, that the last 14 years really had happened, that her life wasn't just last night. And this morning. Elise felt a sudden sense of personal peril. If there were no police, and the hooligans still were out, what was to stop them from robbing her? Or, she shuddered, raping or killing her? She thought of the guy in Craig's bar fight and quickly turned around. There were just a few random people walking by. One had a coffee in his hand. Other than the smoldering ruins, the street looked like it always did at 8 AM. Maybe that was the problem.

After a while, Elise gave up and headed back to her condo. The TV was broadcasting an emergency signal to remain indoors, everything was under control, and so on. If everything was under control, where was her shop? She turned on the radio. Several stations were broadcasting pundits with wild speculations. Glasgow was under quarantine, it had been deserted by the Scottish government, a gang had taken over, and on and on. Everything short of zombies, and Elise was pretty sure that was next on the docket. As far as she could tell, there was a simple explanation. A bunch of hooligans had run amok and the police were off dealing with them. It was like the London riots — disconcerting because nobody expects it to happen at home, but ultimately just a bunch of kids. Nothing worse. *It always gets worse.*

Elise beseeched the phone to ring, shatter the isolation, favor her with a call from one of her friends, her parents, the police, anyone. It remained silent. She tried calling Helen. "All circuits are busy, please try your call again." She had no better luck with anybody else. She checked the internet; her connection was down. She doubted it was anything major, just that the infrastructure in Glasgow wasn't the best and could easily be overwhelmed. Still, it was disconcerting not to be able to talk to anybody. Especially now, when she most needed somebody to talk to.

The telly message changed. "We advise all persons to remain home. A curfew will be in effect throughout the following neighborhoods from 6 PM tonight," followed by a list of neighborhoods. That did it; if they locked down the city, she'd be stuck here. Even if there wasn't anything sinister to worry about, Elise didn't relish another night of rioting. In fact she didn't relish another moment in Glasgow, period. Not after what it had done to her. Best to get out while she still could, but there were some practical issues that required consideration. Elise didn't have a car. She wouldn't be able to order a train or bus ticket from home without the phone or internet working. And it was a good bet that credit card machines wouldn't work either. The only useful information she gleaned from the radio was a mention of added capacity out of Buchanan Station.

Elise kicked herself for not having listened to Craig; she should have gotten out last night, like the old man told her. It's not as if she had saved the shop by sticking around, and she very well may have doomed herself by doing so. Elise took a deep breath. She couldn't have known. People came into her shop and said crazy stuff all the time. Besides, things really weren't *that* bad. If this was all it took for her to panic, how would she deal with a real crisis? Sure, the lack of phone and internet made things inconvenient. But Glasgow was a small city, a walkable city.

That was one of the reasons she had loved it. *Had*. The thought made her sad. Had it ever really loved *her*? Well, she just would have to walk around town and see what was open. Elise packed lightly: a spare shirt, her laptop (just in case), the phone, and the requisite device chargers. She had a total of 147 Scottish pounds, cash. Normally she didn't keep that much on hand, but luckily she just had been to the ATM two days earlier. That was another thing which probably wouldn't work; the ATMs doubtless had been emptied, one way or another.

If she stuck to the high streets, Elise felt she probably could move about safely during the day. Nonetheless, she brought a small knife and filled a perfume spritzer with alcohol. It wouldn't be great protection, but could buy her some time to run if necessary. Dammit, she should have applied for a mace permit. As a shop owner and single woman, she probably could have gotten one. But she didn't want to change the way she felt about her city, begin her negotiation with life on the assumption of violence. How naive. Elise shook her head: too late for that, though. She distributed the cash amongst various pockets and bags in case someone robbed her.

It turned out there were few signs of disorder that day. It was as if the city had spent its rage, vomited itself empty. *It always gets worse.* There would be more to come. She had to leave before nightfall, even if it meant walking. For all its attendant dangers, the road could still be safer than her condo. And without police around, it wouldn't matter where she was; if she stumbled on the wrong people, it would be bad.

But which route should she follow - the road famously less trodden or that taken by the throng? Elise decided her chances were better with the throng. Even after the riot, she had enough faith in her fellow Scots to believe they would stop anything too horrible from happening to her right in front of their eyes. At least she could count on them not to jump in. Who could tell what she may find on the smaller roads. Best to stay with the official evac route — if that was what one could call it.

As Elise walked she gave some thought to a destination, though she wasn't sure there would be any choice in the matter. It was easy to see that Edinburgh would be the best option. Her family was there, it was on the ocean, and the city offered many possible avenues of escape if need be. Escape? Escape from what? It bothered Elise that she now thought this way. Besides, who knew what sort of greeting she'd get in England at this point? The English were very mercenary; she had learned that on her few holidays there. Without money, Elise quickly would find herself in a difficult spot. After walking nearly two blocks, she noticed something lumpy in her pocket. She subconsciously must have known the answer when packing; it was the key to her parents' house.

Predictably, the car rental shops were closed. They all were located on the same street, so Elise had decided to take a small detour and check them. By now she had passed the M8 and was at Anderston Cross. The doors were shut, and she peered through the windows to see if anybody was around. Reflected in the glass she saw a man approaching from behind, and she spun around.

"Oy, what you lookin fer?" The man was wearing a brightly colored reflective vest. Clearly he was some sort of worker. Elise relaxed her grip on the item she reflexively had clutched in her purse. She realized from its feel that it was lipstick. So much for self-defense.

"Are there no buses running, then?" she asked. It may have sounded a bit peevish, but the man didn't seem to notice.

"Not here," he explained. "There's a staging point on Castle Street by the Royal Infirmary. You need to take ... " He began illustrating the path with a hand gesture.

Elise stopped him. "Thanks, I know the way." He seemed in a hurry and was about to leave, or maybe he felt unwanted because she had interrupted his directions. But she needed some more information.

"They mentioned Buchanan Station on the telly," she asked before realizing it wasn't a question.

The man waved impatiently, "they've all relocated to Castle Street."

"What about trains?" Elise persisted. She didn't care if he was busy; she needed to know.

"Don't know about them," he replied brusquely. "You can check Central, but best stay home if you ask me," he pointed in the direction of Central and started off. Then he seemed to have second thoughts and turned, adding apologetically, "sorry, things keep changing. Good luck."

Elise waved to him and decided to head to Central. Everything was on the way to the alleged staging point anyway, and it only was 11:12 AM. She proceeded down Argyll to Central Station, but fared no better there. The several entrances all were chained shut, and even the stairs down had been blocked. There didn't seem to be anybody official around, so Elise just asked a passerby in a suit what was going on. The man, a nondescript yuppie probably in his 30s, just shrugged and returned to muttering into his earpiece.

"Sorry," Elise mouthed, before remembering there was no cell service. Had it been restored? She whipped out her phone and tried again. Not even a signal. By now Elise had reached the East side of Central, so she made her way a bit farther and then headed up Queens St to the eponymous train station. There were a few police officers there, probably to direct people away, but there didn't seem to be any people to direct. She walked over to one, who greeted her in a peremptory tone.

"Whoa there missy — no trains are running."

He sounded a bit the jerk, but she couldn't help being grateful to have found someone in authority. "What's going on?" she asked. Even if the cop was officious, he probably would have some idea what was happening.

"All we know is that people are supposed to stay home. Safest place for you is home," he grumbled unhelpfully. So much for the myth that Scottish cops were nice. She had found the one asshole.

"Listen, I need to report a crime. My shop has been burned."

"Did you call it in?"

"Call it in? The lines are all busy."

"Well, there you have it then," he replied infuriatingly.

"Where is everybody?" she asked. "Why aren't you guys doing your jobs?" Elise felt her temper rising, never a good thing, and especially bad with a cop on a power trip.

He put out his hand as if to block her. "Listen missy, just go home and this all will be sorted out soon."

"Am I required to go home?" she asked contentiously.

The cop seemed puzzled. "Well, no. Curfew isn't until six. Just get about your business and be done with it quick." Then he softened. "It's really not safe out here for you, missy."

"It isn't safe at home either."

"Man abuse you?"

"That's not what I mean." She began to walk away, but then turned back and asked, "what's this I hear of a staging area at the Royal Infirmary?"

The cop rolled his eyes and put his hand on her shoulder. "Listen, you don't want to go there. It's a huge mess. Just go home, and this all will blow over. Everybody's in a panic. You don't want to go there. Trust me."

Elise smiled and thanked him. She obligingly turned around and walked two blocks before rounding a corner and heading back to Castle Street. She was within her rights to ignore the policeman's advice, but felt it would be impolite to let herself be seen doing so. By this time, she had walked at least four miles and was getting a bit tired. Elise took a sip from the thermos she had brought. Then it struck her — no stores were open. She'd need food and water, and if they didn't have any at the staging area it could make for a very unpleasant journey.

As she proceeded up Castle st, she prayed that the government had some sort of evacuation plan in place. Or even that a simple bus was running. She just wanted to get out, disaster or no. She probably would be fine if she went back to the condo, but she didn't want to. Elise just needed to get away from this city. Why was that so hard? It had become like a noisome ex, and she wanted some time apart. Maybe they'd reconcile when all this was over, maybe not. But for now, she wanted nothing to do with Glasgow.

As Elise walked up Castle Street, her hopes rose. There didn't seem to be a crowd or big line. Perhaps she could just hop on a bus, after all. She had cash. Maybe it even would be free, given that they had shut everything else down. Then she noticed somebody standing in a very short line by one of the doors.

"Where does the bus to Edinburgh leave from?" she asked, her voice strained and tired.

The man nodded reassuringly — "You're in the right line, miss." Then he seemed to have an afterthought. "You have a ticket right?"

"No, I'm afraid I don't." Her stomach sank. The dreaded Maitre'd's, "You *do* have a reservation, don't you?"

"Are they all sold out?" she asked hesitantly, fearing the answer, the futility of her quest, and the long walk home defeated through the city that had spat on her. It would laugh smugly, 'I knew you couldn't do without me.'

"No, they're guaranteeing everyone a ride." He smiled wanly, "it just may be a bit of a wait."

"Where . . . ," she began to ask.

The man pointed. "Just follow the road around the back side and go in through the doors."

"Thank you so much," she beamed, relieved that a seat was guaranteed. She didn't care if it took an hour or two, as long as she got out.

As Elise followed the indicated route, it occurred to her that she should have asked the man other questions: What was going on? Is there food? It was so hard to find somebody helpful. It was the fear of being a nuisance more than exhaustion that kept her from going back and importuning him. She never had felt shy before, but now Elise was humbled. The city hated her, she was on her own, and she had almost nothing. At least she could get a ride to Edinburgh. This was enough to keep her going, she felt, as she walked through the doors. In a few hours she would be safe at her parents' place.

Then she saw the line. It would be longer than a few hours. A lot longer.

CHAPTER 8

Day 730 — Near Yining, China

"Come here," the guard gestured curtly to Yu Feng's corner of the cell. Feng looked around to see at whom the order was directed. The cell was a forty by sixty space with a few straw mats strewn about and a couple of buckets in the corners. It resembled a temporary holding pen, and that had been Feng's assumption when he first was brought here. Instead, it became his home for the last four years. About a year in, a guard told him there had been a trial but he didn't know the sentence. The only noticeable difference was that the weekly beatings had stopped. Apparently, things were better for convicts. This turned out to be true in many ways.

The longer Feng was there, the more he knew about the workings of the jail. Contrary to his preconception of such places, strict order was maintained. There was no scrum for food, and fights weren't tolerated. Even a raised voice or threat against another prisoner could land you a drubbing or a month in solitary. So far Feng had managed to avoid both, though with some difficulty at times. Aside from a few long-term tenants, there was high turnover. The average stay seemed to be around six months, and the pen usually held close to a hundred prisoners.

Newcomers didn't know the rules, and still had some residual pride. It was easy to get dragged into a fight when they were aggressive. This was why Feng stayed in the corner by the waste bucket, even when the cell was nearly empty. He could get used to the smell of feces and the noise and indignity. What he couldn't get used to was constantly having to defend his space against newcomers, and risk beatings for doing so. Nobody disputed the corners.

"You," the guard barked impatiently, pointing at him. Feng blinked in disbelief. It was his turn. Finally. This shouldn't have surprised him; there only were three people left in the cell. The other two were feigning sleep near the opposite wall.

The guard drew his nightstick and began to stride menacingly across the room, but Feng didn't need coaxing. He rose to his feet, smiling. It was *his* turn. Finally, after waiting so long, it was his turn. His legs had atrophied from scant use, and he limped over to the guard. Even though Feng was complying, the guard had to make a show of authority. Mercifully, he was satisfied with a rough grab of the head and some desultory shoves, and didn't resort to the club.

"Is it my turn?" Feng ventured sheepishly, glancing sideways at the guard as he was marched out the door.

"Your turn," the guard replied brusquely without pausing.

Over the last few months, the flow of prisoners had changed and there was a buzz in the air. The cell was more crowded, and most prisoners stayed for shorter periods of time. Feng and his fellow "longies", as they were known, speculated about this ad nauseum. When stuck in the same cell without intermission or reprieve for years, there really wasn't much to do besides speculate and sleep. Any casual topics had long since been exhausted by the longies. They knew everything about one another: pasts, loves, the bastards who put them there, what they'd do when they got out. They didn't pretend to be innocent or victims. Feng was guilty.

One could dispute whether his crime should have been considered a crime, but that was true of any action in any society; under some moral systems it was a crime, under others it was not. Likewise, one could argue whether he deserved a greater or lesser punishment or was receiving precisely his due. That too was a question of moral philosophy, an abstraction that need not be answered the same way twice. But such considerations were of little solace to Feng, however often he revisited them. The concrete reality was that he had received a specific sentence under a specific law and was in a specific smelly cage serving it.

He felt it would have been nice to know what that sentence *was*, though. But he never had been told. None of them had, in fact. Whether this was intended as kindness or cruelty was unclear. Perhaps it was not intended at all, simply a residual neglect. There was no need to tell them, so they didn't. It just was the way they did things and always had.

Initially, speculation about the influx of inmates had centered on judicial reform. Perhaps there was a move to clear the prisons. But as a former historian, Feng was well aware that leniency rarely has been exercised from a sense of humanity. There usually was an economic motivation. Even in self-described enlightened democracies, long prison sentences for minor offenses often were deemed fair and just and necessary. Until the cost of the trials and prisons and police were tallied, then suddenly they were not. In another life, Feng had written a paper critical of this Western hypocrisy. It even won praise from two local Party officials.

Of course, it made sense to Feng that such economics would have even greater import in a place like China. There were few advantages to democracy, and efficiency was not one of them. On the other hand, a centrally-managed government was much like a corporation: efficient but subject to many of the same pressures and fads. Perhaps a new department head needed to make a name for himself, and cutting costs was a good way to do that. Or the new watch-word was "budget reduction". Or it just became popular to seem like a kinder, gentler society. Whatever the reason, there definitely had been such drives in the past. However, despite the optimism of his fellow longies, it seemed unlikely to Feng that this was the cause. If so, there would be an actual reduction in population rather than just high turnover.

Another possibility was a drive in the opposite direction. Perhaps there was a large move to quash certain behaviors. Or there had been a big protest and the participants now were trickling in. In that case, it was possible the system was overwhelmed and they actually were using the cell as a holding pen as they processed large numbers of offenders on their way to longer-term detention centers.

Feng had questioned quite a few of the transient prisoners as they came through, but most weren't very communicative. The few who did talk hinted at something bad happening outside, though nobody seemed to know what it was. Some even sounded like they were fleeing *into* the prisons. But of course, that was absurd. People didn't flee into cages; they were put there by other people. From what little Feng had gleaned, the new prisoners weren't political and mostly seemed to have come from other prisons. Which led to his reshuffling theory.

Reshuffling was the other thing that large organizations periodically did to create the illusion of progress. Nobody respects the status quo. If the world were paradise, people would blame god for not innovating. There has to be a sense of motion. This is understandable; time moves us from birth to death, so who wants to stay in one place? While nothing we do actually makes any difference, we can pretend it does. But you can't pretend that doing *nothing* makes a difference. So we respect motion and commotion and a great show of change, even if that change is away from something that we really liked and worked just fine and was quite necessary.

In the criminal justice system, reshuffling serves another important purpose. It keeps prisoners confused. Irrespective of the country or its politics or pretenses, keeping prisoners confused is important. It isn't not just about demeaning them and their families. It's about control. When people stagnate in one another's company for too long, they form relationships and cliques and bonds. Bonds between prisoners are dangerous. A few men cannot control many if those many collude. Sure, guns help; but instability and ignorance are the best tools. Reshuffling seemed to Feng a very likely candidate.

But then, almost six months before he was taken from the cell, the influx abruptly stopped and the cell's population stabilized at one hundred and fifty four prisoners. It may be hard to count a large number of people in a crowd, but here it was easy. There was no shortage of time, and the prisoners didn't move around much. In fact, Feng could have provided a detailed day by day tally of the cell's population over the last few years if some statistician perversely had asked it of him.

Some of the newer prisoners proved more talkative once they settled in. They didn't know much, but seemed less apprehensive about being moved again. It occurred to Feng that things were very different for those stuck in a cell and those passing through it. The former were desperate for change, for conversation, for new bonds. Those in transit, however, viewed such people as mere furniture. Why bother interacting with them, when they knew nothing? Why build a bond when you would move on? As always, nobody respected the man who stayed in place, even if it was not his choice, even if he would give all he was and had and had been just to have the chance to 'be' again. His fellow doomed care nothing about this; they looked down on him until they finally took his place.

Once the flow stopped, conversations started. The main rumor was that there indeed had been a large reshuffle. A couple of new major holding facilities were constructed post-haste, and the prison population had been consolidated from several old ones. Of course, there were many possible reasons to do such a thing. A natural disaster or chemical spill could necessitate a relocation. Or, a mandate for some structural or political change could be involved. It was impossible to know for sure, and all Feng could do was accumulate the mostly contradictory rumors.

CHAPTER 9

Day 283 — Washington DC

There was an uneasy tension in the air. Robert Halifax felt it palpably. He could imagine many circumstances in which uneasy tension is desirable — the grasping expectation of romance after a first kiss, the awkward vacuum created by a deliberately comedic faux pas, and the interstice preceding the announcement of a much anticipated award. However it almost never was a good thing during a special session, especially when the Joint Chiefs of Staff sat in dread of the next words to be spoken.

Robert thought of a cancer patient. However many days the doctor gave you, however angry or resentful or seemingly insouciant you may be, each of those days still is precious. And if they are taken away, if the cancer spreads a tiny bit faster or the medicine proves a tiny bit less effective, the pronouncement of this new doom is as dreadful as the first.

This is not surprising; after all, there is no real meaning to the words "your illness is terminal." All of us suffer from a terminal illness, the question simply is how long we have. We decry the injustice when that number is dropped from thirty years to one. It is just as painful when it is dropped from one year to half that. Never mind that each passing day draws our death closer, each moment a proclamation, killing us a little. We do not notice that little, only the grand announcements. That the world is taking something from us, and there is no court of appeal.

This was the nature of the tension, the moment between near death and nearer death, between being told we have little, and being told that even that little would be taxed by a universe which gave nothing in return. Robert wondered what the prognosis would be this time? They would see soon enough. At bottom, everything known about the Front was mere assumption anyway. For all they knew, it could speed up, stop, split into a million fragments, or a second Front could appear in the middle of the room that very day. Once one impossibility had occurred, who could pretend to know anything?

Someone gave a bronchial cough, and Robert cringed before realizing that his instinctive response was obsolete. Even if that cough heralded a deadly disease, the plague would find itself forestalled. Something grimmer had come, quietly standing between the shadows.

"Our previous calculation of the progress of the Front was based on a flawed assumption."

Lilly cleared her throat, and it was a few moments before she continued. Robert wondered whether this was intended to draw out the suspense. No, a consummate scientist, she would have no flavor for theatrics. He suspected she was giving the room time to prepare itself, to digest the information presented and anticipate that to come. It wasn't from a sense of delicacy or roguishness. It simply would better allow subsequent information to be assimilated.

As an experienced manager and speaker, she clearly knew how to break bad news. More importantly she knew how to break it to important people who were not used to bad news they couldn't deflect onto others or evade or confront. Robert sensed how difficult that must be, especially given the personalities involved. Would *he* ever get to the point where he was capable of such a feat? Even if he could, the Front ensured he wouldn't.

"Our previous calculation of the progress of the Front was based on a flawed assumption," she repeated. "Albeit one which appeared justified within statistical significance by the evidence available until recently. Unfortunately... ".

She paused and wiped her left eyeglass in what could have

been mistaken for an attempt to collect herself, but quickly continued without wavering.

"Unfortunately, the evidence now supports a new model. Before explaining the new model, I will provide the three critical pieces of information that support it."

"Just tell us how much goddamn time we have!" snapped the Navy Secretary, Jim Hyatt.

Lilly contemplated him with a blank distracted look for a few seconds, as if calculating something unrelated before realizing she had been spoken to. "Less," she responded curtly before proceeding as if nothing had been said.

"After a short initial period of confusion, all civilian and military air traffic has been kept a safe distance from the Zone." She was talking about Z-day, Robert realized. Why rehash such basic information? Surely, everybody here knew what had happened. Then again maybe not, if Lilly Tao was taking the time to go over it.

"Therefore, it is to that short initial period of confusion that we must turn for certain information. After the Front appeared but before the threat it posed was understood, a number of flights were affected. Altogether, these spanned a window of approximately two days. Counter-intuitively, the majority of useful information derives from the latter portion of that period. In the sixteen hours after the Front first presented, most nearby air traffic was either grounded or diverted due to the sudden increase in incidents."

"The natural supposition was that a coordinated terrorist attack or some sort of EMP or coincident equipment failure was responsible. Protocol required immediate grounding of locally originating flights, and diversion of all flyovers and incoming flights. After an initial investigation, civilian traffic was restored for reasons which are not entirely clear to us. Most likely they were of a political nature. Six hours later, restrictions once again were imposed and, as it turned out, these were permanent. As a result, we have very little information regarding the actual effect of the Front on air traffic. Almost all the relevant data comes from that six hour period between bans. However, that data is quite telling. Frank."

She looked at Frank Brauwer, Director of the National Transport Agency. The NTA was the bastard offspring of the old TSA, INS, and FAA. Or perhaps it would be more accurate to say it sprung from their skull's full-grown. It had been formed as part of an early attempt to restructure government agencies along jurisdictional rather than functional lines, back after Z-day when 'efficiency' was the new catchword.

The general initiative ultimately proved abortive and politicians moved on to other sound bites, but by then the NTA had taken on a life of its own. It had been given a very broad mandate, which it interpreted even more broadly. By now the NTA had become one of the most powerful agencies, and had responsibility for all aspects of transportation, customs, and immigration. It even had its own military force, nominally drawn from the old Coast Guard. In government circles the NTA privately was joked to stand for "No Tolerance for Anything" (or sometimes "No Talent Allowed"), and its enforcement branch was derisively termed the "New Gestapo." From what Robert heard, this was not undeserved.

Frank looked surprised. Although Robert did not know it, the department heads had been told as little about the nature of this meeting as he had. Lilly called it, and when she called they came. Frank pressed the microphone button briefly and responded inaudibly, before realizing he had to hold down the button while speaking.

"I'm sorry, Madam Director" So *that* was her official title, Robert noted. It often was hard to know how to address senior officials. One person could have a dozen titles, and everybody seemed to shuffle positions constantly. Today's Interior Secretary was tomorrow's AIS spokesman. And if you called him something, it was a good bet that he was something else and would take offense. Robert unconsciously slid back into his seat. One more opportunity to make a jackass of himself, one more reason never to get called on.

"What was your question?" Frank asked, irritably fumbling with the button as he did so.

Lilly responded matter-of-factly and somewhat pedantically, "I didn't ask a question."

She continued, "please explain to the room your findings regarding Z-day flights," and paused, yielding the floor to him.

Frank seemed relieved; clearly this was a topic he knew well. It occurred to Robert that maybe they both felt the same way about being called on. In fact, maybe Frank was Robert in thirty years. *That* was an unsettling thought, and Robert almost was glad that he never would find out. Almost. Frank nodded in acknowledgment, then typed on his texting device for a few moments before sitting back. Evidently, Lilly and his colleagues understood what was going on and waited patiently.

After around thirty seconds, during which there was silence broken only by a few hushed murmurs, one of his three support staff rose. It was a tall blond man, probably Robert's age, and wearing glasses. He seemed neatly composed. The man furtively stepped forward, and handed Frank a folder before hurrying back to his seat. He almost tripped over a step while doing so. Apparently, Robert wasn't the only one eager to avoid the spotlight.

Frank perused the document for a few moments, clearly weighing the quickening discomfort of silence against the danger of misspeaking. When the two curves intersected, he leaned forward and quietly held down the button.

"Madam Director, please let me know if I can clarify any of the particulars..." it was an unnecessary nicety but bought him a few moments to compose his sentence. After a deep breath Frank continued, frequently consulting the documents that had been handed to him, and at times appearing to read directly from them.

"We do not have records for most flights. EU regulations prohibited the storage of data on US based servers due to our information acquisition policies at the time. Judging from historical ratios, there likely were around four hundred and sixty flights that came within a three mile radius of the Origin. That area represents the extent of the Zone at the time of the permanent prohibition on air traffic. Most of the flights had Glasgow Airport as their origin or destination. A number of smaller craft, mainly originating from Prestwick, also are included in the figures."

"Despite the EU restrictions, we have full information for all U.S.-based airlines, continuously relayed, except for MultiContinental Airlines, which used a different system. Information for non-US based airlines is limited. We have basic proximity info relayed from our own airplanes for all flights within 12 miles, some intercepted chatter from UK-based airlines, and an intelligence stream from two German airlines. An examination of satellite feeds during that time provided no additional information, and no data regarding early flights has been retrieved from within the Zone itself. Efforts to reconstruct flight trajectories and timings using enhanced optical imagery, published timetables, and other information have yielded some additional insight." He paused.

"And what are your findings?" Lilly inquired didactically.

"We have complete flight path information for one hundred and sixteen flights, almost exclusively larger craft, and partial flight information for two hundred and twelve flights, including some smaller craft. Of the former, only forty three intersected the Zone. Of these, forty crashed."

Frank allowed some time for this to sink in, waiting for the inevitable reaction. After a few moments of expectant silence, he realized that the inevitable reaction wasn't so inevitable, and everybody simply thought he was going to continue. Nobody seemed to notice the problem. Or maybe nobody wanted to seem the fool by asking the obvious question. With an almost inaudible sigh, Lilly did so for them. "To clarify, three flights intersected the Zone and were unaffected. Is there any consistent explanation?"

Robert noticed that she emphasized the word consistent.

"No," responded Frank.

"What about autopilot?" offered one of the people at the main table, Robert wasn't sure who.

"Autopilot was not activated for any of those flights. We have complete records," Frank emphasized.

"At what altitude were the flights?" Lilly guided the exposition. She had a point to make, and Frank seemed to have gleaned it.

"Of the one hundred and sixteen flights, eighty four had a sixteen thousand foot ceiling while over the Zone. This largely was due to the proximity of Glasgow Airport to the Origin. These flights either were in a holding pattern, were on an approach vector, or had just departed. The remaining thirty two flights were fly-overs and maintained a deck of thirty to thirty-two thousand feet."

"And what of those that intersected the Zone?" queried Lilly.

"We have computed the likely locations of intersection of all forty three flights." Frank signaled one of the attendants and handed her two sheets of paper. She brought these to the podium and showed them to Lilly, who nodded and pointed at one. The attendant carefully placed it in front of a camera, and its image appeared on a large overhead screen that Robert hadn't previously noticed. The writing on the picture was reversed, and the attendant quickly flipped the sheet over. A pair of axes formed an inverted T, with both labeled in feet. The vertical had ticks that were multiples of 5000 feet, while the horizontal ticks were multiples of 1000 feet. Three clusters of points were visible, with a few outliers above the rest.

Frank continued, "As you can see we've plotted the points. There is no obvious pattern." He paused before adding that "the clusters correspond to standard approach and departure vectors," lest everyone frantically strain to see a pattern which did not exist.

"However," he continued, "there are two very interesting things to observe. First, all the intersections were of flights below the sixteen thousand foot ceiling." He paused and looked at Lilly who signaled the attendant. She placed the second picture in front of the camera, this time with the correct orientation. It appeared to be an identical image, except for three distinctly-colored and oddly-shaped blobs which been drawn around the points. Each had a label.

Frank quickly explained. "The second interesting thing to note is that all three survivors are outliers: M15, M29, and M7 on the chart. The only apparent explanation is that, for some reason unknown to us, the Front did not instantly rise to the edge of our atmosphere. Rather, it expanded to that level over time. Based on the data, we deduced the range of heights that the Front could have reached at the five hour, ten hour, and fifteen hour marks. The curves represent those boundaries. They're very rough, of course."

There was a pause, as Lilly impatiently waited for someone to ask the right question.

"So it rose with time? They don't look uniform." It was Robert's own boss, Doug Harving.

Lilly smiled. Apparently, it was the right question. For no good reason, Robert felt satisfaction that his boss had been the one to spot it. As if he were proud to be a bench warmer on the winning team. Except that there was no winning team, of course. This was the fun sort of game where everybody lost, and apparently more quickly than previously anticipated.

Lilly clarified "That's the problem. The Front did not rise uniformly as it expanded laterally. The curves are not inaccurate."

There was silence.

"So how is it expanding then?" It was Doug again, perhaps emboldened by his previous success. Robert smiled. It seemed that approval-seeking was just as prevalent among movers and shakers as schoolboys. It made sense, he supposed; all that changes is whom you seek approval from. Or maybe Lilly just was a force of personality, the rare type of person who could make a room full of self-important bigwigs vie for acknowledgment. He suspected there was an element of this as well.

Now that Robert thought of it, she *was* quite attractive. Older, but there was something about her. He regained control of his thoughts, and wondered if this was on Captain Raymond's no-go list. He suspected that if speaking to Lilly would be off limits, thinking inappropriate thoughts (which sounded vaguely Orwellian, when put that way) would land him in a heap of trouble. And she wasn't 'Lilly', she was Madame Secretary or something to that effect. He could see himself being hauled in front of a firing squad, defiantly declaring it was worth it. Did they even use those anymore? Firing squads seemed so old-fashioned. He almost thought 'quaint', but it probably would seem less so if you were in front of one.

No, these days they would feed him to the Front. Well maybe not just for getting an erection. He had slunk so far down into his chair that he doubted anybody would notice. On the other hand, with all the surveillance in this meeting, there probably was some military goon dedicated just to watching him, taking notes, judging. 'Inappropriate arousal, possibly treason? Google it later.' Or just snickering. He hoped just snickering. 'How is it expanding, then'? It occurred to him that

Doug's question could be taken as a double entendre. Would they share a cell, awaiting execution together? Could be a good networking opportunity. What would the goon watching him think?

Suddenly Robert was very self-conscious, and sat upright. He froze, worried that someone might notice the sudden movement, but everybody was absorbed in the graph. It occurred to Robert that this was a tragedy of being male, that a small fluctuation in hormones can translate the most somber and momentous proceedings into a source of juvenile hilarity. Women had the glass ceiling, men the portable gutter. Which more profoundly impacted career and prosperity would be hard to tell. Robert caught himself at the beginning of a smile, and desperately focused on controlling his face. What if Lilly pointed at him and demanded, 'something *amusing* about this, Mr. Halifax?' It was unlikely she even knew his name, but Robert was certain that such knowledge somehow would manifest itself to better humiliate him.

Instead she just seemed to ignore Doug and Doug's comment and Doug's support staff and barreled on. "We will hear from Information Assessment." What was 'Information Assessment' Robert wondered? It suddenly occurred to him that he probably was not the first male audience member to get aroused by her, and that it probably was too dark to tell anyway. Not to mention the obstructed line of sight. What was wrong with him? His reverie was interrupted by a flashing light on his desk. The text display under it read "Look lively. Our turn next." Apparently *somebody* noticed that he was distracted.

Robert's stomach sank. Our turn for what? He didn't *know* anything. He wondered whether *he* would trip when scuttling back to his desk. Would he make better time than the blond guy? Robert was pretty sure that he would win a competition to be noticed less. He replied by text, "What should I prep?" There was no reply. He looked down and could feel Doug's tension. Was he more worried about taking the spotlight or the Front's newly discovered behavior?

"Doug, would you give us a rundown on the latest ISS intel."

What did this have to do with the ISS tragedy? Robert wondered in the small intervals between panicking and checking his text display. At least it explained why he was here, though. One of his recent projects had been spreading conspiracy theories about the ISS airlock failure. When given the assignment, he naturally had assumed that NASA desperately wanted to divert attention from its own incompetence.

Robert actually was quite proud of this piece of work, it was one of his best. Also one of the funnest. Some of his inventions had been quite creative. His favorite was that Captain Konarski and Dr. Ying had planned to crash the station into the Zone as part of a suicide pact, but the crew thwarted them so they spaced (a term from some sci-fi movie he had seen) everyone in desperation. Another had been that the Zone really extended all the way to infinity, but somehow the space station had avoided it — until somebody sabotaged their controls and secretly sent them through it.

There also was a Planet of the Apes scenario, dripping with sarcasm and chock full of ironic allusions to classic sci-fi. Apparently, nobody had noticed or censored it. At what point did ironically being ironic cease to be ironic? It had become one of the most popular theories out there. If there was one thing Robert had learned long ago, it was that the dumber something seemed to him the more likely it was to be the next big thing. Sometimes he wondered if the Front wasn't a blessing for humanity. The only problem was that it purged the few smart people along with everyone else.

Doug began, "a number of competing theories have been

disseminated. Our numbers show a 12% damage attribution to NASA, well within acceptable bounds." Doug began to rattle off Robert's creations in order of popularity, but Lilly interrupted him.

"We need a change in tack."

Doug seemed confused and began to stammer something about NASA.

"We want NASA to take the blame. All of it. You have been misinformed," she continued.

There was a gasp in the room. Matt McDonald, under whose purview NASA fell, rose to his feet red-faced.

"Sit down, Matt," Lilly commanded in a calm voice, and the murmuring quieted. "The furor will die down. NASA is the most plausible culprit. Incompetence is a good excuse."

There was an uneasy silence. "Why would we want NASA to take the blame?" Doug ventured.

Lilly looked at him as if puzzled that it wasn't obvious. "Because *we* sent the ISS into the Zone, of course."

The room fell silent. Robert could not tell whether it was from shock, fear, or disgust. The "we" in that sentence carried a special connotation. One does not use "we" in such a context to refer to a bunch of employees. It meant somebody higher than her, somebody who had her back. Nominally, there were many such people. Just as, nominally, the U.S. had been a democracy for the last century. In truth there were very few people to whom Lilly actually reported, and none were in the room. Which meant that she was their voice in this matter.

This was one of the reasons she would not be arrested or confronted or shown overt disapproval by anyone present. The other was more sinister. It was obvious to everybody there, even Robert, that "we" included them. They had all been made party to this. The government of which they were a part just openly admitted to murdering the entire crew of the International Space Station, the most public and visible symbol of global unity in the face of an extinction level crisis. This decision was made by the most senior members of that government. Either the institution was sociopathic or they were.

Either way, it was best to give little cause for complaint. It was best to listen on and pray that whatever followed would offer some means of rationalization. A way to believe that it was a necessary evil, that each person in the room could continue to exist knowing what they do and thinking themselves a good person without risking that existence. The problem with having the courage of one's convictions is that it can get one convicted. Or worse.

Then somebody pointed out the obvious. "But, the Front doesn't extend that high. How could you do that even if you wanted to."

The room breathed a tentative sigh of relief. Of course, there was no *good* answer to this. Lilly either was incompetent, insane, lying, a murderer, or some combination of these. All that remained to be seen was which.

Lilly ignored this implication and responded curtly. "As mentioned, the shape is different than previously thought."

The tension returned. This was no mistake, she was serious. All the previous considerations were back, exacerbated by lost hope.

Lilly continued, oblivious to the enormity of her confession or the existential dilemma it posed for everyone. Fortunately, her next sentence raised the prospect of *some* justification.

"From this we gleaned an important piece of data." But then she pulled out the rug, left them all villains. "It was the final verification of our hypothesis before deeming the evidence statistically conclusive." Translation: we murdered them just to double-check our results. There was an audible gasp. Robert revised his opinion of her. Either she was a psychopath, or she was entirely unable to relate to her audience. Didn't she realize she had just removed their slim remaining hope of justifying this act, of not kissing their children good night as murderers.

Lilly changed the topic, giving them little time for emotional prevarication. "This analyst of yours, Doug. He came up with the existing scenarios."

"Yes, Robert Halifax." Doug responded with as much composure as possible, but noticeably failed to address her as "Madame Director" this time. Robert's head jerked up, attentive. Were they talking about him? Like almost everyone else in the room, he still was coming to grips with Lilly's words.

Lilly waved dismissively, clearly uninterested in extraneous details such as his name. "His most popular scenario hit the mark." Uh oh. Robert felt his stomach turning. Was she going to charge him with treason, with somehow knowing or leaking this information?

To his relief, she gave an awkward laugh instead. "It's rather insightful of him." Robert suspected this was as close to humor as she could come. And what better time for humor than right after you announce a crime against humanity?

"Have him manage the revised campaign," she ordered. Doug's face twisted. Department heads didn't interfere with one another's fiefdoms, didn't poach employees. This would not end well for Robert's career. Perhaps aware of this, she continued, "the best man to undo it is the one who did it." Did she just make that up? It sounded pithy, but inane.

"And when you're done, have him transferred to my department." Doug grimaced in anger, but said nothing. Robert suspected that he was kicking himself for mentioning him; otherwise, he could have foisted some schmuck on her. Then again, until an hour ago Robert probably *was* just some schmuck to him. Doug probably hadn't even known his name, and a few hours from now probably will have forgotten it.

"Yes, Madam Director." Apparently, she had cowed him. Robert had heard about this sort of ego-wrangling, but never seen it in person. Lilly didn't care whether she made an enemy of Doug. Then again, after her announcement everyone in the room was her enemy.

The light above Robert's display lit up. It read "Looks like you made a friend." Robert glanced down to see Doug grinning wryly at him. No, Doug would not forget his name.

CHAPTER 10

Day 9 — Edinburgh, Scotland

The dining table looked out on Braid Avenue, an idyllic tree-lined street. It was such a beautiful place, why hadn't Elise noticed before? Why hadn't she moved here years ago? Her parents would have loved it, maybe that was why. She could have relaxed here as often as she wished, listening to the patter of rain on the glass of this lovely limestone. There even was a sitooterie in back. Who actually had a sitooterie these days? How much better than her tiny Glasgow condo, how much more serene. But wasn't that what she had wanted: noise? Had she confused noise with life? Friends with *a life*? Well, it certainly had gotten noisy. Elise cradled the makeshift cast on her arm. Or maybe she just was bitter because of how her own city had treated her.

Even now she couldn't relax, enjoy the silence. Her parents' home was empty, and she needed to figure out what to do next. The trip here had been hell, though she felt a bit spoiled even thinking such a thing. What about those kids in Africa who ran twenty miles every day to school, hiding from violent rebel factions? A 47 mile bicycle trip between two cities in Scotland hardly seemed comparable. Nevertheless, Elise wouldn't relish a repeat. All told, she had been very lucky.

The problems had started when she queued up at the staging area in Glasgow. The line was long and most of the people seemed sullen and uncommunicative. Or at least those near her did. The trouble with a line is that your immediate vicinity remains with you the entire way, defines your experience. For the duration of her time there, it was her universe.

She honestly couldn't understand this reticence. All the standard tools for avoiding social interaction were unavailable.

Cell phones didn't work, there were no emails to send, no texts to write. And they were stuck with literally nothing to do for what promised to be a very long time. So why not chat with other real people here in the real world? Perhaps they were too absorbed in private sorrow or reflection. It was understandable, she supposed. But weren't they at least curious about what was happening?

Unless they already knew. Unless all that needed to be said *had* been said, before she arrived. Elise suddenly had the suspicion that she was the only one who didn't know, a possibility which tormented her until she finally managed to speak with the man behind her.

Of course, when she first arrived there hadn't *been* a man behind her. And the one in front made it quite clear he had no desire for conversation. During the next thirty minutes nobody else arrived, and Elise began to wonder whether she was late to the party, perhaps even last. Still, better the last in the door than the first locked out. Or maybe the police were doing a good job steering people away. Just as Elise began to wonder whether she should have taken their advice, somebody got in line behind her.

He turned out to be a young man with a slightly shady look — shaved head, hoodie, baggy jumpsuit. Precisely the type which seemed likely to throw rocks through shop windows. But Elise couldn't afford to be judgmental. Besides, she prided herself on keeping an open mind. It occurred to her that if you pride yourself on a quality, you probably don't possess it. Deep down she knew that, like everybody else, she was wildly inconsistent in the application of her principles.

When she first sensed the man's arrival, Elise instinctively turned and offered a disarming smile. The man didn't smile back, but neither did he turn or scowl. She wanted to play it cool; it is not considered good form to conversationally pounce on somebody, especially a captive audience. It would be as rude as lighting a cigarette, which the guy promptly did.

Elise was pretty sure that smoking was prohibited. At the very least, it was terribly inconsiderate. There wasn't anybody official around to alert about this, and nobody else in line seemed to care or want to make a fuss. Elise simply was too tired to confront the man. Other than an exaggerated waving motion and a few affected coughs, she made no allusion to the cigarette. But any qualms about annoying him had vanished. If he was going to be inconsiderate, so would she. In fact, she hoped she *would* make his wait unpleasant. Nonetheless, she opened as politely as possible.

"Looks like this isn't going anywhere fast, eh?", she ventured.

He looked at her and then up and away. "Nah." Obviously a First in English, this one. Then she caught herself: *no judgments*.

Elise got right to the point. "Any idea what's going on?"

"You don't know? Why are you here?" He seemed mildly puzzled, but mostly bored.

"Well, the riots obviously." Elise tried not to sound too annoyed; she had little patience for people with attitudes, but was desperate for information.

"Right, that makes sense."

It occurred to Elise that this guy may not be running from the riots; he may have been part of them. He took a puff and blew the smoke vertically up by protruding his lower lip. Was that an attempt to be considerate? It would be a typical smoker rationalization, she fumed. 'If I crack open a window in this tiny room, none of the twenty other people will even notice while I fill it with burnt tar.' Elise took a breath to calm herself, but almost gagged on the air's acrid texture.

"Well if not the riots, why are *you* here?" she demanded.

"Don't be daft. You know, the toxic spill," he replied in his lackadaisical voice. Elise bristled at being called daft. But she wasn't going to let this punk irritate her. Besides, he didn't seem dangerous on closer inspection. In fact, she was pretty sure he was dressed in rather expensive designer clothes. She knew the type.

"No, I *don't* know, actually. Nobody told us anything," she replied peevishly.

"Ok, ok, no need to get mad." He stamped out his cigarette. "It's like this. There's a big spill up North. Some nasty chemical in the Clyde. And it's slowly making its way down here."

"They told us to stay home!" Elise's voice was raised in disbelief. A couple of people in line glanced at her and then returned to staring straight ahead.

"Well, they would wouldn't they?" he smiled.

"So why isn't anything running?"

"It is, just," he pointed ahead with a patronizing look "this is it, isn't it?"

"Buses?"

"Army transports. But it don't matter. The M8 is one big parking lot from what I hear. They ain't going nowhere."

She paused in thought and turned around. Then she turned back. "What about trains? Trains should be running nonstop."

The guy shrugged, "That's what *I* asked. Got some bollocks about worker safety rules. They said you can't run the trains either way unless dispatch at both ends is clear. Well, that's pretty stupid ain't it? So, they're just sitting there."

Elise faced forward and thought for a few minutes. Wait a second, the Clyde flowed West through Glasgow. How could the spill be carried upstream? She turned to point this out, he gave her a pleading look to leave him alone. At least he didn't light up again.

An hour passed, and the line hadn't moved at all. By now it was past 2 PM. After waiting a few minutes more, Elise finally concluded this wasn't going to work. Besides, if the man was right then even if she got on a bus it would end up stuck in traffic. With a sigh, she decided to head home and try again the next morning. Why make a ten hour trip today that only would take an hour tomorrow, once the traffic had cleared. She left the line and headed for the door. After a few feet, she decided to be polite and turned. Before she could wish him good luck, the man in the jumpsuit snorted, "I ain't savin' your place," and shuffled forward. Elise rolled her eyes and walked out.

It was almost 3 PM. With only the contents of her daypack she wouldn't make it far on foot, and it sounded like the trains were out and the roads jammed. As much as she hated doing so, Elise would have to go back and stock up at her condo. She felt defeated. To distract herself, she decided to take a different route home. She also didn't want to see the smug look on that cop's face when he saw her return, thwarted. She could just hear him: 'That's right missy, you head home like I told you in the first place. Mind you, next time you may want to listen to your betters when you're told what to do.'

Elise made her way over to the University. Besides being on her way home it would have a toilet, which she badly needed by this point. The campus seemed deserted. She tried a few doors before finally finding one that was open. In the hallway the restrooms were locked, but she spotted a water-fountain and drank her fill. Elise was surprised how thirsty she was. Outside, the campus was beautiful. It was a perfect summer day, and one could almost imagine that nothing was wrong. After basking in the normalcy for a few moments, Elise sighed and began the walk home.

Without her earlier detours, the trip back actually was rather short. On an ordinary day, she wouldn't have given it a second thought. But this was not an ordinary day, and Elise already was both physically and emotionally exhausted. On the flip side, that kept her from ruminating on her shop and her safety and the toxic spill and the next day. It was a blessing of sorts and made the walk home less unbearable, despite the urgency lent by her bladder.

She didn't get back until around 5 PM. By then the streets were deserted in anticipation of the curfew, except for the odd straggler hurrying to or fro. To Elise's vast relief, her condo building displayed no outward sign of vandalism or forced entry. She quietly made her way up the stairs, wary of the elevator under the circumstances, plopped down on the bed, and promptly passed out. She hadn't even locked the door to the flat.

Elise's sleep was troubled. But despite this, or perhaps because of it, she awoke the next morning with renewed energy and a sense of purpose. After a long shower — it very well could be her last for a while — she set about gathering supplies for the journey. As she did so, it sank in that there was no way she realistically could hike the distance to Edinburgh. It was around fifty miles, a five day journey at the maximum pace she could reasonably hope to sustain.

If conditions along the way were anything like in Glasgow, then the shops would be closed or empty. Elise couldn't count on finding food or water. To be safe she would have to carry enough for the whole trip. There was no way she could manage to fit five days' worth of provisions in a single pack. Even if she did, she certainly wouldn't be able to carry it. At best, it would slow her to the point where the trip took far longer, requiring yet more supplies. Unless, that is, she was willing to break into homes or shops along the way — and Elise couldn't see herself doing that.

But how in the world could a simple walk to Edinburgh be so hard? Didn't people hike hundreds of miles all the time? Heck, she herself had hiked the whole 95 miles of the West Highland Way a few years back. Well, a decade back. When she was fit. And when there were stores and hotels and restaurants and other hikers willing to help if things went amiss. And when she could purify water from streams and lakes. But now she had no iodine tablets, no reconstitutable food. Most of the route consisted of dense suburbs; she couldn't hunt or fish, even if she had known how. Elise marveled that civilization could be less navigable than the wild.

On the other hand, there was no alternate mode of transportation. She would be stuck in Glasgow until this thing blew over, after all. She simply would have to pray that the rumors of a toxic spill were wrong or that it had been contained. Elise felt a growing sense of frustration and futility. But something from yesterday stuck in the back of her mind and gave her hope. Like a seasoned showman, it waited until her emotions had reached a crescendo before revealing itself. Suddenly, she realized what she must do. It was almost 11 AM, and she would have to hurry.

Before committing to this course, Elise wanted to make sure that there indeed was no other option. After filling her backpack with supplies, she looked around her condo and bid it a silent farewell. Then she locked the door and walked out. She was much better prepared than yesterday, and was confident that the supplies would prove adequate to the task. Assuming she wasn't robbed along the way, that is. The streets were even emptier than yesterday, but there also didn't seem to be any obvious troublemakers. Maybe the curfew made a difference.

Elise walked straight to the staging area to check whether the wait had become tenable; perhaps she could just take one of the government transports, after all. The doors were chained and there was no sign of anybody around. *Better the last in the door than the first locked out.* Elise wanted to kick herself for her pride and impatience. Why hadn't she just waited in line, dammit?

But the self-recrimination was short-lived and half-hearted. Hadn't she expected as much? The evacuation either was over or could not be continued for some reason. And that line hadn't moved an inch while she was there yesterday. No, *that* door had been locked long before she came through it. Elise would have to pursue her other plan.

The nice thing about a town with lots of students is that there are lots of bikes. Once Elise made her way back to the University, it took only a few minutes to locate a suitable candidate in one of the bicycle racks. No lock, filled tires, good condition. It was a bright green Specialized road bike. Elise had worn pants in anticipation of the ride, but still chose a step-through frame from habit. The selection made, she looked around carefully. There was nobody.

Of course, who knew where the video cameras were hidden? Most town centers had complete coverage, but did the University? And for all she knew, there were countless eyes behind the inscrutable faces of the buildings. Elise was fairly sure that the campus was deserted, but she also suspected that being "fairly sure" was the easiest way to get caught. It was another beautiful day, and she was tempted to abandon the plan and just linger here until the crisis passed. She could have a lovely picnic on the lawn.

Elise cleared her head. She casually took the bicycle as if it were hers, walking it unhurriedly around the corner of one of the buildings. She expected somewhat to scream "thief" at any moment, or for a whistle to sound and police to come pouring like ants from the buildings. When she was out of sight of the bike rack, she mounted the bicycle and peddled hard. Doing so, Elise almost let out a laugh. This had to be the lamest getaway in the history of crime.

The streets were empty, but she stopped at each intersection just in case. It was the first time she had stolen something — well, at least as an adult. She would get caught, she knew it. Her face would appear in the newspaper as that worst of all things, a looter. Elise was sure that the theft would be reported, video footage would show her, and they'd radio ahead to Edinburgh. She'd be arrested by nightfall. She would go to jail and lose her family and shop and ... wait, there was on shop anymore.

How could something like that slip her mind? Fuck this

city. It owed her at least this, a way to survive, a single bicycle. Besides, nobody would miss it. Should she sit here quietly waiting for poison to kill her simply because nobody was around to give permission to use their bike?

When she had gotten through this, Elise would find the owner and apologize. It was an understandable thing to do, and she was sure that it would be fine. But what if the owner had desperately needed the bicycle to escape themselves? What if they were trapped, and died because of what she did? Would that make her a murderer? No, it would make them an idiot for not stealing somebody else's bike, she decided. She still felt awful about the whole thing, though.

The journey to Edinburgh was more strenuous and less eventful than Elise had anticipated. The M8 wasn't well suited to bicycle traffic, so she mostly kept to the service road. However there was a ten mile stretch where this disappeared, and she had to get on the motorway itself. That was when she finally realized what had been bothering her: the traffic on both sides was heading toward Edinburgh. How had they managed that?

She mostly rode in the breakdown lane, which thankfully graced this portion of highway, though sometimes she had to weave between cars when it vanished. The going was quite slow on those parts, but the traffic itself wasn't moving and Elise didn't have too much trouble. Until around mile 8.

Then somebody swung open a car door and hit her. The bike didn't flip, but she bashed her arm pretty badly when it fell over. Hence the arm-cast. The door had closed again by the time she got up, and she couldn't be sure which car it was. All the drivers were intently looking forward, and clearly nobody was going to identify the culprit. It didn't matter; what would she do if she found him?

Elise had been lucky that she was at the edge of the outer lane when hit, or she could have fallen under another car.

Not that any were moving, of course. After wrapping her arm — which throbbed quite badly — in a spare shirt, she continued. Nobody offered to help, but nobody harassed her. She suspected she had been hit intentionally, but at this point it really didn't matter. From then on, she watched the cars carefully and steered clear of suspicious looking ones. The next two miles took nearly 45 minutes, not least because her arm was useless. Fortunately the sun wouldn't set until around 9 PM, and she almost was there.

Contrary to her expectation, nobody tried to attack Elise or steal the bicycle or stop her. Other than the injury from the car door, she met with no misadventure. And that incident could have happened under ordinary circumstances too. No, she had made the trip relatively easily, all things considered. She was lucky; those people on the road weren't going anywhere. She wondered when they had set out. Elise hadn't paid attention, but the government transports could very well have been trapped in that morass. In fact, they had to be. She thanked heaven she hadn't gotten on one.

Elise arrived at her parents' house around 8:30 PM. Six hours for 47 miles? How pathetic, she thought. When this was over, she would have to get back in shape. Almost immediately, her arm began to throb intensely. It would have to be looked at, or at least dressed properly. Her mom was an ex-nurse and would know what to do. But first, she wanted to think up a game plan. She doubted a toxic spill could reach all the way to Edinburgh. How much of the stuff could there possibly be? On the other hand, if the winds were just right who knew. She laughed. That would be her new catchphrase: a shrug and "who knew?" Maybe she could get her own sitcom. Suddenly Elise felt faint. She barely made it upstairs, before falling onto the first bed she found.

Around 4 AM, Elise woke up freezing. It didn't get very cold in August, but she was shivering uncontrollably. Suddenly she panicked and tore the shirt off her arm. There was no obvious sign of infection. She felt her own forehead. Would that even work? Her hand felt cold, but it didn't seem like a fever. The heat was out. No lights — the power was out too. Elise sighed. So much for a hot shower. Dammit, her premonition had been right; last night *was* her last shower for a while. And now she was clammy and smelly and cold.

She instinctively called out "mom", then "dad", before realizing that the house was empty. It had been since she arrived; otherwise, they would have come to her immediately. But why would her parents still be away at 4 in the morning? Elise looked out the window. The street lights were on, so it wasn't a blackout. It had to be something local. Low heat, power off — the house had been prepped for an extended absence. Her parents weren't just out, they had gone on a trip. She'd have to figure it out in the morning. But at least this meant she probably could take a shower once she switched the power back on. Later. She snuggled under the blanket and dozed off again.

CHAPTER 11

Day 314

The following are selected excerpts from an earlier version of Dr. Jan Markov's critical essay on the Front

⋮

To date, no physical mechanism for the Front has been determined. Though the literature has been rife with speculative theories, none has shown any promise and most have been debunked. The most notable early attempt was the Anomalous Discharge theory of Mary Delphi, which gained quite a following. The theory posited that the Front was the result of interaction with a hitherto unknown form of dark matter. Delphi was a physicist at Harvard, and her book quickly became a bestseller. However, under closer scrutiny a number of flawed premises were identified.

Nonetheless it remained the sole focus of the physics community for nearly a year, finally losing favor as a result of its stubborn resistance to calculation as well as a clear lack of predictive utility. To this day it still boasts adherents in certain circles.

It has been suggested that Delphi's persistent promotion of her theory in government circles diverted resources, squandered the critical months after Z-Day, and ultimately may bear responsibility for the end of humanity. Despite any controversy, Delphi continues to enjoy widespread popularity. After a brief stint as Director of the Taskforce for Front Physics (TFP) under the auspices of the Department of Energy, Delphi returned to Harvard.

⋮

Neither the causation nor the teleology of the Front are understood, though there has been a great deal of speculation about both. The Front itself often has been attributed to supernatural or unnatural causes. Popular theories include the wrath of God, an old wizard in the woods (usually of Druidic origin), a government experiment gone awry, an immunological response by the planet Earth, a triggered failsafe mechanism (divine or man-made), an act of environmental terrorism, various apocalypses, and that perennial favorite — an invasion by aliens.

These sorts of rumors gain traction precisely through their unverifiable nature. The apparent incompatibility of the Front with our existing knowledge of physics lends such ideas credibility in unscientific eyes, but also holds the promise of opening new avenues of understanding to scientific ones. Unfortunately, the latter has yet to be realized.

⋮

The Front expands circularly along the surface of the Earth at a rate of 0.2013 miles per hour. Reported fluctuations in the measured rate variously have been attributed to statistical measurement error and possible refraction through geological features, but there has been no evidence to suggest anything other than a constant underlying rate of progress. From its early effect on airplanes, the Front is known to extend to an altitude of at least 24 miles. It is not believed to extend past the upper atmosphere, in evidence of which the ISS station traveled over it a number of times during the first two weeks without effect. Attempts to burrow under the Front have uniformly failed. Its effect on bunkers and mines also has demonstrated penetration to a substantial but unknown depth.

⋮

The Front has no noticeable effect on anything other than living human beings. It exhibits no known mode of physical interaction and does not affect any other form of matter. While initial evidence seemed to point to an energy field of some sort, later inspection of video footage revealed that the destruction of equipment, failure of communication, fires, and other effects ascribed to its direct action were in fact ordinary consequences of the elimination of human life within the Zone. No effort to circumvent the Front from above or below or to locate lacunae has been successful.

All scientific measurements and apparatuses are based on identifiable physical interactions: particles interacting with detector plates, light interacting with optical media, and chemicals interacting with specialized substrates, for example. To date, no known physical interaction has been identified by which the Front may be detected. It is for all practical purposes invisible to modern science. The exception is its effect on living humans. The precise mechanism of this interaction is not understood, and it appears to adhere to no known physical laws. However, its progress has been studied extensively.

Naturally, the ability to observe is limited by the attendant dangers and, not least, the ethical challenges associated with the use of living humans as subjects. However, some information has been gleaned from electronic observation during cases of unavoidable or accidental contact, as well as from certain nations that exhibit a flexible moral attitude.

The latter cases have prompted public outrage, though sanctions have yet to be imposed. On the contrary, some speculation has arisen that the United States has condoned or participated in such work, believing the information gained more valuable than any potential political fallout.

Whether it is the Front or the Zone which is fatal to humans remains an open question. It is entirely possible that the much-talked-about Front is merely the abstract edge of the Zone. Alternately, the Zone may be viable for humans were they able to survive the passage of the Front. Practically, the effect is the same. However, it likely would prove much less difficult to find a means of surviving the short passage of a deadly Front than a means of surviving in a continually inhospitable world. To date, there is no evidence that a human can survive in the Zone once the Front has passed.

Endeavors to detect the Front have focused on two main lines of inquiry. First, there is an ongoing project to detect a physical basis for it. Our inability to identify a means of inter-action (other than with living humans) renders an empirical approach difficult, and limits the theoretical side to speculation.

Efforts to elicit interactions with non-human biological proxies have failed. Two attempts have been made to leave equipment behind as the Front passes, and subsequently incubate living human fetuses from frozen sperm and eggs in a completely automated manner. One attempt proved abortive due to equipment malfunction. The second failed, as the frozen eggs were destroyed by the Front. However, certain non-germinal frozen stem cells are known to survive the Front.

A notable experiment by Russian scientist Sergei Oligov reported positive results using electrically stimulated human hearts. This led to an in-pouring of hearts, many of which came from questionable sources. Subsequent attempts to reproduce the results failed, and it is widely believed that Oligov was the victim of fabrication by an overly zealous graduate student of his, one Elya Miksha. Nonetheless, he was deemed ultimately responsible and was fed to the Front in an action half-heartedly condemned by colleagues overseas.

:

The effect of the Front on living human beings is known as HLD, Hetero-Lytic Decomposition. More precisely, HLD refers to the process initiated through contact with the Front. The exact mechanism of HLD is unknown. However, it proceeds along the same lines as advanced fungal decomposition of a corpse. Analogies have been drawn with necrotic poisons and necrotizing fascitis, such as those associated with streptococcus A (all of which are based on a certain class of phospholipases).

Because the action takes place on living humans, there have been numerous recorded and transmitted accounts of the experience, as well as a plethora of measured data relayed by body sensors. Apparently, the process begins with a body-wide tingling accompanied by sudden dysphoria. Moments later, a number of sensory phenomena may begin. There have been multiple reports of sparkling lights, halos, the smell of corn, an odd sense of compression, and a grinding whine. The skin begins to burn, and blisters form.

These rapidly putrefy over the course of a minute, while organs begin to deteriorate. Eyesight fades quickly, and the vitreous humor itself may solidify. At this point, the pain becomes unbearable. Unfortunately, neural decomposition occurs last, and it is likely that the mind is clear and aware while the body decays beneath it, with all the suffering this necessarily entails. The process continues past the point of death until the entire organism has dissolved. The residue contains no discernible human genetic material and no intact cells.

There has been much interest in determining precisely what is considered human and living for the purpose of interaction with the Front. Barring an intelligent agency behind the Front, it is reasonable to assume that these criteria are specific and reproducible. Once determined, they may reflect simple char-acteristics which can be masked to protect living humans from the Front. So far, there has been no known instance of a human surviving contact with the Front, either through the absence of HDL or its arrested progress.

The HDL process, once initiated, always advances to completion. Curiously, it involves active mortification of the organism long past the point where first contact with the Front would not have triggered HDL. This has led to the assumption that the Front involves some sort of radiation-like mechanism or induces a chain reaction. The point of "decision" is the initial contact. Most recent research in Front-circumvention technology has focused on the criterion to initiate HDL. If we momentarily can obscure or divest ourselves of whatever attribute triggers the reaction, then we may pass through the Front in safety. If only the Front is deadly, this alone will suffice. Even if the Zone proves deadly, there may remain means of permanently obscuring our presence within it.

As the Front has no effect on a dead human, numerous experiments have been performed to determine the life/death boundary. As mentioned, such a determination could provide clues to the mechanism by which it operates and means to thwart it. To date, no consistent determinant has been identified. It has been ascertained that if a living person has any contact with the Front — however brief or tangential — HDL will be initiated. However, if they immediately remove themselves from contact, the process slows by a factor of two in speed.

There has been a growing argument that efforts to understand the Front from a physics standpoint are misguided, and that we should focus on a biological approach to managing it. Even if "fooling" the Front is not optimal as a permanent solution, it may buy us time to better understand the phenomenon. Unfortunately, research on biological interactions are limited in the United States by legal considerations. The FDA has refused to approve live subject testing, even in voluntary circumstances.

⋮

Most efforts to counteract the Front, excepting those founded in superstition, have been along the same lines as efforts to detect it. In fact, the latter may be viewed as a necessary, and hopefully sufficient, prerequisite to the former. By this school of thought, all energies should be devoted to understanding the physical mechanisms in the hope that even an 11th hour discovery would enable nearly immediate response to the Front and the consequent survival of the species. Despite this appeal, it largely has been superseded by the biological school of thought.

.
.
.

While the language employed by the media often implies confrontation with a possible active or passive sentience, there is no evidence of such a proximal cause, or of any teleology at all. For practical purposes, leaders have emphasized the importance of viewing the Front as a phenomenon rather than an enemy. While philosophically there may be little difference, pragmatically there is.

Were a sentience involved, it would behoove us to divide efforts between investigation of the Front and identification of its creator. It also would stand to reason that the Front is either a weapon or an unanticipated consequence of some non-hostile action. If hostile, dealing with the Front alone would not protect us from other, possibly more lethal, attacks. We would need to either defeat or placate the enemy, gaining permanent relief or at least some breathing room to plan a next step. On the other hand, if the Front is unintentional then its creator may be able to disable or reverse it, and efforts should be directed toward establishing contact or advertising our plight.

The argument is not purely academic. Given the limited time available, an allocation of resources must be made between directly dealing with the Front itself and treating with its potential author. To make matters worse, a major debate has arisen concerning the allocation of resources overall.

.
.
.

One school of thought holds it to be unfair to use resources contributed by the doomed to prevent the death of others rather than ease their own passage or improve their remaining time in this world. Proponents of this point of view believe that rather than a species-wide pooling of resources to save a small number of remaining people (as well as the species), countries close to the Front should engage in unrestrained hedonism and spend every last penny before dying.

Whether this view is morally palatable depends on one's degree of hope for an eventual positive outcome. If counteracting the Front is deemed impossible or the survival of the species of lesser importance, then wasting one's last hours in a vain effort to save somebody else may seem foolish. On the other hand, to those for whom the survival of the species is of paramount importance or who hold hope that the Front may be dealt with while a sizable population remains, such a view is irresponsible.

From a scientific standpoint, there are two potential success scenarios. The first is that we completely restore human access to the Zone. Under the deadly-Front theory this could be accomplished by eliminating the Front or finding a mechanism to safely pass through it, while under the deadly-Zone theory it would involve reversing the Front or somehow removing the causal element for the Zone or finding a means to safely exist within it. The second scenario is that we halt the progress of the Front and simply coexist with it, writing off the Zone and living outside it. Clearly, the first scenario is more desirable.

Scientists have pointed out that without knowledge of cause or mechanism we cannot rule out the possibility of a sudden change in the behavior of the Front or the emergence of new Fronts from other epicenters.

⋮

CHAPTER 12

Day 283 — Washington DC

The meeting had taken an odd tone, perceptibly toxic. Perceptibly to Robert, that is; Lilly Tao inexplicably seemed oblivious to it, or perhaps she hoped to quell the outrage simply by refusing to acknowledge it. About a third of the audience's emotional brew was suppressed pride, an inevitable byproduct of Lilly's personality and the various egos involved.

The remainder was a mixture of fear, confusion, guilt, and not a little resentment. The latter stemmed less from the revelation that the entire crew of the ISS had been murdered than from having been left out of the loop. And apparently, everyone in the room *had* been left out of the loop.

Only six minutes had passed since Lilly announced their unwitting complicity. No, it had not been announced, not even demanded; it simply had been stated. Apparently, damnation now was part of the benefits package for a government employee.

Time seemed to move very slowly for Robert, and even the three minutes since Lilly's exchange with his boss, Doug Harving, felt like ages. Then again, these days everything did. They had to or there wouldn't be time for anything. The Front had given new meaning to "life is too short." And Lilly still hadn't told them the result of her analysis, what it meant for them all as people rather than officials.

Were they going to die in five minutes? If so, Robert imagined somebody would kill her on the spot, not least for wasting those last few precious minutes. Or maybe the Front would come upon them unawares, and she mercifully had distracted them to the last. Clearly she didn't anticipate any consequences from her admission.

It felt as though some of the palpable reverence the audience had for her was lost. After all, they certainly were the equals of a murderer, probably even her betters. No doubt many felt that instead of dictating their doom from a pulpit, she now must defend her actions. They had become her judges, and it didn't help that she was unaware of it.

Lilly continued with a tedious list of technical clarifications and caveats, immune to the complex stew of emotions in the room. Perhaps that was her forte. Finally she paused and looked around. It seemed clear to Robert that she was about to move on to the third and, presumably, final piece of evidence.

"Dick, can you explain the deviation statistics?" She was looking at Dick Tung, a former Professor of Computer Science at M.I.T. and now one of four senior data scientists who reported directly to her. He was one of the few in the room who could not afford to indulge in resentment. He looked up and smiled before answering.

"Over the last nine months, we've traced the progress of the Front as best we can. Here is a chart." He put up a graph with two axes and two plots. The vertical axis was the distance from the Origin, and the horizontal was the time from Z-Day. Neither unit was specified. The Origin/Z-Day point was in the lower left. A bright red line proceeded from that point up and to the right at a 45 degree angle, bisecting the quadrant.

It was the sort of trend-line that demo graphs boast: pure, linear, and optimistically reaching for some form of transcendence. The type of graph that makes sales managers drool and investors cough up millions. Or an illustration of the inexorable progress of death toward one's person. Robert wasn't sure what the second, blue, line represented. It tracked the red one pretty closely until about half way up the graph and then veered up away from it. There were no accompanying numbers to clarify its meaning.

Roger Headworth, director of an agency Robert knew nothing about, pressed his microphone button angrily. "And it took a Professor and six PhDs a whole year to plot *this*? Seems like something any kid can do."

"Only in China." Tung joked uneasily, but it fell flat. He quickly moved on, adopting an impatient expository tone to regain control of the presentation. "I'm sure even you could plot this, Jim." This time a few chuckles, but he waved them away. "The technical challenges aren't plotting the graph or fitting it. They lay in obtaining and extracting the data."

"As you know, most of our data points are approximate and many are based on anecdotal accounts or remote feeds. Other than certain countries which directly measure it..." He paused meaningfully, before continuing. "The data is very noisy. We have had to cross correlate it with many other sources to determine precise timings. In truth, most of the work consisted of hand-cleaning each data point."

"This said," he added, "we also had to combine tailored versions of a number of machine learning algorithms". After considering for a moment, he explained. "Ordinary Bayesian techniques, PGMs, back-propagation, dimensional reduction methods don't work very well here. The data is too heterogeneous. What we've done instead is use those techniques to teach algorithms what to look for in obtaining the data."

Lilly interjected to clarify. "So rather than using Machine Learning to fit the small set of directly-applicable quantitative data, you build algorithms which extract additional data from the vast amount of other information available."

"Sometimes in ways that we wouldn't even have imagined ab initio. Yet, as you see, once we have the data the pattern is pretty obvious. In truth, it's a fascinating use of AI — about as close to the vision of intelligent machines as we've come..."

Lilly cut him off. "Thank you, Dick."

She turned and addressed the audience. "This graph is what

we desperately struggled to construct, and desperately hoped would turn out differently." She paused, not for dramatic effect, but in seeming recollection of a painful memory. Her frustration was visible, but it didn't make any sense to Robert.

"The red line is a simple linear extrapolation based on a constant circular rate of expansion. It is what we are familiar with. We had hoped the second line would differ." Robert was puzzled for a moment, but quickly understood. He had a pretty good idea what the blue line represented, and the difference wasn't that large. They weren't all going to die tomorrow. It had to be something more. Then he realized: Lilly didn't care about the magnitude of the reduction. She had not undertaken the research to more precisely identify their X-Day. She must have entertained a serious hope that the Front was decelerating or that they could detect some sort of interaction, a way to impede its progress.

Robert wanted to believe that this was her motive. It gave greater meaning to the sacrifice of the ISS, possibly even offered some justification. If she had found what she sought then the world could have hope, greater hope than a handful of people floating through space would offer.

Instead she had found this. She would much rather it had been a waste of time, that the graph had shown only a straight line, that the ISS had been destroyed in vain. But *this*, well this only added insult to injury. It was a necessary insult, a useful insult, but an insult nonetheless.

She continued: "The blue curve is the actual data. We had hoped that this would lay below the original one and exhibit evidence of some sort of asymptotic leveling. We had hoped that the Front would slow."

She lifted her head. "As you can see it does not. It shows signs of acceleration."

There was a sudden murmuring from the audience. She motioned them to be silent.

"However, the acceleration is not random. As those of you with mathematical backgrounds have probably figured out."

Robert had recognized the pattern. He mentally anticipated Lilly's next sentence: "It's a power law." He was glad that his anticipation had been purely mental, however, because that's not what she said. Technically he still was correct, though.

"What we are seeing is that the Front is spherical," she explained. "It began from the origin and expanded outward in a spherical pattern. This is why all attempts to circumvent it have failed. This is why not all air traffic intersected it during the first few critical hours. And this is why until recently it appeared not to be a threat to the ISS."

"From an abundance of caution we nevertheless had kept the ISS away from airspace above the Front, and this turned out to be wise. At approximately Z+52 days, the Front reached the minimum altitude at which the ISS operates. Approximately one day later it had traversed the full range of altitudes between which we move the ISS. When the other evidence had been compiled and the conclusion appeared unavoidable, we used the ISS to conduct one final test."

"What most people don't know is that the ISS actually passed over the Front twice in the first few days, before its behavior had been established. The ISS was not affected during either pass. This is why we had been so confident that the Front did not extend to that altitude. Now we needed to know for sure. First, we had the ISS follow a path that would not intersect the Front under either our original hypothesis or the spherical one. Nothing happened. This was no surprise, but established that the Front did not uniformly extend above the ISS altitude." She paused for a moment before continuing.

"Next, we guided it over the Origin itself. In almost any plausible scenario, this would be the point at which the Front would reach the highest altitude. It only would intersect if our original assumptions was wrong. The ISS was perfect for this in a number of ways. We could control its orbit with sufficient precision, and the crew all wear medical monitors that continually relay data. We obtained a very precise reading on the time of intersection with the Front. We also obtained slightly more precise physiological readings during the process than hitherto had been furnished from other sources."

"So the ISS perished directly over the Origin?" Doug interjected incredulously.

Lilly smiled. "1285 miles from it, in fact. Precisely consistent with a spherical expansion of the Front. There were 37 seconds between when the ISS intersected a radial cone passing through the Front's circular edge on the surface and when it intersected the Front itself. If we had waited a few months to conduct the test, that interval would have increased, but for our purposes it was sufficient. Our biological monitors have a resolution of around two seconds." She paused for any follow-up questions, but there seemed to be none.

"This was a difficult decision," she offered in response to the silence in the room. Her tone was explanatory, not defensive. "Whether to reserve the ISS for future purposes and as a symbol of hope or to use it in this capacity. The need was too dire, however."

"So you killed the only people who may have survived the Front. You killed humanity's ace in the hole," Jim blurted out.

Lilly looked perplexed. "If the Front was circular and of limited vertical extent, they would have survived our test. A spherical Front would have killed them anyway, when it grew large enough. Either way, the experiment resulted in no change to our prognosis as a species."

"But isn't that a good thing?" Doug interjected. In response to the shocked looks around him he hastened to clarify. "Not the killing of the ISS. But if it's spherical doesn't that mean the Front must pass through thousands of miles of dense rock and magma? Isn't it likely to get absorbed or impeded by the Earth as it passes through it? Maybe it will stop in time." Doug was on his feet, looking around anxiously for encouragement, some sign of support for this optimism. Instead, he was greeted with silence.

Lilly responded gently, "that's not what the data shows. For all practical purposes, the Front does not interact with matter."

"What about the core?" Doug shot back desperately.

"What about it? If nuclear weapons have no effect, why would we expect anything from the far lower temperature of the core." She saw the look on his face and added, "but of course, we cannot know for sure. After all, the core is much greater in extent. At present, we have no evidence to support this hope, though."

Tung chimed in inquisitively, "you said 'for all practical purposes'."

Lilly seemed surprised and gave him a warm smile. "Ah, you picked up on that, Dick." She briefly adjusted the microphone on her lapel before continuing. "As you know, there is a lot of apparent noise in the data."

"Apparent? It passed all our randomness tests. It's just an information theoretic artifact of...," Tung began to object, before falling silent. His boss had adopted an expression of distaste, and he obviously thought better of continuing to contradict her in front of the whole room.

Lilly seemed a bit hesitant before responding, and Robert assumed she was furious with her subordinate's impudence. After a few moments, she smiled at Tung. "The Department of Information Acquisition has stronger randomness tests than you have access to. It is not random."

After a bit of murmuring had died down, she continued. "There is evidence of a very minor," she emphasized the last word, "interaction as the Front passes through the Earth. It is consistent with a form of refraction given what little we know of the distribution of mass throughout the Earth."

"But," Lilly quickly added, lest this inspire undue optimism, "it does not appear to be something we can take advantage of or otherwise replicate." She turned to Doug. "But it does lend some credence to your hope regarding the core." She paused and looked around at the audience before offering, "If you need hope, let this serve." She handed a sheet to an attendant, who placed it in the projector. The page contained several numbers. Robert looked away and tried not to listen as Lilly explained, "this is our new X-Day." It was a lot sooner than he had imagined.

Disappointed as Robert was, the real problem wasn't the small amount of time lost to him. He clearly perceived the source of Lilly's frustration. It wasn't just that the outcome of her analysis proved to be undesirable. Nor was it the specific downward revisions to which the U.S. was subject, though these surely would not go over well with the public. The real problem was much more serious.

Every moment until the end there remained the possibility that a solution would be found, the Front stopped or negated. Even if only a few people survived by that point, the species would endure. But once Earth was encompassed, it was over. The time until that happened had been reduced by a third, from almost 6 years to less than 4. Humanity's chances just had dropped significantly.

CHAPTER 13

Day 9 — Edinburgh, Scotland

When she awoke, Elise felt much better and the chill was gone. It must have been exhaustion from the long ride. The first priority was getting the power back on. She didn't intend to stay for long, but a hot shower definitely was in order. This wasn't the house she had grown up in, but she had visited enough times over the years to know her away around fairly well.

She tried to remember her father's instructions regarding the power and water. Whenever her parents traveled, Elise was enlisted to keep an occasional eye on the house. And each time, her father emailed detailed instructions before leaving. Very detailed instructions. Sometimes Elise wondered if they were aware she was an adult. An adult who ran a successful business and was old enough to be a parent of her own. If she had wanted to. For two decades her parents thought her adult enough to pester continually about having children. Apparently, she became a child again once it became clear she wouldn't have any.

The care-taking instructions particularly irked her. Once, her father even added additional information about locking the door on her way out, something she faithfully had done every time for years. As Elise read it, she shook her head in disbelief. What next? Would he actually explain how to turn the key in the lock? And then he did. But, she supposed, all parents were crazy in some way. She wondered if her kids would have thought her a loon or a pain or resented her. No, they wouldn't, she smiled. *They* didn't exist.

Those ridiculous instructions now were of paramount importance to Elise. There was some weird system with a water level and two valves. She had to turn one, add water to the level, and then turn the other before restoring power to the pump. But she couldn't recall which was which, and there definitely was something else she had to do too. For years she had nagged her dad to replace the boiler, but once he had a system in place he wasn't one to change it unless absolutely necessary. Why should he spend money just because she was too lazy to follow a few simple instructions, he would grumble.

As Elise tried to remember those instructions, she felt pretty sure she would miss some minor detail and flood the whole house. It would serve him right; maybe he finally would upgrade. But once she was in the basement standing before the contraption, the procedure came back to her. It still took Elise about an hour to get everything working properly, though. She prayed that the city power wouldn't go out before she had her shower.

Once Elise had showered and eaten, she felt ready to confront reality. Her right forearm felt much better. It boasted an ugly bruise, but seemed functional. Elise was pretty sure it wasn't broken, but she wrapped it tightly anyway. Then she proceeded to a thorough search of the house. After her experience in Glasgow, she was acutely aware of the possibility that she may have to leave in a hurry. This time, she wouldn't underpack.

By noon she had gathered a variety of items. The pantry hadn't been terribly well stocked, but she located matches, a proper knife, crackers and oatmeal, several water bottles, and some basic medical supplies. There also were plenty of clothes, and she picked out a couple of her old shirts, a sweater, and two hats. In a moment of panic, Elise realized she absentmindedly had left the bicycle outside last night, but breathed a sigh of relief when she saw that it still was there. No need to tempt fate, however; she brought it around back and inside.

In case she didn't have time later, Elise wrote a note of explanation to her parents should they return. It wouldn't do for them to think the place had been robbed, especially by her. She apologized for the things she had taken, and promised to replace them later. On the other hand, she supposed her parents would much rather see her safe than worry about a few missing odds and ends. Besides, she was pretty sure they would be in touch before they got back.

In her exhaustion Elise hadn't thought of it before, but perhaps there was cell reception here. She dug out her phone. It was dead, drained by her frequent attempts the previous day. After a few minutes of charging, it had enough juice to boot up. No signal. Elise left it charging, while she pondered her next move. Even when fully charged, the cell phone continued to register no signal.

Suddenly Elise remembered the house phone, a landline. That was the most reliable type of connection, designed to function even if there was a power outage. And since there still *was* power, the phone was bound to work. Elise was a bit embarrassed she hadn't thought of it right away. It's just that nobody she knew even had one anymore. She thanked god that her parents were so old-fashioned. Who else actually would have a landline? Elise didn't even know how one would go about getting one. Probably one of the cell companies, or would it be the government? Oddly, this made her even more hopeful. If nobody used landlines, then the circuits wouldn't be busy. But didn't they have unlimited capacity anyway? She would have to look this up when things returned to normal. For the first time in a while, Elise felt positively giddy.

She created a mental list of all the people she would call. Even if useless as a phone, her cell held many of the numbers she would need, and she was glad it was charged. By now she had reached the front hallway, where the old phone resided. It was a generic beige plastic block with a sloping rotary dial and U-shaped receiver. Elise wondered whether her parents had found it at a flea market. Or maybe they had it all along, and she never noticed.

Elise cradled the receiver in eager anticipation, before gingerly lifting it from the cradle and drawing it to her ear. Silence. In disbelief, she tapped the hook-switch repeatedly. Silence. Frantically, she checked the cord and the connection. She even went to the basement and traced the phone line. There had to be something. Maybe her dad turned off the phone while they were away. Suddenly Elise was angry. It was just the type of thing he would do: pedantic and pointless. It wouldn't even save him money. Now she'd never be able to get it to work. Elise felt hopeless. After a while she gave up and returned to the bedroom. The last thing she checked was the broadband connection. Unsurprisingly, they did not have one.

Elise considered several possible courses of action. She could look for public transportation. It was unclear whether the city had been evacuated or her parents had fled of their own accord. Fled? Why did she assume that? For all she knew, they happened to be on vacation. Then again, she would have received an email if this was planned. Of course, they could have made an emergency trip for some other reason. Could Debbie be in trouble?

A sudden flight down to London to help her sister would explain everything. Could the toxic spill have reached London? Surely not, if Edinburgh was still okay. Or it could be a completely unrelated emergency. Elise's imagination teemed with possibilities. No, if they had rushed out the door for an emergency, her parents wouldn't have meticulously closed down the house. At the very least, it was a considered decision. Perhaps impromptu, but considered.

Suddenly Elise had a horrible presentiment. What if they had attempted to travel to Glasgow to check up on *her*? It was the type of thing they would do if they couldn't get through by phone. Elise remembered the M8, Eastbound on both sides. They would have had to take some roundabout side road, and those probably were just as bad. Or maybe they had come halfway when the Westbound lanes were reversed.

How did that happen anyway? Did the government just divert traffic, creating a big pileup? It sounded like the type of thing they would do. Elise almost laughed at the image. No, they probably just blocked traffic and rerouted it or directed it to turn around somehow. For all she knew, her parents were in that traffic jam waiting to be overtaken by whatever horrible toxic waste was headed their way. Was it some sort of Chernobyl? Nobody would admit it, if it were. Then again, hadn't all the nuclear plants been closed by the SNP right after Scotland seceded? It was part of their platform. Wouldn't it be ironic if her parents had been the ones to knock her bicycle over? Her dad never did pay attention when he opened the car door. Elise decided to have a hot cup of tea and clear her mind.

After tea, things weren't much better but Elise did decide that worrying served no purpose. Her parents probably were fine. They would get in touch when they could. For now, all she could do was keep herself safe. As in Glasgow, the TV and radio had nothing useful to say. There wasn't even any local news about Edinburgh; all the signals were from afar. The immediate choices she faced were whether and when to leave the city. She felt safe here. She had a home here, a home in a very upscale part of town. Then again, her shop had been in an upscale part of town. But this was Edinburgh, not Glasgow. It was a civilized city, and it also was the capital. Even if they didn't care about anybody else (and Elise was fairly sure they didn't), the government would try to keep Edinburgh safe.

That was when something vague in the background noise caught Elise's attention. She had kept the radio on, just in case anything useful was announced. There was a soothing quality to the background chatter as well; hearing another human voice, even a reconstituted one, somehow lifted her spirits. Elise turned her attention to the radio. The pundits had stopped talking, and some official-sounding announcement was being broadcast over and over.

Elise walked over and turned up the volume. The reception was terrible, and she felt like a spy from the 1940s trying to tune in the resistance. It took a minute before Elise managed to locate a fully audible version of the message and hear it out.

The Prime Minister was dead. No word of any disaster, just some sort of plane accident on the way to Glasgow. Of course, she probably was heading there for a post-riot photo op. Cynicism aside, Elise actually had liked this PM. She was one of the originals that had been around since the secession. A founding mother, so to speak. And with the PM gone, that asshole Campbell would be in charge. Who knew what he would do, probably sell Scotland back the UK. She wondered if that really would be so bad.

Elise sat down on the bed and began to cry. It couldn't be the news about the PM, could it? She didn't really care about her *that* much. She just felt really sad. It was as if her country, her way of life, the world she painfully had learnt to navigate over forty years — as if it all was falling apart. She realized she probably would have to leave Edinburgh soon, but simply was too tired. That was it, she just needed some rest. She would stick around for a few days, gather her wits, and see where things stood. Maybe the whole mess would sort itself out by then. Maybe her parents would be back. If she waited, maybe she wouldn't have to leave. Maybe the choice no longer would be hers to make.

CHAPTER 14

Day 730 — Near Yining, China

Three months passed, and they started removing prisoners once again. This time, however, it was a slow trickle out and nobody took their place. Each day, they removed two. One longie (a farmer named Wu) seemed very excited by this and explained that he had seen it before, many years earlier, when he had first been imprisoned in Chengdu. It was a repatriation program. The courts processed a few at a time and then filtered them through re-education schools — much like half-way houses — and back into society. Feng asked why they would do so, and Wu admitted he wasn't sure. When it first happened, he had been told that it was a rehabilitation program for non-politicals. Apparently, he was too new at that time to qualify for sentence reduction. But he was pretty sure that this was the same thing. It had happened just this way.

Such news buoyed Feng's hopes. Every prisoner hopes for freedom, even if they do not expect it. If this indeed was a rehabilitation drive, it was quite likely Feng would qualify. His offense had been a property crime, not violent or political. While it always was possible that the victim knew somebody important, most likely Feng just would be deemed a non-troublesome individual and released. After close to four years, he definitely would be eligible. For all he knew, his sentence would end soon anyway. Then again, China was not known for the leniency of its penal system.

For the next three months, one or two prisoners were removed each day. And each day, Feng's hope rose when the guard entered and sank when he left. It wasn't always the same guard, of course. The worst was the tall one with the missing tooth. He was meaner and tended to kick the prisoners. Rumor had it that he even had beaten a man to death. That was in another cell, though. Another cell, another world. This was not the guard who came for Feng. It was the other one, the short one with the wide face. He probably was from up North.

After so long, Feng had grown certain he would be the last person called. It almost would be disappointing to be next to last. To have waited all this time, and not have the distinction of being last. For some reason it didn't bother him that other cells may have held other prisoners, that he would have no way of telling whether he actually *was* last. Feng was certain that the last would come from his cell, the only cell that mattered.

What he feared most was that they would stop just short of him. Perhaps they would meet their quota, or perhaps he wasn't on the list at all. Was there a list? He wondered if the cell itself was the list. The remaining three all were longies, but a few other longies already had been taken.

As always, Feng had no idea what to make of it. He knew there was no point to worrying or wondering, but what else could he do? Of course, the same could be said of life in general, for which Feng's cell was an allegory — though to his mind rather an ugly one. Such thoughts depressed Feng. His world was concrete and shit pails, and surely what lay beyond was better than concrete and shit pails even if he had a hard time remembering it. Allegories were a luxury of those on the other side of walls.

Feng wasn't disappointed when his turn came, just bewildered. His mood usually went through many cycles during a given day. As it happened, he had been ruminating on how to handle a solitary life in the cell. He supposed he could move to the center of the room; there would be nobody to shove him aside. But he would take the bucket too, otherwise it wouldn't feel like home. He had become convinced he would be forgotten there.

An hour earlier, he had believed just as firmly that he

would be the very last taken. Perhaps there would be a special ceremony when he was removed. Feng envisioned a strange ribbon cutting, in which he was guided out into the blinding sun and camera flashes (he couldn't tell which was which) and presented with a huge pair of scissors. As the last prisoner released, he would have the honor of triggering the demolition of the now-empty prison.

Before his fantasy could explain how scissors would be used to accomplish this, he grew melancholy and decided he never would be released. Perhaps they would demolish the building with him in it, not from spite but simply because they had forgotten him. Because somewhere on some form his name accidentally had been omitted. The guard never would trust the evidence of his own eyes over the official documentation. Feng would cry out in vain as everyone pretended not to hear him, that he didn't exist, because the list said so.

None of those scenarios came to pass. Instead, Feng was led through a series of gray hallways with sliding barred doors. At each, the guard went through a ritual, conveying his name, prisoner number, and various information to the person on the other side. The door then opened, the guard signed some sheet, and they moved on. There seemed to be an endless sequence of these. Feng couldn't remember whether he had come this way years before. His arrival had been a blur of terror and disbelief.

They had told him he just was wanted for some questioning. Despite the general belief to the contrary, questioning usually meant just that. Feng knew this quite well. His shop fronted for a popular gambling den. Everyone turned a blind eye to it. In fact, a number of local officials were regular customers (he made sure they were comp'ed, of course). For form's sake, the police raided his place every now and then, and hauled him in for questioning.

Usually, he'd just pay a cash fine. If things were slow at the station, they sometimes asked him to give them a few busts.

They'd supply a list of names and he'd nod at this one or that, later alerting them when those customers showed up. To their shock, the police would be waiting to arrest them when they came out of the club drunk and with a lot of incriminating cash. Feng would get a ride home, and the customers he'd fingered would get six months or (more often) pay a handsome bribe. It all was a big hustle as he saw it, the price of doing business.

So when they brought him to the station for questioning that night, he assumed nothing was amiss. It was a name-picking night, so he pointed them to a couple of people who had won a lot recently. Why not lighten his load a bit too? The cops had seemed pleased with his cooperation, and he looked forward to a late dinner. The problem was that the ride home had taken a detour. Next thing Feng knew, he was shoved onto a prison transport, taken to the facility, and processed into his cell. The latter part of the night was a fog of confusion.

Over the subsequent four years he had played the details over and over in his head. He identified countless subtle deviations from the usual script that should have cued him in to his danger. A slightly more officious tone, a sidelong glance between officers, a sinister double meaning to something that was said. Who could tell if these things were real? In the absence of the obvious breadcrumbs a filmmaker may drop for his audience, the mind is left to seek signs, any signs. To create them if necessary. Had Feng's imprisonment been foreordained? Or had the night simply gone south?

He always had viewed the officials as a gang of shysters and petty crooks. He had no doubt they could be nasty if you crossed them or were arrested for a real crime. But for the most part, he saw them as a normal and generally harmless part of his ecosystem. Had he been mistaken all along? Perhaps they were much more dangerous and unpredictable than he had assumed. There was an old saying: do not fear officials until they officiate over you.

Every remembered interaction could be cast in a sinister light. Feng preferred to think they had gotten the order from above. That it wasn't something he said or did, that he hadn't named the wrong person. That the officials whom he had socialized with and paid so well had done their duty reluctantly and were very sad to see him go. Perhaps they had argued for him, defended him to no avail. But something told him this wasn't likely.

His suspicion often took over and he imagined it was his bartender, his maitre'd, his mahjong parlour's bit boss. Perhaps even his own sister. Maybe the officials had hated him the whole time, sneered behind his back, waited. Maybe they relished the moment they could destroy him, cruelly pretending he would be okay.

But it didn't matter now. Feng would find out, get to the bottom of it. Carefully, of course; he wouldn't want to end up right back in prison. He wouldn't make any motion to take back his business or start a competing one, he wouldn't accuse anyone. He would dissemble. It wasn't to take revenge; years of not having a clear target for that revenge had blunted his thirst for it. But he still would like to know who had done this and why. Surely, they would tell him that. Perhaps not right away, but after time. After he had shown he was no threat.

CHAPTER 15

Day 844 — Near Denver, Colorado

A couple of days after their own arrival, Dwight and Brad were joined by two other men in their little tower. Or, more precisely, by one man and one woman. The latter, squat and sullen, wouldn't normally have been anybody's "type". But for a bunch of guys stuck on top of a mountain, it isn't long before anybody becomes everybody's type.

The barracks were located a small distance from the choke point, which consisted of two towers overlooking the remains of the road. Technically they were guard towers because they had guards in them, but they resembled fire towers more than anything. Nor were they rustic or ancient. They had been assembled from some sort of prefab army kit. Dwight actually was impressed that such sturdy structures could be built from simple, lightweight components. The army always got first dibs on the best toys. Some sort of special polymer, he guessed. Heck, they'd probably be making bicycles out of it in a year or two. Dwight's face sank a bit, as he remembered. No, they wouldn't.

Julie was the female soldier's name. She hadn't offered a last name, and nobody cared to ask. That was the way things were these days. No dog tags either. It took a while for the vast Army bureaucracy to change its way of doing things, but they finally realized that dog tags were pointless. "No man left behind" had changed to "Lie where you die." It wasn't even proper grammar, but when had that stopped the Army?

Once things had settled down, Julie turned out to be soft-spoken and kind, though a bit moody. Dwight guessed that she had been a manager in her former life, perhaps in HR. Not that he was one to judge; his own greatest claim to fame was a two year stint as assistant manager at an OfficeUSA superstore in Denver. His department had been ready-to-assemble furniture. Dwight was amused to think that the stuff they sold was harder to put together and far less sturdy than the army prefab. In fact, there was an old joke that just because furniture was ready-to-assemble didn't it mean it actually could be assembled.

Whatever Julie may have been, it probably trumped Dwight's illustrious career. But she never spoke of it, or exhibited attitude. However, it wasn't her personality which warmed Dwight toward her; it was that her presence finally caused Brad to shut up. Apparently, he was too self-conscious around a woman to yammer on and make his usual crude comments. The new guy, Jim-something (he had shared the something, which Dwight promptly forgot), was thoroughly uninteresting and hardly said a word. In fact, there had been very little conversation in the three days since the newcomers arrived. Apparently they had been brought in for a reason, and it wasn't to talk. Mull was even more business-like than before.

The fort, if it could be called that, now was fully staffed: two towers with four soldiers each. Mull had been joined by an NTA colleague, Dave. Dwight suspected that Mull outranked Dave, but it was hard to tell. The NTA dispensed with most military trappings, including insignia of rank and salutes. Apparently this was deliberate, though Dwight had no idea why.

One thing was clear, Dwight had been given specific instructions by his superiors to follow NTA orders. This made him uncomfortable. Nobody liked the NTA even back when it was the INS, when they just glowered at you in airports and resentfully stamped passports. Over time, they had grown stronger and nastier — at least if the media reports were to be believed. In the years leading up to Z-day, deportations had been stepped up. Worse yet, rumor had it that ordinary Americans were having their citizenship revoked for a growing list of reasons. Since Z-day, the rumors about Dwight's new boss only had gotten worse.

But whatever dread the NTA may have inspired, Mull and Dave themselves seemed fairly unimposing. They certainly didn't loom large in jack boots and long leather coats, barking directives with sinister finality. In fact, both seemed a bit overweight and wore what could be mistaken for tan park ranger outfits. Maybe that was the idea, Dwight mused. They wore side arms, standard issue Glock 19's, but he had never seen them even unholster a gun to practice.

The soldiers, on the other hand, were required to do so continually. Every hour during daylight, a two man contingent went off into the forest and practiced for about ten minutes at a makeshift firing range. In theory this amounted to around four sessions per day per person, but in reality they barely managed three. The ostensible purpose was to both keep the men ready and deter anybody from approaching. Dwight thought this was dumb; it just would encourage incomers to time their entry between shooting sessions. If the idea was to deter people, this was the wrong way to do it. Especially the type of people who were likely to try.

Beside the guard towers, there were several small outbuildings. Mull and Dave had decided that an incursion was most likely to occur during daylight, so the towers were fully manned during the day — about eight hours at that time of year. The crew of each tower took turns sleeping in a nearby heated cabin during the night, leaving the other tower to keep watch. Dwight wasn't sure if Mull or Dave ever slept. They always seemed to be there to give him grief if he dozed off or started an interesting conversation, true to the NTA mission of sucking the fun out of everything.

Dwight had been quite lucky, all things considered. He was visiting friends in California when F-day had been announced. After the East-Coast riots, the government had imposed martial law but still allowed free movement within the country. This probably stemmed more from practical considerations than any regard for freedom. The United States simply had been a single entity for too long to make a policy of geographic segregation feasible.

After the riot-control measures had been taken, the country seemed to take a deep breath. The chaos of the mass westbound migration was replaced with more orderly travel. As people saw that the world hadn't actually ended, and that the ordinary modes of transport were accessible in the ordinary ways, an attitude of business as usual seemed to prevail. There were no surprises, as there had been for the East Coast, and people had the time and opportunity to evacuate well in advance of the Front. For a blissful couple of months, the illusion of normality could be maintained.

Then the government announced Freeze-Day, known as F-Day for short. That acronym caught on, and it quickly became known as "Fucked-day" in popular usage. In retrospect F-Day was necessary, of course. The country could not sustain an indefinite migration West. Everybody knew that something had to give, but it always would be tomorrow not today. Then tomorrow came.

The reaction was as to be expected when two hundred million people are told they must sit and die wherever they happen to be. To the government's credit, the announcement of F-Day preceded it by nearly three weeks. Most likely, the idea was that people could use that time to return to their homes and families. Dwight believed it was intended to allow a gentle and voluntary reshuffling before the cast was frozen and destinies fixed.

Unfortunately, the premise that people had accepted their fates with equanimity was flawed, as surely it must be. People are not built for acceptance or equanimity, they are built for panic and survival. Predictably, the announcement that travel would cease by a certain day caused it to cease almost immediately. The major highways quickly turned into parking lots, and all other modes of transport were booked beyond capacity.

Within two days, transportation had been blocked more effectively than any edict could have accomplished. Perhaps this was the actual goal of the announcement, but Dwight liked to imagine that the intentions had been good. Naturally, frustration and fear led to violence on the roads and chaos in the cities.

A second major set of riots followed, this time in Denver and most other urban areas East of California. Inevitably, the military was deployed. Nonetheless, it took almost two weeks to quell the last of the rioting. When it finally rolled around, F-day itself proved uneventful. By then, the fury had passed. Those who wished to riot were either dead or spent.

What puzzled Dwight most was that people had rioted in the first place. Mere months earlier, everybody had seen how the government responded to the East Coast riots. Sure, the military was a little hesitant at first, but it quickly found its footing. Hellfire missiles, assault helicopters, cluster bombs. All the stuff reserved for the worst enemies. And the F-Day riots were the same, but with less restraint. This time, the army had blown up most of the major roads. After all, F-Day was approaching so why not kill two birds with one stone. It almost had a ceremonial quality, like the severing of old ties. There really was nowhere to go. But people tried anyway.

Of course, the announcement of F-Day was a choice, even if a necessary one. To that extent, the government bore some responsibility. With the East-Coast riots, it just had been the messenger. Sure it had waited until after the fall of New York to pass that message along, but by then it had no choice. SA-Day was a necessity, and the only argument that could be made (and it *was* made by lots of conspiracy theorists) was that the government had known about it but kept the information secret. On SA-Day the American people learned that the Front was moving faster than expected — speeding up, in fact. Apparently, it was expanding spherically through the Earth, though how that was possible escaped Dwight. The gist was that the Front would reach everyone in the U.S. a month sooner than previously believed. People in California cared less, those on the East Coast more. Especially since the Front already was upon them by that time. It also probably didn't help that the entire government had safely relocated to San Diego a year earlier. There was a lot of anger and confusion when New York fell three weeks ahead of schedule, and the announcement of SA-Day only added fuel to the fire. The government responded decisively to the riots, and then allowed the survivors of that response to flee West in an orderly fashion.

That's what got Dwight about the second set of riots. Everybody already knew how the government would react. And this time, there would be no post-response evacuation. The whole point of F-Day was to *stop* people from evacuating. For a measly thirty extra days, millions of people rioted and cast away whatever time they *did* have. It was a tragedy, but then so was everything and therefore nothing.

Dwight quietly pondered this. He had heard rumors of what conditions were like in Denver toward the end of the riots. That was almost three months ago, and there had been an embargo on news since. He only could imagine what it was like at home now. If Dwight hadn't happened to be visiting friends in California when the fateful F-day announcement was made, he never would have gotten out. As it was, he ended up overstaying his welcome by about three months. His friends were friends no longer, though they had grudgingly tolerated his involuntary exile. To be fair, what couple would want a third wheel ruining such a sizable chunk of their remaining time together? Still, it was better than having been stuck here. Yet here he was, just a slightly different here than the here he would have been.

All the while, the U.S. didn't even have it so bad. New Zealand got it worst. Sure, they seemed like the lucky ones, the last on the chopping block. But that wasn't the right way to look at it. First, they would have to wait for everybody else to die, see it coming from afar. Many people envied this, but not Dwight. To him, it seemed like that would be a most horrible sensation. Each and every other person on the planet dies before it is your turn.

Of course, there was the small chance the Front would stop short of them. A bunch of superstitious people even had moved to Oban, New Zealand in the belief that it would be spared — the seed for a new world — since the Front had started at its antipode in Oban, Scotland. Of course, it really hadn't and they really wouldn't. No, New Zealand would watch and wait and, if strong enough, kill itself before the Front got there.

There also was another special gift, courtesy of the Front. When it turned out to be that new shape, they lost over two years. Americans only lost a month. Of course, from the vantage point of waiting, maybe it was a blessing. Two fewer years on death row, with no hope of reprieve.

Then there was the way that other countries dealt with the Front. The Chinese had tied prisoners to posts to watch its progress. When they ran out of prisoners, they moved to farmers or anybody who happened to be at hand. They didn't even try to hide it; he had seen the videos, widely circulated. They were uploaded by soldiers involved — not to show the world how abhorrent it was, but for fun. Some had even posed in the videos.

Hadn't this always been the benchmark? When in its history had the United States not been guilty of oppression or injustice or excess of some egregious kind? The thing that made it such a wonderful country was that everybody else was worse. Much, much worse. Before the Front appeared, it had looked like this finally was changing. Northern Europe had begun to look better, even parts of Asia, and to be frank the U.S. had been doing pretty badly the last few years. Now Northern Europe didn't exist, and the U.S. once again was the lesser evil. For all its faults, that was something to remember.

Dwight heard Dave briefing the new soldiers, and was grateful that he hadn't been required to attend. Then again, *somebody* had to sit watch. He remembered Mull's speech. That time, it had been just Dwight and Brad. An intimate speech, it felt special.

You have been mobilized as a last line of defense for your country. yada yada. No shit, Dwight had thought as he listened.

You probably haven't been told much, and I'm afraid I cannot share all the details of this operation with you. What you need to know is that the enemy will come up that hill. It sounded like the speech from some bad old war movie. Then again, maybe that's where Mull had gotten it. Dwight just had met Mull at that time, and the man struck him as the type who watched bad old war movies, who would rip them off, who practiced in front of a mirror.

They may look like your friends, the people you knew, the people you grew up with. They may look like Americans. But they are not. Dwight had wanted to punch Mull in the face. What were they then? Maybe this shit worked back when they were convincing Texans to shoot Mexicans... though the Texans he knew really didn't need any convincing.

It sounded like typical propaganda BS. It occurred to Dwight then (and on many subsequent occasions) that if he shot *Mull*, nobody would know. Brad wouldn't say a word. They could just say he bought it from some civilian. Nobody would check; they obviously didn't have anybody extra to send. He half regretted not taking the opportunity. He had an itchy trigger finger quite a few times those first days. But, annoying as he was, Mull never did anything to merit execution. Nor was Dwight the executing type. Of course, once Dave and the six new soldiers arrived, such things became impossible anyway. But it had been fun to think about for a while.

Dwight didn't remember most of the other stuff from the speech. There had been lots of the same ra-ra nonsense they spouted on TV these days. The importance of law and order, how the US still was the greatest nation, and so on. At least they didn't claim the Front was God's wrath or a way to deal with homos or some such. Dwight could stomach quite a bit, but he would have a hard time if they tried to use the Front itself for political ends. Perhaps they had, just not overtly.

But what it really came down to, the reason he had come when they called, the reason he didn't shoot Mull, the reason he sat here every night peering into the woods at the decayed remains of civilization was that it simply didn't matter. That was the liberating thing about the Front. Nothing mattered. So the answer to all questions was "why not?"

For all Dwight's dismissive contempt, there was one thing Mull had said which he *did* remember.

When you're wondering whether to pull the trigger, think about exactly what you are facing. These aren't choir boys. They're not nuns. There has been a massive quelled riot in Denver. The city has no natural supply of water or food. They've been under effective quarantine for three months. It's dead winter at an elevation of 10000 feet. The roads have been destroyed at several points, and there are two outposts ahead of you. When you see somebody coming, don't ask whether they are innocent or guilty. Think about the sort of people who will make it this far. Think about what will be coming up that hill.

At the time Dwight almost had laughed. Apparently they had moved from bad old war movies to bad old zombie movies. But something bothered him about the way Mull said it. Especially that last line.

Think about what will be coming up that hill.

There had been a hint of reminiscence, a hint of disgust in Mull's eyes. This wasn't the first time he had done this. The same situation must have arisen with cities farther East. Maybe it wasn't a mountain pass, maybe just a toll booth or a rest stop. Mull had seen the refugees as they fled. He knew something more than he was saying. Since then, Dwight had pondered this quite a bit. What on Earth had he seen?

Mull finished on what he deemed a humorous note, though to Dwight it had a sinister sound.

And don't worry. We've got plenty of ammo.

Mull didn't ask if there were questions.

CHAPTER 16

Day 15 — Edinburgh, Scotland

Before Elise left her parents' house, she cleaned the dishes and made the bed, turned off the water and power, and ensured that everything was as she found it. Minus the supplies she took, of course. Elise walked out the door and stood on the sidewalk, looking at the house for nearly a minute, wondering if — no, when — she would see it again. She locked the door and tucked away the key. She hoped that she would need it again, soon. Or better, that she wouldn't because her parents would be here next time.

She carefully strapped on the heavy pack and mounted the bicycle. Elise had always thought that panniers and saddlebags looked silly, slowed a cyclist down. Now, she really wished she had some. Crouched over the handlebars, she could tell that her back would be very unhappy very soon. But it still beat walking.

It had been two days before Elise was in any condition to leave the house. There wasn't because of her injury, just a general emotional paralysis. She felt lethargic and exhausted and really didn't care what happened. There had been quite a bit of crying and a few bouts of near hysteria, even some vomiting.

Elise was grateful nobody was around to see her in such a state. Then again, if there had been somebody around she may not have felt this way. Although ashamed of her lack of composure and afraid of the uncontrolled panic she sometimes felt, Elise sensed she was undergoing a natural response to the grief and uncertainty she had experienced.

One hallmark of a prolonged anxiety attack, and what makes it so difficult to quell, is a sense of pervasive and inexplicable dread. The presence of anxiety itself becomes a source of anxiety, self-perpetuating. However when anxiety has a real and obvious cause, it is explicable. This does not mitigate the pain, but prevents the episode from assuming a life of its own. It lends finite duration. After two days of real grief and real fear and real sadness, Elise found herself whole once more.

By this point it was getting dark, so Elise treated herself to a bath and went to sleep. The next morning she was ready by 10 AM and decided to start exploring the city. It would be like a vacation. She pretended that she was seeing Edinburgh for the first time and had rented her parents' place. Her first venture was a small, local one. She made sure to bring the key her parents had given her. Not that it would matter if she had to break back in; it *was* her parents' place.

But she'd rather not be taken for a looter. What if they didn't give her a chance to explain herself? Heaven knows what they did with looters. Elise walked around a bit but kept within a small radius of the house. She also brought a kitchen knife for protection. This probably violated a dozen laws, but she really didn't care. If things got to the point where she found herself being searched by the cops, a knife probably would be the least of her worries. Besides, who could fault her under the circumstances? Then again, she bet judges heard *that* refrain all day long.

It turned out there was almost nobody around, and those whom she did pass seemed more worried about her than vice versa. It reminded her of that nonsense the park rangers spewed about wild animals: 'they're more afraid of you than you are of them'. But they aren't really, are they? At least not the one that ends up slurping out your innards.

What a morbid thought. Was she becoming like Craig? That last conversation with him must have disturbed her more than she realized. Who knew that an avuncular old man could say such things? Then again, he had been right. Maybe she *should* be more like him. Elise tried to be observant as she made her tour of the neighborhood. There were no obvious signs of looting, but all the stores were closed. That wasn't a good sign. Then she realized it was Sunday. But not just any Sunday. In all the chaos, she had forgotten. It was her birthday.

Back at the house, Elise stood in the large empty dining room. Happy 42nd, she thought. Happy goddamn 42nd. She wasn't sure what was more depressing — having a 42nd birthday, or spending it like this. She sensed the onset of another attack of depression, and tried to ward it off. She was safely at her parents' place. If she left, it would be her choice. Nobody was forcing her. *Like Glasgow?* She had the bicycle and could escape again if needed. She was alive and well. What about her shop? Was it alive and well? Enough self-pity; the shop was a practical matter that could be dealt with.

The back and forth went on for some time. But eventually, its arguments rebutted, her anxiety receded into the shadows, awaiting a more opportune moment, a new weakness. Elise felt more confident now that she knew she could keep the panic at bay. *'Have' is not 'can'.* This was true, she couldn't count on always being able to regain control. She sensed that as her departure grew more urgent, this imminence would feed the anxiety. And if she had an attack at that late hour, the paralysis could prove fatal.

No, she would have to leave while the choice remained her. It would have to be soon. But today it was her birthday, and she would make the best of it. Besides, the only worse way to spend a 42nd birthday than alone in the midst of a disaster was alone in the midst of a disaster *and* depressed. Well, there always were worse ways. Wasn't this the gist of Craig's philosophy?

That got Elise thinking about the other things Craig had said. His warning. Stay away from cities. Wasn't Edinburgh a city too? Why did she think things would be different here?

Even if it seemed empty, couldn't that change quickly as waves of people moved through. Or if the few who remained were of a bad sort. Suddenly she felt very unsafe. She had to get out. Why had she even come here? Was it to find her parents? To see if they were okay? Or was it to be comforted by them, told that she was home now and everything would be all right. They would protect her. Maybe she *wasn't* such an adult after all, running to mummy and daddy at the first sign of trouble. Or did she hope for the same succor from Parliament? To come to its home and be comforted. 'You're inside the walls of our fort now, nobody can come get you, little sister.' No, they would be the first to flee. They were politicians, after all.

But why *was* it so empty? What had happened to all the people who should be coming through? Where were all those drivers from the M8? Even if the jammed traffic moved very slowly, it still should be flowing into Edinburgh. Why was there no traffic at all? Had the government blocked the roads? Nobody was *that* callous. Perhaps they intended to keep them open, but simply lacked the manpower to manage the traffic.

Would they really leave all those people stuck in their cars for days on end? What if the toxic spill caught up? It didn't make any sense, there had to be more to it than that. Elise was tempted to retrace her route in, and see what the end of the highway looked like. But she was worried that things could be pretty hectic there, possibly even nasty. And if her misgivings were correct, she really didn't want to see what the highway was like by now.

Foreboding and speculation and suspicion aside, there were no signs of imminent unrest or danger nearby. Elise slowly calmed herself and took a deep breath. Rushing out the door would solve nothing. She had to decide where to go. And she needed to proceed cautiously. Things seemed comfortable enough here, but if she fled without a plan she easily could find herself in a situation far less to her liking.

There were three directions in which Elise could travel from Edinburgh. North would be problematic if the toxic spill — or whatever it was — had spread. Scotland was very narrow at this point, but quickly widened as one traveled North. The Eastern coastal road could get her past whatever was plaguing Glasgow, or it could take her straight into the disaster zone. The problem was that Elise had no clue as to the origin or shape of the spill, or the direction in which it was spreading. For all she knew, volcanic gas was blowing down from Iceland. Even if she made it to the far North, she would be trapped on the sparsely inhabited tip of the island.

There *was* something very disconcerting about being confined on an island. The continent seemed to offer a certain ephemeral freedom, the flexibility to flee in whatever direction one wished. No ocean, no obstacles. Just a big open area on the map. But on an island, Elise could be trapped ever so easily. The quickest way to remedy this would be to find a boat to Europe. That certainly would open up a lot of possibilities.

Elise didn't know her way around Norway or Denmark, but hopefully she could at least access her bank accounts from there. As a last resort, she knew a few people in Paris and probably could manage something if need be. Most important, she could watch TV or use an internet connection and learn what actually was happening. It probably would turn out to be something embarrassingly mundane. But she'd rather appear ill-informed and panicky than get killed by poison or radiation or rioters. The third choice was to head South into England. London was much more convenient to the continent, especially if her destination was Paris.

But before deciding, Elise wanted to determine what was available. So she made a quick bicycle tour of downtown Edinburgh. It was empty. The docks were devoid of ships, the train stations were locked. The only good news was that the roads seemed clear. Perhaps the city had evacuated early enough. Once again, she wondered why she didn't see cars from the M8 coming through.

Come to think of it, that was different from other traffic jams she had experienced. When she bicycled to Edinburgh, the cars hadn't been moving at all. Not even inching along. Why was that? The service road was empty, because every entrance had been blocked. That was a blessing for her, of course; she simply lifted her bicycle over the concrete step barriers. But surely there were other ways around? Why was everyone stuck on the M8 West of Edinburgh? And where had everybody who lived here gone? Even the government buildings seemed deserted. They were probably the first to leave, she mused cynically. One thing was for sure: when this mess was over, a lot of MPs would lose their seats.

Without any ships or trains available, Elise's only option was to head south. She briefly considered stealing a car, but decided that this would be crossing a line. Why did she have *this* line, and where did it come from? Why was a bicycle on one side and a car on the other? She wondered at this, but the decision was clear to her. Maybe the line would move after another day or two of bicycling. She suspected that lines had a way of doing this when necessary. At least she hoped so, because she also suspected that lines could get you killed. Not that her qualms mattered in this case; Elise had no idea how to steal a car.

The city actually was quite beautiful with nobody in it. Well, there probably were a few people, but Elise didn't run into them. It felt like she was the Queen of her own land. She considered cycling up to the old castle and parking herself there to wait out the crisis. She probably would be arrested when everybody returned, but it would be worth it to be Queen for a week. And if the poison came, she would be the last ruler of this land. How poetic. The reverie over, Elise decided she would rather live than be poetic.

It was another three days before she finally mustered the resolve to begin her journey South. Once her sense of imminent danger had passed, it was difficult to find a good reason to leave. She was comfortable in her parents' home. When she found herself starving and homeless in a few days, she would wonder why she left. It made her think of those hustlers in the train stations. 'Please, I just need a pound to get back to ... wherever.' She always wanted to tell them there *is* no going back to wherever. There's never any going back, only forward. Maybe her parents would chance upon her in a few years, toothless and diseased on some street, and wonder why she hadn't just stayed safely at home. Then they would toss her a coin and move on, ashamed to acknowledge her as their own.

Elise decided she was being a bit melodramatic. But it did raise a legitimate question. She had seen many disaster movies. Sometimes the people who stayed behind were the survivors, but usually the ones who kept moving made it while those who stubbornly remained behind learned of their error too late. Of course, motion made for good drama, and Elise didn't want to base a real decision on bad movies.

She always could return if she was wrong about leaving, but she couldn't always leave if she was wrong about staying. At least until she figured out what was happening, she should keep moving. Why was that so hard? Millions of people immigrated to foreign countries and started new lives. They had no money, didn't even speak the language. If they could do it, Elise could get off her duff and bicycle a few miles south. A few miles? London was a few hundred. Come to think of it, where *would* she go? Should she go *anywhere*?

Maybe it *was* one of those movies where the people who stay behind survive. She would sit in her lawn-chair with a lemonade in hand, greeting the tattered refugees as they straggled back into town. She would try not to judge them too harshly or lecture them on the wages of cowardice. Yes she would stay, do the sensible thing. Then she remembered the anxiety attack, felt a slight turning of her stomach at the mere thought of it. That ended the debate. She would go. Now.

Elise took out the map she had found in her parents' house, and spread it on the dining room table. It would take a bit longer, but she could follow the A1 down. That would keep to the coast part of the way, and there could be ships. She wanted to avoid any big roads, but the A1 wasn't too bad. Then again, the coastal route *was* quite roundabout, and Elise wasn't sure how long she could endure with a heavy pack on the bicycle. She prayed that along the way she would find a bus or some means of renting a car. That probably wouldn't happen until Newcastle, though. That's where she would head. Newcastle. At the very least, it was a fun town. She decided on a direct route: the A68. For some reason she felt safer inland, nestled. It was 10 AM the next morning when Elise finally began the long journey South.

CHAPTER 17

Day 850 — Near Denver, Colorado, 12:30 AM

Unlike Brad, Dwight did not believe the Guard had been called up "just in case." He was fairly certain that people would come. Before he had been requisitioned (that was the word they now used, as if he were a canteen or a flashlight), Dwight eagerly had followed the news regarding Colorado. When the government announced the change in shape of the Front, it also released a revised timetable for the remaining major cities. At first, this had surprised Dwight. Like many, he subscribed to the view that the government deliberately withheld information for the longest time, and he saw no reason to believe their numbers now. One couldn't trust the media at the best of times, and most likely they were wholly government-run at this point.

But there were enough other sources of information, most prominently the Australian Broadcasting Service, and they seemed to corroborate the revised schedule. After some consideration, Dwight thought he understood why the government had, on this occasion at least, been forthright. They probably decided that fear of the unknown was more dangerous than fear of the known. Among other things, it would distribute the chaos. People tended not to react until a threat was imminent. If everybody panicked at once, the country could spiral out of control. The military so far had proved adept at keeping this from happening. But they too were human, as were their commanders. At some point, they would prefer to join the chaos than engage in aggressive crowd control. That was when Dwight stopped blindly hating the government, despite all they had done.

It wasn't easy; their actions inspired hatred. They had been the first to tuck tail and run when the Front threatened DC. Then they had kept everyone else from doing the same. They were rumored to have ordered air strikes on Americans, organized mass executions, even deployed nerve gas, long before the actual riots. But rumors were just that. If Dwight were called to serve in the Guard, as he worried he might be (and ultimately was), then he may as well do so with pride. He never would like the government, but he would tolerate them. He would give no ear to rumors, and assume that they did their best to maintain a steady, if firm, hand.

After all, they were dealing with an impossible situation: the Front on one side and a rabble of terrified and confused people on the other. People in a democracy are dangerous at the best of times, and now ... well, it couldn't be easy. Power is the perception of power, and stability is the perception of stability. If either teeters, the whole will collapse. A single sharp blow to the entire system could unravel everything. But if people only fled when the danger approached their own city, the military could focus where needed. The situation could be contained.

Apparently, Denver had proved more difficult to manage. Or perhaps Dwight had been brought in because another crisis elsewhere had spread the army thin. He could not recall whether any other cities were scheduled to be hit around the same time. All he had paid attention to were the time-lines for Denver and Boulder. The Front would reach both at roughly the same time. This had seemed odd to him until he realized that the Front originated in Scotland, at a much higher latitude. It was approaching from the Northeast, not the East as most of the media imagery misleadingly implied. In fact, it was the ultimate 'Noreaster.

Dwight struggled to remember precisely when Denver would be hit. He thought back to the news reports. Why couldn't they just post a simple list? That would have been easy and painless; but no, there had to be drama. He suffered

through all the blather about the various cities that were
detailed in the government release. The news network had a
long segment on each, with copious commercial breaks (mostly
government sponsored messages) and lots of flashing words
and infographics. Dwight remembered wondering at the time
whether some cities would be gone by the time their segment
aired.

After about two hours, it was Denver's turn. Dwight was
thankful that it was classified as a "major city" and began
with a 'D' (he had to read a later press release to learn about
Boulder). A woman with beauty-pageant-blonde hair and an
obscene amount of makeup came on. Who looked like that
anymore? Dwight wondered. Was she supposed to be some
Mid-Western stereotype? Did they realize that Denver wasn't
in the Mid-West? And it certainly wasn't in the 1950s. Were
that it were, he sighed.

"Denver, a city with a long history of," she began and
proceeded to drone on as if reading from a bad guide book.
None of it sounded anything like the Denver that Dwight
knew. Finally she wrapped up, "and now over to Bob Bower
for the latest."

Bower was an ex-football-player cum sportscaster. These
days he specialized in swirling his arm around in a weirdly
exaggerated gesture and shouting "SLAMMED". The news
loved to use action words — "slam", "crush", and "wipe out"
— when talking about the Front. In reality it was far more
banal.

This reminded Dwight of horror movie posters that
featured a huge skull. To Dwight, that detracted from the
horror, trivialized it. It clocked you over the head, crushing any
hope for nuance and wiping out whatever dread the unknown
may otherwise inspire. See, this is a horror movie. Let's make
sure that even the biggest idiot realizes that. And that poster
with the big boobs is a porno movie. We're all safely inoculated

against the unexpected. To Dwight, the horror was where you didn't look for it. The horror *always* was in the banal.

Bob began his schtick. A large wheel of cities rotated, to reveal Denver followed by several empty slots. Helpfully, other cities were not visible — obscured by the wheel itself. It wouldn't do to let people know when they would die without appropriate panache. Dwight briefly considered walking into the studio and shooting it up. It would cost him only a few months of life, and everyone probably would thank him for it. Heck, in the old days he'd probably have lost more of his life just for having some weed.

In the end, though, he couldn't muster the energy to get off the couch. He wondered how many American massacres had been averted over the years by a similar sentiment. The couch was a lifesaver. Besides, his guns were back in Colorado. So, he just kept watching.

First, Bob explained that Denver (by which they always meant first contact with the outer 'burbs) had previously been scheduled for Jan 21. He enunciated the month and day as an alliterative 'oh-one-twenty-one'. Then he did a little roll and they had a "wa-wa" sound in the background, at which point he announced solemnly "but they've got a new date. Not THAT sort of date. A date with DEATH. That's right, this December 9, they'll be", there was no alliteration here. He sucked in a lot of air and did a big wind up before whirling his arm violently. Dwight clicked off the TV just before he shouted "SLAMMED."

CHAPTER 18

Day 727 — Dwill, Utah

Contrary to the predictions of countless armchair philosophers over the years, the "thin veneer of civilization" did not come crashing down at the flimsiest excuse. At least not at Dwill. Nobody could argue that *this* excuse was flimsy, yet things had continued with as great a semblance of normality as could be hoped.

Nor was the normality superficial, masking some lurking horror. Neighbor did not turn on neighbor. There was no hording of food and guns, no tyrant seized control, and no roving hordes or violent invaders threatened the people of Dwill. None of the presaged dystopias emerged.

The people of Dwill did not pretend and did not hide. Other than the very young or mentally feeble, everybody knew what was coming. The routineness wasn't a delusion or farce, born of ignorance or religion or fear. There simply was no point to doing anything differently. The police were a bit more vigilant in keeping an eye on the occasional visitor, but on whole the town experienced little trouble.

In part this may have been because of Dwill's location, far from the main roads. What once had been a bane to commerce and growth now proved a blessing. There simply was no reason to live in Dwill unless you always had, and even less reason to pass through it. It wasn't on the way to anything.

As for the people who *did* live there, the same reasons explained their reluctance to leave. Most had expected to die there eventually, and if eventually came sooner than hoped, so be it. Besides, there was nowhere to go. The government's restrictions on travel had closed all paths of egress. Even those who wished to leave had no obvious way to do so.

Supplies were growing tight, but were adequate to last for the foreseeable future. And the future *was* foreseeable. There simply was no reason for the people of Dwill to do anything differently. The cynics would have to look to big cities for satisfaction. In Dwill life continued as always, albeit with a slight pallor.

Marissa didn't look up from her writing when Josh entered the kitchen. He had long ceased expecting her to.

"At it still, I see," he observed while opening the refrigerator. "Are we out of milk?" he asked the side of her head.

Marissa didn't respond, scribbling furiously instead. Josh walked over, gently stroked her hair and placed his hands on her shoulders. She tensed and shrugged him off without looking up. Not the response he had hoped for, even now.

Josh sighed. He didn't hold it against her. They each dealt with things in their own way, and he couldn't begrudge her this. He just wished they could cope with it as a family, share the experience. That was *his* way, and part of him resented her for denying him this, for unilaterally deciding to do it her way.

Marissa looked up as if suddenly aware of his presence. "Did you say something?"

"Nothing worth noting." Josh quietly kissed her on the forehead. "Carry on."

She gave a wan smile. "You, know, I have to finish this." And then she was back to the urgent scribbling, punctuated only by small pensive interludes.

Josh watched her for a few moments longer. He didn't have the heart to remind her that nobody would read anything she wrote, that there would *be* nobody to read it. She had been writing for over a month. At some point the paper would run out, and she'd probably start writing in the margins. Maybe even over her previous words, a thought which unsettled him for some reason.

He never read what she wrote; it was too private. Maybe it

just was "all work and no play…," endlessly repeated. What if what she actually was writing would make him wish it *was* "all work and no play…"?

Regardless, it was compulsive. He supposed this was how a patient might react to the news of a terminal illness. The need to write all their thoughts for posterity before it was too late. Thoughts that hitherto had never borne recording, had been trite or redundant or personal. For a posterity that never before had deserved consideration, and never thought *she* deserved consideration.

Josh envisioned billions of people posting their hopes and dreams and bathroom habits into the vacuum, imagining that somebody was listening. Wasn't this what people always had done? They just used to call it prayer.

It all boiled down to narcissism, of course. The desire to preserve the self in some form, to pretend that the end wouldn't *be* the end. As a psychologist, Josh imagined himself too self-aware to adopt such a conceit. His challenge was a different one: to refrain from presuming to analyze those he loved, especially at times such as this.

It was a danger for someone of his background, and one of which he was acutely aware. Though his formal training spoke against it, most people entered the field from a desire to do precisely that. Few tried, and fewer succeeded, but it was a difficult mistake to avoid.

Josh understood that Marissa needed a distraction. He had hoped to *be* that distraction, but apparently he was part of what she needed distraction *from*. Part of the very grief she was about to suffer, or perhaps already had.

Marissa was one of the strongest women Josh knew; which was why he had been attracted to her, married her, maybe even loved her. It was possible she loved him too, for a time, though he was experienced enough not to assume that.

As the old adage went: "a man loves his wife, a woman

loves her children." In his practice and life, he had seen little evidence to the contrary. It wasn't as terrible as it sounded. Josh much preferred that her affections find a home with their daughter Rielle than some other man. Or, worse, no home at all.

He felt alone, and it had nothing to do with his wife's coldness. He had a growing sense that there was no amount of love could bind him closely enough to Marissa and Rielle. However tightly he clutched them, the force would be insufficient and they would be torn asunder, each to perish miserably in their own cell.

Was this all there was: a fleeting approach, orbit, and then departure? Three particles which briefly intersected and then scattered to infinity? At least it was quiet outside, he sighed.

The scribbling continued, unabated.

CHAPTER 19

Day 730 — Near Yining, China

The guard led Feng through a final door. He thought about how films required rain when someone entered or left a prison. In fact, it was quite sunny. Feng's eyes hurt. There were no flash bulbs or scissors or demolition crews. Then he remembered that there still remained two prisoners in his cell. He smiled; it was "his cell" no longer. One of those two would be given the scissors or forgotten as the building collapsed. Feng was led into a small prison van.

Like all such transports — including the one which had brought him — the windows were blackened. Feng viewed this as a small mercy; he would have been mortified if somebody from his previous life saw him in prison garb. But what if they just left him on his doorstep? That truly would be humiliating. He hoped they at least would give him back his old clothes.

The van drove for around 45 minutes, turning a few times on its way. The wind was strong, and it felt like they were buffeted around. It didn't occur to Feng until later, but he didn't hear a single other car during the trip. The van stopped a couple of times at what Feng assumed were checkpoints. At each, there was some official bustle outside and voices he couldn't quite make out, before they moved on.

When the van finally reached its destination, it coasted to a slow halt. There was a long pause as the driver fiddled about outside. Then the back door burst open and light flooded in. A sunset. Feng lapped it up. He had forgotten that such beauty existed. But he didn't get to dwell on it for long. The driver, a uniformed guard, unchained Feng and told him to get out of the van. He then fiddled about a bit more in the back and closed the doors. They were on a stretch of highway in the middle of nowhere, but it was a beautiful nowhere surrounded by trees. Feng could hear all the sounds of the woods, and they brought back memories of childhood excursions. The outside world was real again.

The driver put a placard with a number around Feng's neck. It read "841". Feng understood. It was a photo op. They weren't just content with releasing the prisoners; they wanted to prove they had. This must be to satisfy some international human rights group or for propaganda purposes. The guard motioned him to the nearest highway marker: "3994". Feng stood in front of it, but the guard walked over and gently moved him next to it, adjusting his position and posture and straightening the placard a bit. As the guard raised his camera, a small Japanese digital model, Feng reflexively turned his head. The Americans were fond of publicly humiliating their prisoners, but China was civilized. They made you pay for the crime physically, but hid your shame away. Except for the occasional show trial of a high ranking official, and Feng was far from that.

The guard must have understood his concern. He lowered the camera and explained, "For official records only." This definitely meant he would be set free. No guard would bother explaining anything to a prisoner. Feng was a person again. He smiled and turned to the camera. The guard casually pressed a button. There was no flash. After checking the photo on the back of the camera, the guard nodded, "Ok, stay there," took the placard, and walked to the other side of the van. Feng looked around and relaxed. He had to pee, but knew better than to do so without permission. The road stretched for kilometers in either direction, lined by trees and the occasional distance marker. He couldn't make out what it was, but there was a square object on the road much farther down the highway. It seemed a little small for a car, and did not appear to be moving.

While Feng basked in the fading sunlight, the guard

retrieved something from the passenger side of the van and brought it over. It appeared to be a small cage. Below it was a metal box, the width and length of the cage, set on vertical springs. A device which looked like a walkie-talkie was attached to the side. The cage itself seemed cheaply made but strong enough to hold somebody. Its top opened from a hinge and had a few bars as an opening. The sides had some small holes but were otherwise closed off. Weld spots were visible on the corners.

The guard opened the top and ordered Feng to get in, only to be met with a bewildered stare. "Get in," he barked gruffly, drawing his side arm and waving it at Feng. It took a few moments for him to understand what the man wanted, during which the guard grew visibly impatient. Feng wanted to object, but was afraid to argue with an armed and angry soldier.

He gingerly stepped into the box, hesitating as it wobbled and sunk under him. It felt like getting into a canoe, and the instability was disconcerting. After a few seconds, the floor seemed to level and Feng heard a click under the cage. The springs must have fully depressed under his weight. "Down," the guard ordered, motioning with his gun for emphasis. When Feng was in, the guard holstered his gun. With one quick motion he stepped forward and slammed the lid shut. A latch snapped into position, and it automatically locked shut.

"But I'm supposed to be be freed," Feng protested.

The guard laughed and lit a cigarette. "Yes, you are free. Not only are you free, but we're giving you all this." He gestured magnanimously at the surrounding woods. "All yours."

The man muttered beneath his cigarette as he fiddled with the walkie-talkie and an object in his hand. He then retrieved a couple of other items from the van. Feng heard some drilling around the cage, but the floor remained stable. Were they bolting it shut or bolting it down? Once satisfied that everything was set, the guard went back to the van and retrieved a small bottle of water and two sandwiches. He ate one and drank half the bottle, then went off to take a piss by the sign post. When he had relieved himself, he walked back to the cage and kicked it gently.

"Hey, you alive in there?"

Feng whimpered a "yes".

The guard dropped the remaining sandwich and half-empty bottle of water between the top bars. "Here's one for the road," he laughed half-heartedly as if regurgitating a tired old joke. "Can't have you dying in there."

So they *would* be coming back for him, then. Was this some sort of publicity stunt? Feng had heard of crazy artists who put on huge performance pieces. His mind raced with possibilities.

"Won't a car hit me?" he objected as the guard began to walk away.

The guard turned around and stood over the cage looking down at him contemplatively. He almost seemed sympathetic. "There's nobody to hit you on this road." He took a drag of his cigarette and was about to throw it away, when Feng wiggled his hands through the bars pathetically. The guard shook his head, looked at Feng disapprovingly, and dropped the cigarette on the ground. As he stepped on it he chuckled, "don't you know these things will kill you."

As the sound of the van receded, Feng felt a sudden spasm grip his body, and he began shaking uncontrollably. He screamed and flailed around wildly for a few moments, but quickly stopped when cramps set in. There wasn't much space to maneuver, but after a few tries he managed to find a kneeling position that wasn't quite as painful. Then he had some time for reflection. The loss of control and subsequent jitters were very disconcerting, and it took Feng a few moments to realize he had experienced a panic attack. This itself calmed him. Maybe it wasn't so bad. Didn't they just put a bullet in your head if you were to be executed? Why the cage? Why the contraption?

For the next 16 hours, he had nothing to do but wonder. Even in his new position, the cramps grew unbearable. The cage didn't keep bugs out, and they had their way with him throughout the night. Fortunately, it was a cooler time of year and they weren't as prevalent, but that also meant he got cold quickly. It didn't help that he had urinated on himself soon after the van left. Once the initial warmth of the pee faded, it served to dampen and chill him. There was no place for it to drain and, as his earlier fit had taught him, the cage was indeed bolted to the ground. There was no way he could tilt it and get rid of the fluid. He basically had to sit in a wet, metal box. There was little chance of sleep during the night, but he did manage an hour or two once dawn arrived and the sun lent some warmth.

When Feng awoke, the sun was strong and he was parched. He drank the water but decided to keep the sandwich for later. He had no idea how long he would be there, and something told him that this choice would be critical to his survival. Were he trained, he would have realized that the opposite was true: water was essential, and the sandwich an unnecessary luxury. In fact, it likely would have sped his death by further dehydrating him. But he never ate his sandwich.

Feng was used to the smell of stale urine, and after years in a cell almost nothing could ruin his appetite. But the distant scream did. There was a quality to it that shocked him. Movie screams almost always were melodramatic shrieks. Even the screams he heard in his cell had been simple reactions to quick sharp pain. Aside from soldiers and doctors, only the unlucky get to hear the scream of a grown man in unbearable prolonged agony. And only the truly unlucky get to hear it puncture a silent forest amidst the chirping of birds and cadence of crickets. While locked in a cage.

The scream came from the box Feng had seen down the road. He could only hear it faintly, an agonized shriek that chilled him to the bone and he was powerless to stop. And it went on and on for almost a minute. Then it faded in a gurgling and ended. Feng vomited. A few kilometers away, the radio squawked and a red light flashed in the guard's van. "Right on time," he muttered, pressed a relay button under the red light, and kicked the idling van into drive.

CHAPTER 20

Day 841 — Near Denver, Colorado

Dwight had been called up the day after Thanksgiving, too late to ungive his Thanks. He reported to the Point Loma Joint Staging area (called the "Jasper" for short) on November 30. It was an impressive structure, built on the foundation of an existing Naval installation. He had seen it from afar while staying in San Diego, but had no idea how vast the complex really was. They had called out the entire National Guard, or at least it seemed that way. He was surprised they didn't seem to care that he was from Colorado, not California. And he was even more surprised when they shipped him the following day to his old training ground in Alamosa.

At first he suspected they were stationing everybody near home, but on reflection this made little sense. When a regime needs to act with force against its own, the prudent course is to bring in outsiders. You send soldiers from Colorado to Montana and vice versa. He remembered that from history; everybody from the Assyrians to the Soviets had done it this way.

It also was why the army tended to be more effective than the Guard for such purposes; any local flavor was diluted in the overall mix. There probably had been individual instances of mutiny, but collective defections were unlikely. So far there had been no news of any, but Dwight was certain such events would be dealt with quietly and decisively. In the old days, accounts of the horrific deaths of traitors quickly would circulate. But in a modern military, ignorance is a more powerful tool than fear.

Once back in Colorado, Dwight's speculations were quashed. This may have been his old stomping ground, but most of the Guardsmen he met were from California, Arizona, and Washington. Except for Brad. Alamosa had become a surprisingly busy place, and it only was the following morning that Dwight noticed him. It was that familiar laugh: abrasive, grating, and just what he needed. There was no mistaking it. Dwight turned and, sure enough, there was Brad.

They didn't have much time to chat because ten of them promptly were loaded into a special transport. A journey which would have taken about two hours in the old days took nearly six. The roads were passable for the most part, but there were stretches which had been destroyed to prevent travel, as well as occasional scarring and debris from some of the riot control measures. Many stops were necessary, and the group had to labor quite a bit to get past some of the larger obstacles.

They finally arrived around noon, and the whole crew immediately was put to work. Mull already was there, but just kept to himself while they labored. Dwight had assumed that the whole contingent would remain, but once basic guard towers had been installed and the gear unloaded, only he and Brad were posted.

The rest moved on, to heaven knew where. Actually, Dwight had a pretty good idea. There weren't any real choke points for traffic farther along, other than the Kenosha Pass. It was the only logical destination. Then again, logic didn't really apply when it came to this stuff. The drivers weren't forthcoming, or genuinely didn't know, and Dwight decided he didn't care enough to badger them. He and Brad were here now, and that was all that mattered.

Mull chatted a bit with one of the drivers and signed some paperwork. Then he beckoned to Brad and Dwight, and the driver bade them all good luck. By then it already was dusk. When the truck had departed, Mull introduced himself without much ado. He asked whether Brad and Dwight were aware that he would be their commanding officer, which they both affirmed.

Dinner was eaten in relative silence, after which he told

them to take it easy that night because they would start early the next morning. After the bustle of the last two days, the sudden quiet was disturbing to Dwight. It felt like a trip he had taken in Italy once, when he had decided to stay on for an extra few days after his friends returned home. Those were the loneliest days of his life.

Dwight was glad that Mull was there, even if he was a sullen prick. Otherwise, it would feel like they had deserted, or been deserted. Wasn't that what marriage was all about, Dwight chuckled, sticking with a prick because you're afraid to be alone? Guess they were married to Mull. Well, at least there was Brad. He seemed eager to catch up, and Dwight would have liked to but simply was too exhausted. Instead, they just went to bed.

CHAPTER 21

Day 769 — Dwill, Utah

There were few benefits to being around for the end of the world, and one of them was not having to go to school. In lieu of a future, hope, and adulthood, a child at least deserved the consolation of unlimited playtime. It was unconscionable to deny them this. Rielle simply could not believe her ears.

Of course, Rielle did not *know* that any of these things were true. At five, she had little concept of finality. As a teenager she would decide that life had no purpose because it had an end. In college she would realize she probably did not exist at all. And as an adult she would come to learn that she did, that she wished she did not and, with a great deal of effort, could pretend she did not until she actually did not.

A few profound sources of angst would be replaced with myriad practical ones. Through the tedium of life, purpose would be restored. Or more precisely, the absence of permanence would be replaced by simple absence.

None of this resulted from the Front, of course. What *did* result from the Front, was that she never would experience any of it. That was what bothered Marissa most. Her daughter never would get to be miserable for her own reasons in her own way.

Such things were part of a distant future, one Rielle could not possibly understand. What she *did* understand were five words, the cruelest which could be uttered.

"Today is a school day."

Rielle's view was simple, as befit one of her tender years. She knew little, but she knew it with astonishing vehemence. And she *knew* she shouldn't have to go to school. The reason was pure, clear, and incontrovertible. Her friends didn't have to go, so why should she?

Marissa had trouble explaining to herself, let alone her daughter, *why* she required Rielle to continue in school. Josh probably could have come up with a convincing bit of psychobabble to explain her reasons — that was his forte — and Marissa was ready to give him hell if he tried. He did not.

She would have liked to believe it was for Rielle's sake. If the world didn't end, Rielle would be behind her class. She would be academically inferior, ill-prepared for the complex demands the world would place on her. And *she* would be the mother who let that happen.

If Rielle could not get straight A's in school (even in Dwill, especially in Dwill), then how could she hope to get into a top college? Without attending a top college, she wouldn't get into a good graduate school. There would be no good job, no future. The world would have ended for Rielle, Front or no. Besides, what better way to distract her from what approached.

Marissa knew this was dishonest, though. She was doing it as much for herself as Rielle. No, more so. She needed Rielle to disappear each day to avoid frantically clinging to her, never letting go. This way she was forced relinquish her every morning, only to be reunited that afternoon. It was proof that the end *hadn't* come, that Rielle always would return to her.

But there was more to it than that. If she removed Rielle from school, it would be a defeat. She would be acknowledging that it was over, disowning hope. Marissa took Josh' general silence on the matter as agreement. Besides, they both were happy to have a little time to themselves. Wasn't that what school was for, after all?

Unfortunately, nothing could make those five words any less cruel to a child. The snow had fallen, the town blanketed in a billowy, silent, and impassible white. It was that most lovely of days: the snow day. Rielle could go back to bed, worry no more about homework or class.

It would be a terrible injustice to deny her a single snow day, force her to trudge to school when all her friends had been excused. And this was infinitely worse. Her friends had been excused *permanently*. They told her so. To them, school was no more than a distant horror.

That could mean only one thing. *Every* day was a snow day, and *her* life should be free from care or worry or schoolwork. But no, it was not to be. She had been denied that paradise, without reason or recourse, by the very two people who professed to love her most.

Rielle was not happy. What followed was one of the largest tantrums she ever had thrown. Nor was she to be cowed by the threat of lost TV or game-time. The stakes simply were too high: a lifetime of freedom or a lifetime of drudgery.

People through the ages risked everything for such a choice, or so the stories told. Rielle held her ground. Nothing else mattered. The greatest ill in her life could be cured if she just remained steadfast.

After two hours of wrangling, including some physical wrestling, Marissa sat with her head in her hands, nursing a migraine. Rielle was in her room, sulking and probably plotting her next strategy.

Marissa wondered whether it always would be this hard, whether her own daughter would drive her mad long before the Front arrived. Mostly, she wondered where the goddamn hell Josh had been, and why he wasn't pulling his weight in this thing called parenting.

The pills helped, though. There were benefits to having a shrink as a husband, though even in this regard he was half-useless. The little shit couldn't even prescribe anything; he had to go through a friend with an MD.

If only she had paid closer attention, and married a psychiatrist instead of a psychologist. She scoffed at this as she began to nod off. If she had it to do over she wouldn't marry a psycho-anything. No, scratch that, she wouldn't marry an anything. Period.

CHAPTER 22

Dwight wasn't quite sure how fast the Front moved these days, but if it was at the original speed of about 0.2 mph — which is what everyone still used as a rule of thumb and had thoroughly ingrained in their heads — then it would take about four days to cross Denver. He was stationed around 45 miles from West Denver, and it was a fair bet that when the Front hit the bigger Eastern suburbs, panic quickly would spread. Some of the more intrepid types may try to get out early, but the government blockades would serve as a general deterrent.

Most people don't really appreciate danger until it's at their doorstep. It was a phenomenon Dwight was well acquainted with. He suffered from it himself, and wouldn't fault others. But it did make it easy to anticipate the course of events.

At some point, the imminent approach of the Front would overcome complacency and fear of the government. When that happened, the proverbial wall would come crashing down, unleashing a torrent of desperation. Panic would spread, and people would feel less vulnerable joining the mob. Isn't there safety in numbers? Surely the government would be forced to relent if enough people were involved. Dwight knew better, of course. But he wondered whether he would behave any differently.

Once the exodus started, the rise in looting and general lawlessness would motivate holdouts to leave as well. Communication and power blackouts would help slow the spread of panic, but in a city the size of Denver word surely would spread fast.

Assuming the whole city went crazy at once, most people would try for I-70. Or maybe not, since they may still remember what happened there during the 2nd riot. Dwight wasn't quite sure, but the passes northwest of the city, along 34 and 36, probably would be hit by the Front before anyone could get to them. Of course, that wouldn't stop some people from making a fatal error. Then again, what wasn't fatal these days?

The only plausible escape routes would be South or Southwest. There only were a few tenable passes over the Rockies, and Dwight was pretty sure they all were manned by units similar to his own. 285 was the most viable road, and the Kenosha Pass was the first major choke point west of the city.

No, the flood definitely would come this way, and he was the dam. Or the third in a sequence of breakers, perhaps. If the two forward posts couldn't hold back the mob, they'd pour through that nice quiet forest, desperate and angry and quite likely armed. The terrain was difficult, but it was early in a winter which promised to be mild. Travel was not challenging enough for Dwight's taste. He gave it only three days for the vanguard to make the journey.

The Guardsmen hadn't been allowed radios or any other civilian communication devices, so he couldn't quite be sure of the situation in Denver. If Dwight remembered correctly, the Front was due to hit the outskirts in the next day or two. There would be a few before then, people with ATVs — though he doubted that there was much gas to be had anymore — and some who had the foresight to beat the rush. Of course, they'd get blocked at the first two outposts. It was the pedestrian onslaught he dreaded.

Hiking to the pass was tough, even along paved road; it probably would spread the crowd out and make the influx a bit less overwhelming. But when they piled up and started clamoring to get through, things could get ugly. Hopefully, they wouldn't get out of hand. Dwight laughed. How could they not get out of hand? What else possibly could happen?

And to make life even more exciting, the Front itself wouldn't be far behind. The Kenosha Pass only was about 10 days farther out than Denver. All he had to do was fend off a bunch of civilians until they were overcome by the Front, and then run before it caught up with him. Of course, he wasn't holding out much hope on that last point.

In fact, there was a thought that had been bothering Dwight more and more, a gnawing doubt which threatened to undermine him. The question he kept asking himself was this: if the government had no problem trapping people and letting the Front devour them, or bombing its own to prevent waves of refugees and maintain order, why would they show more concern for some random group of National Guardsmen. Especially when some of them were from Colorado anyway and by all rights should die along with the locals. This probably was why they were using the Guard instead of regular army: expendable labor.

Dwight was pretty sure there was no plan to get them out. He wondered if anybody else in their detachment had reached the same conclusion. No, they probably weren't even thinking about it. Thinking ahead was a dying art. Along with a lot of other things. Brad probably was oblivious, and Dwight wasn't going to bring it up. Sometimes it's best just to let people pretend in their own way. Ignorance, bliss, and all that. Wasn't that what religion was all about? He guessed that Mull knew. But Mull and Dave had been through a number of these... scenarios... before, right? Maybe they had orders to shoot him when the crisis had passed. No, that wouldn't work, and it would be pointless.

Then it occurred to him. Where was the next place they would need such a blockade? There weren't a lot of densely populated areas remaining between Colorado and California, and California was where it ended. This was the last time. Mull knew it. Dave knew it. Maybe they even wanted to die here, maybe they had *volunteered* for this group. It was just Dwight's luck to be picked for the suicide squad.

But then why didn't they just let all those poor civilians through? There couldn't be that many of them left, and it was doubtful most could make it to California. It was winter and there was a lot of dismal terrain to cross. Perhaps rules had to be enforced, or maybe it just was a way to give everyone something to do. You people attack, and you people defend, and before you know it the Front will have swept everyone away. Just a tidy way to kill two birds with one stone. Or a few million birds. To Dwight, the only thing worse than dying for nothing was knowing he was dying for nothing. But wasn't everybody?

CHAPTER 23

Elise stood in the courtyard and stared at the drab barracks in which she had spent the last two nights. They were ugly buildings, brick and industrial but not the type of brick and industrial that commands obscene prices in the newly fashionable parts of a city. These were devoid of charm. Elise doubted even a skilled architect could transform them into something desirable, something that didn't suck the color from life. This must be what it felt like in prison, she thought. But it wasn't prison, just a camp.

The first fifty miles of the journey South had been easy. Or as easy as fifty miles on a bicycle with a heavy pack can be for an out-of-shape 42-year-old. Now, *that* was a depressing thought. Forty two. Elise couldn't believe it. She had spent her birthday completely isolated from everybody she knew. No, that made it sound as if she were lost in some distant and dismal country. She had spent her birthday at her parents' beautiful home in Edinburgh, but isolated from everybody she knew. It was a home she now regretted leaving, though she suspected she wouldn't be alive if she had not.

Scotland was under martial law, and all the roads had been closed. Elise had learned this when she finally stopped in a small town just south of the border. Like the motorway and all the towns she passed while on it, the border-crossing seemed abandoned. If they didn't care, then neither would she; Elise simply proceeded through it. The problem was that the next stretch of road traversed a nature preserve.

She had enjoyed a weekend there many years earlier, but was certain it would prove anything but enjoyable under the present circumstances. She was tired and sweaty after cycling all day, her water was exhausted, and she really needed to find a town soon. Worse, her knee was hurting, and she dreaded getting stuck on such an isolated stretch of road. Isolated? What stretch of road *wasn't* isolated at this point? She had not seen a single car on the way down. For all she knew, she was the only person left on the whole island.

When she set out from Edinburgh, Elise had hoped to reach Newcastle by nightfall. Intent on this, she peddled those first 50 miles with few breaks. It hadn't occurred to her to stop for information in any of the towns she passed; there simply was no time for it. They seemed empty anyway, and if they weren't she certainly didn't want to meet their occupants. The sort of people she wanted to meet wouldn't make a place seem empty.

Somehow being on a bicycle made her feel safe, as if nobody could catch her. But now she realized how dreadfully she had underestimated the length of the trip and overestimated her own stamina. She would stop in the next town, regardless of its appearance. If nobody was there, she would find some sort of shed and shelter over for the night. Thank god it was summer. If worst came to worst, she could sleep by the side of the road. Animals always stayed away from the road, didn't they?

Fortunately Elise did reach a town soon after, and it wasn't empty. As she approached, there were a few people visible in and around their houses. One waved, and she waved too but didn't stop. She would double back if they turned out to be the only people around, but she was intent on reaching the town first.

Then she saw the stone house with a parking lot. Its hanging wooden placard was illegible from afar, but the place unmistakably was a pub. Her knees ached, and she decided that town could wait, after all; a pub would do fine for now. As everybody knew, the center of any small English town is its pub. She would find what she needed here, or at least get pointed in the right direction.

It was 5 PM, and Elise was ecstatic finally to have reached

civilization. Perhaps because she was exhausted, this pub seemed particularly inviting. Elise wondered whether this was how weary travelers of old felt when they finally came across an inn. Were pubs what truly had civilized England all those years ago? She pulled into the parking lot, but was hesitant to leave her bicycle in plain view; so she gently leaned it against the wall around back. She was less concerned about leaving it unlocked, though. Now that she was back in the real world, she didn't expect to have much further need of it.

Only later, and to her great annoyance, did Elise realize she had failed to note the name of either the town or the pub. She simply was happy to have found them. Besides, one town pretty much was the same as the next; and charming pubs were largely interchangeable — at least to a visitor.

The pub itself had a homey atmosphere, old wood construction bathed in a warm yellow glow. As much as she would have liked a stiff drink, Elise didn't think it wise after such a strenuous cycle. Instead, she decided to focus on more pressing concerns — food, water, lodging, information, a shower, and a phone. Maybe after everything had been attended to, she would return for a Scotch before bed.

The bartender was a portly blonde woman, probably in her 50s. She did not seem particularly friendly, but the English rarely were. Elise shuddered to think how disheveled she must appear after cycling fifty miles. No wonder the woman wasn't thrilled to see her; she probably looked homeless. It didn't help that Elise started by asking for a glass of water. The woman sighed and gave her one, which she chugged.

Elise was ashamed to present as such a mess. Present as? She *was* such a mess. And she *was* homeless, at least for now. She bristled at the woman's judgmental look. Well, let's see what *she'd* look like if this had happened to *her*. But she really couldn't blame the woman for wrinkling her nose. She would realize soon enough that Elise wasn't a bum. What was the old phrase? A person of substance. Elise was a person of substance.

Though she wondered what that substance was and how much of it remained.

She asked if there was a phone, and to her delight the answer was yes. Who actually had a pay-phone in this day and age? Apparently, some rural pub with a scowling bartender. Elise remembered those old BBC dramas where the outsider was viewed with suspicion and hostility, generally because they had stumbled upon some sinister local intrigue. But that was before tourism. These days, the outsider was viewed as a wallet.

The pay-phone was located in a small hallway around the corner from the bar counter, next to the toilets. Only after she had walked over to it, did Elise realize she had no coins. The bartender grudgingly agreed to make change, but gave a particularly sour look when Elise handed her a Scottish five.

Things really hadn't been the same since the divorce, especially near the border. The woman gave her three one-pound coins and four fifty-pence ones. Despite the grumbling, she had been nice enough to ignore the exchange rate. When Elise last checked, one Scottish pound went for around 0.9 of a British quid — and surely it had depreciated significantly since.

Elise left her backpack next to one of the bar-stools, and dialed her sister.

"The number you have dialed is not valid, please try again."

Crap, she forgot to leave off the country code now that she was in England. Her second attempt went through, but nobody picked up. Eventually a message came on.

"This is Deb, yo. Let me know."

Really? At 39? Elise always had been embarrassed by her younger sister's "phases", varying affectations at being young or hip or ethnic or whatever. Couldn't she just be herself? Or maybe that *was* herself, and Elise just was jealous. That's definitely what Debbie would say, if confronted. But right now, Elise just would have been glad to hear her voice pretending to be anything. Anything alive and well, that is. Elise hung up;

she would try again later. Then she changed her mind, and called again.

This time she left a brief message that she was okay and to please let their parents know. While doing this, Elise turned to ask the bartender the name of the town, but she had disappeared. So instead, she explained that she would be in Newcastle the next day and would grab a train down to London. Of course, Debbie would not be thrilled to have a guest on such short notice. But then, her sister had no right to complain; she wasn't the one who lost her home. By now, the bartender had returned and was shaking her head slowly while cleaning a glass.

Elise walked back to the bar and tried to strike up a conversation. She apologized for her appearance, explaining that she had bicycled a long way. The bartender laughed, "Oh, so that's it. I thought you had walked." Was that sarcasm? It was hard to tell with the English, they could be glib under the best of circumstances. Elise brushed it off, and ordered a cup of tea and a meat pie. Nobody likes a freeloader, and she hoped this would lend her legitimacy as a paying customer.

But as the bartender took the order, it was clear from her attitude that she was concerned about getting stiffed by Elise. Well, soon she wouldn't care what some provincial pub owner thought. For now, she would don a shopkeeper's imperishable smile and remain ever so polite.

"How far is it to Newcastle?" she asked when the tea had been served.

"Is that where you're headed, then?" the woman responded in a pleasant but decidedly patronizing tone.

"Well, I need to visit my sister in London," Elise clarified.

"So I heard," the woman smirked. Ah, the joy of a small village pub. Elise wondered if they included "eavesdropping busybody" in the job adverts. The woman *was* an anachronism.

"Ah, yeah. She's not home. Just letting her know I'm coming. See, she doesn't ... " Elise began.

The woman interrupted with a knowing look, "She wouldn't, would she?"

Elise wasn't sure what to make of this, and adopted a puzzled expression. The woman didn't say anything else and just stood with her hands on her hips, the very picture of a displeased matron. Elise sighed.

After sipping her tea, Elise asked if there was an inn nearby. Before the question was out of her mouth, she realized her mistake. Many pubs took lodgers, and it would be difficult to politely decline if the woman offered a room. She may have no choice but to sleep here. Elise probably would have to worry about the innkeeper spying through a keyhole or something equally comical. This was why she had lived in... She stopped herself. Maybe things were broken everywhere, and she just hadn't noticed before.

Much to Elise's relief, the woman pointed down the road. "Two B&Bs down the road about a mile."

"Do you think they have space?" she ventured, hopeful.

"Probably," the woman shrugged, "We haven't had much traffic lately."

Before she could ask any more questions, the woman turned and headed to the kitchen. "If you need anything just give me a shout."

How English. Elise frowned, but then thought of what had happened in Glasgow. Was she going to snipe at English manners after what her own people had done? Elise found she had surprisingly little appetite, and just picked at the pie. What she really wanted was another glass of water, but was reluctant to call the woman back just for that. Better thirsty than scowled at.

About five minutes later, a pair of local policemen sauntered in and planted themselves on either side of Elise. Well, she thought, it *was* that time of day. After a few seconds, one of them turned and smiled at her.

"Nice night for it, eh."

Elise wasn't sure what "it" was, but he seemed nice enough so she smiled back. "It certainly has cooled down."

"Yeah, you get that out here. Best not to be in the forest at night."

The other one chimed in, "You driving?"

Ah, that was it. They wanted to make sure she wouldn't be drink-driving. "No, bicycle." She tapped her glass, "Just water, though."

The one on her right laughed, "If *I* was driving to Newcastle, I'd want a Guinness for the road."

How did they know she was going to Newcastle? Elise's stomach sank. She had grown so accustomed to it that she forgot the bicycle was not hers, that she was a thief. The bartender must have seen her image on TV, and called the police.

"Bicycle, eh?" the one on the left elbowed her jocularly, "Where are you down from?" Here it came. She may as well just go with it.

"Glasgow," she replied tersely. Elise remembered what the lawyers always said: keep your answers short and to the point, don't give them anything extra to work with.

"Really?" The one on the right genuinely seemed surprised. "You just came down from Glasgow?"

"No, I was in Edinburgh for the last few days." So much for brevity; she just had confessed the timing.

"Ah," the one on the left nodded to the other. "Tell her?"

"She'll find out soon enough anyway," the one on the right shrugged.

The other cop hesitated, then shook his head slowly. "You probably don't know then."

"Know what?" Elise suddenly had a bad feeling. Was this about her parents? Did these cops know *everything* about her?

"Glasgow's gone."

"Gone?" Elise must have had a stupefied expression, because they didn't say anything else. "What do you mean gone?"

"That's all we know, miss. Glasgow's gone. You were lucky to get out of there."

Lucky? That wasn't a word Elise would have chosen to describe any part of her adventure so far.

"Where did everybody go? There was nobody in Edinburgh either," she almost screamed.

The policeman on her right gave a sympathetic look. "Things are bad. Nobody's quite sure what's going on."

The one on the left chimed in, "Or they're not telling us, anyway." The other cop shot him a sharp glance.

"Don't mind Lloyd here, he likes to think everything's a conspiracy."

Lloyd shrugged.

"But you've made it this far. At least that's something," the cop on the right continued. He then stood up, and Lloyd followed suit.

"The good news is that we've got a place for you to stay," he smiled and held out his hand. "I'm Reggie, by the way."

Elise instinctively shook his hand. He had a firm grip, and held it for a little longer than was comfortable.

"But I could just stay at the hotel down the road," Elise pointed out.

Reggie waved dismissively, "You don't wanna stay there. Besides, they'll charge you a boatload. This is free."

This is cruel, thought Elise. *If you're going to book me, just do it.*

"You got any stuff, missy?" Lloyd asked. Elise pointed to the bag, and he hoisted it over his shoulder with no apparent effort. As they walked out the door, Elise mentioned the bicycle around back. May as well come clean, she supposed.

Reggie thought for a moment. "There's no room in the car for a bicycle. But it'll be safe here."

Just to be sure, he yelled toward the back, "Hey, Elise, don't let anybody nick the bike in back." It struck Elise as an odd coincidence that the bartender was her namesake. She wasn't certain how she felt about that. A muffled "sure" came from inside.

Reggie explained to her, "You can pick it up after," as they got in the car.

After what? They hadn't cuffed her, and apparently they didn't care about the bicycle or even seem to know it was stolen. Were they really just Good Samaritans? Maybe the bartender simply had called them to help her, called them because Elise seemed to *need* help. And to be honest, at this point she really could use some. Maybe these English weren't so bad after all.

CHAPTER 24

Day 462

From an essay by the Reverend Talbert of the Second Atheist Church of Medford, MA.

There comes a point in any thoughtful individual's life when time takes on new meaning. It ceases to be a distant abstraction, and its contemplation assumes a certain urgency. We understand, rather than simply know, that we have a distinct beginning and a distinct end.

The manner in which we approach that end may vary, much as the formative manner in which we evolve from our start varies. But the fact remains that there is a time before which we did not exist and there will come a specific moment at which we cease to exist. Whatever the cosmologists may tell us, time is not without end. We are, each of us, precisely demarcated.

Of course, the *truly* thoughtful individual also realizes that we do not exist at any of the points in between. Nonetheless, our physical presence traces a small path through space and time. The effects of our thoughts and actions propagate a little farther before being lost in entropy. Thus time changes from something which we tell into something which tells us. We appear to exist, most of all to ourselves. And what is more important than keeping up appearances?

This is the angst attendant to an abstract consideration of our own mortality. Each of us has an end, but we don't know *when*. What if we did? That in itself would pose various psychological and philosophical conundrums. Yet fear and grief, companion to each of us, remain personal to each of us. As the saying goes, we each die alone. But what if we didn't?

What if we knew not only when we would die, but that we all would die together? Or, as fate would have it, in groups.

That mere fact transforms the personal into the social. We experience various rites of passage - birth, schooling, marriage, parenthood - most keenly with those who happen to share our time and place and velocity in life. We move through that life in unison, our existence measured by tandem events within each little group. Now, death too may be shared.

Of course, this hardly is a unique circumstance in history. Many believed they knew the time and place of their death, and others have shared a time of death due to cataclysm or war. But never before has everyone *truly* known it and *truly* shared it. Never before have we been partitioned into precise groups which will die at precise times, an intimate bond both appealing and appalling.

Never before has every man, woman, and child been able to point and say — I will die there and I will die then and so will he and he and she. And while the correlation with geography is high, it is not absolute. Nor does it matter whether some of us choose to take matters into our own hands or join a different group.

We all know that by a certain time we shall have ceased to be. There is a hard bound, and nothing we do can change this. A frantic struggle for a few extra moments will seem futile to most of us. We would fight for survival, but not a mere day or two, unless fighting for fighting's sake is what we desire.

There is an exception, however. Those who possess that rarest of gifts: hope. An ever dwindling hope, to be sure, but is that not better than no hope? Is not delusion better than disillusion?

We must thus accept our fate, except for those with hope. And of that, rational man does not partake. Those who possess this gift, this simplicity, are to be envied and pitied, much as one may envy and pity a well-fed pig ultimately bound for the slaughter. Would you deny them their madness? Would you not wish it for yourself? Perhaps. But such are childish thoughts, and the thoughts of children are of little account.

We see a commonality of all, for the first time. That humanity as a whole shares a single purpose, a single goal, a single fate. We are, all of us, not merely to die but to to die *soon*, and that makes all the difference in the world. Is it not something grand? Something hoped for, but never expected?

For centuries, we have warred and bickered and competed with one another to make more of *us* than *them*. Now it does not matter. There will *be* no us or them. Children will not bury their parents; they will perish by their side. We have something in common — young, old, poor, rich — and it is something that actually matters. The prospect of a universal dying has brought us closer than millennia of living. Who could have imagined that death would grace us so?

Let us not blame fate or curse the wind, but instead embrace the Front. Much as the New Year is ushered in around the world, passed from city to city like an Olympic torch, so too let us celebrate the Front's progress and the passage of each successive group. Let us celebrate their being and having been, their history, their accomplishments, their aspirations and struggles, what they meant to be but never will be, what they were and pretended not to be, their future that wasn't, and lastly their end that was.

Let us toast them one last time and speak of them no more. Let old acquaintance be forgot. And when it is our turn let us not flee or lament or cry out in terror, but embrace one another and quietly give thanks to fate for bringing us together, binding us in this way, freeing us. Let us thank her for a death we only could have dreamed of, before we dream no more.

CHAPTER 25

Day 852 — Near Denver, Colorado, 5 PM

It turned out that Dwight was partly correct. The wave of humanity did indeed arrive in a trickle, but it started two days late and was not heralded by distant gunfire. Dwight suspected that Mull lied about the two forward guard posts. After all, this was the first pass. There may have been a couple of stations behind it, but it wouldn't make sense to have any in front.

The dreaded invasion began with a few college-aged kids straggling over the crest in tattered fleece and down coats. They slowly made their way toward the sentry posts. Brad was the first to see them, and sounded the alarm. Dwight wondered why they just carelessly sauntered into plain sight of the towers. Maybe they figured that these had been abandoned and could serve as shelter. Spotlights flicked on from the other tower.

Mull entered, and adjusted his uniform. Apparently, it wouldn't do to have the enemy think you untidy. He gestured to the other tower that he'd take this group. Dave nodded back and calmly spoke to the civilians through a bullhorn.

"Please remain where you are. This is the United States Army. You are prohibited from proceeding."

It certainly sounded imperious. Dwight felt he would have been intimidated by that air of authority had *he* been confronted with it, were he coming over the hill instead of having spent the last two weeks experiencing firsthand how ordinary the soldiers with the rifles really were. Of course, how you view soldiers *always* depends on which end of the gun you are standing.

The kids just squinted in the light and stared blankly. They didn't make any attempt to run or turn. A few more were visible in the distance, laboriously making their way up. One, probably the leader of the group, waved his arms across one another in the universal signal for help. Mull made his way down the line of soldiers whispering in each ear. Dwight was third from the left, and Brad was last. When Mull reached Dwight it was, "Cover the one in red, 2nd from the right." All four soldiers had their assignments.

Dwight didn't like this. Why were they assigned to specific people? What about the rest? This made it personal, uncomfortable. Mull then spoke slightly louder, so all four could hear.

"You've been trained for this. On three, take your primary, acquire a secondary, and keep going until you're out."

Everybody shuddered. This wasn't what they had signed up for. They just were supposed to contain them, use force only if necessary.

"Julie, you stay on reload when you're done."

Dwight could feel Brad tensing, twitching. C'mon you dumb redneck, you've dreamed about dropping college boys your whole life. These are the yuppies that would have pissed all over you. Just do it.

Of course, he was having his own problems. His target was a girl, about 20 and pretty, if a bit mussed. She probably was some granola chick. Maybe he would have asked her out if they met in a cafe a few years ago. The one next to her looked a bit like a kid, Jack Frill, that he and Brad had gone to school with. On closer inspection through the scope, he seemed about their age — but it wasn't Jack.

He and Jack had gone to the same school, lived roughly the same life. Jack even was a Guardsmen, just like Dwight. But he hadn't been called up because he still was in Denver. If Dwight hadn't happened to be visiting California when they announced F-Day, he'd be walking up that mountain too. He and Jack. Two paths that had diverged only to reconverge here, where they both would be anyway, but somehow inverted. The same person, but he was on this side and Jack was on the other.

He forgot that it wasn't actually Jack. Jack was there looking at him and he was looking back. The same person, except he happened to be the one with a gun in his hand. He heard a distant "three".

What were they hoping to accomplish, these dumb kids? What would their lives buy? By now there were around fifty people congregating, not just college kids: men, women, even a few older children. None appeared armed, though Dwight couldn't figure out why. Just turn and run, won't you. Why do this just for a few months of extra life? Please don't make a murderer out of me, he begged silently. He wouldn't do it, even if it cost him his life. He was a good person, and good people did not do such things.

He heard Brad muttering to himself, and turned to look at him. Something was wrong; he seemed to be squirming uncomfortably. Suddenly Brad pushed back from the rifle. He stood up in agitation and turned around, only to find Mull's Glock pressed firmly against his forehead. The back of his head exploded, spattering Dwight with gore. Brad collapsed on the back of Dwight's legs, and he kicked the body off him. Then he squeezed the trigger. The girl fell.

Dwight only stopped firing when the slide popped back. As he ejected the empty magazine, Julie handed him a fresh one. It turned out she had been the fastest to burn through her own ammo, and he wondered whether she just had fired into the air. Mull probably wished he'd put Brad on reload duty instead, he bet. Dwight reloaded and began firing again.

The people were like zombies; they didn't run, they didn't scatter, and they didn't charge. He supposed they had nowhere to go. But why didn't they fight, dammit? It made him despise them. Maybe this was what they wanted? Well, he would give it to them. A murderer was a murderer, so he may as well do it right. It reminded him of those vampire movies he used to love. He always wondered what he would do if he became a vampire. Would he be willing to kill just to live a few days more? No, he was willing kill to live a few more minutes. Besides, it was kind of fun once you got into it. He just wished he had some popcorn.

For the next two days, the shooting was nearly continuous. A few people tried to shoot back, but they quickly were taken down. Some latecomers attended to the sound of gunfire and hid behind trees when making the approach. They tried to find an inconspicuous way around. But the advantage of the choke point was that there *was* no way around. And Mull had been right about one thing. There was plenty of ammo.

CHAPTER 26

Rielle hated when mommy and daddy fought. It wasn't the abstract notion of conflict which disturbed her; she didn't have one. It was the raised voices, and the tone of those voices. Mommy and daddy didn't sound like mommy and daddy. They sounded like other people, other people who didn't like each other very much. Rielle's world consisted of certain givens, and the places of mommy and daddy were two of the most important.

Fortunately, such scenes were rare. Marissa and Josh had agreed early on about the importance of presenting a unified front to their children. They would not undermine one another, they would not vie for favor, and they would not act at cross purposes. These rules had been followed with surprising success, but an occasional row was inevitable.

From what Rielle could glean, daddy wanted to go on vacation with some of the other men from town. Mommy didn't want to take a vacation. This probably was because mommy was mean and wanted Rielle to suffer every day by going to school. She wasn't like the other mommies.

Sometimes Rielle wished she had one of *those* mommies, but then she really didn't. They had been nice when she stayed over, but were different from *her* own somehow. Mommy looked like she needed a vacation, and Rielle said so. That made her even more angry, and she blamed daddy for dragging Rielle into it.

This time daddy mentioned that something bad was coming. Some sort of storm. A long time ago another daddy had said something too, but mommy grew upset when she heard. Rielle didn't want to anger her, and didn't bring it up again.

But now it was worse. Mommy was furious, and daddy looked sad. He went upstairs and brought down a suitcase. He must *really* have wanted to go with his friends. Mommy said that they weren't allowed to go, that they would get in trouble.

Why would he be in trouble for going on vacation? Maybe he was supposed to be at work. If he was skipping work, maybe *she* could skip school. Rielle jumped up and down and shouted that she wanted to go on vacation too. Daddy hugged her, and took her by the hand. She was going to get to go! Rielle was so happy.

Then Mommy kneeled and told Rielle to give her a hug goodbye. Daddy clutched her hand hard, but Rielle pulled free.

"Why don't you come too?" she squealed, jumping into her arms. She was so glad that mommy and daddy weren't fighting anymore.

Mommy said nothing, but stood up, clutching Rielle tightly to her chest with one hand. She drew the gun with her other and pointed it at daddy. Rielle wasn't sure where it came from, but she had seen guns in movies. You pointed them at people and they fell down. She wondered how long they stayed down.

Daddy suddenly changed his tone. He adopted an expression Rielle never had seen before. He didn't argue with mommy or yell at her or rush over and take the gun (it would be easy, just like in the movies).

He simply looked at Rielle sadly and mouthed, "I love you." He gave mommy a long hard look, saying nothing. Rielle didn't like that look. Then he picked up his suitcase and slowly walked out the door without turning around.

Mommy kept the gun pointed at him until long after he had driven off in the car. Rielle squirmed free of her grasp, which was so tight it hurt, and ran outside shouting, "Daddy." But mommy didn't move. She slowly lowered the gun and walked outside and took Rielle firmly by the hand. They went inside, and she locked the door. But Rielle knew that daddy would come back for her.

CHAPTER 27

Day 17 — North England

"Camps are places where they put unwanted people. Children for the summer, refugees for the winter, undesirables forever. Only the rare individual leaves a camp the same as he went in. It sometimes is regarded as good fortune to leave at all, for part of us — diminished beyond recognition — to continue in some form. This is a common mistake."

Elise had not paid close attention to the approximately 30,000 pages of literature and history she had been forced to consume as a student. Even the books she read freely as an adult received scant attention, with scanter retention. But it is in our moment of desperation, when all else has been devoured, that we must turn inward, rely on that which we once had and pray it dwells within us still. Or something poetically pretentious to that effect.

It would have been a useless but palliative vanity for Elise to recall every word on every page. But of course, this was not possible. Most had been lost or amalgamated, irrevocably disfigured in the transmuting furnace of memory. Yet somehow this particular passage left an impression. She could not recall who had written it, or even the book or course. But it spoke to her then, as if presaging some need in which it would emerge, a harbinger of hope or despair.

There was some consolation in knowing she was a mere part of the endless repetition, that beneath those somber words lay a note of promise. She must persevere, struggle to become the rare individual, unchanged in the crucible. Or perhaps it would be best to change. To shed the parts which had been naive and weak, which had believed and hoped. To be diminished in all the right ways. Is it necessarily bad to be transfigured beyond recognition? What if you don't like being recognized, don't like what is recognized as you? What was left would be lean and light and compact.

She knew that she was reading the prophecy to her own advantage, knew what unfailingly happens in stories when one does that. But how else was Elise to read it? What availed understanding if understanding wrought nothing?

To be precise, *her* camp was in the second category: refugees. She often had watched the scenes on television, or read of them. A distant bombing of a village, people fleeing from here to there or from there to here. Her country had hosted such refugees. The images always seemed the same: people dressed in crappy jeans and sneakers and sweats, with a touch of ethnic baggage — a scarf here, a shawl there.

Some were prettier, some less so. But they all essentially were the same. A horde of gibbering primitives from some backwater. You could dress them up, give them internet access, even money — but they never would have culture. They wouldn't have a thousand years of civilization behind them. It didn't mean they were undeserving of help. That's what good Christians did. But the refugees still were despicable: hands out, needing, wanting. She just wanted to spit on them. *Those people.*

And now she was one of those people. Or more precisely, it was happening to "these" people. Elise suspected the English felt the same way about her. Heck, she didn't have to suspect; they declared it on a regular basis. Many hurtful things had been said in the runup to secession, and many more since. To the English, *she* was some gibbering primitive just recently down from the mountains. Never mind that they'd shared a monarch since James I, that she probably had more English blood than most English did — especially these days. In fact, despite all the rhetoric about keeping foreigners out, Whitehall pretty much was run by them. That's how Rome fell wasn't it, letting foreigners run things? How ironic that England should end up a colony of Pakistan.

Elise clenched her fists and rubbed them vigorously against her sides, partly to keep warm and partly to cleanse her mind. She wasn't that sort of person. A bigot. Maybe everyone was, when it came down to it. That's the sort of thing those PC Americans always were on about. The more righteous you seemed, the more you secretly harbored racist thoughts.

To her, this smacked of an inquisition. The more devout you seem, the more likely you're secretly in congress with the devil. Actions were no defense against a charge of heresy. One misspoken word outweighed a lifetime of piety.

Was that what had happened to her? Had she lapsed, had a bigoted thought? Was she really a bad person? Or would the inquisition judge her such? Or perhaps the diminishing already had begun. Perhaps she was being cleansed, and would emerge as the Elise who was meant to be. The Elise who should have been, so many years earlier. She said goodbye to the self-indulgent self-congratulation, the smug hypocrisy. She would turn this experience to her advantage. She would emerge scathed, scarred, and formidable.

Then she heard the meal siren and scrambled for the mess tent, pushing and shoving her way toward the front of the mob. She wondered which of the men she elbowed aside, who pushed back with equal violence, had once been professors, poets, fathers, and thugs.

Once? *once*? Was she that pathetic? It wasn't the dim and distant past; she had been bused here two days ago. Two days. How would she feel after a week, a month, a year? A year. Elise shuddered at the thought. If there was no arrest, no trial, no conviction, then what determined when she would be released? Could they hold her forever?

Elise collected a food tray, carefully guarding it from her fellow detainees. She was more concerned about somebody accidentally knocking it over than stealing it, but you never could tell how people would behave. No, here there were no professors or poets or fathers or thugs. Here there only were mouths. Little rags with mouths.

CHAPTER 28

Day 855 — Near Denver, Colorado, 2 AM

The thing about shooting people you don't know is that it can get very tiresome.

Dwight quickly had learned that it wasn't like those video games featuring an endless onslaught of zombies. There, the positioning, the supply of ammo, the design of the game all conspired to create an atmosphere of tense uncertainty, of urgency, of real peril. Sitting in a tower, with a well-nigh unlimited supply of bullets and an Armalite AR10 sniper rifle, picking off from a hundred yards slow-moving targets that never seemed to fight back, those elements were conspicuously absent.

There even was an M240 belt-fed machine gun in case things got "hectic". They had been admonished by Mull not to use it unless necessary because it, "burned through ammo like a bitch." That was the only time Dwight heard Mull use profanity.

Nor was there any aspect of the endurance horror which an endless stream of weak opponents may lend a video game. Dwight had six comrades all doing the same thing. When he tired out, he just rested. In a pinch, even Mull and Dave could be counted on to hop in.

Dwight grimaced. He bet Mull was saving the M240 for himself, selfish bastard. It *would* be fun to unload on live targets, though. Shooting machine guns was one of the reasons he had joined the Guard. It wasn't illegal for civilians— there were regular machine gun shoots in Colorado all the time — but it *was* expensive. Very expensive. Even at its slowest setting of 600 rounds per minute, an M240 would burn through ammo, well, "like a bitch." You didn't need quality ammo just to play around, but even the Czech stuff was almost a buck a round.

Of course, the army wasn't allowed to buy the cheap stuff. It probably had to pay three times the going rate for the very best. But then, the army never really cared about cost. Dwight looked down at his AR10. Or quality, apparently. Why did they give him this crap? It jammed all the time, and a 0.308 was overkill against targets like these. It just doubled the cost of ammo, and made no sense. Not that he minded having longer range capability, especially since he was an exceptional shot. But the AR10 was a lot heavier too. If he had to evac in a hurry it would be better to carry something light. And an evac in a hurry was just what Dwight had in mind.

It wasn't until the 3rd night after the shooting started that Dwight decided it was time to make a move. Ever since the contingent became fully manned, the soldiers slept in 6 hour shifts, three to a cabin with one sentry for "their protection." If that really was so, why was the sentry *inside* the cabin?

The two Jims (and, before he was shot, Brad) had the 1st shift, 6 PM -12 AM with Dave in command and Wayne on sentry. The 2nd shift was Dwight in the left tower, Russ and Warren in the right tower, Mull in command, and Julie on sentry. Dwight waited until his shift.

The rate of arrivals had decreased during the 3rd day, and this lent some urgency to the situation. They were a necessary distraction; once the supply of incomers ran out, it would be much more difficult to escape unnoticed.

Over the last three days, Dwight had noticed certain patterns. People always approached in clusters for some reason. Maybe they got lonely on the way up and gathered together, or maybe it was a continuous stream but something had happened to the ones in between. Even as the frequency of clusters declined, the sizes had not. He roughly could tell how many people to expect in a given group by the early arrivals.

Not the first two or three; they generally were a bit quicker but not quick enough to completely separate from the group. It was the few after them which served as the best indicator. If there only were one or two, the group likely would be small. If there were more than four, the group would be large and spread out. A bigger than anticipated group wouldn't be a problem for Dwight, but an unexpectedly small one could. He needed at least 5 minutes of continuous fire.

It wasn't until around 2 AM that a large enough cluster appeared. The first three arrived, and about a minute later there were six more. If history was any indication, he could count on about 8 to 10 minutes of continuous shooting. Unfortunately Mull happened to be in Dwight's tower, sitting in a corner and looking bored. Dwight fired a few shots and then signaled that he had to go to the bathroom. Mull gave him a sour look, gesturing at the shooting, but said nothing. Dwight just shrugged. You've got to go when you've got to go. Mull rolled his eyes and went back to staring into space.

Dwight left his gun and casually headed off in the direction of the outhouse, then doubled back to the supply depot. This was a small shed behind the sleeping quarters. His watch showed 2:07, and he counted one minute down so far. He was pretty sure nobody could hear him above the shooting, but was very careful anyway.

He quietly removed a spare AR10 (once again he wished there were some lighter M16s), ammo, MREs, a flashlight, batteries, a med kit, and a shovel. Toilet paper too. Never underestimate the value of TP. He loaded the AR10 but left the safety on, and propped it against the shed. He grabbed the shovel, put the rest in a large duffle bag, and left it ready next to the AR10. Dwight then proceeded to the side of the cabin and peeked around the edge.

The cabin's door, around the corner from him, was in plain sight of the sentry towers. It wouldn't do to let anyone see him go in. He probably could explain it away as wanting to see Julie or some-such, but it would put a crimp in his plans and he would have to pray he could get to the duffle before anyone noticed.

As it was, he didn't see anybody above the waste-high bulwark. Mull still was sitting. Keeping a careful eye on the towers, Dwight waited for the next burst of gunfire and then reached around and knocked on the cabin door. He had to rap twice, probably because Julie could hear him over the shooting. After a few moments the door finally opened and she greeted him, bleary-eyed, with the business end of a glock. Had she been dozing?

She seemed startled for a moment, but then realized it was Dwight and reholstered the gun. He darted inside and pulled the door shut, pretending to catch his breath as if he dashed over. When his eyes had adjusted to the dark a bit, he turned to Julie and explained that Mull needed everyone out there.

As she stooped to wake Dave, he clocked her on the back of the neck with the sharp edge of the spade. He marveled that she hadn't even noticed he was carrying one; clearly she wasn't meant to be a soldier. As Julie collapsed, he saw that she had managed to unholster her Glock. That was close, he gulped in surprise as she lay twitching on the ground. For good measure, he brought the point of the spade down on the back of her neck. He then gently removed the Glock from her hand.

By now he could make out the interior of the room quite clearly. Dave was in a sleeping bag on the floor not far from where he had killed Julie. Why the hell didn't he sleep in a bunk like everyone else? Dwight let out a slow breath. Another close call; he almost had stepped on him. He stood over Dave contemplatively for a few seconds before slowly pressing the tip of the spade into his windpipe. When Dave's eyes opened and his hands flailed, Dwight leaned hard on the spade, then pulled it up and smashed it down into his left eye. He grabbed a pillow from the upper bunk and proceeded to the other side, where the two Jims were sleeping.

There only was one way to do this, and he had to be quick. Outside, the gunfire remained strong. He took Julie's Glock, placed the pillow over the muzzle, and fired one shot into each soldier, then quickly turned as Wayne woke from the lower bunk on the other side. He fired one shot without the pillow into Wayne. Then he quickly fired a 2nd shot into each of the three soldiers, Dave, and Julie, once again using the pillow to muffle the shots. Best to be sure. If they hadn't heard the unmasked shot, they wouldn't hear these.

There was no going back now, and he had to move decisively. Dwight discarded Julie's Glock and drew his own. Safety off, 15 shots, 1st chambered. He crouched, flung open the door to the cabin, and scrambled to the side. Peering around the corner, he saw no worrisome movements in the guard towers. He just prayed they weren't quietly flanking him. He heard a couple of staggered shots from the 2nd Tower. They weren't aimed at him. Thank god, the shooters still were busy.

That left Mull. He couldn't be sure, but he suspected Mull hadn't moved from the 1st Tower. To be safe, Dwight kept his Glock out and ready. He gingerly reached around the side of the cabin and pulled the door shut while watching the towers. No reason to alert them unnecessarily. Suddenly the hairs on his neck bristled and he sensed Mull was sneaking up on him. He spun around and pointed his gun. Nothing.

Dwight quickly retrieved the AR10. He looked around carefully and checked the outhouse and depot shed just in case. Finally he felt confident that he wouldn't get ambushed from behind. And he was pretty sure that Mull wasn't going to snipe him from the woods; he just didn't think that way. Not once in three days had he seen Mull fire a rifle. No, Mull was in the tower waiting. And that meant he too had to wait. He couldn't risk going back to the tower to shoot Mull. He would do it from here.

He placed the AR10 on top of an inconspicuous rock and brought it to bear on a point above where he remembered Mull sitting. Even if Mull stood up and happened to stare right at him with binocs, it still would take a few seconds to make out Dwight in the dark. And it probably would take a few more to register what was happening. Unless Mull was seasoned and cynical, which he probably was.

Dwight furtively glanced at his watch. 2:13. The whole operation had taken 6 minutes so far. It felt like a lot longer. Not the cliched "lifetime", just a lot more than 6 minutes. Before, he had been worried Mull would grow suspicious too soon. Now he needed him to. If he didn't get up before the shooting stopped then things could get ugly. Russ and Warren weren't crack shots, but he had no desire to go up against two highly armed soldiers intent on killing him.

Or would they be? Maybe they'd just run off on their own. Or insist on joining him, which could be worse. He groaned. C'mon, stand up. Be an asshole. Stand up and tap your watch like the prissy shit you are. As if in answer to his prayers, Mull did stand up. He didn't seem the least bit concerned that the incomers may shoot at him. He yawned and stretched and then looked around. Dwight carefully aimed from a prone position. This was a critical shot, there was no need to rush it. He was sure Mull wouldn't sit down; if anything, he'd probably come looking for him.

Dwight squeezed the trigger on an exhale, but nothing happened. Safety was on. He never would have done that if he wasn't nervous. He reacquired. Mull turned just as he fired, and he had the pleasure of watching the front of his face explode. He wondered whether Mull had seen him in that last moment, not that it mattered.

The gunfire abruptly stopped. Oh shit. Had they noticed? There was red spattered all over the 1st Tower, but Mull had collapsed to the floor. When daylight came — or if they used a spotlight — they'd see the blood.

Dwight supposed he could just wait, and take his comrades out one at a time when they went to the bathroom. But he didn't want to wait. Besides, they probably would be useful in keeping the rabble at bay. It wouldn't do to be overtaken by a herd of civilians, even if they weren't particularly dangerous. In two days, the Front would wipe out Russ and Warren anyway. He wasn't friends with them, but had nothing against them either. And in some small sense he had fought beside them. *Fought?* Well when had there *ever* been such a thing as a fair fight, so why not lump this in with all the rest.

No, he'd leave them their remaining two days. Dwight waited five more minutes before moving. When there was no reaction he grabbed the duffle bag and made a beeline for the woods, always keeping a watchful eye on that second tower. He walked about a mile, then hid twenty feet off the road and waited half a day.

Nobody came. They just didn't have the manpower, he guessed. Of course, they may have radio'ed ahead. The next choke point was a few miles farther. Heck, it may not even be manned. But as Dwight began the hike toward it, he knew one thing for sure. He wouldn't just stand there while they shot at him.

CHAPTER 29

Day 23 — North England

Over the past week, Elise had learned the personalities of the four guards with whom she had regular contact. The camp was much larger than the area in which she resided; of that, she was certain. At one point, she overheard somebody mention the number 600,000. If that indeed was accurate, the facility was far more extensive than she previously had imagined.

This had little impact on her day to day existence there, though. Whatever its true size, the camp clearly had been partitioned into manageable groups. Doubtless this division was based on some criterion, but Elise was at a loss to identify it. From her observation of fellow inmates, she could discern no obvious commonality. Besides being Scottish.

For all she knew, the assignments were random. Come to think of it, that approach probably would serve to best balance the sub-populations. Of course, the English never did anything because it was the best approach; they did it because it was *the* approach, the one stated in the rule book. Whatever their reasoning, her own movements were restricted to one particular holding area. If there were 600,000 inmates, she never would meet 598,000 of them — at least not here. And from what she had seen of the 2000 refugees she *could* meet, it really didn't matter. Refugees ... she almost had thought "prisoners". But that was unfair, at least for now.

It always gets worse. Elise wished that Craig never had said that — not because he was wrong or it was depressing, but because she was sick and tired of remembering it every time some new piece of unpleasantness revealed itself. Like some tired Country and Western song. Yes, things had been going downhill. She got it. Maybe she would restate his words, make them funnier. 'Like shit, it only dribbles down ...' That just was awful; Elise decided she was no good at being funny. *It always gets worse.* No shit, Craig. Next time he came into her shop, maybe she would shove the scissor into his eye. 'See, it just *got* worse, didn't it?'

This was bad; she was beginning to sound like him. Besides, she didn't have a shop anymore. No shop, no scissor, no Craig. Just those things which always got worse.

The holding area consisted of a set of nearly identical bunk buildings, each housing approximately 200 people, as well as a yard, some outhouses, and a mess/recreation hall. It was very much as she had envisioned prison, or perhaps a military barracks. That probably would be a more accurate comparison. She wondered whether it *was* a converted military base. If there were anywhere near the purported number of refugees, the English would be hard put to find places for them all. Even if they had been on the best of terms with Scotland, she doubted they could do much better. And they most certainly were *not* on the best of terms.

Suddenly Elise felt ashamed of her country. The first sign of trouble, and the whole population flees south. Independent in name but not spirit, or maybe just a nation of cowards. It made her think of a kid dashing behind mommy for protection. And the actual problem wasn't even serious, just some sort of chemical spill. But they had *made* it serious by panicking. What must the English think of them now? Pretty much what they had thought all along, no doubt.

But maybe only a few Scots were as skittish as she. Maybe everybody else still was at home, scratching their heads and wondering what was wrong with her, wondering why she wanted to sleep in some smelly English camp instead of her own comfy bed. In fact she hoped those people *were* still home, safe. She remembered the M8, the empty streets of Edinburgh, and had the terrible sinking feeling that they weren't anywhere now.

What was it the cop had said? *Glasgow is gone.* Like countless refugees in countless past crises, Elise began to wonder how many of her countrymen still existed, whether her *country* still existed. Or had it too been lost along the way? Attrition. That was the curious and technically inaccurate term they always used on TV. How clinical.

Elise remembered reading somewhere that this was a sign of psychosis, a frequent misuse of uncommon words. Was the TV psychotic? She suspected it was more like a schoolyard instigator with poor impulse control. Would they start broadcasting lists of dead or missing persons soon? It seemed like the sort of thing they would do. Or should do.

Elise felt an urgent need to find a TV. What if she missed hearing the name of somebody she cared about? Then again, seeing an interminable list of the lost would be terribly distressing. To hell with the rest; she would settle for knowing that her parents were safe. Maybe they would see *her* name scrolling by on TV. Elise wondered if she would attrite before this all was over. If it wasn't a word, it certainly should be.

There were a total of sixteen guards assigned to her area, though she was certain that many others would rapidly appear in a pinch. Elise's daily movements placed her in almost exclusive contact with four. She thought it odd that she already had a routine; it had only been a week. She was reminded of a nation which just experienced revolution. A young nation imitating its elders, pretending to their dignity, and imbuing its institutions with artificial pomp and ceremony. 'This is the place where President Zimbatwebongo declared us free and ate of the traditional warthog spleen'. Last month.

Nonetheless, there was a certain timelessness to this place. It would as easily have been at home in the 1940s. Heck, for all she knew it had been. Yet there were certain things which helped mitigate the stark appearance, offering some hope that inmates were viewed as unfortunates rather than undesirables. They were allowed to retain their clothes; there were no camp uniforms. And although the original bouquet of color and style rapidly faded to grey amidst the general grime and lack of ... amenities, it did help dispel the gloom such a camp necessarily breeds. It also helped people retain a vestige of their former life, fostering hope that this soon would be over and everything would return to normal.

The downside was that if you arrived with just a T-shirt and jeans, you were stuck in them. And it wasn't warm. Other than a few old coats and shoes — which Elise imagined were charitable donations — there wasn't much to spare. This said, nobody had died of starvation or disease or exposure — to her knowledge. Then again, it still was summer.

It couldn't be easy to support so many refugees, even if the true numbers only were a fraction of what she had heard. Despite all the hardship she had been through, and the fact that she was here involuntarily, Elise felt she was making a dreadful nuisance of herself, unpardonably imposing on her hosts. It was not in the nature of Scots to be reliant on others.

She supposed she would do the same for others were their situations reversed, but really wished somebody would set her mind at ease anyway. Tell her to come in and sit by the fire and have some hot soup, that it was no trouble at all. Perhaps somebody *had* said something to that effect; but there were no radios or televisions here, and the message would have been denied those who most needed to hear it. Or maybe that just was her.

Nevertheless, the guards themselves gave some hope that she was in sympathetic hands. Though they never assuaged her guilt outright, their unfailing politeness had an effect. It made her feel more the guest than the ward. Though none were overly friendly, they did their best to answer her questions. Unfortunately, their best wasn't very good; they seemed to be in the dark as much as everyone else. What else would one expect of soldiers?

There are few countries that bring bureaucracy to the level of an art, and an English functionary is as close to an automaton as philosophically possible. Most employees of most agencies in most governments are unhelpful and bureaucratic. However, they typically act this way to get a bribe or to avoid work or simply because they are miserable human beings.

The British do it from the purest of motives: a precise adherence to the rules. This can swing both ways, however. If a single 'i' is not dotted or 't' not crossed on any of the incomprehensible tangle of forms necessary to complete even the most basic tasks, they prove more inflexible than any substance known to science. Skyscrapers could be built from them, diamonds cut with them. But if you can demonstrate that you *did* strictly follow the rules, they will admit every consequence of those rules, however absurd. Show that a particular form, properly completed and timely filed, confers the monarchy, and you will be coronated.

In Elise's case, the interactions were polite but unhelpful. Requests for information, release, communication with a lawyer or relatives all were denied, most likely because provision never had been made for them. There simply existed no procedural regulations for such an unprecedented situation. She was sure that every other refugee was contending with the same issue, having the same conversations.

Didn't the soldiers tire of endlessly repeating, in subdued but firm tones, that this or that was impossible? Nor did they seem to have any ability or desire to determine whether there *did* exist a means of addressing the requests.

Another quality of the English official is their inability to answer the question, 'how can I do something?' They will explain at great length why X or Y cannot be accomplished; but if the goal is Z, they never will consider the means by which it *can* be accomplished. It's not that they do not wish to help or don't care; it's simply that the question makes no sense to them. After all, a question has yes or no as an answer.

That morning's conversation was no different than the countless others which preceded it.

"Robert, how are you this morning," Elise bubbled, mustering as cheerful an expression as could be expected.

"I'm fine, thank you," came the quiet reply. Robert never remembered her name, though she was pretty sure he recognized her face by now.

"A bit of the weather we're having, then." Elise kicked herself for this idiotic attempt at small talk. Her voice had the shrill timbre of a middle-aged woman hitting on a younger man. She supposed that in a sense this was not inaccurate. The principle was the same, though it wasn't romance she was after. Not that she found Robert unattractive. Quite the contrary, and in spite of her feminist leanings, she apparently did have an eye for a man in uniform. Especially an unflappably polite, if unhelpful, man in uniform. She just wished he remembered her name.

"Weather's always like this around here, ma'am." Stiff, formal. Unfortunately, Elise had nothing to warm him up. She couldn't offer him a cup of tea or a spot of something. This must be what it was like to be homeless, she considered. Then she remembered, she *was* homeless.

"Any word from the party, Robert?" This was her running attempt at humor. She referred to the inside as 'the madhouse' and the outside as 'the party'. Robert never laughed. It was an allusion to an old television series that featured a cast of loveable lunatics and their comically inept caretakers. At the end of each episode, the staff would get ready to leave after having narrowly averted whatever contrived crisis was stewing. But one of the inmates was convinced they were going to a party and he needed to come with them or he would miss it, so they always promised that the big party was tomorrow.

Even back then it didn't make much sense, and Elise couldn't figure out why inane references to it kept popping into her head. Sometimes she giggled out loud. Robert probably thought she was crazy or slow, though it occurred to her at one point that he may have taken "the party" as some sort of snide political allusion. If he did, he showed no sign of it.

"No word, I'm afraid," he replied in the same tone. Wasn't he the least bit curious, she wondered? It made her think of those old movies where the line of soldiers marched up the hill, muskets in hand, dropping like flies. He did what he was told. If they told him to lay down and die, he probably would. Or maybe he did what he was told so that he *wouldn't* die.

"So, no news on when we'll be freed?" she asked hopefully.

"You're not prisoners, ma'am. Just awaiting placement."

"Can't you at least let me make a phone call, let my parents know I'm all right?" She always made the same plea. Active tense, 2nd person, involve the audience, establish an emotional rapport — just like she had learned in that sales course. Too bad there hadn't been a course on camp life. The rest of the conversation was predictable to the word.

"I'm afraid I can't allow any calls without authorization."

"How can you get authorization?"

"You'd need to fill out a form 3467i, which requires one of four special circumstances."

Elise corrected her earlier assessment. He only would lay down and die if provided with a properly completed form to that effect.

"Where do I get one of those?"

"The command office would have them, or you could obtain one through a licensed solicitor."

"Can I go to the command office to get one?"

"I'm afraid not, ma'am."

"Why not?" As the old adage goes, the one question you

never ask a bureaucrat.

"Security reasons. There is no protocol for an escort to be put into place." Why did she need an escort if she wasn't a prisoner?

"When will there be a protocol?"

"The situation is fluid, ma'am. I'm sure there will be one soon."

"What about a solicitor. Don't I get a lawyer?"

"You're not being detained." By what definition of "detained"? she wondered. Perhaps if she argued too much, she *would* be "detained." Then again, that may be good. She could get a lawyer. Or it could get worse. Much worse. At least they were being polite now.

"So how can I get a solicitor?"

"You can call one."

"I can?"

"Yes, but you'll need an authorization."

"How do I get that?"

"Form 3467i."

And so it went, every day.

To their credit, Robert and the other three guards never raised their voices or grew angry. Or maybe they just didn't show it. Maybe Elise would be the first one they dragged out back and hacked to pieces when the "authorization" arrived. Though, in that regard she probably wasn't at the top of any list.

Most other prisoners were far less courteous, and some could be downright belligerent at times. The guards never used force unless absolutely necessary, and then only minimally. Shortly after she first arrived, Elise saw a large woman get quite aggressive with a guard, pushing him, spitting, and even threatening to "tear his sass'nack shait face off". Another guard quietly appeared from behind and held the woman's arms, while the target of her fury wrestled her down and handcuffed her.

Nobody would have blamed them for roughing her up a bit or accidentally bouncing her head off the nightstick a few times "on the way to the guardhouse". If you attack a cop, you have to expect to end the night worse for wear. And if you attack a military camp guard ... suffice to say, there have been very few times in history when *that* ended well. A small crowd of bystanders had gathered in almost gleeful anticipation of some excitement.

But once the woman had been securely restrained, they just escorted her away and wrote up the incident. She didn't disappear. She didn't return covered in mysterious bruises.

The guards' attitudes reminded Elise of what she had read of lunatic asylums. When a suicidal individual was brought to an upscale private institution, they treated her courteously but firmly. Of course, at the public ones they probably just would beat, drug, and cage her. How odd then, that *this* was the public institution. She wondered quite a bit about that.

For all their courtesy, she sometimes wished these soldiers just *would* lay down and die. Then everyone else could leave and get on with their lives. Elise was disgusted with herself whenever she had such a thought. It was an unbecoming thought, a terribly ungrateful thing to wish ill on her hosts. It was unworthy of her.

Well, maybe tomorrow would be different.

CHAPTER 30

Day 703 — San Diego, California

Once again, Robert Halifax found himself anxious and ill-prepared. A lot had happened over the past year, and by all reasonable measures his career had taken an exponential leap forward. First, he had been placed in charge of the most significant disinformation project since Z-Day. This had proved an immense success. Too much of a success, in fact. When New York fell almost two weeks ahead of schedule, there was a great deal of confusion and unrest.

The government finally was forced to disclose that the Front was spherical rather than circular, and revise the official timetable accordingly. However, they did not do so immediately or people would suspect they knew all along. Instead, they waited two weeks to give the impression that the revelation resulted from an investigation into New York's premature fall. When the announcement was made, on what came to be known as SA-Day, the public was taken completely by surprise. It was a perverse reflection on Robert's skill that major riots broke out in most East Coast cities less than a week later.

Robert had informally reported to Lilly Tao during the campaign, and officially was transferred to her division when it ended. For the past two months he had worked there, under lock and key. It was the most exciting research project of his generation, and he was given almost complete autonomy and an enormous (to him) budget.

He appreciated what this impossibly rare opportunity: the chance to be humanity's savior, though he suspected it would be an unsung savior. Robert was uncertain whether others were pursuing similar research in parallel, but he hoped they were. As flattering as Lilly's sole confidence would be, he much preferred not to bear complete responsibility. Then humanity would not perish when he failed and proved himself the fraud that he knew he was.

One thing Robert did not understand was why the government had waited over a year to make its announcement. Whatever the reason, it had cost the U.S. dearly. Both Boston and New York had fallen, one to the Front and the other to chaos and *then* the Front, before most people could evacuate. Why so many people had waited until the last minute was another mystery; perhaps they had mistaken the appearance of normality for safety. The lesson was a sharp one, and he doubted others would repeat that mistake in the coming months. The deaths of all those people had been a grievous loss from many standpoints, and it dealt Tao's effort a major blow. Much of the nation's scientific and technical talent was gone. Sure there remained some reservoirs in New Mexico and California, along with the odd pocket elsewhere. But much of that remaining talent suffered from an additional problem — a problem which, however synthetic, rendered them as useless as the dead. That problem was the government's definition of "acceptable talent".

Despite all that had happened since Z-Day, the vast government bureaucracy remained intact. Robert could attest to this through his daily struggles, despite having top priority and a direct line to Lilly (albeit, one he was loathe to use except in the utmost extremity). One of the idiosyncrasies of this machine was a strangely antiquated notion of what constituted a 'good' citizen.

Violent crime was far less damaging to one's prospects for government work than were drug or other 'moral' offenses. Doubtless this odd prioritization was rooted in old-fashioned religious sentiment, a Puritanical notion of what was proper. But it remained ingrained long past the point where society had ceased to entertain such views. Naturally, a rationale evolved to justify its continued application.

In modern times, it was 'to avoid blackmail'. Yesterday's sin was today's shame, and shame could be exploited by enemies. It never was clear to Robert why somebody would be ashamed of things no longer considered shameful by anyone outside the U.S. government. In essence, it was like saying "you may not know that eating peanuts is a sin, but we think so, and thus an enemy can blackmail you if they find out you are a peanut eater."

The argument was circular and made no sense, but apparently it gave somebody the excuse they needed to keep out those they deemed undesirable. The consequence was that the government remained comically inept in a number of critical areas: the absurdly misnamed "cyberwarfare", various areas of intelligence gathering, and even basic translation and cultural awareness in regions where it had been actively engaged in conflict.

It was no small wonder most Americans viewed it as woefully detached and anachronistic. Nonetheless, it *was* the government, the instrument of rule as empowered by the people. And it had both the responsibility to govern and the power to do so. It was an opinionated grandfather that held socially awkward views, but one who held the purse-strings and a big gun.

In the present circumstance, the problem was that the definition of 'acceptable' excluded much of the remaining talent in California. There had always been a certain collaboration between Silicon Valley and the government, but it was an uneasy one. Two business partners smiling in front of the cameras with arms draped over one another's shoulders, while each held a knife to the other's back.

There was some hope amongst the public that private enterprise would achieve what the government could not; this much Robert knew from the NSA briefings (and by perusing the chat groups). He sighed. How little they knew. The vast gulf in resources between the private and public sectors made this unlikely — even if the big companies were more efficient in their use of them. And there was that pesky missing element: information. The government had much more of it, and it wasn't sharing.

This wasn't motivated by stinginess or pettiness. It simply was due to the complex tangle of regulations governing the release of information. Some rules did not allow certain information to be disseminated at all, while others required it to be released to everyone at once to avoid favoritism. The red tape was enormous. The steps of locating, redacting, approving, and actually conveying a piece of information each took time and had a high likelihood of failure. And while the government had great trouble recruiting talented engineers, scientists, and thinkers, it had no shortage of talented lawyers. In fact, in Robert's estimation it was almost entirely composed of them.

Thus the answer to any question was no. Except for the question of hiring Robert into his present role. For once, the government inanity had worked in his favor. He already had clearance, already had been vetted, already was known to be an acceptable person. He was chosen from the very limited pool of talent to which Lilly had access. For all her clout, she was helpless against true bureaucrats. Robert sometimes joked that the Front would be no match for those bureaucrats. Without the proper signatures, they simply would refuse to die.

Robert was acutely aware of the absurdity of the situation. He was a smart guy, but cringed at being chosen over thousands of better qualified individuals. This was a tremendous responsibility, and he felt that both humanity and those scientists were injured by his preferment. Nonetheless he would do his best, however inadequate that may prove.

He spent every waking hour studying and analyzing and

catching up on the necessary bits of geology, physics, biology, and whatever else conceivably could serve. Three recent college grads aided his effort and helped fill any gaps. Quite frankly, Robert was embarrassed to manage them. In fact, he deemed at least one of them better suited to his own role. But this was the government. You didn't question the star on your shoulder; you asked for another.

Yes, Robert's career had advanced beyond all expectation or reason. At least the remaining few months of it, he laughed. Perhaps Lilly was like a general trapped in a trench with a private. Before they both died she decided to promote the soldier as a kindness, a caprice, a mockery. It never occurred to Robert that Lilly actively preferred *him*, that he wasn't simply the least undesirable choice at the time.

Whether as General or Private or AC3-level analyst, Robert dreaded this meeting. It was his second private one with Lilly (though nobody referred to her as anything other than Madame Director or Dr. Tao). He had learned from their first meeting that it was impossible to prepare for her, though he suspected everybody felt the same way. Well, not *everybody*; most people never even got that far.

Dr. Tao met with only a few people a day. She brought to mind a mafia boss from some movie, and Robert felt both honored and terrified. He clutched his notes. The Front was a distant terror, Lilly an immediate one. He imagined that a meeting with a mafia boss wouldn't end well if one displeased him. Robert only could hope that his findings would please Lilly.

No, not please. She wasn't the type to be pleased or displeased. He hoped they would interest her. That was the most he could ask for, and he was confident these would.

CHAPTER 31

Day 840 — Dwill, Utah

Marissa crossed her arms and tried to look as stern as she could.

"No," she told her daughter.

"But Moooooom, everybody else gets to stay home," Rielle whined, shuffling her five-year-old feet in support of the argument. It wasn't strictly true, but even being one of three kids in school was unfair. And the other two weren't right.

Charlie didn't speak, and just stared off into the distance. Maybe his parents wouldn't let him talk because he didn't speak well. Marissa had drilled into Rielle the importance of proper speech. "You won't go anywhere if you don't speak well," she emphasized. Rielle wasn't sure where mommy wanted her to go. Clearly, not on vacation.

Even Blake got to go on vacation, and he couldn't speak well at all. It was very confusing. Suebee (at least, that was what everybody called her) was the third child in their little class. She seemed normal, but sometimes got very angry.

Once Rielle borrowed a crayon without asking. Suebee tried to shove it down her throat. The teacher explained it was a good idea to leave Suebee alone when she was like that. Most of the time she was nice, though. But you never knew when.

Rumor had it that Suebee's daddy had stayed when the others left. Rielle was a bit jealous, but she had never seen him so it probably was a lie.

"It doesn't matter." Marissa held firm, as she had for months. It was getting harder, though. Things were beginning to fall apart. It was important not to let that happen. Despite herself, she really missed Josh.

Marissa clenched her hand. She had to keep to a familiar rhythm. An imperceptible trickle of blood formed on her palm before she relaxed her grip. There were no more meds. There only was Rielle.

"But there's only two teachers left and they said we could stay home," Rielle insisted, adopting an impressive pout, and imitating her mother by crossing her own arms firmly.

Such recalcitrance. Marissa smiled and thought how alike they were. But if Rielle ever wanted to learn words like 'recalcitrance', she would have to remain in school. Marissa had been a school teacher for several years when younger. Before. She remembered when they dropped that word from the SAT. Recalcitrant. It was back in 2016. The SAT itself disappeared only a few years later, replaced by the RET, which emphasized team-building skills and dispensed altogether with traditional memorization.

Things just had gone downhill since then. Still, a low-quality education was better than no education. Rielle only recently had entered the school system, and Marissa had fretted that its faults would become her faults. None of that mattered now. It was increasingly certain there would be no SAT or RET or anything else for Rielle.

But it wouldn't do to abandon all discipline. Even if she spent all day memorizing lines from soap operas, it was better than the alternative. Besides, what if the Front stopped somehow? Where would they be if the Front stopped and the world was filled with dunderheads. Maybe that was what the aliens wanted, or whoever started the damned thing.

"I promised daddy you'd stay in school until he got back," Marissa explained. Her self-loathing grew with every use of this particular lie. Despite herself, she teared up.

Rielle wondered why mommy cried so much. Once, she opened the door and saw mommy sobbing on the bed. She quietly closed the door. It was important to leave mommy alone sometimes.

"When's daddy coming home?" Rielle demanded, switching topic with bewildering speed.

"Soon, honey. And then you can stop going to school."

Rielle pouted once again. "He better. I'm sick of school."

Things *would* get better when daddy got back, she was sure of it. Rielle bet that mommy secretly wished they had gone on vacation too. Daddy even gave her another chance. Rielle was supposed to be asleep, but saw daddy from her window two days after he left.

He was in the backyard, and put his finger to his lips when he saw her in the window. That was the secret spy sign for not telling. He also blew her a kiss. Rielle hid under her blanket, waiting to jump up when he came in the room. He always was scared when she did that.

There had been loud voices, and then everything was quiet. Mommy must have yelled at him again. That was just like her. She was so mean. After that, daddy hadn't come back. He would, though. Rielle just knew it. She never said anything to mommy about seeing him, though. Daddy had signed her not to.

"Will we get to go on vacation when he does?" she suddenly bubbled, bouncing up and down.

Marissa smiled, and mussed her hair. "Yes we will."

Rielle gave her a skeptical look. "Promise?"

"Where's this from, all of a sudden?" Marissa wondered, laughing. "But yes, pinky promise."

She had gotten mommy to promise. Now, when daddy came back, they'd be together again.

CHAPTER 32

Day 35 — North England

It now had been over three weeks, and the routine was beginning to wear thin. Uncertainty was taking a toll on both refugee and guard, but the latter continued to act with admirable restraint. Elise would not have been surprised were there frequent outbursts of violence, but there hadn't been. Any group is bound to have a few bad apples that stir trouble, steal what little is to be had, or simply are crazy. But if her section had them, they remained surprisingly inactive. Even the large woman whom she had seen get into a fight with the guards early on had caused no further trouble.

Elise wasn't sure why she had lucked into the quiet section, but was grateful she had. She wondered if things were much worse in the men's bunks, if the guards treated women better from a sense of chivalry. A few weeks after she had been immured here, there were some riots in other sections. Elise could hear the commotion in the distance, though it was some time before she learned what caused it.

During the tumult, gunshots were fired, but only sparingly; she suspected they were warning shots. Nor had she heard of hangings or shootings or other reprisals afterward, though it certainly was possible that appearances were being carefully managed. During the riot, the soldiers in her section remained unperturbed, evincing neither impatience nor sympathy.

Eventually, Elise learned from the camp gossip what caused the riots. Edinburgh was gone. Most of the rumors were noise, a hodgepodge of competing assertions and claims. But this was consistent. The guards even confirmed as much, which meant it must be common knowledge. They were the last to know anything, but what they knew usually was true.

By now, Elise had resigned herself to an indefinite stay. Unlike some of the inmates, she remained well-disposed toward the soldiers. They only were doing their jobs, and they probably were as afraid and homesick as their wards. Everyone here was a prisoner. She also sensed that Robert was beginning to warm to her a bit. How could people fail to develop some sort of bond when they were thrown together like this? On the other hand, she hadn't become friendly with the other refugees.

More precisely, they hadn't become friendly with *her*. Were her fellow Scots always such a prickly lot? Elise wondered whether they resented her familiarity with the guards. Did they think she was some sort of informant? What could she possibly inform on them about? The only one she exchanged pleasantries with was Mrs. Dunster, an old lady whom Elise befriended when she first arrived.

Many of the detainees had arrived around the same time, at least in this section. There had been much conversation back then, as everyone tried to figure out where things stood, where *they* stood. But after a few days, that energy dissipated. There simply was nothing more to say, and people settled into cliques. In this regard, it was a lot like the first few days of school; once established, the social structure was largely immutable. However, there was none of the exclusion or bullying that she remembered from school. Most individuals were polite enough if approached, but made little effort to establish any sort of connection. Perhaps they had located familiar faces, or their group already filled some quota of essential social interaction.

Elise didn't care; she was happy by herself, especially since everybody seemed so sullen. Even within the cliques people hung around silently. Like an encampment of hobos, she imagined. With no hope, no future, no outside, what was left to drive conversation? Only when a particularly alarming rumor made the rounds did the volume of chatter rise.

Elise wondered where such rumors came from — new

inmates, guards, somebody's deranged imagination? But even then, the gossip mill never maintained momentum for long. Like a snowy shroud, this place dampened mood and thought and speech.

There always was a village loudmouth, of course. But even they could only hold unrequited conversation for so long. With no booze and with the sexes segregated, what was the point? The gender separation had bothered Elise a great deal at first. It seemed insulting and archaic. But as far as she could tell, women and men were given equal treatment in all other ways. In fact, she suspected that the female sections were better kept than the male ones. And though it was inconvenient to admit as a feminist, she felt much safer this way.

Safe or not, a camp certainly was no place for the elderly. Elise felt compelled to check on Mrs. Dunster frequently, much as she would look in on an infirm neighbor. Or maybe Elise *was* lonely, after all. She never heard tell of a Mr. Dunster, and suspected she was the woman's only friend. As loathe as Elise was to admit it, Mrs. Dunster was hers too. Except perhaps for Robert, but could one ever count one's captor a friend? She never really was certain how much of his conversation stemmed from forbearance, pity, or ennui.

When Elise first arrived, there was a general sense of foreboding. Everyone was convinced that some sort of threat approached, but nobody knew what that actual threat was. For want of a better term, Elise continued to refer to it as a toxic spill. It wasn't even clear whether the detainees were under quarantine. That would imply some sort of contagion, and wouldn't the soldiers be in danger too? She fared no better with subsequent queries along these lines than any other.

The news about Edinburgh made clear that the threat was spreading, whatever it was. If it had destroyed both Glasgow and Edinburgh, then it wasn't something local. No, not "destroyed". Both times, she had been told that the cities were "gone". What did that mean, 'gone'? Nobody had been able to clarify, and the few inmates she asked seemed irritated by her pedantry. What was she, a teacher? Who cared what word they used? It all was the same.

Elise supposed it all *was* the same. It was the fact of the end which was important. Any end was an end. The form the end took only mattered to the people experiencing it, and then not for long. This almost made her laugh, but for some reason her stomach turned instead. If only they hadn't confiscated the cell phones. Not that hers worked any more, but what if the signal returned? What if her parents called? Elise felt very lonely during those first few days.

Today, Elise found herself chatting with Robert in the usual vein, though she was too bored to reiterate the customary pleas. Instead, they were having a normal conversation. Trivial, boring, and utterly pointless, but normal. It was one of those conversations in which she could not recall a single word that had been said so far, but was inexplicably delighted that they *had* been said.

Then she heard a scream. Not another riot, she sighed. There had been only one so far, and she was fearful that another could strain her nascent friendship with Robert. Worse, it could force her to sever it. When called upon to make a choice, she would choose Scotland every time. Did her fellow inmates understand this? What if she now was English in their eyes, and they never accepted her back? What if there was no place for her anywhere.

Moments later, Robert's walkie-talkie began squawking unintelligibly. Unintelligibly to her, that is; Robert clearly understood. She began to nervously joke about the noise, when he interrupted stiffly, "excuse me, Elise, I have to attend to this." Then he was off in the direction of the scream. Friendship? At best, she was a persistent nuisance. He had started calling her by name, though. At least that was something.

One thing which puzzled Elise was the apparent absence of any backlash against refugees like her. Given the UK's past behavior, she had expected a great deal of violent denunciation by politicians. While there was no way to tell what was going on beyond the camp walls, Elise was fairly certain that such vitriol would infect the demeanor of the guards. Perhaps the bonds of kinship with Scotland were stronger than she had imagined. Were she to get through this, Elise would try to think better of her southern neighbors.

Of course, a variety of more cynical explanations also came to mind. She suspected that politicians had to strike a very delicate diplomatic balance. Scots weren't really foreigners, and many families spanned the border. Most people in England still viewed the separation as a mere formality, a short-lived rebellious phase, or a harmless nod to quaint Scottish pride.

But surely this must be a dream come true for the current British Prime Minister. Unlike his predecessor, he had been a staunch foe of the Scottish referendum. His party had gained quite a few seats in the aftermath of the separation, spurred by anti-Scots sentiment. Why weren't they exploiting this? Or perhaps they were. Without access to radio or television, Elise only could guess which camp rumors were true.

Unfortunately, there was a great deal of time for rumination and very little information to ruminate on. Naturally, this led to some wild speculation. One possibility which Elise entertained, though she thought it a bit far-fetched, was that the crisis had spread beyond Scotland. Maybe it was big enough that the UK worried it could soon find itself in similar straits, possibly begging at the door of the European Union. If that were the case, they wouldn't want to set a dangerous precedent.

Elise had expected Robert to be occupied for some time with whatever crisis was brewing. Instead, he returned almost immediately. By now there was a lot of commotion in the distance, and the unrest was spreading fast. Nothing was so certain to create a terrified stampede as a toxic cocktail of uncertainty, helplessness, and a steady chorus of agonized screams. Every nerve in Elise's body told her to run. There are screams, and there are screams. The falsetto screech of a

panicked woman, the grasping disbelief of a man unable to
save a loved one, the wail of a child startled in the night, the
exclamation accompanying a sharp pain — these all could be
characterized as screams.

But even to one who never has heard it before, there is no
mistaking the sound of a man dying in agony. There is nothing theatrical about it. It brushes aside all thought and feeling
and replaces them with a single sentiment: I don't want that
to happen to me. That can't happen to me. I'll do anything to
keep it from happening to me. Only with great effort may that
injunction be defied, but the sound cannot be forgotten and
cannot be ignored. Much like the gurgling and gasping sounds,
subdued and all too human, which followed and marked not
the end of agony but merely the end of an ability to articulate
it. What Elise heard was a crescendo of such screams at varying
stages, almost musical and certainly sonorous.

It was over such a chorus that Robert addressed the restless
crowd in front of him. His voice carried an authority that was
both unexpected and desperately needed. Elise was impressed
that this young man could rise to the occasion, and she felt a
modicum of hope. But only until she looked closely at his face.
It was the face of a man desperately trying to seem in control.

Elise wished to believe that Robert was no coward, that
he wouldn't feign confidence just to maintain authority. No, it
was an effort to let the crowd pretend a little longer. A father's
attempt to mask from his family the ills which beset them. She
wondered if he *was* a father. Was he a good father?

There was so little she knew about him. What does one
ever know about another, especially one who must keep you
at a distance? She felt he was a good man, just a tired one. She
hadn't realized how this wore on him. How it wore on them
all. But she was certain he would stand by them, defend them
against whatever was coming. She was glad he was there to
protect her. Despite everything, she felt safer than she had since
leaving Glasgow.

The screams were getting closer. Robert ordered everyone to quiet down, and surprisingly they did. Once again, Elise was thankful she was in the docile section; heaven knew what was happening in other areas.

"Everyone get inside. Whatever is coming, we will deal with it. You are safest inside."

People were hesitant, but something in Robert's tone comforted them. They wanted to believe that the walls of the bunker would protect them, that he would. By now, the other three local guards had joined him.

He was trying so hard, and Elise almost didn't have the heart to speak out. It felt like betraying him, so she waited until almost all the inmates had gone into the bunkers. Then she confronted the guards.

"Let us out. We can run. Whatever is coming, we can run."

The soldiers looked at one another and, for a moment, she thought they would do it.

"There's nowhere to go. The gates are all shut," one of them explained. Robert said nothing.

"So open them," she enjoined.

"We can't. We're to protect you and keep this camp running smoothly until further orders come in."

"What if there are no further orders?"

"There always are. We just need to hold things down until reinforcements are sent."

"We're all going to die." She didn't sound panicked, just matter of fact. A statement of what was going to happen.

"If you're afraid, go inside," one of the other soldiers chimed in. His tone was pleading, not derisive.

"Look, just give us a choice. Open the gates and let us through," she implored once more.

Robert finally spoke. "We don't have authorization to open the gates."

It was the same thing the other guard had said, but firmer. Did he resent her for challenging him?

Elise made as if to run, but Robert lightly tapped his gun and shook his head. By now the other three guards had scattered to manage the other inmates, most of which had returned to the bunker as instructed.

Robert looked at Elise, and turned to join them. He tapped his gun again.

"We're not authorized to open the gates. We're also not authorized to use deadly force."

He gave a tight-lipped smile and walked away.

Had they known all along? Well, they certainly knew now. Maybe not what was out there, but that they couldn't fight it. That they were going to die. She hid next to the bunker. It was dark, and nobody would see. Besides, if they were not authorized to shoot ... that didn't mean they *wouldn't* shoot. For the first time, she prayed that the English were indeed as rule-addled as they seemed.

Elise ran fifty yards to the boundary with the next section away from the approaching tumult. There was a large barbed wire fence, but there didn't seem to be anybody on the other side. They probably were fleeing from the direction of the threat as well. At least she hoped so.

She wrapped her shirt around her hands, as she had seen in a movie, and began to climb. The problem was that the top tilted inward. Here, Elise's weight worked against her. After a couple of failed attempts she decided to follow the fence to the gate. Nobody was around, and she wondered why nobody else was trying to escape. Of course, *they* didn't know that the guards couldn't shoot. For the second time, she corrected herself: *shouldn't* shoot.

Suddenly, Elise heard a large number of screams coming from the bunkhouse. Why weren't people pouring out? Then she realized, the entrance was on the other side. Whatever was killing people had gotten in, and nobody could escape. Elise saw the gate, and predictably it was chained shut. She had no idea how to pick a lock, but the gate had to be the weak point.

Nobody was looking, so perhaps she could just kick it open. After six kicks she gave up. She would have to climb. The top was not tilted inward here, but the gate mesh was finer; her feet could not find a purchase, and she lacked the strength to pull herself up.

Elise noticed that somebody was watching from about 40 feet away. Her heart stopped for a moment, but it just was Mrs. Dunster. Why didn't she help, dammit? Then she saw why. Mrs Dunster was convulsing in agony. Elise lost control of her bodily functions, but quickly recovered her wits.

It wasn't over yet; she still could get out before that thing killed her. It was unfair, she wouldn't even know *what* had killed her. At the very least, they should tell her that. Suddenly she grew angry. Why hadn't Robert given her the damned key! He just could have dropped it in front of her. Now he was dead, and she was going to die because of *his* stupid rules. Because he had too big a stick up his arse to break them. Elise softened for a moment. But he *had* broken them, in his own minor way. She supposed that counted for *something*.

Then she heard the sounds Mrs. Dunster was making, and all other thoughts vanished. Elise's body moved of its own accord, uncontrollably tearing at the gate. Whatever this thing was, she didn't want to die like that. She wished that they *had* been ordered to shoot. But by now there was nobody left to shoot her, of that she was sure. It occurred to her that there hadn't been *any* shots, even when the guards must have been dying in agony. Elise almost wanted to laugh at this tragic absurdity. Then she started screaming.

CHAPTER 33

Day 703 — San Diego, California

"Let me first ask you a question," Robert began. He said this without thinking, a necessary preamble to his presentation. But as the words came out of his mouth, he cringed in anticipation of the response. One simply did not put one's boss in the hot-seat. At best it would be regarded as coy, at worst presumptuous. Lilly's face remained blank. After an awkward pause he continued.

"How certain are you of the effect of the Front as it moves through matter?"

Lilly looked disappointed; perhaps she had been expecting something novel. Was he the umpteenth person to go down this same dead end? Nonetheless she humored him, responding without hesitation or annoyance and almost by rote.

"Surface matter has no effect, transverse propagation through mountains for over three hundred miles has no effect, water to a depth of four thousand feet has no effect, direct subterranean immersion has no effect to a depth of three thousand feet. Passage through the Earth is unimpeded as indicated by adherence to a spherical form."

She crossed her hands, the very picture of a school teacher expectantly awaiting a pupil's next halting question. But she wasn't a schoolteacher; she was the second most powerful person in the government. If Robert didn't give her something, this likely would be their last meeting. He could imagine her tart explanation that his new assignment three miles from the Front would better allow precise, personal observation of the phenomenon which so effectively eluded him.

Well, she wasn't a cat-petting megalomaniac with a penchant for rewarding failure in particularly unpleasant ways. But she *had* demonstrated a certain moral flexibility regarding the health of others, and definitely was not the sort of person Robert wished to disappoint. By now there was no turning back, no scurrying from the office in a tangle of papers, so he moved forward.

"What direct evidence is there for the passage of the Front through water and earth?"

Lilly responded quietly. "We have precise information."

"But how? There would have to be people..." he blurted out without thinking.

Lilly fixed his eyes and reiterated firmly, "We have precise information."

Robert hesitated, then took a different tack.

"How certain are we that the Front is unimpeded while passing through the Earth?"

The "we" was meant to avoid placing the burden of correctness on Lilly, allowing for the consideration of alternate possibilities without loss of face. Or so he had read in some book. In Robert's experience, it paid to read books when placed outside his comfort zone. Books didn't yell at him or complain when he forgot what they said or resent it when he ignored their advice. And sometimes their advice was quite handy. Especially when he had to deal with a clinical sociopath, even one he liked and admired despite his better instincts.

Robert was proud of his strategic tact, but gazing into Lilly's unblinking eyes he realized tact was as irrelevant to her as he was. He decided to get to the point without waiting for a reply — especially since one wasn't forthcoming. Apparently, she thought the question rhetorical or too trivial to waste time on.

"What if it *is* impeded?"

"We have no time for idle speculation. We know it is not. I encourage thinking outside the box, but I fear this is a fruitless pursuit."

She rose to leave. He realized there was no room to be timid; if he didn't explain now, he never would have another opportunity. And that could be a disaster for everyone.

"I have strong evidence that this is not correct. A more precise analysis of existing data hints at this and..." Lilly looked as if she was about to object, so he motored on.

"We have acquired substantial new data as well." If that didn't do it, then nothing would.

Lilly sat down, and Robert breathed a sigh of relief. He had bought an extra 10 minutes of her valuable time. For a typical executive, this would be a matter of ego, a careful rationing of coveted attention. But with Lilly, there wasn't a matter of station or power. He had bought Lilly's attention until she reached a conclusion about his work. This could take five seconds or twenty minutes, so he spoke quickly. There was too much at stake to risk losing her.

Robert was reminded of something he once had been told about female management consultants. Before taking a government job, he had interviewed with an MC firm out of college. The interview was a group affair, presumably representing a realistic competitive environment. The recruiters claimed could identify the best candidates by their behavior under fire.

He remembered eight candidates and six interviewers, four male and two female. They had started with a presentation about the firm, and then proceeded to answer questions by the applicants. The men had differing styles, but all spoke clearly and confidently. But the women sounded like locomotives. Their staccato speech, without punctuation or pause, lent a certain inexorable force to the flow of words.

Afterward, Robert joked about this odd behavior in passing to a friend. The fellow briefly had worked as a management consultant himself, and explained that it was a common phenomenon in that world. The men tended to be loud and assertive and had no qualms about interrupting one another.

They could jockey amongst themselves on an equal footing, but women were at a marked disadvantage. They tended to be more thoughtful and hesitant at first, and barely could get a word in. The successful women were those who adopted a style which didn't admit interruption.

Robert thought this apocryphal, but his few data points seemed to bear it out. Fortunately his present argument had far more data behind it, though the effect also was more subtle. It occurred to him that he was sitting before a woman whose silence could drown the voices of most men. He wondered what strategy *she* had adopted when first starting out. Or was she always Lilly Tao?

"New data?" she asked quietly.

"As you know, I came from disinformation. Creating memes and viral campaigns."

Lilly waved him on impatiently. Robert remembered his undergraduate thesis adviser warning him about this. His instinct had been to explain everything, free his readers from the need to struggle with the material as he had. He wrote his initial draft in such a manner, providing extensive background material. It weighed in at 94 pages, and he was quite proud of it. Then his adviser slashed it down to 6 pages. 'You don't need to waste everybody's time, just discuss what's new,' he explained.

Robert got to the point. "This can work for other purposes as well. I created the online FOG movement. FOG stands for Flower of Good. It allows people whose X-Days are approaching, those who cannot escape or who wish to die, a chance to give their death purpose. To lend us their deaths, so to speak. We provide open-source instructions to create a special kind of biosensor from a variety of commonly available devices — fitness gadgets, tablets, smartphones, or even directly from basic components. We reserved a specific transmission frequency range and co-opted an array of receivers for this purpose. A participant can wire their device as instructed and download the software. It uses our knowledge of the precise sequence of biological processes attendant to intersection with the Front."

Lilly winced and quietly commented, "That's restricted information."

Robert was ready for this.

"The software does not disseminate such information. It simply monitors all the necessary signals, along with a lot of unnecessary ones. Technically, the software is self-decrypting. The code is available, but its effect cannot be deduced."

When Lilly didn't respond, he elaborated.

"The code has been path-obfuscated using a Hishijima-Netado algorithm. One can read it, or execute it on a given set of inputs — which include a large set of unidentifiably extraneous variables — but deducing its general operation is computationally hard. Provably so."

He looked at her. "Of course, some would say that people selflessly helping humanity shouldn't be begrudged such knowledge."

"It does them no good," Lilly noted. "But as long as they cannot deduce the profile, I see no problem."

She paused for a moment, thoughtfully, and smiled at him. "I will put it through a security review. I assume it will pass muster."

It wasn't a question, but Robert nodded. Lilly motioned him to continue.

"We gathered data over one month from 812,354 participants."

Lilly raised an eyebrow, and Robert assumed for a moment that she was impressed.

"Human participants are unreliable, of course," she observed.

Robert nodded again. "Yes, we created a reliability model

based on the expectation that certain individuals would prove unreliable or deliberately attempt to sabotage the effort for various reasons. Our data analysis algorithm accommodates this and many other noise channels."

Lilly didn't say anything, so he went on. "We constructed a Bayesian Network and employed a specially-constrained Markov Chain Monte Carlo approach over an aggressively-pruned state space."

"The effect would have to be tiny, given our existing data. I don't see how you could discern it," Lilly objected, almost rhetorically.

"We used specialized software produced by LIGO."

"Gravity waves?"

"What could be more difficult to detect?" Robert smiled. "Their software was publicly available, and we adapted it to our purposes. We also made use of a number of specialized signal processing tools that are classified, mostly adapted from technology for low-bandwidth ultra-long-wavelength submarine transmissions."

A brief glimmer of pain crossed Lilly's face, as if from an unpleasant memory. "And your conclusion?" she asked, regaining her composure.

"The wave refracts through matter. It is a very small effect."

"How small?"

"Small enough that we don't know whether we are seeing refraction through a medium or diffraction off of particular features."

"It's not diffraction," Lilly declared.

Robert looked puzzled by her certainty.

"Otherwise we would have seen some scattering when we detonated a 2 Megaton device on top of the Front," Lilly explained. "The explosion core was extremely dense, even if not particularly massive."

"But only if you were looking for it," Robert noted after a

thoughtful pause.

"How certain are you?" Lilly asked, ignoring his objection. It was the only question which mattered.

"It passes the 5-sigma test," he smiled.

"That's all I need to know." Lilly rose. "Send everything to my office within an hour. We'll verify your results."

Suddenly she adopted a stern expression. "I needn't tell you how disappointed I will be if this turns out to be a ploy for attention. It better check out."

Had others tried such a thing? Robert shuddered to think how *that* turned out. Were they among his 812,354?

"It will," he promised.

"Good. Then we have nothing more to discuss." She rose, signalling that the meeting was at an end.

"There is one thing," Robert added. If not now, he may not get another opportunity to ask. Lilly turned with an air of impatience.

"I'd like permission to visit my family for a week."

"Now's not the time for vacation," she snapped and turned to leave.

"Then when?"

"When we win," Lilly quietly responded as she walked out the door.

CHAPTER 34

Day 1592 — Melbourne, Australia

A small group of men stood in the crisp morning air, rubbing their hands and stepping in place to keep warm. They wore a variety of colorful outfits, mostly spandex or Lycra, and each had a large number printed on waterproof paper pinned to their chest. The numbers ranged from 12 to 6974, but seemed to have been assigned at random. Below the gathering was the entrance to a large viaduct, open on top and stretching as far as the eye could see. If curved, it wasn't easily perceptible.

George Beckstein didn't mind the cold. It would warm up quickly once they started running. In fact, when the sun came up, they probably would feel too hot. He glanced at a couple of the other runners; they definitely would need to shed a layer.

There weren't many places where one could hold a proper marathon any more, and he was glad to have the opportunity to participate in what likely would be the last. Of course, these days it wasn't really a challenge to get in; there were no traditional qualifiers. If you could make it to the starting line, you could run. They *did* encourage people to register ahead of time so they could arrange suitable transportation at the end point, but generally weren't too strict. Everyone was pretty lax about things these days. If they didn't have enough van support, they'd just do their best. Why worry about such things? Life was too short.

It had been a long time since George ran a marathon, and the last was old-style: rules, qualifying times, and a full twenty-six miles through some city with thousands of sweaty people. He'd made it in 4:10. Not terrible, but not great. Things had changed a lot, he considered, looking around.

For one thing, running a marathon these days carried a lot

more cachet. Sure it always had been impressive to complete one, especially a major like Boston or New York. But those were no fun. The same people always won — all from some tribe in Kenya or Ethiopia, George always forgot which. They'd run marathons every day just for the heck of it, and that sucked out all the fun for everybody else. Or it did if you were at all competitive.

George had decided not to be competitive many years ago. Whether it was from wisdom or because he just never won anything was unclear even to him, but it had worked well. He wondered what had happened to all those competitive people, those Kenyans and Ethiopians. They could run faster than everybody else, seemingly forever. They all were gone by now. He wondered how far they had run before the Front caught them, or if they had run at all.

But this was more like it. A bunch of guys, most in good but not peak condition, and nobody whom god had designed just to run. They all stood a chance of winning. And since there weren't many people left, they very well could end up as world champions. That was quite a thought, the last World Champion... with a time of 4:10. Well, he hoped he would do much better than that. After all, this course was only eight miles long.

There were two major challenges when organizing a marathon, beside the general shortage of manpower. The first was finding a long stretch of viaduct or canal or natural canyon. One would think subway tunnels would be ideal, but they generally were too short, had too many exits, and tended to have abrupt turns. They were tried in the early days and found wanting. Blocking exits was one of the most important preparations for a marathon. There had to be no way in or out before the end. This meant that the walls needed to be pretty high, and any existing entrances had to be sealed. Otherwise, there was no point to the whole affair.

The second challenge was ensuring that the course was properly aligned relative to the Front. Precise calculations were important here, but George had confidence in the government predictions; they had been dead-on for the last two years. The layout of the course was important, though. The starting line had to be hit by the Front first. This made turning back impossible. Merely blocking the entrance once the marathon started wouldn't do. It would be artificial.

The peril must arise naturally, otherwise why not just have an ordinary race where the losers were shot? That wouldn't make for good entertainment, or at least not *as* good entertainment. Also, it would be demeaning to be chased by some artificial timer like a lab rat. This actually had been tried in South Africa at one point, and the ratings were abysmal. It turned out they had miscalibrated the timers for that course, and everybody was shot before the end. No, it was the Front and nothing else which must lend urgency to one's feet. There was an almost religious aspect to this, hearkening to days when gods decided the right of one's cause through chance or combat.

So the Front had to intersect the starting point first, and shortly after the race began. The remainder of the course was designed to allow runners to evade it if they behaved strategically. The Front itself wasn't particularly fast, even now, so there would be no drama or risk if everyone simply ran away from it in a straight line. To be exciting, the course had to closely follow the contour of the Front itself. It also had to have a shape which realistically allowed escape.

This was accomplished by defining a 'livespeed', a pace which, if maintained from start to finish, guaranteed survival. The Front wouldn't cross the course at any point ahead of you if you maintained the livespeed. Beyond this there were no guarantees — except that once the Front crossed the end point anybody remaining was doomed. A well-chosen course had a livespeed that was difficult to achieve consistently, but nonetheless allowed escape even if portions of the run fell well-below it. Runners often had to plan quite carefully. There was much more to it than simply optimizing the overall running time.

Certain bends had to be cleared by certain times. The finish wasn't the only place where a slow runner could be trapped. If one ran too slowly early on, saving energy, then the Front could intersect a bend ahead. If one started slow to conserve energy, then a later bend could prove problematic even if the livespeed subsequently was maintained. On the other hand, a quick start could tire a runner out, causing too long a drop below the livespeed later on. The precise speed profile could make or break a runner. There was much greater room for cleverness than in an old-style marathon, and that was part of the appeal.

The commission announced the course layout a month ahead of the run, so there was ample time for preparation. The problem wasn't mathematically difficult, but it wasn't entirely trivial either. Most runners chose to adopt a more heuristic approach, and George was no exception. However, this didn't mean he neglected preparation. By the time of the marathon, he had become quite conversant with the layout. Despite its initially linear appearance, the course *did* curve quite a bit. There was one critical bend which he needed to make in time. That was what made it such an adrenaline rush; there were stretches along which you were running *toward* the Front. It was the ultimate sense of imminent peril.

George looked at his watch. Three minutes. The support van already had departed for the finish line. It would take a safer route. He glanced around; only runners remained. Nobody spoke, each knew his life was in his own hands. There wasn't so much a sense of competition as an unspoken mutual respect and camaraderie.

Two minutes. There were no spectators, just video cameras,

but George knew that lots of people were watching. Heck, probably 90% of the remaining population. Or perhaps he was flattering himself. Maybe they all were cultivating private sorrows and had no time to watch people throw their lives away. There was a fine line between bravery and idiocy, or no line at all. George noticed that the crew had left the gates open, a last minute out for those with second-thoughts. It was a kindness, though he doubted anyone would avail themselves of it. Nobody did.

The sound of a gunshot issued from the overhead klaxon, and the runners were off. They kept in a clique for the first two miles, almost as if everybody were ashamed or afraid to pull ahead or fall behind. The livespeed for this course was 10 mph, a six minute mile. But they only needed to keep to it early on and make a critical bend at the 3.4 mile mark. George suspected that if he cleared this, even a 9 minute mile would suffice for the remainder of the course.

The group maintained a solid 11 mph pace for those first 2 miles, with only minor dispersion amongst the 16 runners. Apparently, everybody realized the peril and was fit enough to adhere to the same plan. Then two of the group began to fall behind, at first a little then a lot. The group spread out, with George toward the middle. His calves burned; he never really *had* learned to run properly, but 3.4 miles at that pace should be eminently doable. Heck, he *deserved* to die if he couldn't maintain a 6 minute mile for under 30 minutes.

George focused on the ground in front of him. Experience had taught him that it was best not to look too far ahead, lest he anticipate the effort involved. That only would serve to reduce his endurance. Suddenly somebody sprinted past him in the wrong direction, barely avoiding collision. It took a moment to register what had happened. A suicide.

He had heard of such people. It was a way to meet the Front on one's own terms. Some did it privately and some publicly. There even had been a few widely reported cases of ships sailing into the Front, passing to the other side with quiet dignity, while the unfolding horror within remained shrouded in steel. George wondered whether those ships had intended to cross the Front, whether the passengers had agreed to it — or even knew of it, or whether this was a fiction purveyed by the media, a generous lie to mask acts of incompetence or madness or murder. There were no shrouds *here*, no lies. Had the man planned it, or was it impromptu? As he heard a distant screaming behind him, George wondered why somebody would want the world seeing *that*. It just seemed so … indecorous.

A first bend at the 2.8 mile mark was approaching. The course snaked into a small curve followed by a large one, and George was on the lee-side of the former. He made the bend, and sprinted past it. A little over half a mile to go. He heard screaming in the distance behind him. Jesus. He nearly panicked. George hadn't realized how close the timing on that first bend was. He was lucky he made it. The fear lent him speed, and he rushed toward the front of the pack, making it third past the second bend. That was the big one, the 3.4 mile marker, and he breathed a sigh of relief without slackening his pace. The wiggle now took him away from the Front, then back toward it a little before opening out onto a continuation of the original straight track.

As he heard some more screaming behind him, George struggled to remember the exact shape of the remaining course. It had been so clear this morning. Straight for about 2 miles, then one small wiggle, then a 2 mile straight stretch to the end. He could afford to pace himself now. No, he *had* to pace himself now if he hoped to make it.

George slowed a little and gulped air, barely registering the puzzled looks two runners shot him as they passed. By now he had forgotten the calf pain, and plowed on at a steady 9 mph.

He wasn't worried about averaging to the livespeed because he knew that the rest of the course was safe. There just was that one minor bend up ahead.

Going into the lee-side of that last small curve, George considered whether, to be safe, he should pick things up to 8 mph once the course straightened. He had just decided to do this when he felt a strange sensation. As he stared at his hand in disbelief and before he started screaming, he wondered whether he had misjudged the angle of the course. He wished he had done the calculations, or at least stuck with the pack. Then he remembered he was on camera. At least he would try to die with dignity.

He didn't.

CHAPTER 35

As any scientist can attest, there is a great difference between knowing how to solve a problem and actually finding the solution. And as any engineer can attest, there is a great difference between knowing the solution to a problem and implementing it in the real world.

Robert was neither a scientist nor engineer by training, but he had become intimately familiar with both of these principles. He now was working alongside Lilly Tao, and was in charge of mankind's greatest endeavor, and most likely its last. Over 1200 researchers and engineers reported to him, most of whom he would have been thrilled to even meet a mere year ago. His resources were those of the United States, such as they were. And despite all this, he felt completely helpless.

Two weeks earlier, his group's results had been confirmed by two independent teams. The data indicated a pattern of refraction as the Front passed through the Earth. The effect was minute, and it had taken the very latest computational methods and technologies to identify it. Robert wondered at the serendipity which led to the appearance of the Front at precisely the point when humanity could hope to deal with it.

Of course, 'hope' was the operative word. Three weeks later, there still was no indication they *could* deal with it. At first, Robert had considered that the Front may have been triggered by some alien species based on the indicators of human progress. Perhaps it was a cleanup mechanism or a fail-safe, the plot device for countless bad science fiction stories. But then it occurred to him that *any* civilization could perceive itself to be in a similarly exceptional position. It was an illusion, of course.

The side of a mountain looks the same regardless of where one is, and without a sufficient vantage point it would be natural to assume that what one sees is the entirety of what actually is, that the phenomenon fits precisely into the epistemological paradigm to which one is bound. One would then suppose that their particular technological or military or religious knowledge, their arcana, could tip the scale, but not until that very moment.

Each people would have their own perceived hope of thwarting it — a special incantation, a sacrifice to propitiate the gods, a machine to destroy it. There was an anthropic element to the whole situation. And perhaps Robert's world was as deluded in their hope as any other would be. For all their efforts, all their technologies, they had been able to detect only the weakest interaction with matter. They had detected it after much of humanity was gone, with little time remaining. And they had detected it by the slimmest of chances and most improbable conjunction of people and events.

He was part of that conjunction, perhaps even an important part, but that didn't make him any more 'special' than the computer he worked on or the seat he worked in, or even the signals he received from dying souls the world over. Did this knowledge really give them anything? Was it more useful than the knowledge that some gods were angry or an evil wizard had doomed them?

The internet had advanced every imaginable theory, revisited them frequently and tirelessly, beaten them like dead horses, and then some. That was the scope of human knowledge, a field of dead horses and the men who kicked them. But did it matter? Robert suspected they were no closer to understanding the Front than some medieval society would be. What if they were as far from saving themselves with all their scientific knowledge as some primitive beating a drum to a silent god?

This was the perennial quandary that everyone faced: how to use their time. When we find ourselves in this world with no knowledge but the lies others teach us and no purpose but the fictions others invent, how do we define time? How do we use it? All it takes is one wrong turn for a life to be spent in futility, a fly trapped in a room fruitlessly searching for the way out. The problem was that all turns were wrong, and all were right. Robert rubbed his forehead vigorously and took a swig of coffee. These weren't new considerations. They had occurred to him every night for the last few months, with ever increasing urgency. The great questions hungered for answers, and soon there would be nobody to provide them. Must they be the *right* answers? What if he winged it, like a test. Would he be judged amiss?

The most frustrating thing was that there *did* exist a magic number. There was *some* pace at which the Front could have been defeated or escaped, just not *this* one. Maybe if they had ten years or a hundred or a thousand. Even if the Front itself proved unstoppable, nonnegotiable, inexorable, mankind could develop the technology to flee it, to survive beyond its reach. That was the unbearable thing: never knowing. Then again, could anything truly be named 'unbearable'? Death lent finite duration to every torment, and anything in finite measure was bearable.

Perhaps escaping the Front only would serve to prolong mankind's agony; perhaps the Front was the universe showing mercy. Robert hoped that when he died, God finally would open the books and reveal the truth. "See, you were so close. If you hadn't made that one sign error in the calculation...," or, "It was amusing to watch an ant try to stop a tractor." Besides, who was to say that the Front *hadn't* been there all along, tiny, waiting or moving incredibly slowly. Maybe over the years, the odd passerby had died, unremarked, when they walked through it. Or maybe nobody happened upon it until it grew large enough; there still were many places in the world that never had been touched by humans. And now, many never would be.

Suddenly Robert was shaking violently, spasming. It was happening. Somehow, they had misjudged. The Front was here, and it had him. The pain would start soon. He prayed it would be over quickly, though he knew quite well that it wouldn't. He slowly would decay, and (to the best of his knowledge) remain conscious the whole time. There was nothing for it, but to allow the Front to take its course. Once it had touched even the slightest part of him, he was doomed. But he had been doomed long before it touched him, even before the Front existed. It just came down to a matter of time, more or less. And his clearly was spent. Maybe somebody would save the rest. All he could do now was wait. And scream.

The shaking grew more and more insistent, until finally Robert's eyes snapped open. It was Amanda Ricodi, his personal assistant. He was leaning back in his rolling office chair and staring directly up into her hazel eyes as she leaned over him. In any other situation, this would have been quite intimate.

"Meeting is in five minutes, sir," she informed him.

There was no sign of embarrassment or judgment, and Robert felt oddly unabashed in front of her. She wasn't just an incredibly attractive girl his age, she was his employee. Still, it was hard to ignore that side of things.

A few weeks ago, he was some schlub she wouldn't even have glanced at in a bar. Heck, he probably still was. But now she attended to him and called him 'sir'. Ironically, now that he had the opportunity to get to know her, even was in constant close quarters with her, there was no possibility of romance. However much he impressed her, nothing could happen. This was precisely why the rules existed; things went a lot more smoothly without that possibility.

In practice, Robert could have gotten away with anything at this point. Nobody was going to jeopardize the effort over something like that. If there was a problem, Amanda probably would disappear and Lilly would give him an annoyed talking-to. He wasn't sure which part appalled him more. But the whole thing was a moot point. Power and prestige had done little for Robert in this regard. He simply was too shy to do anything untoward, even if his character had allowed it.

Robert's position afforded him a compensation though. Up until then, reproduction had been of paramount importance, a man judged almost entirely by his ability to attract a mate and propagate the species. But the Front made evolution irrelevant. There only was one way for humanity to endure, and he was their best hope. Until the Front was disarmed, sex was of no importance — whatever small consolation that was.

"I'll be there," Robert croaked.

Not that he was in any condition to hit on her anyway. He became a bigger and bigger mess each day, and must already have seemed quite frightful. That's what 20-hour workdays did. That and cause a wide array of psychological issues, none of which Robert hoped would visibly manifest themselves. Maybe right before the Front hit, Amanda would grab him and tear his clothes off. Wasn't that what people *did* when the world was about to end? There would be no repercussions, no awkward afterward. Of course if the world *was* about to end, it meant he had failed and why would she want to spend her last moments with a failure.

This pretty much quenched any remaining fantasy. Somehow, wild sex seemed less appealing when followed by prolonged agony and death. But it probably would beat *no* wild sex, followed by prolonged agony and death. Robert almost laughed, but caught himself, mortified that Amanda may notice. It was difficult enough to talk to girls in general, but to be under the constant scrutiny of an attractive young woman was very disconcerting.

Robert was sure *somebody* would be turned on by the idea of HLD during sex, though. After all, there was an internet fetish site for *any* perversion. But there was something about the imminent and unavoidable prospect of a horrible death which dampened most libidos. *Unavoidable.* Was that what the head of mankind's last effort should be saying? If he couldn't keep the faith, who would?

It was more than that, though. Robert sensed that over the last few weeks everybody had come to look at him a certain way. It was as if they were pinning all their hopes on him, as if they believed he actually could do it. Was this how a General felt among his soldiers, a star quarterback before the big game? He remembered a scene from some movie. A young man was introduced to Stalin, who offered him a cup of tea. When he took the cup, the man's hand was shaking. Stalin asked something to the effect of, "why does your hand shake? Mine did not shake when I met you." The man replied, "because you are our father." It probably was the only answer which wouldn't get him killed.

Robert realized the absurdity of comparing himself to a homicidal dictator. He may hold the key to life, but they all faced death together. There could be little fear of him under such circumstances, he hoped. Perhaps they viewed him as their father in a good way. As much as his ego would have rejoiced at this, the thought made his stomach turn. Being a father was a grave responsibility. He was no saint and he was no scientist. He just was a techie, a techie way out of his depth. A techie who had been paid and promoted for deceiving everyone at the government's behest. A techie who probably still was deceiving everyone, just with a different type of lie. But such thoughts would not do. There was a meeting, and he must have enough hope for everyone. A meeting? He would have to decide what to do, the perennial burden of leadership.

A meeting. Something about a meeting. With an start, Robert awoke from his reverie. He looked, unblinking, at Amanda for a moment.

"Am I late?"

She shook her head, and he exhaled in relief. He did *not* want to keep Lilly Tao waiting.

Robert left his office and gently closed the door behind him. A small guilded plate announced "Deputy Director" in oddly misaligned calligraphy. He proceeded down the hall, past the mahogany desks and the smiling faces, turning left at the end, as he had countless times over the past few weeks, and mechanically nodding at everyone as he walked by.

When he reached the end of the hall, he looked at the door. It had a small guilded plate in a cleaner non-cursive font, which stated "Director". Robert entered, gently closing the door behind him.

CHAPTER 36

Day 637 — Broadcast NY, VBTV Channel 5

We now return to our original show, already in progress...

[*Show features two men arguing.*]

Man1: Ok, but that's absurd.

Man2: To you, perhaps.

Man1: Look, it's there, expanding, killing us all.

Jim1: [*interjects, grinning at the audience*] That's a fact.

Man2: Nobody's arguing that it's THERE. You can wave at it all you want, but that doesn't prove your point.

Man1: So you still insist that there's no God.

Man2: It's a big stretch from what you're arguing to a God. To YOUR God.

Man1: [*smugly*] He's OUR God, whether you acknowledge him or not.

Man2: It's your nonsense, whether you acknowledge it or not.

Man1: [*heatedly*] Look, you can say what you want, but I think any rational person...

Man2: Any rational person would look at the facts. You've got an agenda.

Jim: [*smiles at audience knowingly*] Don't we all.

Man2: You people are all the same.

Man1: You people?

Man2: You know what I mean.

Man1: Do I? It sounded to me and [*gestures expansively at audience*] I think a lot of us, well, pretty racist.

Man2: Another attempt to distract from the real issue, eh?

Man1: You said it, not me.

Man2: Indeed, and I'll thank you to let me finish it.

Man1: [*points at man2 menacingly*] It better not be anything nasty. These people don't want to hear that sort of crap.

Man2: [*ignores him and rolls his eyes, looking at the audience then back at Man1*] You people [*said emphatically*] take even the slightest uncertainty about anything and twist it to support your view. If science explains 99% of what we see, you point out that it can't explain everything and must be wrong. If religion fails to explain 99% of something but you find 1% that doesn't directly repudiate it, you deem your particular doctrine proven.

Man1: Lots of big words there, prof. But they don't change the Plain Truth.

Man2: Which is that you're an idiot.

Jim: [*smiling*] Let's keep it civil.

Man2: So, your argument is that you're right because I used big words. Do you want me to put it simply?

Man1: Please do. We're all good simple folks here. We keep to the simple truths.

Man2: Excellent, then I'll keep it really simple. There's no evidence of any intelligence behind it.

Man1: It ONLY kills humans. It can't be explained by science. Those sound like pretty big pieces to me.

Man2: Let's not confuse "can't be" with "hasn't been".

Man1: Sure, if you stop confusing the Plain Truth with some desperate attempt to shore up the mess that is science.

Man2: You can say what you want, but the only reason your words even can reach viewers is because of science.

Man1: And the only reason you're around to lie to them is God.

Man2: As for your basic premise: yes, it only kills humans. But why is God the only explanation?

Man1: Because it's the right one. Because it's always been the only explanation. Period.

Man2: Punctuate away, it doesn't change the fact. Or as you like -- the Plain Truth. There exist perfectly legitimate explanations that have nothing to do with God.

Man1: Ok, shoot. I want to hear your perfectly legitimate explanations [*said sarcastically*].

Man2: Well, first, there's the possibility of a man-made disaster.

Man1: Sure, but that could as easily have been God's agency. The tools he uses to punish us can be of our own devising.

Man2: It doesn't matter if God COULD also be an explanation. The point is that he needn't be. We could have done this of our own accord.

Jim: Let me interject here. I'm no scientist, but doesn't that seem unlikely? We can't explain it. Even if there was a vast conspiracy, they'd want to stop it before it killed them, right? We can't even interact with it. How can we have created something like that and know nothing about it?

Man2: Accidentally. There's no reason that the Front need be something we anticipated creating. Perhaps we just triggered it, by doing something we thought we understood.

Man1: Ok, then I can counter that God put in place certain fail-safes. Don't eat from the tree. You do, and boom -- you're expelled. Don't do this thing -- whatever it was. You do, and boom -- you're dead. We already had 2 strikes if

you count. Original sin, and killing our
Lord and Savior.

Man2: We've done a lot more than just
those two. Wouldn't he have killed us
before this?

Man1: Leans toward audience. Personally,
I think it was Gay Marriage. Once that
took over, God decided we were beyond
redemption.

Man2: What the hell does that have to
with the Front? You think Gay people
having sex triggered it? I hate to break
it to you, but that's been happening for
a long time.

Man1: Not like this. Now it's legal,
accepted, encouraged. We tell our
children to do it. With each other. You
ask what the hell it has to do with the
Front? I'd say everything. Hell is where
the Front is sending us. Or those of us
who have fallen from grace.

Man2: You think it won't kill you?

Man1: Not eternally. I will be saved, as
will all those who have faith.

Man2: And you think the billion people
killed so far all deserved to die.

Man1: I am not privy to the Lord's
thoughts. It is my hope, my prayer,
that a great many were saved and now are
blissfully enjoying his grace.

Man2: That's fantastic, but it doesn't
help us understand the Front.

Man1: Of course it does. You can't fight God. You shouldn't fight God.

Man2: So ... you'll be jumping into the Front -- just to help his will along, right?

Man1: I'll stay with my flock as long as they need me. [*looks intently at Man2*] I'd strongly encourage you to, though, and rid us of this offensive crap. If enough of you do, perhaps the Lord will see fit to spare the rest of us and let us carry on with our lives.

Man2: [*laughing*] Carrying on *does* seem to be what you do best.

Man1: You said you had a few arguments. Is this the best you can muster -- some government accident. Why not some other far-fetched theory. If you're stretching, reach for the stars. [*turns to audience*] We all remember Mary Delphi's illustrious AD theory. That's what scientists give us.

Man2: Ok, well here's one you didn't think of. If thinking can describe any of what you do.

Man1: [*sits cross-legged with a posture of exaggerated attention*] Please, enlighten us.

Man2: You mean enlighten *you*. I'm sure these fine people [*waves at audience as Man1 had*] are quite enlightened already. What if the reason the Front kills humans isn't by any design or because it specifically targets us or knows us as humans.

Jim: That's not an explanation. It's just a "what if".

Man2: I'm not finished. It's perfectly possible that the Front acts by a mechanism that happens to only affect humans.

Man1: You mean ... like a SOUL? [*looks around triumphantly*].

Man2: Well, that would be your answer to pretty much anything. I was thinking something more prosaic. We differ even from the next species on the evolutionary chain in many ways. It could operate on any of those things. If another animal happened to have the relevant characteristic, whether it coevolved or happened to converge to it, the Front would do the same to it.

Man1: Even though it doesn't operate by any known scientific principle? According to you people, all we are is atoms and chemicals and cells. If you don't believe in anything else, then what is it interacting with that you can't otherwise detect.

Man2: I can't speak to the mechanism of interaction, obviously. But the criteria may involve a complex set of constraints that only are satisfied by humans. Or there may be other things affected but we just don't notice because they are rare or difficult to observe or we're just too busy fretting about our own plight.

Man1: Sounds pretty far-fetched to me. A real reach to avoid the existence of God.

Man2: And the stretch from SOME intelligence to the particular beliefs of the 3rd Baptist Ministry of Louisiana, that's NOT a reach?

Man1: Faith always is a reach. It is the only way to reach the divine. Oh, and [*reaches over and pats the back of Man2's hand gently*] - you forgot to mention aliens.

Man2: I think aliens would want to steer clear of this place. Well, the good news is we'll all be reaching the divine soon enough.

Man1: Not all of us. [*turns to the audience*] NOT ALL OF US. You must have faith. [*turns back to Man2 and speaks gently*]. I know we have our differences, and I've spoken harshly. But I really want to save you too.

Man2: Well, that's a relief. For a minute, I thought you had a stake ready. But seriously, [*turns to audience*] if you want save me, and you want to save yourselves, tell your Congressmen to keep funding our efforts to stop the Front.

Jim: You've heard the arguments. You know the deal. YOU decide. WHICH is the Plain Truth? Thank you Reverend George Tanner of the 3rd Baptist, and thank you Professor Gimlick.

CHAPTER 37

Day 734 — San Diego, California

Lilly looked up from the papers crowding her desk, and glanced at the neatly framed photo. Three small children seemed to frolic happily in front of a palatial building. They actually *hadn't* been frolicking or happy at the time. Lilly knew this because she was the middle child. They were in the midst of one of the myriad conflicts which defined childhood.

There was an unceasing array of active disagreements, dramas, and perceived wrongs from which to draw each day's fodder, all utterly inconsequential in retrospect. Lilly sighed. She'd had little patience for that sort of nonsense, and escaped into her books at every opportunity. Fortunately, Chinese parents encouraged such studiousness. Unlike *these* people.

She never understood the utter contempt Americans had for education. Or, for that matter, how they accomplished anything. Navigating the American political hierarchy had only served to heighten the mystery. It seemed as if every aspect of American culture was designed to thwart real success, to stifle real ideas. Lilly understood the likely answer. She had read of such things happening toward the end of a country's life cycle. Such confusion was a common affliction during such times.

It was the way some of the great Chinese dynasties fell, as well. The Han had emerged as a cultural force after establishing military hegemony. To an observer in their heyday, the sources of their ascendancy were manifest: a universal and uncorrupt system of examinations through which talent was tapped, economic support for scholarship, and a culture which venerated learning and the arts. In short, a court which lent the nation an enlightened personality. The same observer living in the latter days of that dynasty would see equally evident signs of decline: a weak monarchy mismanaged by self-serving eunuchs and venal officials, rampant graft and favoritism, a capriciously corrupt justice system, disdain for true scholarship, and the elevation of obsequious flattery to an artform.

Lacking historical perspective, he would marvel that such a civilization could have flourished in the first place, that men so small could have achieved *anything*. It was the illusion under which everyone labored: that their time and place somehow were representative of what had been or would be. Lilly decided she simply had arrived late to the party. She missed the birth and wedding, and was just in time for the funeral.

Throughout her childhood, Lilly hid in her books and successfully cloistered herself from the pointless bustle of the playground. Nor were her fellow children the myth of propriety that American parents seemed to imagine them. Her brother had suffered permanent brain damage at the age of eight when an otherwise inconsequential bully hit him on the head with a brick. She looked in on him every few years, at least until the Front made travel impossible.

The bully later got a scholarship, and worked on Wall Street when last she checked. Lilly did not feel resentment toward him, or revel in his likely demise when New York fell. Nor did she abhor the injustice which left her brother a drooling, wheelchair-bound vegetable for the last forty years while his assailant prospered. She realized the subjective nature of justice.

It wasn't for Lilly to judge, simply to observe and from those observations deduce. Or more precisely, induce; for science is by nature inductive, and only a fool confounds the two. Lilly almost was certain her brother had perished in the recent upheavals in China. She probably could have used her influence to rescue him, but did not. What purpose would it have served? Living or dead, a vegetable is a vegetable. She had made her choice. Regret ceased to have meaning once the Front appeared, along with a great many other things.

When the photo was taken, the children had pretended to be happy for a moment, a minor concession to their parents. This was the true difference between Chinese and American children. It wasn't respect or diffidence or any of the other qualities which Westerners commonly ascribed to them. The grass always is greener, and the greenest grass sits atop the bog. No, the difference was of a more practical nature. Chinese children knew the art of appearance, to smile when needed, to dissemble. And Chinese parents accepted this. American children and parents had warred for centuries, but never came to this obvious and honorable truce.

In ten minutes, Lilly would meet with her principal researcher, a protege of sorts. He was utterly unlike her, and she wanted to keep it that way. Would it be more merciful to kill him? She seriously wondered this sometimes. Well, not exactly *wondered*. Like most thoughtful individuals, Lilly concluded early in life that killing people almost always *was* the right thing to do. Her current concern was of a more pragmatic nature, one of myriad internal debates which occupied her rare idle moments.

There were eight principal investigators, each working separately and each reporting directly to her. None had been told there were others, though Lilly would have been disappointed if they didn't consider that possibility. This was the system she had settled on with the President, though it made her wonder whether she too had secret counterparts, perhaps even with the same title and budget. Lilly had done some rough calculations, and the available resources of the government would at most support two such efforts. She doubted they would spread themselves so thin, especially with the present military demands. Unless there was something significant she didn't know.

In Lilly's experience, there *always* was something significant she didn't know. It was the nature of science, politics, and knowing. Lilly wasn't sure how she felt about a doppelganger, though. When she had been tapped to lead the effort, she didn't balk at the responsibility. She was under no illusion what it was or would become, though the title and scope were more modest back then. With crystal clarity, the path shone before her. Until the Front was remediated, the need would grow more and more dire. Her team ultimately would be the last line between humanity and oblivion.

This was what she was born to do, and it seemed natural that she had been chosen. Besides, there were no other real contenders. Ever since the crucial missteps of the first year, superfluous considerations had vanished. Perhaps not from the bureaucracy, but certainly from the thinking of senior leadership. They wanted to live, and all other considerations were subordinate to this. It was that simple. The choice had to be the best one. There was no cronyism, political correctness, favor-mongering, or good old-fashioned politics. To survive, they needed to put the right person in charge. Not the one best at convincing people they are great or winning grants or publishing papers. The one actually most likely to save the world.

Lilly was not surprised that this was her, she just was surprised they had the sense to figure it out. Roman history abounded with such examples. The Senate and people's Tribunes bickered and quarreled until they brought the Republic to the edge of destruction. But when disaster truly was at their doorstep, fear did what wisdom could not. They appointed a dictator, a great General of their age, to contend with it. However unworthy the elected leaders may have been, at least they acknowledged the existence of greatness and begged its help in direst need. It was this and this alone which saved the Republic time and time again from the fruits of perfidious democracy. As much as she knew herself to be the natural choice, the only choice, she still was surprised to see that choice made by people such as these.

Lilly rarely found it useful to form opinions of politicians. They were largely interchangeable, and all operated according to simple principles. If she *had* troubled to form an opinion of President Larisse, or Maggie as she knew her, it would be that she was marginally worse than average. In politics, that was saying a lot. If they *did* survive, she was sure that all sorts of maneuvering would ensue. Who could say whether Lilly would emerge as the savior of the world or an inconvenience to be discarded, perhaps even vilified? It didn't really matter. She had died long before any of this happened. All that remained was to see whether anyone else would live. How she was viewed posthumously was of no consequence.

One of the advantages of being at the top is the view. It also is one of the dangers. The distilled view which underlings choose to present may omit or distort important details. It is a view seen through the eyes of others, assembled piece-meal according to their taste. An avid student of history, Lilly was well-aware of this, and found it best to inform herself. Without drawing attention to the fact, she often examined the raw data directly, read her subordinates' unfinished files, and perused their analyses. As Director, she had unfettered access, but preferred to be discreet. The last thing she needed was an atmosphere of intrigue and suspicion.

She wasn't worried that someone deliberately would keep something from her. While she couldn't rule out such a possibility, it was the unintentional lacunae which concerned her. But there was more to it than that. It was precisely the ability to see the bigger picture that allowed a leader to draw conclusions, make decisions, transcend those they commanded. It wasn't a matter of politics or power, but of effectiveness. Perhaps she could see something they could not. And though the groups didn't know about one another, she still could act as a means of sharing information, focusing inquiries, and preventing unnecessary duplication.

The pattern wasn't obvious, even from the top. Lilly's suspicions had grown over time, and several recent pieces of data had confirmed them. In particular, certain implied parameters seemed inconsistent between different sources of observation. Inconsistency is the engine which drives discovery, and this was no different. Over the last month, suspicion became hypothesis, and hypothesis became near-certainty. Further tests would be required, of course. One couldn't rely on mere observation; active experiments were necessary.

Even if everything she theorized was confirmed, there remained the question of what could be done with this new information. There was no doubt in her mind what it implied. Hope. A very slim hope with countless attendant caveats and assumptions, but hope nonetheless. And any hope was better than no hope. Perhaps she finally could offer it in earnest, instead of the merciful lie purveyed so far.

It did not surprise Lilly that none of her teams had detected the effect, nor was she disappointed. It was mere accident that led her to spot it, however obvious it may have seemed once fully discerned. Besides, nobody else was in a position to do so. Nor would they be. This hope was hers and hers alone, for the moment. She had analyzed it in detail and produced a report of her findings. It reminded her of the good old days, when she actually did research that people read and understood. Back before her job became distilling complex truths into succinct lies for the fools that other fools had voted for. Back when she wasn't Madame Director, which made her feel so terribly useless.

Of Lilly's eight direct reports, Robert was her favorite. From the beginning, he reminded her of her younger self. Doubtless he was destined for similar disappointment, especially in a country like this. He was incredibly bright by her estimation, and her estimation was not a forgiving one. She had little patience for his self-deprecation, though. By now she was pretty sure it wasn't an affectation, though she would have preferred that it were. Instead, it was a pointless obstruction to the clear exchange of information.

Information. Yes, perhaps she would give the file to *him*. She had debated whether to give it to all eight groups at once, but decided to start with just one. There were arguments in favor of both approaches. Her discovery could be of critical importance, but it also could be a red herring. If she revealed it to everyone, other potentially fruitful paths of inquiry would be abandoned. On the other hand, the chances of successfully making use of it would increase. The strategy she settled on was a simple one: reveal it to a single group first, measure their progress, and proceed from there. She could share it with some or all of the others as circumstances dictated.

Yes, the initial recipient would be Robert. He had the least formal training, but exhibited the greatest faculty for flexible thought. He also knew how to keep his mouth shut. And the best part was that he had no discernible ego. Lilly learned long ago that the greatest obstacle to success in any field was ego. She had one in the distant past, and she intended to keep it there. Her present actions were directly attuned to the problem at hand, it did not matter to whom credit was assigned. This was one benefit of being dead.

CHAPTER 38

Day 873 — Dwill, Utah

Marissa held Rielle by the shoulders and explained quietly, as she did every day. "You have to learn, honey. One day you may need what you learn."

"But why doesn't anybody else need what they learn?" she replied with impeccable child-logic.

"Because they have gone away."

"On vacation?" Rielle wondered.

"That's right, but not a good vacation. The bad kind." Rielle had not known there was such a thing as a bad vacation. If it was bad, then it wasn't vacation. It was school.

It was getting late, and Rielle knew that mommy would be angry if she was late for school. Today she wouldn't win, but tomorrow she would try again. One day soon, mommy would let her go on vacation too.

Before she left, Rielle turned.

"Mommy, Suebee said that bad things are coming. She said they would get us soon. I'm scared."

Marissa squeezed hard, and pressed her cheek against Rielle's. "No, honey. While we're together, we're safe. The bad things will just pass us right by. You'll see. We just have to hold each other and never waver in our love."

This time Rielle could feel the wetness on mommy's face.

Marissa stood up and wiped her eyes. "Never mind mommy, Rielle."

She suddenly brightened, and smiled at her daughter. "No, the bad things won't get us ...," she gently patted Rielle's behind, "but only if you go to school and learn how to stop them."

Marissa handed her daughter a lunch basket, and saw her

off. She waved cheerfully from the front door, a picture perfect mom in a picture perfect home. Except for the thigh-high weeds covering the lawn. There was no bus, so Rielle would walk. Marissa didn't worry about such things, not like she used to be. For her part, Rielle was proud she was old enough that mommy would let her walk all by herself.

The streets were empty except for the odd light in a house here or there. Rielle wasn't sure, but the homes seemed less crisp and clean than when she was younger. But at five she almost was grown up. Maybe things got messier as she grew up, or maybe she just noticed messiness more. She was unsure, but it didn't bother her.

When she got to school, the door was open. Nobody bothered locking it these days. There were so few people around, and they all knew one another. Besides, there was nothing to steal.

Rielle went straight to classroom six. It was the only one in use. For a while there had been a class in room three, but one day the teacher left. This made Rielle sad. What if he came back, but all the kids were gone? What if there was nobody left to teach? Maybe he would join them in room six. Three teachers and three students, it would be like having a new daddy. Suddenly, she was sad.

Room six looked like it always did. Mr. Brendon was clean-cut, and had a permanent smile plastered on his face. To an adult it may have passed for genuine, but not to Rielle. It was like one of those masks clowns wear. She always felt a bit icky looking at it, but still was glad he was there.

He taught them interesting things about god and aliens. Sometimes they discussed the government too. She never told mommy the things she learned, but mommy never asked. It seemed to be enough for Rielle just to learn things.

The school day was unremarkable. The teacher read a little from a Polish history textbook. Apparently, Poland *was* history, whatever that meant. Then they did some drawing.

Ms. Gonnelly didn't show up, and Mr. Brendon said that she would be back next week. He also said there would be a test, and it was very important to focus on studying for the next few days.

This made Rielle nervous. Nobody had mentioned tests before. She would have to ask mommy about this. Suebee was in a sullen mood, and didn't say much. But toward the end of the day, she came over and gave Rielle a furtive little hug before running out the door. Mr. Brendon waved as Rielle left for the day. It made her feel good. He never waved before.

When Rielle got home, she found the door open. Like the school, mommy didn't bother locking it anymore. There was no need to. When daddy first went on vacation, she kept it locked. But one day she stopped. Just like the gun. A few days after he left, she stopped carrying that too. Maybe she didn't want to scare him when he came back. Rielle hoped it would be soon.

She went inside and called out, but nobody answered. Upstairs, mommy's door was closed. That meant mommy was sleeping, so she went back down and looked around. Usually there was dinner when Rielle came home. But mommy must be tired, so she let her sleep.

Suddenly, she had an idea. She would be a grown-up girl. She would make dinner herself. Rielle looked around, but all the cupboards were empty. She wondered where mommy kept all the food. She would have to ask, even if it meant waking mommy.

Rielle went upstairs and opened the door. Mommy was on the bed with her gun in her hand and lots of red goo next to her. Rielle went over and shook her. She didn't wake up. Then Rielle saw a note on the table. Sometimes mommy left notes when she was going to be away.

It read, "Tell dad I'm sorry."

Rielle went downstairs, and sat on the couch. She wondered when mommy would wake up to make dinner.

CHAPTER 39

Day 734 — San Diego, California

Every time he entered her office, Robert instinctively expected Lilly to look up and smile. Or at least offer a hint of acknowledgment as he stood there, waiting. She had, after all, hired him and promoted him and given him an unholy level of responsibility. What else could she be working on? There was one thing that mattered, and only one. It wasn't as if an election approached, or she had to prepare a speech or work on research of her own.

Robert wondered whether she was writing something personal, perhaps a letter or memoir. But for whom? There would be nobody to read it. He always had viewed her as a machine, calculating and rational but without emotion or any notion of personal investment. It occurred to him that she wasn't Spock. However dignified and dispassionate, she was a real person with a past and with people she cared about. Maybe she had private griefs too. In fact, it was certain she had private griefs. Many private griefs. Everybody did. And nobody could have done the things she did without other sorts of feelings too.

It was a testament to her composure that Robert hadn't even considered the burden which knowledge of her coming demise must place on her seasoned mind. Everything he felt, she probably felt as well. They both were astute cancer patients.

He caught himself. It would not do to pretend familiarity. He should not assume she was without feelings, but he also should not presume to know what those feelings were. If she kept them hidden, it was for a reason, and it was not his place to pry.

Lilly looked up and seemed to notice him for the first time.

"If you're going to linger, sit down." She distractedly motioned him to a chair.

"We have a meeting," he began uncertainly. So much for the lofty title, he instantly became a hesitant child in her presence. He wondered if there was anybody *she* felt that way around. Robert looked at his watch to make sure. "At 9:30," he noted. It now was 9:45.

Lilly seemed confused and irritated for a moment, but then grew attentive and put the cap on her pen.

"Yes." She gave no apology or explanation for making him wait, but he had grown accustomed to that.

Robert began to speak, but she waved him to stop.

"I know what you are going to say."

"But, I...," he began.

She gave him a stern look. "There is no means of producing a meaningful impediment to the Front."

Robert seemed surprised, and Lilly explained.

"It was pretty obvious when you first explained the effect. Anybody with an ounce of sense could see it."

He wanted to object that she had agreed with him, had shared his hope. But she hadn't directly accused him of being obtuse, and he would appear defensive.

Lilly smiled. "You forget that I have the benefit of both a great deal more knowledge than you, and a great deal more data."

"Then why...," was all Robert could stammer.

"I thought it would be obvious," she replied. Then, almost to herself, "no, I suppose it wouldn't be — that's why it works."

She looked at him. "There never was any real hope. You know that, and I know that. Everybody here knows that too."

Lilly waved in the direction of the hall to indicate the 'everybody' of which she spoke.

"We all know this, but nobody wants it to be true," she continued. "And if you don't want something to be true, it must not be. This is the basis for all philosophy and religion."

She cupped her hands together and raised them as if throwing flowers in the air. Then she blew on the imaginary petals. "Thus, there is real hope."

Lilly fixed Robert's eyes. "Not a real chance, just real hope."

She slid back into her seat and sighed. "This is the difference between us. Between me and you and them." Once more she gestured. He never had seen her exhibit any physicality, and this was unexpected. "For me, there is no hope — real or not. There only are the facts. And the fact is ... "

"There is no solution." Robert finished the sentence for her.

"Your words, my sentiment." she smiled.

"So all this is ... "

"To keep hope alive, to keep busy, to give purpose. To create a fiction we may die with." Once again, she sighed. "Or, at least you."

"And what of you?" Robert blurted out, instantly appalled that he had the temerity to ask such a personal question.

Lilly smiled. "What of me? I will die too, but I will die in reality." There was a melancholy pause before she added, "it is not my choice, but it would be my preference."

"So, what should I do? Now I know too." It was unfair that she had dragged him down with her. He was supposed to keep hope alive for everybody else. How could he do that now?

"You've known all along. You came here to tell me. This would have implicated you."

"Who cares? How am I supposed to face everybody now?" He was angry and didn't care if he pissed her off. She had betrayed him, betrayed everyone, wasted all their time, kept them working for her, bound, unnecessarily, when they could have used those last few invaluable weeks for something more important. More important? What could possibly matter? Deep down, Robert knew she was right and hated himself almost as much at this moment.

"That same question existed before I told you anything. And now, you have not compromised yourself. You will not have to lie. You can die uncompromised." Lilly stood and walked to the window.

"How? When I walk out that door, people will ask me."

"Then do not walk out that door. Use the window."

Was this her form of humor, asking him to commit suicide? She was Asian; isn't that what they did when things went wrong?

"I don't think it actually opens, though," she continued, smiling.

"Or, you can walk out that door and tell them what I say to tell them. They will hate me, and that is fine. I gave you your burden when it suited my purpose, and I will take your burden now that it suits my purpose."

"But why not keep *me* in the dark? Why not let me present my findings, and just object to something technical, as you always have? According to your theory, I would latch onto any hope, however implausible, and pursue it."

Lilly softened. "Because I like you, Robert." She paused and faced the window, dreamily gazing at the harbor. A slight fog rose from the water. One almost could think that all was right with the world. As if it ever had been.

"Go home to Dallas, Robert. You weren't cut out for this. You asked for leave, and now you have it. That is where you would like to die, and that is where you should. I've arranged transport."

Robert looked horrified as she turned to face him.

"Do not be so upset. I say this not from anger, but from observation. It is clear to me." After a moment she quietly recited a poem in Chinese. In answer to to Robert's bewildered look, she translated, "it is better to die where you are now, than where you are not later."

Without warning, Lilly's expansive tone vanished, and she

returned to normal.

"Listen carefully. You value your integrity. I do not, but I will help you preserve it. You must say exactly what I tell you, nothing more and nothing less."

Robert listened attentively.

"You have been reassigned to a new initiative in Dallas. You are forbidden to discuss its nature with anybody. In your absence, I will assume direct responsibility over the project. I have several new ideas I will present at a project-wide meeting on Tuesday."

"But those are lies," Robert objected.

"Are they?" Lilly asked as she sat down and looked at her papers, clearly signaling an end to the meeting. "Everything I have instructed you to say strictly is true. If others assume that the new initiative will save us, that is *their* choice."

"What new initiative?"

"Let's call it project don't look a gift horse in the mouth." She smiled before beginning to write.

As he opened the door, Lilly looked up and quietly added, "For what it's worth, I would have chosen you to lead the effort even if success was a real possibility. I think you could have achieved it."

Robert turned to say good luck, but he realized those words were without meaning. As he walked down the hall, dreading the future, he suddenly felt free. He was a student who just failed a final exam. There would be consequences, but for now his time was his again.

CHAPTER 40

Day 1511 — Australia

Dave shook his head and wiped his brow. The car just wouldn't start. God, he hated this shit. Why did everything constantly have to be "improved"? There was this restless assumption that motion was progress, that there is such a direction as forward. For centuries, people made do with the same functional technology. The wheel worked, why change it? No need to prove you're doing something innovative, demonstrate growth for shareholders. Just build more of them. It was that simple.

But in recent years, if you ran a solid company with solid, consistent profits, you'd get ousted by some activist fund. And if you found something you liked in the store, better stock up; chances were it would be gone when you needed another, replaced by some "new and improved" piece of crap.

Nowhere was this more pronounced than with cars. In the old days, cars were tools, adaptable, usable. Now they were big plastic toys. Just like phones and computers and all the other dumbed down pieces of garbage Dave had in his life. Just when you found something you liked, something that *worked*, it was gone. Of course, it's not like there *was* any forward anymore. Well there was, but only for one thing and nobody called it an improvement.

The problem with cars was that they needed fuel, and the problem with *modern* cars was that they needed a very particular kind of fuel. Fuel could run out at the most inopportune times. Worse, there was no substitute for good old gas. Or good new gas, as it were. Modern cars were ultra-safe, finely-tuned, eco-friendly. They did one thing very well, but if you needed to run them rough in a bind you were shit out of luck.

And Dave *was* shit out of luck. Gas was scarce, but he

had brought several large jugs of cooking grease just in case. Now he discovered they didn't work. He just couldn't believe it was as bad as everybody said. In the old days he would have screwed around a bit, and the thing would run on paint thinner, alcohol, kitchen grease ... pretty much anything short of piss. These days, he had to get a factory firmware update for even the slightest change. There only was one thing he could do with a modern car when it stopped: get out. And that's exactly what Dave Gorland was forced to do.

As invariably is the case when a car runs out of gas, it did so in a bad spot. It was more than just a "bad spot", in fact. It was a *very* bad place in space and time. The road ran transverse to the Front, and he had been racing to get past the point where it curved away. Not that this mattered now.

The Front was creeping along at its leisurely pace, and he no longer had any chance of making that turn. So Dave was forced to do what he desperately hoped to avoid, what he planned to do only if he found himself on the short end of time. He would walk.

He had fretted about that possibility ever since embarking on the long stretch of road. The problem was that he didn't know exactly *where* the Front was. And there was no touch and run; if it made contact, he was done.

Dave did not have nerves of steel, was not the stereotypical Aussie, trading punches with bikers and killing venomous snakes with his bare hands. In fact, he'd never met a stereotypical Aussie. Most of his friends were quiet yuppies. No, Dave wasn't tearing along on an adrenaline-fueled high. With every passing moment he grew more and more anxious. And now his fear had made the worst happen. No, second worst. It wasn't over yet.

The car wouldn't make it a hundred meters off-road in this terrain, but *he* could. He'd entered the two hundred kilometre stretch of road with only a half tank of gas. He estimated about 30 litres. Based on experience, at 100 kph he'd get decent mileage and a range of over 240 kilometres, well past the bend and into the next town.

Of course, "town" was a euphemism. There weren't real towns out here, but there *would* be a store and gas station. Hopefully, there even would be gas. That's why he had avoided the major roads. Sure there were more service stations along the highway, but those facilities had to be long dry from the steady stream of evacuees.

Dave was late to the party, and would find nothing there. However, nobody used the back roads. There were fewer supply points, but they were more likely to *have* supplies. According to his map, the next station was right past the bend where the road veered away from the Front and toward safety.

The problem was that Dave didn't have the nerve to stick to 100 kph. It took effort. Every time his will slackened slightly, his foot leaned on the gas pedal. And when he *did* manage to keep to 100, the tingling in his spine grew stronger and stronger. He envisioned a towering red wall bearing down on him. Surely that was how the Front really looked, if you could see it.

This was the big problem, what made it so scary: that you couldn't visualize it. That the mind could not comprehend or classify or locate it. He couldn't say, "there it is, and it looks like such and such." There was no form, no *being* to it. Even monsters had form, looked like something that somebody could describe. It *truly* was an unknown in every sense of the word.

Come to think of it, maybe the Front was closer than he thought. Dave's peril suddenly seemed imminent, and an overwhelming sense of urgency enveloped him. A panicked need to run as fast and hard as he could. He brought the car up to 110, then 130. It held steady, but rode a bit rough. He edged higher, but the car didn't like it and he eased off.

There was no reason not to stick to 130. Nobody would

mistake the road for a highway, but it was paved and straight. Moreover, Dave could see far ahead. Going 130 seemed a safe bet. At least until some shredded truck tires by the side of the road made him less sanguine. He decided not to push his luck; there was no spare tire, and the last thing he needed was to end in a ditch. He dropped back to 100. Forty five minutes later, Dave noticed something wrong. The orange fuel light was glowing.

What the hell? It took a few moments before he realized his mistake. At 130, the car's mileage dropped significantly. Why didn't he think of that, dammit? The head-wind probably hadn't helped either. It was ok, though. He still had enough fuel. And there always was his special reserve. That made it sound like a fancy drink. This was the opposite of a fancy drink: two five-gallon jugs of rancid cooking oil he had set aside when the fuel shortage first started.

It had been a purely precautionary measure, and he never expected to use them. Dave hadn't driven much recently, in fact. He had stayed home, stoically planning to meet his end there. At least until he awoke in a cold sweat one morning, terrified that it was too late, that he had missed the proverbial bus. As it happened he narrowly beat the cutoff, and very well may have been the last person to make it South. If he made it South. This was the third leg, and the critical one. After that, the rest of the trip was away from the Front.

Even when the fuel light came on, Dave was certain he had at least a gallon or two in reserve. He had come 176 kilometres so far, and if he kept to 100 kph he'd be fine. At kilometre 179 the car began convulsing, and quickly sputtered to a halt.

Dave stared at the gauge in disbelief, feeling betrayed. His old Toyota always had two gallons in reserve when the light came on. But this was a Subaru. Why would they do that? Why would they trick him, and leave no safety margin? Some engineer's stupidity was going to kill him. He wanted to check the user-manual to see if he was right, but his stomach wouldn't let him. He had to move quickly. First he would try the emergency cooking oil, and pray it worked. It didn't.

After spending five minutes trying, Dave had to make a choice. His body decided long before his mind caught up. It only was with effort that he stopped himself from dashing off without any supplies. He hoped the Front had gotten the engineer who did this to him. No, the whole damned company. Of course it had, but he didn't feel any better.

Dave already had a bag packed for emergencies, and he grabbed anything else he thought could be useful. Damned car. Thankfully, it was 3:45 PM and the desert sun wasn't at full furnace. Heck, at night it even could get cold. If he made it until then. Dave didn't need to guess what would happen next. For the last few years the TV lineup had been filled with dumb plot devices involving people running from the Front, or thinly veiled metaphors for it.

It was just as bad with literature. Dave was a buyer for Great Abandon Press (as in "wild abandon," not "abandon a baby," he always pointed out), small but established. They had been inundated with manuscripts over the last couple of years. Family running from a radioactive cloud. People waiting for a meteor to hit. His favorite was the man running from time. Wow, deep ... if you're a freshman in college. Next!

Why did anyone even submit these things? Or write them, for that matter. The real Front would take them long before their cheesy allegory saw print. Even if the world's greatest manuscript *was* published, it wouldn't achieve immortality. There wouldn't be anybody to read it. The only reason Great Abandon stayed open was to keep themselves busy, take their minds off the obvious.

He thanked the submitters for taking his mind off his impending doom by writing endless bad variants of how it would arrive. Why didn't anybody write love stories? Not ones that ended tragically with the arrival of a deadly solar flare. No, just plain love stories. Guy, girl, emotions, crisis, denouement, happy ending. He really should have quit his job, and spent his time reading old books at the library.

The one benefit of reading and watching all that schlock (as well as the news, which often was worse) was that Dave had a very good sense of what to expect. At it's original speed of 0.32 kph, the Front would cover 8 kilometres per day. But that was then, and this was now. When the Front hit Darwin back in August, it had been traveling over 0.6 kph per hour. Almost two months later, it had blown through Perth at around 0.8 kph. It had sped up a bit in the two weeks since then, gaining velocity as it approached the antipode.

Dave thought of the people right near the end, on the Southeast coast of New Zealand. Those Kiwis always seemed like a nice bunch, though he'd run into a few of a rougher sort from Invercargill. That would be one of the last places hit, but it was a real shit-hole and he wasn't sorry. They were Scots by descent. Dave loved Scotland; he had been there twice, and always enjoyed it. It was kind of sad that this whole thing had come out of that beautiful country, to his mind.

But in Invercargill it was different. For some reason he couldn't help but remember that line from the Lord of the Rings: "a terrible and mutilated life form." It was as if some evil wizard had taken those lovely people from Scotland and deformed them into ... something else.

Perhaps an antipode inverted things. Not just summer and winter, or the direction to the equator, or the constellations. Other things too. Less easily defined things, but crucial nonetheless. Did the Front do something similar? Maybe it absorbed the best parts of us and left just the residue. Unpleasant or not, none of the Kiwis deserved this. Sure they got a little extra time, but when it came the end would be worse.

Even in Australia, he still could think of the Front as a wall. It was a defined thing coming to get him. He just had to run fast enough to keep ahead of it. And when he came to the sea he could fling himself in and keep swimming. But in New Zealand it would emerge from the ground, consume them from below. There was no running, nowhere to run *to*. He shuddered at the thought.

Here and now, there *was* somewhere to go. Dave just needed to keep up a solid 20 kilometres per day. He could do that, as long as he didn't injure himself or get sick. And hopefully, he could make it to an abandoned town and grab a car. At least he knew what direction to walk: straight away from the Front. Once he'd gotten about half a day's head start, he'd check the map and come up with a plan. But for now, he'd already wasted time and didn't want the Front catching up with him before he even started. Dave suddenly got spooked. He started hiking, barely pausing to zip up the pack.

There are many types of desert, some more passable than others. The word solely is defined in terms of average rainfall. Dave remembered the trick question they used to ask in elementary school: "what's the world's biggest desert?" The answer was Antarctica, of course. Or at least it was before changing weather patterns cost it that title. Now, the Sahara was the largest. Fortunately, Dave wasn't in the Sahara, or the Great Victoria Desert or the Great Sandy Desert or any other Great desert. Deserts with 'Great' in their name generally were bad news. They tended to have lots of sand-dunes and other features which made them impassable. Not that *any* desert should be taken lightly. The first rule of wilderness survival was that a man can die twenty yards from his car. Well, that wasn't really a rule but definitely something that had been drilled into him. Never underestimate nature.

Fortunately for Dave, the terrain in which he found himself was eminently navigable. It mostly consisted of a mix of scrub, brush, and flat hard soil with a thin layer of sand. In fact he wasn't sure whether he even was *in* a named desert, or just one of the interstitial areas. But whatever its formal designation, no desert was *easy*. Heatstroke, sunstroke, and dehydration were constant threats. And on a longer journey — which Dave very well could be facing if he missed the town by even a kilometre or two — food would become an issue. In theory. Dave remembered what his camp instructor told him in high school: people only die of starvation among other people. In the desert, thirst would take you first. Only when all other needs had been satisfied, did starvation have the leisure to ply its art.

Dave had good boots, a hat, and enough gear to manage for a day or two without trouble. If he didn't find the town by then, he would have bigger problems anyway. It was early Spring and the sun wasn't too bad. Temperatures could reach into the high 40's C in the deep desert, and he prayed they wouldn't have a heat wave. So far so good, though. It was around 27C during the day and probably wouldn't drop below 16C at night. If he had to be stuck on a long hike without proper gear, the conditions were about as good as could be hoped for.

Dave made it about 10 kilometres before deciding to take a breather. His watch read 6:28 PM. The temperature had been cool and the terrain flat, and Dave hadn't pushed himself or sweated profusely. Dehydration wasn't an issue ... yet. However, the sun was setting, and he wasn't sure what to do. He checked his compass and map, and confirmed that his bearing was directly away from the Front. However, he would have to veer left 30 degrees to reach the village, and the longer he waited the greater the detour. Dave decided he was more afraid of the Front catching up than of walking an extra few kilometres later. He could hoof it then, if needed.

Once in town, he would not require much time. Even if the place wasn't abandoned, he doubted anyone would give him trouble. He would find a car, hot-wire it if there was no key, and fill it up. Then, off at a reasonable clip toward the Southeast.

The problem was light. Dave wasn't sure when the moon would rise, if at all. He also wasn't sure how long his flashlight would last. It was an LED model, advertised at about 80 hours on a full charge. But that could be a lie. Besides, he had no idea how much juice was left in the batteries. After the car, he wasn't going to assume anything about the invisible levels which governed his fate. One unseen menace was enough.

The stars would provide some light, but from his experience it would be too little to hike safely. If there was one thing he didn't need, it was a broken ankle. All the wilderness training in the world wouldn't help him limp away from the Front in time. And wasn't night when all the really dangerous stuff came out? Dave didn't think there were any large predators in these parts, but wasn't sure.

There was a saying that there was nothing in Australia which couldn't kill you. Come to think of it, couldn't that be said about anything? Of course, it just was marketing meant to impress tourists with the Aussie's rough and tumble image. Mad Max and all that. If there were rough and tumble Aussie's, Dave wasn't one of them. But after some consideration, he decided to take his chances and continue hiking. All those things *plus* the Front could kill him while he slept. At least on his feet he was one threat down. He decided to try for 20 kilometres before taking a brief rest.

As it turned out, Dave's concerns about the night were misplaced. If there were any animals, they paid him no mind. Between the stars and his flashlight he could see just fine. This turned out to be a mixed blessing, however. The problem was Dave's body. He had planned on pacing himself — walking, resting, walking, then sleeping. As long as he kept to that regimen, the Front wouldn't catch up with him.

That made sense, but sense had nothing to do with how he ultimately behaved. A wall of death was coming for him, and it was getting faster. If Dave stopped, he was frittering his life away. And what if he dozed off and overslept? Would he even know, if the Front caught him sleeping? The worst would be if it became a race between him and the Front. What if it caught him just as salvation was in sight, and he would have made it if only he hadn't indulged in a bit of shut-eye. When lost in the woods, all one's learned wisdom vanishes. When fired upon, all one's training goes out the window. And when an invisible wall of death approaches, however slowly, no amount of reasoning or intelligence can keep one from panicking. And Dave *was* panicking. It didn't happen all at once, with a dramatic flailing of arms and hysterical screaming. This was more insidious, creeping up on him unawares. Slowly, like the Front and perhaps just as deadly. So Dave walked without slackening, without breaks.

Of course, this could not continue. Dave knew this, but couldn't help it. He tried to sleep once, but was unable. He simply was too agitated. So he just kept going until physically unable, then he rested for a few minutes and continued. Besides leading to bad choices, panic itself took energy. And water. Dave was dehydrating quickly. He had exhausted his two liter supply, but hadn't touched any food.

Finally he sat down, and forced himself to take a bite of a roll. There wasn't much food, but he had to have *something* to keep going. All he needed was to make it to town, a car would do the rest. The bread stuck to his palate, and he couldn't swallow. That's when he realized how parched he was. He had iodine tablets, but he'd need a water source to make use of them. Even a puddle would do. He laughed. A puddle. The average annual rainfall was only a few inches. There wouldn't just be a puddle sitting around. He looked at the map.

It was a road map, not a topo map — but it showed some major features: large bodies of water, mountains, a few rivers. Dave noticed a thin blue snake on the map. It probably was just a stream, but it would do. He couldn't quite make out how far it was, maybe another ten kilometres. In the dark, the real thing wasn't visible from where he was standing. However, there was no danger of missing it. The stream curved around, and he would have to ford it anyway in order to reach the town. He just hoped it wasn't too wide or difficult to cross. Worst case, he'd follow it toward the town a bit and cross at the easiest point. At least he'd have water.

According to the map, there was a small spike of rock right before the stream. It turned out that Dave had come farther than he thought, and after only four kilometres he spotted the formation. In the strong moonlight preceding dawn, there could be no mistaking it. Dave saw the tell-tale spike, but no river. Maybe things weren't quite to scale; it *was* a tourist map, and probably exaggerated the size of the spike. Dave barely was able to keep his footing by this point. If it didn't show up in another kilometre or two he would be in big trouble. He supposed there were ways to get water from the desert scrub, but had no idea how. It probably would turn out to be poisonous, anyway. Then Dave heard a faint gurgling. He lurched forward and, with what little energy he could muster, dragged himself toward the sound.

The gurgling grew louder, its chords rich and lyrical. Dave stopped, his stomach a knot of despair. It was an ancient despair, one which has been with travelers since there first were any: the siren's call, the long trek to a dry oasis, the last failure of hope. Before him was a deep chasm extending as far as he could see in either direction. And at its bottom a little stream babbled pleasantly. It seemed to be laughing, oblivious to the despair it caused or perhaps because of it. There was no way down, no way across, and no way around.

Dave sat down to cry, but could muster no tears. It wasn't just dehydration; he was the sort of guy who couldn't cry even if he wanted to. It was like being nauseous and unable to vomit.

That was something else he wished he could do at the moment, but simply was too parched.

He faced the direction of the Front. Was there a faint blurring of the air? Dave was sure he could see it, feel it. It would be upon him any minute. But he still was his own master, could choose his death. He couldn't cry or vomit, but he *could* die. He slowly put down his pack, took out a pad and pen, and began to write a note. Then he stopped and let out a hysterical laugh. Who would read it? It was a bit of a relief, that; he never would have known what to say. He should write a masterpiece, the greatest thing ever written — just like all those submitters. In a million years, some alien visitor would find it, wonder what it was, what language it was written in, perceive its beauty and his genius. Or use it for toilet paper. No, he just would write a message. A message to god.

Dave picked up the pen and wrote in big letters "Fuck You". More than anger, he felt embarrassment. It wasn't for letting anyone down. He *had* nobody to let down, at least not anymore. Nor would his death inconvenience anybody. None of his string of choices were at fault either. Not the car or the fuel or waiting until the last minute to flee or fleeing at all. These days, there was no right or wrong as far as such things were concerned. Nobody could be saved, so cowardice and courage had no meaning in a post-Front world. The source of embarrassment was much more basic. It was the shame of being killed by something so slow even a child a could outrun it. *This* was what had defeated humanity? *This* was his conqueror?

Not *his* conqueror. He still had one choice left to him. Dave put down the pen and pad, and stood. It was around twenty meters to the edge. He made a running start, but stopped about six meters short, walked to the edge, and peered down. He put out his arms and willed himself to fall forward, dive gracefully through air and water and stone, deep through the Earth, the

Front, and straight to hell. No, he decided, not that easily.

Dave returned to his backpack, nestled in the sand, and sat down defeated. He looked at the note, and decided it wasn't a message to god after all. Tearing off the sheet, he attached it to his shirt with a safety pin from the first aid kit. Then he turned to face the direction of the Front, and waited.

CHAPTER 41

Day 734 — San Diego, California

The Lilly of decades past bore little resemblance to the present one. She had been obsessive, a trait which remained in distilled form, but also temperamental, anxious, and borderline paranoid. She had been convinced that her colleagues would backstab her or steal her ideas. Despite young Lilly's many endearing qualities, strong grades, and impressive thesis, she had been unable to find a top tier academic position after earning her PhD.

This precipitated a breakdown of sorts, and she disappeared for almost two years. Rumor had it she was institutionalized and then homeless for a time, but she made no effort to set the record straight. In truth she had hidden in shame from her family and friends in the easiest way. She joined the Peace Corps under a slightly different transliteration of her Chinese name, and nobody inquired too closely. Not all her Peace Corps experiences had been good, but that was neither here nor there.

When Lilly returned from her tour, she still had to face her parents. First she visited her brother, though. For hours she sat there, studying his uncommunicative face, eyes open but dulled, mouth permanently gaping. What did her brother perceive, what did he feel? Did he know who she was? Lilly wondered if all this time he hadn't been maturing, just like her but trapped. When his future ended, he had been eight, brilliant, fast accelerating past her. Maybe that was what brought the bully, offended the stars above. Or maybe it just was bad fucking luck.

After four hours, Lilly felt her own eyes growing dull, as if he were drawing her soul out. Or dragging it down into whatever abyss he inhabited. She knew he wouldn't want that. She also knew she never could be whole. It had nothing to do with him, but she *had* lost the one thing which mattered to her. She was like her brother; her body just didn't know it.

Over the next 24 hours, Lilly turned over various options in her mind. Die in poverty. A mediocre career, sucking up to people far inferior to her. A family and children who would fail, like her. An honorable death. As the choices revolved in her mind, this last seemed by far the best one. She had been created to do physics. If she could not do it, she had no purpose. And a person with no purpose is no person at all.

But it was not in her nature to kill herself. Lilly was not clinically depressed, she did not wish to die in a biological sense. It was more of an abstraction, a wish simply not to be. Perhaps it was purely romantic. Sure, she *could* kill herself. But that would be pointless and illogical. If one should have died at a certain time, then everything which happens after is extra, outside the rules of the world. And the *other* option always remains. There is no need for fear, because you already are dead. There is no need for worry, because nothing can happen to you.

The solution was simple, Lilly declared herself dead. Not to the world or her parents or anybody else; they were irrelevant. It was of no consequence whether they held occasional trite communication with her or honored her corpse with a grand ceremony and annual remembrances. She declared herself dead to the only person who mattered. And since she was dead, that person never would tell. The shell which remained could engage in any behavior without shame or fear. The worst that could happen is what already *had* happened. And if ever the need arose, she could align the physical reality with the philosophical one.

The next few years were odd ones for Lilly. She adapted to her new outlook with aplomb. One danger to being dead is that it can breed apathy. However, her unusually energetic personality successfully avoided that pitfall. It turned out the dead Lilly was far better suited to both a career in academia and a political ascent. She was unconstrained by concerns about what others thought; the dead did not care for the judgments of the living. Nor was she hampered by shyness or other hangups.

She calculated what was needed to get a tenured position at Stanford: relentless self-promotion, promiscuous involvement in fashionable projects, and shameless attachment to the right mentors. And she got it. But she didn't stop there. A natural momentum took over. There was a lot of luck involved, of course, but the dead Lilly did not hesitate to make the most of opportunities. She was unhampered by inhibitions, no longer bound by her erstwhile weakness.

The door opened, and Robert entered. Lilly didn't allow this to distract her, and contemplated the papers in front of her a few moments longer. Besides, she had learned it was good to keep visitors waiting a bit. Finally, she shoved the folder into a drawer and looked up.

Not yet. She would decide what to do with the discovery later. To whom this hope would be revealed, and how. For now, she would hear what Robert had come up with on his own. With a bit of luck, he would relieve her of the need to make a decision. Maybe he had the answer.

CHAPTER 42

Day 856 — Near Denver, Colorado

The problem with walking is that it is quiet and solitary. Quiet and solitary activities provide ample opportunity for reflection. Dwight always had enjoyed this aspect when time to himself had been scarce, but now found it troubling. Thought is the enemy of courage, and it wasn't long before he began ruminating on every aspect of his plight.

Not long after he fled, Dwight realized his mistake. He knew there was another guard-post ahead, but wasn't sure where. When he set out, he had assumed it was located where the pass emerged from the mountains, a natural choke-point which could not easily be circumvented. As he progressed, Dwight grew less confident of this. In principle, it could be positioned anywhere along the way. It would not command as expansive a view, but that wasn't particularly germane to its purpose. The guards were there to obstruct traffic *from* Denver, not the other way.

But who could tell how these people thought. Dwight had been with the National Guard for years, and still had no idea. At first he imagined his commanders privy to information or insight he didn't possess, but quickly was disabused of this notion. If Dwight found their behavior unpredictable, it was because he had the misfortune to think rationally.

This realization had been disconcerting enough back then; its implications were more so now. If the guard-post wasn't in the obvious location, every step could bring Dwight into danger. Maybe he would spot the soldiers in time or hear them, but more likely they would see him first. As contemptible as the refugees seemed, Dwight didn't think them stupid. At least not all of them. If *they* had been easy to spot, so would he.

There was little cover along the road, and only a few feet of vegetation on either side before one reached the rock face. Though Dwight was adept at concealing himself while hunting, this was quite different from hiding in a blind. It simply was infeasible to hike ten miles without significant exposure.

Even if he had the time and patience to creep along, Dwight's flank was in danger from his betrayed comrades. He doubted the refugees themselves posed a threat, even if they made it through. But behind them was a more formidable enemy. Dwight estimated he had at best one day before the Front reached his former post. He could outwalk it, but not while playing at stealth. If he observed proper precautions and moved only under cover of darkness, he certainly would be overtaken. He had no choice but to remain in the open and hope for the best.

Whether or not the soldiers ahead knew of Dwight's treason, they probably would not hesitate to shoot him. Maybe the uniform would give them some small pause, *if* they spotted it. But Dwight himself probably would have shot someone in uniform as if they weren't. Anyone could murder a soldier and don his uniform. Without orders, the unit would not place itself in jeopardy to welcome an outsider. And of course, there was that other little thing. He *had* killed people in uniform, and it was possible the other guard-posts had been alerted.

Dwight's major regret was that he didn't kill his remaining comrades before leaving. Besides eliminating any danger of pursuit, it would have opened that side of the pass to civilian traffic. If he had been smart, he now would have a steady flow of civilians blocking for him. He need only have dropped back and waited for gunfire, to know where the guard-post was.

Then Dwight probably could have snuck in at night and blended with the other soldiers, at least long enough to slip past them. But it was a moot point now, and Dwight kicked himself for his folly. Keeping an eye on both his front and rear was nerve-wracking, and made for slower going than he was comfortable with.

It wasn't until noon the next day that Dwight had his first real scare. By then he was tired. He had hiked all night, albeit slowly and without much light due to the cloud cover. A cold wind had kicked up as well. As a result, Dwight wasn't as alert as he should have been. The tower already was visible by the time he noticed it between two trees. With a muttered curse, he ducked to the side. Jesus. If somebody spotted him, he was dead.

Even if they gave him a chance, he doubted he could talk his way out of this, especially if somebody like Mull was in charge. Dwight couldn't have come upon it at a worse time, either. After dark, he would have noticed the lights from afar and been hard to see. Come to think of it, why *hadn't* they spotted him? He wondered at the stillness of the camp. Shouldn't there be *some* commotion, even if they were unaware of him? There was no reason for the soldiers to be silent; a unit always generated a certain amount of hub bub.

After a few minutes, Dwight decided to risk a look. He cautiously peeked from behind the tree. There was no sign of life. Despite his slow pace, Dwight was sure he had put some significant distance between himself and the Front. He could afford to wait until sundown, just to be sure the post was empty. The next few hours were some of the tensest of his life. When it finally had grown dark enough for his comfort, Dwight made his move. There were no lights on the towers, and no sound emanated from any of the structures. Dwight doubted this unit had night vision goggles when his own hadn't. Unless it was an improbably patient trap, the post was deserted.

Dwight remembered a discussion he once had with an IT security expert at his university. When asked how best to secure a computer, the man had joked that he should fill it with concrete. There's no such thing as removing all risk, he explained. You simply protect against the most dangerous and easily addressable threats. You have no choice but to say, "if the enemy does such-and-such, he wins." And there *always* was a such-and-such, often many.

If this unit was clever enough to lay such a trap, Dwight decided, they win. The alternative was to remain paralyzed in fear until the Front won. With great caution, he inched toward the guard-post. Having manned one for some time, he knew there was no good angle of approach. Once in sight, there was nowhere to hide and no way around. There only was one reasonable thing to do. Taking a deep breath, Dwight stood and waved his arms, calling out his name, rank, and unit.

There was no response, but that didn't necessarily mean anything. Even if someone *was* there, they likely wouldn't say anything. Dwight cringed and awaited the gunshot. Well, there was no reason to keep standing and make a target of himself. He had sworn he wouldn't just let himself be killed like those damned civilians. He couldn't snipe at the tower from the trees because nobody was visible, but he could increase his chances by startling them.

Dwight suddenly sprinted toward the left tower, firing into the right one at an angle. He tried to aim where the soldiers would be sitting. Nothing happened. If *that* didn't draw a response, he was safe. And an idiot. He realized he just had alerted everybody within miles to his presence. If the unit was nearby, they would find him soon enough. He'd have to make a run for it. If he made it over the pass, the woods opened to the sides and he could get off the damned road. The problem was that he still didn't know how far it was.

Fortunately, it turned out Dwight had been right about one thing: the post *was* at the point where the pass emerged from the mountains. After another mile, he ducked off the road and made his way through a half mile of forest. Then he covered himself and relaxed. The soldiers wouldn't have dogs, so he should be safe where he was.

First thing in the morning, he would backtrack to the pass and see if anybody had returned. It was risky, but necessary. From this side, he would be able to spot them long before they spotted him. Maybe he even could grab a few supplies if it was abandoned. Dwight hadn't noticed a car at the guard post, but there could be one nearby. Despite his caution, he felt at ease for the first time in a while. The immediate peril had passed, and he had breathing room. In fact, he was fairly certain the entire contingent had deserted long ago. Perhaps they never had been posted in the first place.

Despite his exhaustion, Dwight found it difficult to fall sleep. He realized he wouldn't get far without rest, but that only made it harder. There certainly was time for it, but something about the Front's inexorable advance inspired a primal urge to run until physically unable. It was only with great effort that he managed to quell the rising panic. This seemed unfair. Now that he finally felt safe from men, his own mind wouldn't allow him even a brief respite.

Only when he awoke with a start, did Dwight realize he *had* managed to doze off. Sitting up in the dawn light, he caught himself and quickly flattened against the ground. Before he could recall his plan of the night before, he felt a cold wetness. Had he pissed himself during the night? There was a two-inch layer of snow on everything, and more was falling. He realized how exhausted he must have been to sleep through *this*.

Dwight decided to make his way back to the road, counting on the falling snow to erase any footprints. He knew better than to allow the blizzard to disorient him, and it took only twenty minutes to manage the half mile. Looking up and down the road, he understood why the unit had abandoned their post. The storm had saved his life, but there would be no getting out now. The road would be impassable in a matter of hours, and

he couldn't make it very far by then. The only option was to
wait. He felt he was forgetting something important.

Dwight was experienced at surviving in the woods, and
knew he could weather out a storm — even winter over if
necessary. It wouldn't be so bad. He had ammo, and the
abandoned station probably had supplies. At the very least
it would save him the trouble of building a shelter. Dwight
suddenly felt calm. There was something reassuring about
having only one course forward. He would wait out the storm,
and then carefully flee West. He'd make his way to some place
where nobody recognized him.

As Dwight began the slog back to the station, he
remembered. He wasn't running from the soldiers. Even last
night, he had known that. Was he *that* tired? How could he have
forgotten? He was running from something which the snow
would not stop, something which he now had no chance of
outrunning.

One more gunshot rang out, but nobody was listening.

CHAPTER 43

Transcript from TripleTalk, Episode 112

[*Zooms in on host Brad Palmeri sitting in an old armchair and facing crescent-shaped table with 3 empty seats*]

Brad: Welcome to another edition of TripleTalk, the program where we believe there are three sides to any coin. Tonight, we discuss a topic most of us never thought would garner debate: "Is murder wrong?" We welcome the author of this controversy and the book that spawned it, "Murder isn't a Four Letter Word," New York Times bestseller and winner of the Regent Book Award, Ron Correll.

[*Enters Ron Correll to mixed applause and boos. Brad shakes his hand and he sits in the center seat*]

Brad: Thank you all for joining us. Well [*gestures toward the audience*], you've certainly stirred up some strong feelings with your book. Murder is universally reviled as one of the worst crimes, and it meets with the harshest of penalties from our legal system. Your book argues that this all has changed, and that we should view it differently in light of the Front. [*Holds the book in his hand, thoughtfully*]. What is it that makes murder acceptable now.

Ron: Thank you for having me, Brad. First, I'd like to point out that the word "murder" itself is loaded. We interpret it legally and psychologically in inherently negative terms. But its etymology comes from the ancient "mrtro", which simply means "to die". There's little evidence that it meant anything more malignant until relatively recently, when killing became more than a matter for personal revenge or remuneration.

Brad: So you're saying that the word is at issue?

Ron: No, I'm just pointing out that our use of the word is loaded. And that's part of why I include it in my title. It's like the word "piracy" for copyright violation or "assault" for threatened contact. Also, you aren't quite right about the place this crime holds in our legal system. Murder may comprise one of the biblical injunctions, but in modern criminal law it isn't that serious. In fact, most of what we commonly would consider murder has been assigned lower degrees of culpability. Unless you announce your intention to kill somebody, publish a novel detailing the plan, then kill them in plain sight while writing your name in blood, you probably won't be convicted of the premeditation.

Brad: Isn't that a bit much?

Ron: Ok, maybe -- but you get the point. These days, the average State statute book contains over twenty crimes punished with greater or equal severity to premeditated murder. Federal law contains sixteen capital offenses, and murder isn't one of them (though murder of an active law enforcement officer is). Not long ago, you would be punished equally for kicking down an ex-girlfriend's door during an argument (home invasion), carrying a few ounces of heroine (drug dealing), or defacing the web page of a company (hacking). At one point during the Victorian Era, English law detailed over 200 capital offenses. Pickpocketing carried the same penalty as murder.

Brad: So, according to you, this makes murder ok?

Ron: This all is beside the argument of the book. I'm just pointing out that murder has a special place in our minds as a word, but lacks comparable status in our legal system.

Brad: So the argument is that because we don't punish murder harshly enough, therefore it's ok.

Ron: [*chuckles*] I think you know that's not the case, Brad. You've read the book.

The point I make is that the special
place murder holds in our psychologies
is predicated on many assumptions. I
won't attack all of these, and some are
so deeply ingrained that we're barely
aware of them.

Brad: That's a convenient way to avoid
addressing them.

Ron: [*laughs*] I suppose it could be, but
I do mean to address a couple of biggies
on this show. In today's world, it is
hard to argue for the sanctity of law,
need for social stability, deterrence,
or any of the standard sociopolitical
principles behind condemning murder.

Brad: Though, I suspect that our other
guests will choose to argue each of those
points.

Ron: Let's focus on the moral implications that most of us would agree on.
When you kill somebody you take away
their future, you deprive their loved
ones of their presence and support, and
you deprive society of a member. But none
of these have the same potency as before.
Taking away a few weeks or months of life
from a man is very different from our
concept of a nebulous and undemarcated
future. Nor has that individual any real
potential. He could not have changed
his life, improved, married, had kids,
gotten educated, started a company,
become famous, become rich, or any of the

other things we commonly aspire to. Or if
he could, only in a vastly abbreviated
form. All that really is left him is to
wait and die. Horribly.

Brad: Well, *that's* a depressing thought.

Ron: So in the absence of time and of
future and of potential, does killing
another person really deprive him of
anything substantive?

Brad: I believe so. It deprives him of
the same future or potential as before.
He could have been killed anyway, by a
truck or disease. The fact that he knows,
has conditional information, does not
change his right to that future.

Ron: Ah, but it does. It changes
everything. In some sense, all we have is
time. And now we have much less of it.

Brad: But by that argument, the murderer
should be tried and executed very
quickly, so that he is punished propor-
tionately.

Ron: One could argue that, but it
is pointless to do so. My argument
isn't that murder won't be punished
or shouldn't be punished. Just that it
shouldn't be viewed as wrong in the same
way as before.

Brad: And I look forward to hearing you
elaborate on that subtle distinction
after we introduce the rest of our panel.
But first an important message.

[*Fundraising Commercial for NPR*]

[*Enter two men and take seats on either side of Ron*]

Brad: [*Turns to audience*] Well, Ron Correll's book certainly has an unusual premise. That murder may no longer be indefensible, given the existence of the Front. Joining us tonight to discuss this is Professor Mark Poltinsky, bioethics expert, Professor of History at the University of Michigan, and author of over 11 books, including the bestseller, "Evil's Divine Seed," and His Excellency, Jackricard Dominique Spruce, Bishop of the Diocese of Tucson. [*Smiles at Bishop*] Well, that's quite a mouthful.

Bishop Spruce: You can call me Jack. After all, time is short. [*Grins at audience*].

[*Light Laughter*]

Brad: Welcome to TripleTalk. I'm going to start with you [*pauses, seemingly indecisive*] Jack. You both heard Ron Correll's arguments, and you've read his book.

Mark: [*jokingly mumbles*] It was quite the read.

Brad: [*laughs*] It sure is [*holds up book for audience to see and opens the last page*]. 1234 pages. [*Turns to Ron*] Couldn't you just have explained it like you did here?

Ron: [*smiles*] Publisher insisted on some filler.

[*Laughter*]

Brad: [*Turns to Jack*]. So, Jack, what are your thoughts on this? I know your own views often have met with controversy, framing the debate on abortion to skirt the line between orthodoxy and heterodoxy, the American church vs the Vatican. What do you think of Correll's points?

Jack: [*Speaks slowly, as if hesitant*]. Well, it certainly is ... novel. [*There are some chuckles from the audience.*] I know you probably expect me to invoke the bible and fire and brimstone, but the church has evolved a lot over the last century. This isn't the place to go into it, but I think you genuinely would be surprised by the many progressive voices both here in America and in the New Vatican. [*Speaks in a faux-conspiratorial tone*] And for the record, the schism with the Vatican is highly exaggerated. [*Returns to normal tone*]. The truth is that Ron's views differ quantitatively rather than qualitatively from those most of us hold.

Brad: I think you lost me there.

Jack: It's a mere matter of degree.

Brad: Last I checked, the church did not condone murder under "some" circumstances.

Jack: Well perhaps he phrased it in extreme terms, and that may have detracted from his argument, but the definition of murder *is* somewhat arbitrary. In the old testament, people were killed in all sorts of ways for things that wouldn't even be considered crimes today. One of Jacob's daughters was raped -- or more likely seduced -- by the son of the leader of a friendly tribe, who then did everything possible to make amends. Jacob pretended to forgive the tribe, converted them all to Judaism, and, while they were sore from circumcision, had his people murder the men and rape the women. Even by the standards of the times, this was an atrocity. And that was one of the great patriarchs. It just goes downhill from there. In fact, it's difficult to read the bible without being astonished by how reprehensible to modern eyes our icons were. The notion of murder as a crime is one of both law and of faith. The idea is not to wantonly kill God's ensouled creations. But most of us would agree that under certain circumstances killing is necessary -- defense, war, and perhaps when essential for great good. Is a baby human from the moment of conception? I believe so. Is is wrong to kill it if the mother's life is at stake? I say no. As you know, this is quite controversial; most people who argue the latter, disagree with the former too -- and vice versa.

Brad: That is true, but I imagine you can explain everything with, "the ways of the Lord are mysterious."

Jack: You know, people often think that. It would be convenient to win every argument just by saying that. [*Laughter*]. There's an assumption that the Church holds all this to be the work of God. But we're not a bunch of monks in cells anymore; most of us are connected on the Internet. We're pretty much like everybody else, except for a personal choice to devote our lives to Jesus Christ. As you know, his Holiness does not hold the Front to be an act of God. Even to the superstitious there should have been portents, a sequence of events heralding the wrath of God or the end times. Maybe in medieval times everybody looked over their shoulder for the four horsemen and every wart foreshadowed the apocalypse, but we've come a long way. The doom and gloom of the bible is now understood to be largely metaphorical, a warning for what may be wrought by ourselves *on* ourselves if we're not careful.

Mark: Couldn't you argue that this attitude is precisely why God would be wrathful?

Jack: [*smiles indulgently*] You're not
the first to make that argument, believe
me. There have been reactionaries in
the Church who sought to use the Front
that way. But no. The Lord I know and
have faith in never would do such a
thing, not overtly and not mysteriously.
The Front is something else. There are
many agencies in this world that do
not operate under the Lord's direct
guidance.

Mark: You mean Satan.

Jack: [*grimaces*] And the boogeyman too.
No, Man and Nature. We do not blame the
Lord for natural disasters; we moved
past that long ago. We do not blame the
lord for wars. That too is an old belief.
Why should we blame him for the Front?
Sure, some people have argued that it
could be a fail-safe He left in place and
which we somehow triggered. But if we
blew up a bomb and caused an earthquake,
would that be His fault? I'd just like to
add ...

Brad: [*Interrupts*] Thank you, but I'd
like to avoid getting too far afield.
Let's hear from Professor Poltinsky
[*turns to him*].

Mark: Well, I think it is interesting
to debate these issues philosophically.
However, when it comes to real people
being murdered, the issue takes on
a different tenor. There are many

approaches you can take to both the
ethics of murder and its legal character-
ization, and each of these has had its
advocates and opponents in different
times and places. But there is one
overarching concern which I believe
is more important than the abstract
considerations discussed in the book.
It has to do with the manner in which
humanity proceeds toward its end.

Brad: Then you're not a believer.

Mark: [*Laughs*] No, I don't think this is
anything divine, but I also don't think
we are prepared to deal with it. It's
like a meteor heading toward Earth; if
it happened a few hundred years later
maybe we could escape or divert it. It
just came too soon. But let me return
to the question of murder. To me, it's
not just one of law and stability. It's
one of personal preference. At some
level it does not matter whether we
approach the end screaming in anarchy
or quietly consoling one another. The
Universe won't care. There's nothing
to care. But *we* care, whatever that
means. I personally would prefer to
die in quiet contemplation as the plane
plummets toward the ground rather than
amidst ear-piercing shrieks, flailing
arms, and excrement. It would be less
unpleasant. And that's really what it's
about to me. Dying with dignity. Sure, we
could open the floodgates. Do what you

want, no government, no law. But that just would lead to a very unpleasant last few days for the cancer patient. Isn't it much better to file orderly out the door, last one turn out the lights?

Brad: But that's *your* preference, not everybody's. Why should yours control?

Mark: I never said it should. However, I do believe that it is what most of us really want. There are other reasons too. If there is *any* chance of survival as a species, of stopping the Front, it will be lost if we resort to anarchy. But this all is academic. It is neither here nor there what you think or I think or Correll thinks. We elected a government. It is that government's job to see us through this crisis, even if the end is 'the end.' For all the things which have drawn condemnation and criticism, it *has* maintained order. It has gotten us to the point where, two months after the Northeast fell, and as the Front creeps across our country, we still can debate this in a civilized manner on TV. Most of us don't really fear death so much as we fear pain. What the government is doing is preventing that, by keeping a tight reign on our actions toward one another. Laws themselves may be arbitrary, but the rule of law isn't. It is a binary proposition, something that a society either has or does not.

Ron: Let me ask you a question, though.

If it is pain we fear, why not allow us to end it sooner. The Front is a terrible way to die.

Mark: Nobody is saying you shouldn't be allowed to self-euthanize. I even would argue that you should be allowed to euthanize others who voluntarily request it.

Jack: But where do you draw the line? What if a mentally-ill person requests it?

Mark: Should their inability to make a sound choice prevent everybody else from having *any* choice? The same argument could apply to any right. Besides, as Correll points out, the Front *does* have an effect. If a depressive asks to die while depressed, perhaps they should be allowed. They don't have a lifetime ahead of them. Or if they do, it is a short one. Besides, left to their own devices it is unlikely they will awaken to reason before the end arrives.

Brad: So you agree with Correll's point about potential?

Jack: It appears to be a matter of degree, even for Professor Poltinsky.

Mark: Well, if you'd like me to formally refute Ron Correll, I'll offer a few examples from traditional Ethics theory.

Brad [*looks at Ron, Jack, and audience queryingly, nodding his head*]: I always like those sort of conundrums. Fire away.

Mark: Well, these examples also will serve a purpose. First, there's the old question from Jewish lore. You're in a rowboat and come upon three people drowning: your father, your son, and the world's most holy and learned man. You're the only one who knows how to row and there's only space to save one. Whom do you choose?

Brad: If you jump overboard and drown, you'll never have to make a choice. That's why I never go rowing.

Mark: Well, I can't say I've heard *that* response before [*laughter*]. Don't be fooled, though; drowning to avoid the responsibility of making a choice is *itself* a choice. The traditional answer is your father, because the other two are replaceable. Now consider the question in the presence of the Front. None of them are replaceable. But it also doesn't really matter as much if they die.

Brad: Interesting.

Jack: Or you could teach one to row and dive in.

Brad: You'll be the Holy Man, I suppose, so you're already drowning.

Jack: How unfortunate. And I didn't even get picked. [*Laughter*]

Mark: The next was posed by a prominent twentieth century logician. It goes something like this: Suppose the three of us are in the desert, far from any water. [*aside*] You're safe at home, Brad.

Brad: Or out rowing, apparently. [*Laughter*]

Mark: Jack and Ron each decide to murder me, without knowing the other's intention. Jack poisons my canteen while I'm taking a piss. Before I get back, Ron sneaks over and pokes a hole in that same canteen. I return, find the canteen empty, and die of thirst. Who murdered me? I never drank Jack's poison, and Ron saved me from drinking poisoned water. On the other hand, the moment either took action, I was doomed. To make it even more perplexing, if Jack had poisoned the canteen but I then accidentally spilled it, he wouldn't be guilty because I would have doomed myself. Who is guilty?

Jack: I think it's pretty clear, they both are.

Ron: Well, given that I argued in my book that murder shouldn't be stigmatized, I'd have to say ... it's you. [*Points dramatically at Jack, to laughter*].

Mark: Well, the point is that the notion of "guilt" here assumes the ability to ascribe causality. And causality as a moral or legal notion is ill-defined, it reflects our biases and assumptions and an arbitrary set of principles. Physically the universe is one big quantum field (aside from the Front, apparently), and there is no causality, just a deterministic evolution of state from some initial condition.

Brad: Hold yer horses, Professor. [*Turns to audience*] I always wanted to say that. [*Laughter*].

Mark: The point is that what we call causality from a macroscopic "human affairs" standpoint is just a story we tell ourselves. It may be a convenient story with practical ramifications, but it has no profound significance.

Brad: And how does the Front come into play?

Mark: Well, that conundrum just was intended to demonstrate the way in which our assumptions can fail us. The Front comes into play in this next one. Suppose you have two hundred people in one room and one person in another room. If you don't press a button, the two hundred people die, if you do then the one person dies. You know nothing about the people in either room.

Brad: Is this the sort of thing you guys think about a lot?

Mark: Oh yeah, there's a whole lab under the University, and we go through

students like you wouldn't believe.
[*Laughter*] Well, whom would you choose
to save?

Brad: The two hundred, obviously.

Mark: That may make you a murderer under
U.S. law because your action killed a
person. Under the old EU law, it would
have been less obvious.

Jack: It would be a very difficult
problem, but I probably would not be
allowed to press the button.

Ron: It's a bogus question because the
murderer is the person who created the
situation, not the person who is forced
to choose.

Mark: Who said you were *forced* to choose?
[*smiles*]. But yeah, let's assume that.
And you're right, as most people would
agree. Ethics theory is filled with
variants of this problem in which you
know different things about the people,
have more or less freedom, and so on.
In our case, suppose that you know that
all two hundred people have been given
a poison to which there is no antidote.
They have precisely one week to live.
The single person has a form of cancer
and has at least four years. Which do you
choose?

Brad: I'd stick with the two hundred?

Mark: Why?

Brad: Well, it saves a lot more lives.

Mark: But from what standpoint? The total human time you have preserved is less than if you saved the one person. What if I gave you the same choice one minute before the 200 would die? One second?

Brad: I see where this is going. I'd choose the one, but where do you draw the boundary?

Mark: Exactly.

Brad: And the Front?

Mark: This is precisely the dilemma we face. For all practical purposes, most of us are stuck roughly in place until the Front comes for us. We then run into situations where the lives of three thousand people one third of a mile from the Front together are worth one life a thousand miles from the front.

Jack: Well, that's just ...

Brad: Very interesting.

Ron: Which is why the notion of murder is both antiquated and ambiguous. Your arguments directly support my view.

Mark: Not quite. These aren't arguments for your viewpoint, any more than an argument for an abstract god endorses a specific religious doctrine. [*Looks at the bishop*]. Apologies, Father.

Jack: [*Smiles*] Not at all. Those ARE fun puzzles, though I'll admit [*he looks guiltily at the audience*] I may have heard one or two before. The two hundred people puzzle is the analog of the fetus and mother abortion problem if you value awareness instead of time.

Mark: Sure, they're all variants of old conundrums. But I think that, as with murder, Ron would argue that the Front has given them new meaning, new immediacy [*Looks at Ron for agreement*].

Ron: Indeed. I think one could say without exaggeration that the Front has lent a lot of urgency to everything. The end always is in sight.

Brad: [*Jokingly*] Including for this show. Our time is almost up. Professor, why don't you quickly finish your argument and then we'll hear from Jack and Ron.

Mark: Thanks, Brad. In math, and philosophy to some extent, if you can show that a new situation is equivalent to one we already understand, then the same understanding should apply. So let us consider two situations which I deem morally equivalent to the Front, though we may respond quite differently. I think that our intuitive ethics in those situations should inform how we view behavior in light of the Front.

Brad: Ok.

Mark: First, consider a disease.

Ron: [*Slumps back impatiently*] I address that in the book.

Mark: Bear with me, this is a different scenario. In this case, we're all infected with this disease. It will kill us all at varying times. Not only is there no cure, but we're certain that no cure will be found before it wipes us out. And no, I don't mean this as an allegory for death. Children won't survive longer, and the species will die. How would we react? Would we decide that murder is permissible? The same could be said for any unavoidable disaster scenario. Give or take an element of hope and the dynamics may change, but the core premise is the same. The second scenario is a bit more subtle. Suppose that you are locked in a room with five other prisoners. You all will be executed, no reprieve, no hope. You will die one per day, and you know the order. Would it be ethical to strangle one another in your sleep? This is just a variant of the poisoners quandary I mentioned earlier. But here is where it gets really interesting ...

[*Brad taps his watch*]

Mark: Ok, I'll keep it brief. What if the ethics is based on how long you have to live? One could argue that if the last man to die kills the first it is less of a crime than the converse because in one case a man is deprived of one day while in the second he is deprived of five.

Jack: Or you could argue the opposite,

that the single day is as precious to him as a whole lifetime is to the other. For that is all each of us has, one lifetime, and until recently we didn't know how long it would last or what it would entail.

Brad: Well while you're at it, why don't you offer us your final thoughts on the matter, Jack.

Jack: I'm not convinced, of course -- but then the purpose of this show isn't to convince the guests. [*Laughter from the audience*]. I'm going to stick with my view that killing another person -- whether from anger or greed or even to enforce a law -- and I know I'm going to get in trouble for this -- but even to keep order or to prevent people from fleeing the Front -- that killing another person is wrong. The fundamental tenet of our Faith is, "do unto others as you would have them do unto you." Only if Ron would have others murder him with impunity would that injunction grant him the right to take life. Similarly, only if the government were to remain where it was and allow the Front to wipe it clean could it argue that others should be prevented from fleeing. It moved to California at the first sign of trouble, so I think you know my opinion on that. [*Applause from the audience*].

Brad: And if you were in one of the towns being stormed by refugees and rioters?

Jack: I'd offer them food and prayers, and turn the other cheek.

Ron: The Front doesn't care which cheek it hits.

Jack: [*Laughing*] I expect not.

Brad: And you, Ron, any final thoughts?

Ron: I'll save those for [*checks his watch*] 3 months from now. [*Nervous laughter*]. I should clarify that I don't plan to go out and murder anybody and I don't encourage anybody else to. I just felt that the Front should prompt us to reevaluate the ideals we take for granted.

Mark: Nietzsche would argue we always should do that anyway.

Ron: The purpose of my book is to promote discussion, not anarchy.

Brad: And you don't worry that it may do more?

Ron: If anarchy seeps through the cracks of our society, it won't be because of a coffee table book that very few people actually read. It will be because it was waiting under the surface all along, waiting to boil over. Or for us to sink into its quagmire. [*Turns to Mark*] And for the record, Professor, I share your aesthetics. I'd like a peaceful end. And I hope that the government ensures that by continuing to wisely administer its Gentle Firm Hand policy. [*The participants nod agreeably*].

Brad: And with that, we bring tonight's TripleTalk to a close. Thank you Professor Mark Poltinsky, Bishop Spruce, and Ron Correll. And as always, goodnight as night falls.

CHAPTER 44

The term "deadline" always held a particular fascination for Lilly. Though she had learned English at an early age, there remained a tendency to translate colloquialisms with a perverse literalism before registering them as such. Long before the Front revealed its silent, implacable face, deadlines had seemed sinister to her. Why were they not "faillines" or "losslines"? Were Americans *that* serious about business? Of course they were; it was all they had. But from what she'd read, *most* of history was about business in one form or another. It was unfair to fault the Americans for their peculiar obsession. Whatever its origin, the word "deadline" still sounded ominous. Even before it took on a more significant and personal meaning.

Lilly had been sentenced to death three years before everyone else. This served her well. The world panicked when the Front appeared, but Lilly remained unaffected. What passed for nerves of steel was little more than experience, though. She had three years longer than everyone else to come to terms with her own imminent death. A pop psychologist would say she had passed through the four stages of grief, a pointless and simplistic classification at best.

As does everybody, diagnosed and undiagnosed, she passed through a new stage at every infinitesimal point in time, became a new person, evolved. The countless stages of grief, if it served some purpose to thus divide her existence, were neither more nor less than this. Her being simply adapted to something new, something unexpected. Instead of a future with forty more years of hope and possibility and disappointment and fear, she had three. On the bright side, three of anything was much more manageable than forty. Just ask a prisoner.

The discovery of Lilly's cancer had been a lucky accident. After a week of incapacitating fatigue, she had been prevailed upon by a superior (or, more accurately, ordered) to see a doctor. She made an appointment six months out, the earliest her physician could schedule. The next day she collapsed at work and was taken to a local emergency room.

The doctor on call happened to be reasonably bright. He also happened to recognize her as a former Professor from back in college. Ordinarily, he would have stowed his suspicions, rehydrated her, discharged her with a prophylactic antibiotics prescription, and let her become somebody else's problem the next time she collapsed or worse. As it was, he took the time to call in a friend from Oncology just to make sure. The tests left no doubt, a grape-sized dark spot caressed the edge of her left lung.

It turned out that medical technology had made little real progress over the past century, but it *did* have a few new tricks to improve the prognosis of people who mattered. The fact that Lilly mattered had nothing to do with her government position; she shared the same awful health plan with every other federal employee, and would have been lucky to schedule a checkup before she died. Nor did it have to do with her history or gender or accomplishments. It had to do with the only two things which counted: money and the skill to apply it well.

Fortunately she had inherited both from her father, an astute businessman out of Guangzhou. The details were different in the U.S., but the principles were the same. A friend aptly summarized this to her, after she'd complained to him about some bureaucratic tangle or other.

"The United States," he explained, "is a third world country with a first world economy."

She was certain he was quoting somebody, but never figured out whom. Although initially incredulous, she quickly came to agree. And she had seen nothing to prove otherwise since. Once Lilly had been disabused of the national mythology, life was much easier. The old ways were the best ways, and they worked here too. She scolded herself for ever thinking otherwise.

Years later, this knowledge continued to serve her well. It had taken Lilly only two weeks after the initial diagnosis to identify the only potentially effective treatments and the few physicians competent to administer them, and secure their services.

It was no secret that the general principle of health insurance was to let a patient die before getting to the more expensive treatments. That was the main reason why a long sequence of ineffective treatments had to be tried before "experimental" treatments were approved. Of course, "experimental" didn't actually carry any scientific meaning here; it simply meant costly. Very few patients made it to these experimental treatments, and those that did generally got there on their own dime.

The prognosis was bad. Not as bad as pancreatic cancer or brain cancer, but close. Lilly wondered which industrial chemical was responsible for her death. Was it the stuff she breathed at work, the stuff she breathed at home, the stuff she breathed on the street? Or was it just bad luck? She didn't smoke, had never been subjected to second-hand smoke or (to her knowledge) asbestos. Though she couldn't be sure her childhood in China hadn't contributed, she had not lived in a polluted area. Most likely, it was something random in her childhood which was thought innocuous at the time but later proved deadly.

The problem with cancer was that it still had no cure, only "treatments". There was a reason for this, of course. Lilly was no conspiracy theorist, and didn't believe in smokey backrooms. Smoking no longer was allowed, the rooms were clean and brightly lit, and most of what took place there was far less exciting than anyone imagined.

In her experience, conspiracies were rare and mostly concerned themselves with hiding somebody's personal or financial indiscretion. Even in her modest position back then, Lilly had realized this. Sure, one could argue that by its nature a *real* conspiracy would have been hidden from her. But she didn't need to know *everything* to reach that conclusion. She knew people, and people were simple.

It wasn't that conspiracies *couldn't* exist. People simply were not competent enough to form meaningful ones, and nothing she had seen led her to believe otherwise. Unfortunately, conspiracies weren't the only threats to life and freedom. In fact, even if one existed it probably wouldn't rank close to the top. The biggest threat always was bureaucracy, and the runner-up was market dynamics. It didn't matter which bureaucracy or which market or which dynamics.

As a former physicist, and a top one at that, Lilly had impressive technical skills. But her greatest strength, the one which made her extraordinarily effective in her government roles, was her ability to gauge the difficulty of problems. Anybody could look at a problem and assess whether it would be easy or hard *for them* to solve. They may lie to themselves or others, but unless they were particularly inept they knew.

However, Lilly could determine the difficulty of problems in a more general sense. Nor was it merely a theoretical determination. Whether something is computationally complex is of interest to researchers, but tells little of its actual difficulty. A formally "hard" problem may be challenging only in a few cases of no real utility, while a formally "easy" problem may prove intractable in most cases of practical interest.

Lilly's assessment was more subjective, but much more useful. It wasn't whether a problem could be solved by some abstract machine in some limit, but whether a given set of people could do so in a reasonable time. When the

Front appeared, this skill proved invaluable, especially after several major missteps by politicians which cost critical time and resources. Lilly's talent was recognized, and she was promoted. Even when her assessment was unpopular, it was respected. If somebody was going to take charge of a desperate long-shot, it had to be somebody who understood that it *was* a long-shot, and knew which way to point the gun.

This same skill helped Lilly see things that weren't apparent to others. For example, she understood — to a greater or lesser extent — which technical problems were likely to be tackled or not. Of course, she wasn't *always* right. Outside her area of expertise she had to rely on summaries of research, and the reliability of these varied greatly. Also, new discoveries could be made which changed the landscape. But for the most part, her assessments hit pretty close to the mark.

- Controlled Fusion: Hard

- Colony on Mars: Hard

- Artificial Cognition: Easy

- Cure AIDs: Hard

- Cure Most Cancers: Easy

- Cure Diabetes: Easy

- Stop the Front: Hard

If a problem was hard and lots of resources were being devoted to it anyway, then politics was at play. On the other hand, if a problem was easy but remained unsolved after many years, there could be two causes. Either very little money had been spent because it was an unpopular problem or afflicted unpopular people, or lots of money had been spent, yet little progress made. The latter was the case with her form of lung cancer.

To Lilly, this wasn't the result of some conscious effort to suppress a cure or avoid finding it, thus ensuring greater profits from treatment. It was simple incompetence, money given to the wrong people. But the effect was the same.

As a field, medical research was very primitive. In the 20th century, enormous progress had been made in physics, chemistry, mathematics, computer science, and biology. However, medicine hardly advanced in any meaningful way. The arsenal of tests and treatments had grown slowly, and progress mostly was through technical improvements rather than major innovations. Medicine was *not* a hard problem, but there were strong economic and political forces which pushed it in unfavorable directions.

Cures were expensive to find and tended not to be very profitable. Once a person was cured, they were done. In the worst case, a company could put itself out of business by finding *too* effective a measure. If a disease was eradicated, all the hard work that went into curing it would be worthless.

On the other hand, a lifetime of *treatment* could be quite lucrative, *if* prices were kept just low enough for insurance companies to allow it. This wasn't some sinister cabal's plan, just natural market forces doing what they did best: screwing people.

In Lilly's case there was no cure, just numerous treatments — all expensive, and all unpleasant. However, they increased her life expectancy from three years to almost twelve. She went through a round of chemotherapy, then switched to a cocktail of inhibitive agents. The process was to be repeated every two to three years until it became ineffective. Most patients managed four or five rounds before that happened or the treatment killed them.

The contrast between declaring herself dead in a philosophical sense and being sentenced medically was not lost on Lilly. As much as she had believed she could lose nothing, feared nothing, it simply was not true. She *was* afraid to die. But three years and innumerable well-concealed panic attacks later, she was not. More precisely, she had come to terms with it. From a practical standpoint, the Front was no different than her treatment failing by the third round. That too was a distinct possibility.

So while the world cried out in terror, Lilly sat back calmly, knowing what she had known for three years. She actually felt a perverse sense of relief. At least she wouldn't die alone. For the second time in her life, Lilly felt ashamed. She quickly brushed it aside. The dead Lilly did not feel shame. And she was thrice dead now. She looked out her window and smiled. Welcome to the club, everyone.

CHAPTER 45

Day 1524 — New Zealand

```
++02:55:16 W NOCOM 2 TO CCOM SRCBEAC 1HF42 REL
***** 0 VESS, FLAGSTAT OK, ACT OK

++02:59:11 W NOCOM 3 TO CCOM SRCBEAC 1HF42 REL
***** 12 VESS, FLAGSTAT OK, ACT OK

++03:04:03 W NOCOM 1 TO CCOM SRCBEAC 1HF42 REL
***** 36 VESS, FLAGSTAT OK, ACT OK

++03:10:16 W NOCOM 2 TO CCOM SRCBEAC 1HF42 REL
***** 1 VESS, INCIDENT IN PROG

++03:12:45 W NOCOM 2 TO CCOM SRCBEAC 1HF42 REL
***** 1 VESS, FLAGSTAT UNK, ACT UNK

++03:12:53 W NOCOM 2 TO CCOM SRCBEAC 1HF42 REL
***** ALERT UNK VESS LOC 43.3.37S168.45.48E,
***** BEAR 6.484K@141.36.42

++03:13:12 W NOCOM 2 TO CCOM SRCBEAC 1HF42 REL
***** PROBE HSIG SENT 156.8HZ

++03:13:18 CCOM TO W NOCOM 2 DKFEED34 LLCOM-76
***** ACK ALERT, ACTION WAIT

++03:14:10 W NOCOM 2 TO CCOM SRCBEAC 1HF42 REL
***** ALERT UNKNOWN VESS NOACK
***** PROBE HSIG EXPANDED 157.125-161.925HZ
```

```
++03:14:15 W NOCOM 3 TO CCOM SRCBEAC 1HF42 REL
***** 12 VESS, FLAGSTAT OK, ACT OK

++03:14:30 W NOCOM 2 TO CCOM SRCBEAC 1HF42 REL
***** ALERT UNKNOWN VESS NOACK
***** PROBE HSIG EXPANDED FULL
***** SPECTRUM, 10 SEC CYCLE

++03:14:45 W NOCOM 2 TO CCOM SRCBEAC 1HF42 REL
***** ALERT UNKNOWN VESS NOACK
***** REQUEST ADVISE

++03:15:12 CCOM TO W NOCOM 2 DKFEED34 LLCOM-76
***** ACK ALERT, ACTION CONTINUE
***** PROBE 120 SEC

++03:15:40 W NOCOM 2 TO CCOM SRCBEAC 1HF42 REL
***** ALERT UNKNOWN VESS NOACK
***** PROBE HSIG CONTINUE FULL
***** SPECTRUM, 10 SEC CYCLE

++03:16:02 W NOCOM 1 TO CCOM SRCBEAC 1HF42 REL
***** 36 VESS, FLAGSTAT OK, ACT OK

++03:16:18 W NOCOM 2 TO CCOM SRCBEAC 1HF42 REL
***** ALERT UNKNOWN VESS RESPONSE
***** ON 156.475, RCV HOLD

++03:17:11 W NOCOM 2 TO CCOM SRCBEAC 1HF42 REL
***** ALERT MSG RCVD "SHIP ID
***** US FLAG DURANT II"

++03:17:45 CCOM TO W NOCOM 2 DKFEED34 LLCOM-76
```

***** ACK ALERT, VERIFIED COMMERCIAL CRUISE
***** LINER DURANT II, REG US, ID 45G378B

++03:17:55 W NOCOM 2 TO CCOM SRCBEAC 1HF42 REL
***** ID 45G378B MSG SENT "ENTERING NZ
***** SOVEREIGN RESTRICTED ZONE. DO NOT
***** PROCEED. TURN OFF ENGINES TO
***** SIGNAL COMPLIANCE"

++03:18:03 W NOCOM 1 TO CCOM SRCBEAC 1HF42 REL
***** 37 VESS, FLAGSTAT OK, ACT OK

++03:18:34 W NOCOM 2 TO CCOM SRCBEAC 1HF42 REL
***** ID 45G378B MSG RCVD "REQUEST TO PROCEED.
***** 2800 PASSENGERS. NONMIL.
***** REQUEST MED HELP"

++03:18:42 W NOCOM 2 TO CCOM SRCBEAC 1HF42 REL
***** ID 45G378B ENGINE ACTIVE, NO COMPLIANCE
***** REQUEST ADVISE

++03:19:15 CCOM TO W NOCOM 2 DKFEED34 LLCOM-76
***** ACK REQUEST, REQUIRE COMPLIANCE

++03:19:45 W NOCOM 2 TO CCOM SRCBEAC 1HF42 REL
***** ID 45G378B MSG SENT "YOU HAVE ENTERED NZ
***** RESTRICTED ZONE. SIGNAL COMPLIANCE"

++03:20:14 W NOCOM 2 TO CCOM SRCBEAC 1HF42 REL
***** ID 45G378B MSG SENT "YOU HAVE ENTERED NZ
***** RESTRICTED ZONE. SIGNAL COMPLIANCE"

++03:20:28 W NOCOM 2 TO CCOM SRCBEAC 1HF42 REL
***** ID 45G378B ENGINE ACTIVE, NO COMPLIANCE

```
***** REQUEST ADVISE


++03:21:14 CCOM TO W NOCOM 2 DKFEED34 LLCOM-76
***** ACK REQUEST, REQUIRE COMPLIANCE


++03:21:37 W NOCOM 2 TO CCOM SRCBEAC 1HF42 REL
***** ID 45G378B MSG RCVD "REQUEST TO PROCEED
***** 2800 PASSENGERS. NONMIL.
***** REQUEST MED HELP"


++03:21:45 W NOCOM 2 TO CCOM SRCBEAC 1HF42 REL
***** ID 45G378B MSG SENT "NZ COM TO DURANT II
***** ENTRY REFUSED.  SIGNAL COMPLIANCE"


++03:22:02 W NOCOM 1 TO CCOM SRCBEAC 1HF42 REL
***** 38 VESS, FLAGSTAT OK, ACT OK


++03:22:08 W NOCOM 2 TO CCOM SRCBEAC 1HF42 REL
***** ID 45G378B ENGINE ACTIVE, NO COMPLIANCE
***** REQUEST ADVISE


++03:22:16 CCOM TO W NOCOM 2 DKFEED34 LLCOM-76
***** ACK REQUEST, HOLD PENDING


++03:22:28 W NOCOM 2 TO CCOM SRCBEAC 1HF42 REL
***** ID 45G378B ENGINE ACTIVE, NO COMPLIANCE
***** HOLDING


++03:23:38 CCOM TO W NOCOM 2 DKFEED34 LLCOM-76
***** ID 45G378B DEEMED ACTIONABLE


++03:23:54 W NOCOM 2 TO CCOM SRCBEAC 1HF42 REL
***** ACK, REQUEST CONFIRM KEY
```

```
++03:24:15 W NOCOM 2 TO CCOM SRCBEAC 1HF42 REL
***** ID 45G378B MSG RCVD "PLEASE ALLOW
***** TO PROCEED. CHILDREN. NEED HELP, FOOD."

++03:24:16 W NOCOM 2 TO CCOM SRCBEAC 1HF42 REL
***** 1 VESS, INCIDENT IN PROG

++03:24:30 CCOM TO W NOCOM 2 DKFEED34 LLCOM-76
***** ACK REQUEST, CONF KEY FA17E3A4D97C48A5

++03:24:40 W NOCOM 2 TO CCOM SRCBEAC 1HF42 REL
***** ACK, KEY CONFIRMED

++03:24:50 W NOCOM 2 TO CCOM SRCBEAC 1HF42 REL
***** ID 45G378B ACTION PREP +120 SEC

++03:25:10 W NOCOM 2 TO CCOM SRCBEAC 1HF42 REL
***** ID 45G378B NO LEGAL VESSELS
***** NO WARNING NEEDED

++03:25:16 W NOCOM 3 TO CCOM SRCBEAC 1HF42 REL
***** HAPPY BDAY HELEN!

++03:25:45 W NOCOM 2 TO CCOM SRCBEAC 1HF42 REL
***** ID 45G378B ACTION PREP +60 SEC

++03:26:04 W NOCOM 2 TO CCOM SRCBEAC 1HF42 REL
***** ID 45G378B ENGINES OFF, IN COMPLIANCE

++03:26:15 CCOM TO W NOCOM 2 DKFEED34 LLCOM-76
***** ACK, AUTH PROCEED

++03:26:34 W NOCOM 2 TO CCOM SRCBEAC 1HF42 REL
***** ACK, ID 45G378B ACTION +9 SEC
```

++03:27:04 CCOM TO W NOCOM 3 DKFEED34 LLCOM-76
***** THANKS GUYS, UR THE BEST :)

++03:27:14 W NOCOM 2 TO CCOM SRCBEAC 1HF42 REL
***** ID 45G378B MITIGATION INITIATED

++03:27:23 W NOCOM 2 TO CCOM SRCBEAC 1HF42 REL
***** ID 45G378B MITIGATION SUCCESSFUL

++03:28:06 W NOCOM 2 TO CCOM SRCBEAC 1HF42 REL
***** ID 45G378B MITIGATION COMPLETE

++03:28:15 CCOM TO W NOCOM 2 DKFEED34 LLCOM-76
***** ACK STATUS

++03:28:47 W NOCOM 2 TO CCOM SRCBEAC 1HF42 REL
***** 0 VESS, FLAGSTAT OK, ACT OK

++03:29:06 W NOCOM 3 TO CCOM SRCBEAC 1HF42 REL
***** 12 VESS, FLAGSTAT OK, ACT OK

++03:30:04 W NOCOM 1 TO CCOM SRCBEAC 1HF42 REL
***** 38 VESS, FLAGSTAT OK, ACT OK

CHAPTER 46

Lilly closed the door to her office for the last time and quietly locked it. She walked to her desk and looked out the window for a moment, but only a moment. Then she pulled the shades shut and sat down.

There was so much to think about before she ceased to be. It would not do to waste time gazing idly at the unraveling city below. And it would not do for anybody to see her, though she doubted they could from the street. They probably wouldn't care even if they did.

The same could be said of these precious thoughts she seemed so intent on savoring during her last days. They would not matter to anyone else or to the universe or to some vague posterity. There would *be* nobody else, no posterity, vague or specific, and no universe. Her thoughts mattered only to her, and only for a short time. But that was enough.

There was nothing to fear, she remembered. Lilly died long ago. In retrospect, the whole act of which she had been so proud was just a bit of melodrama, a conceit. But there was a more profound reason. It often is the case that childish vanities later find accidental justification in deeper wisdom. She had come to understand that no finite being truly could be said to live. In an infinite universe anything finite was as naught, and in a finite universe there was no such thing as permanence. In no world did people matter, or even exist.

She was born to die, which is to say she was born dead. Later she declared herself dead. Then she was diagnosed as dead. Now she would be dead. Such was the slide toward entropy, degradation. Sometimes Lilly wondered whether these intellectual gymnastics served only to conceal a reality she wished to deny: that she really would suffer and really would die and really would decay. No philosophy could change that. Nor would death be a dreamlike dissolution, the stuff of the literature of her youth. She would die in agony, the specifics of which she was all too familiar with. Yet somehow she still felt no fear. Only a sense of accomplishment.

The evacuation had been more orderly than would have been expected of a desperate government in disarray. The original plan was to relocate to Honolulu two weeks before the Front reached San Diego. Any sooner would cause panic and a loss of authority, any later would cut it too close. Their top priority was retaining control of the military until the end. Predictably, they failed.

The Seventh Fleet sailed ahead of schedule, under Admiral Roan. Perhaps he sensed the weakness of the civilian government, and understood how dangerous such a witless and wounded beast could become. There had been rumors of gunfire aboard two of the ships. But other than the summary execution of a few recalcitrant officers, there apparently was little bloodshed. The Admiral clearly had planned this for a while, and the actual desertion went smoothly. No doubt, he convinced his soldiers that the mainland was in chaos and they had been ordered to sea. It's what *she* would have done.

Lilly was grateful to Roan for this. The fewer big guns remained, the less noisy these last few days would be. And if anything, she wanted a bit of peace and quiet before the end.

The Third Fleet and other military units did not interfere with Roan's desertion, though it was unclear whether they knew of it. As a precautionary measure, Admiral Bower of the Third was executed, along with thirty-three senior officers. This both confirmed Roan's wisdom in leaving and well-nigh guaranteed unrest among the remaining soldiers. It was a pointless piece of idiocy, just the sort of thing Lilly had come to expect of President Larisse. Unjustifiably murdering the highly respected commanders of the very people with guns who surrounded her. The desertion had not been publicized, so such a move would appear capricious, and meet with disbelief and anger.

Well, it wasn't Lilly's problem anymore. There no longer was a need to indulge Larisse or anybody else. Surprisingly, however, there was no further mutiny amongst the ranks. The Third fleet departed on schedule, and made its way toward Hawaii as planned. Lilly ascribed this to luck and the soldiers' emotional fatigue. In any other time and place, things would have played out *very* differently.

The Seventh had been the last carrier group with sufficient manpower to deploy. The Third consisted solely of transports, destroyers, and a variety of support vessels. Hawaii had been making noises about seceding for some time, and particularly objected to hosting a government they despised. They always had been a bit of an outlier — in many senses — and this seemed just the recipe for trouble. But in the end, Honolulu acquiesced. Apparently, they decided it just wasn't worth the fight.

Satellite imagery indicated that the Seventh was heading for Australia, and the Third fleet steered clear to avoid conflict. There was much speculation about what would become of Roan and company. They probably weren't strong enough to fight the entire Australian navy and force a passage. They had no nuclear weapons, and few remaining planes. The vessels themselves could travel indefinitely under nuclear power, but regular fuel reserves were too low for any sort of air campaign. In fact, the carriers were sitting ducks.

The three accompanying destroyers probably could protect them if push came to shove, but likely could do little else. No, the Seventh probably would get turned away by Australia and end up heading to New Zealand. Whether they would try to fight their way into harbour or just wait out the remaining two years offshore was unclear. If they *did* fight, it was anybody's guess who would win. Maybe the Kiwis would offer them a place to live; after all, that's the sort of people they were.

The civilian evacuation of San Diego was conducted by air. Flights ran continuously on special fuel reserves for over a week. All in all, approximately 8400 government officials were relocated, along with computer equipment, records, and other essentials of the bureaucracy. The President, cabinet, and five surviving Supreme Court justices were among the first evacuated. The remaining 247 members of Congress were included, as well. By common consent, Congressmen lost their vote but not their privileges when the Front passed their district. Senators retained both. Nonetheless, many from both houses had chosen to return home or been trapped by its progress.

The quiet, steady nature of the process helped avoid a mass panic. Nobody realized what was happening until it almost was over. That's when the gunfire began.

Lilly had been invited too, of course. In fact she had been ordered to join the evacuation, along with her team. She arranged for everybody else to leave early with the Third Fleet — the only civilians to do so — arguing that they could use some of the onboard equipment to continue research. She herself had been scheduled to fly out with some of the Cabinet on the eighth flight, but she kept postponing for various reasons. Finally, President Larisse personally ordered her to get on the next plane.

Somehow, the escort detail had been unable to locate her when they arrived. As Lilly had predicted, things were getting ugly fast, and they spent little time searching for her before heading back. They probably resented her, wondering why they were trying to save somebody who didn't want to be saved, one of the lucky few who *could* get out if they wanted. By then, order quickly was deteriorating, and people had begun rioting. Some even tried to storm the base, with predictable results. Everybody wanted to get on the remaining planes, everybody except her.

Once she was certain the soldiers had departed, Lilly emerged from the office down the hall and returned to her own. She closed the door and locked it, though she felt silly doing so. There really was no need to worry about looters or rioters. Nobody cared about some random administrative building downtown. Occasionally she heard a door swing or some glass shatter, but nobody bothered to come in or climb the stairs. Why would they? Everybody was trying to get out, and that meant the base. In the distance, there were the sounds of sirens and steady gunfire. About four hours later, the power failed. It could have been the rioting, but Lilly suspected the military had blown the power station on the way out. It was a parting gift, really. It would ensure a little peace and quiet. By now, the Front was only four days away.

On Lilly's desk lay a thin folder containing some sheets of data and a few paragraphs of analysis. She sat down, opened her center desk drawer, removed a pair of glasses, and slowly put them on. Then she read the documents, as she had a thousand times before. When she was done, she noticed the picture on her desk, the three children frolicking. She had picked it up in some frame shop, mainly because the kids looked Chinese. Some generic family with a generic life. They probably all were dead by now.

She bought it in an emotional moment after her first death, probably for the obvious reason. It had been a silly sentimentality, and not even an accurate one. Lilly only had one sibling, a brother, and no photos of them together. She never really wanted kids of her own, and deemed it no great loss that she couldn't have any.

That had been a small gift from the Peace Corps, a uterine infection after her rape in Uganda. They didn't tell you about that in the literature, or how they generally covered those things up. It wasn't entirely their fault, of course. Such things happened in places culturally at odds with the role women played in the Corps. But it didn't help her self-esteem. Lilly hadn't "found herself" in the Corps. All she found was a local teacher who raped her. He probably thought it was his right since she was his assistant.

Unlike many women, she had not felt ashamed. Nor did she hate her assailant, any more than she would hate a dog which bit her. In fact she'd viewed him as just that, even before anything happened. She viewed everybody that way. It made her wonder why she was in the Peace Corps at all. She didn't particularly enjoy helping people *or* animals. Maybe she had hoped to discover some brilliant kids, enable them to achieve their potential. Or maybe she just was a confused idiot. Lilly supposed it was irrelevant. She was the sum of her experiences. Except for this last one, the one coming in four days. That was the reset button. No, that was the off button.

If anything, her condition was a blessing. It helped avoid distraction. If she had children, she would have done what every other animal on the planet does. She just would have been a piece of meat producing another piece of meat to croon over. She had been saved from that. She had accomplished so much more. She had accomplished *this*.

It is difficult to describe the flow of thoughts while one waits for death. This isn't just due to its volume, but rather its concurrency. Lilly knew this better than anyone. The "I" is an anachronism from a time when we were viewed as skins filled with mystery, a soul, a whatever. A time when they didn't know of the countless voices in each brain, vying for dominance, struggling to be heard. That each of us isn't just a thief, a lover, and so on, but a village, a city, a civilization. Not just one, but an ever changing parade of them. To record all those parallel, competing, contradictory flows is well-nigh impossible. It is tantamount to writing a history of everything everyone has ever said. But in the collective known as Lilly there was a constant, a thing upon which the myriad thoughts agreed. They took pride where pride had long vanished, where pride was repudiated, disdained, condemned, which was itself a pride of sorts.

That pride was the pride of a well-made decision, of accomplishment. The satisfaction of being able to sit back and breath a sigh of relief that, however terrible the contest, you persevered, prevailed, and most important, proved yourself the man you wished to be. Or, in this case, woman.

Every time Lilly looked at the folder, she wondered something. She wondered whether it would have made a difference. If she had shown it to somebody, anybody, everybody, this information that they didn't have, this critical discovery about the Front, would it have allowed them to stop it, survive it? She hoped so.

Or maybe humanity *already* had been spared, and she just didn't know it. Perhaps the Zone was habitable. The few who survived the passage of the Front would be the denizens of a new Eden, the progenitors of a new world. Perhaps a few chosen ones or, more likely, a few lucky ones, had made it through the Front. Unable to communicate across it for some reason or other, they lived there now. In that case, the Front *would* be a reset button, a way to cleanse the infection of culture without altogether extinguishing humanity.

No, that was too unlikely. She simply couldn't force herself to believe it. That always had been her problem. She never could drink the Kool-Aid, believe, simply accept. How much happier life would have been if she had. Lilly almost laughed. Happy, but with the same end. All the believers and optimists, all the philosophies, all the thoughts and brilliance and art and magic and words and politics and laws and agreements and wars and discoveries and inventions. All had led to this.

Simply. Inexorably. It made no difference.

Once again, Lilly looked at the folder. But it could have. This very well could have given them the answer. She needed to believe that. *If* she had shown it to somebody. To Robert, perhaps. He could have done it. Yes, he probably could.

That was why Lilly felt pride. She had made a decision, held to it until temptation was obsolete. Now it no longer mattered. Even if she dashed from her office and found an airplane and reached Honolulu and Robert somehow had survived and she handed it to him. Even if all went perfectly and smoothly and the discovery worked. It. Simply. Was. Too. Late.

Lilly smiled. It was better this way. There were three great things one could accomplish once born into a world: create a new world, understand the present one, or destroy it. The first two were hard problems. But the last ... well, that had turned out to be easy. The Front didn't matter, it was a mindless phenomenon. It was *her* choice which had doomed mankind. She could take credit for ending the world, and nobody would dispute it.

Lilly walked to the closet and opened it. She surveyed the boxes: a week's worth of nutrition bars, vitamins, 64 gallons of water, a bucket in case the toilet backed up, lots of batteries for the flashlight, and some soap. Far more than necessary for the few days which remained. Her private bathroom likely would continue to function in a rudimentary capacity even after the water pressure vanished. She wouldn't look great or smell great by the end, but it didn't matter; she would look and smell far worse shortly after.

For the first time in many years she was alive, and would remain so for a few more days. That was all that counted. It would not do to die before her death. One task remained, but it was an important one. She would drink some Kool-Aid, after all. But only a small, manageable dose. She would force herself to believe that the world would have been saved if she told

Robert. That she had *accomplished* something by not doing so. For this, she had four more days.

Lilly picked up the folder. So little time, and so much to read.

CHAPTER 47

Day 0 — Near Oban, Scotland

The Horse's Head inn in Oban had all the trappings of an archetypal British pub. Nobody could accuse its stone exterior of having been manufactured, or even of the semblance of that regularity which defines modern manufacture. It had character, as an eager real estate broker would gush.

A large wooden door with an equally ponderous brass knocker, solely decorative, opened onto a pair of warmly lit rooms. The coarsely rustic wood interior, with hints of Dutch influence, framed a traditional counter replete with an array of fancifully crafted beer handles. While the top shelf boasted a range of Scotches in varying stages of depletion, the second was home to a regiment of Pimms bottles. A chaotic assortment of liquor, mostly unopened, constituted the afterthought of a bottom shelf.

As Rodney and Louise had discovered, this was one large distinction between British pubs and American bars. In America, the ditty had gone, "liquor before beer, you're in the clear; beer before liquor never been sicker." In Scotland, there was no need for such a mnemonic. The saying was, "beer before beer, then more beer."

The strength of the beer was another major difference, one the couple discovered after their first day hiking in Scotland. Everyone had raved about Scottish cider, and Rodney figured it would be refreshing to have a quick pint when they got back. Then they'd wash up, tear one off, and head for a well-earned dinner.

Unfortunately, there had been no washing, no sex, no dinner. Just sleep. It turned out that a British pint was 20 ounces, not a farcical American 16, and cider was twice as strong as beer, not half-as strong — a natural mistake for one only accustomed to its nonalcoholic namesake — and proper Scottish cider was stronger still.

Louise didn't mind, if she were to admit it. The prospect of a drawn out evening after the hike didn't really appeal to her. Nor did sex; she simply wasn't in the mood. In fact, she had been less and less in the mood as the trip progressed. It wasn't her time of month, it just wasn't her time. Nonetheless, skipping dinner wasn't to her liking, especially after all that exertion. She was upset with Rodney for having to have his stupid cider, and grateful that their accommodations included a full English breakfast the following morning. There was much eating and little talking during that meal. After all, what was there to say?

It took a few days before Rodney tried another cider. This time it was preceded by a quick post-hike nap and plenty of water, and they successfully made it to dinner. Despite the dire warnings they had received, both Louise and Rodney found British food quite to their liking. It differed from the subtle flavors of Northern Italian fare, and wasn't drawn from a lake of butter like French food. Those were cuisines designed to be eaten with wine.

Nobody would have accused British food of being either healthy or light, but it had one great asset: it went perfectly with beer. In fact, it often was cooked with, around, and in beer. While tastes certainly differ, Rodney and Louise began to suspect that they shouldn't listen too closely to those self-appointed arbiters from the Continent. No doubt, it was after careful consideration that they declared their own cuisines perfect and those of their dour Northern neighbors repugnant.

On their first evening in Oban, the couple dined on bangers and mash, a small pork pie, and a disturbingly tender piece of smoked salmon. Hiking builds an appetite, and they finished their meal with gusto before deciding to treat themselves to some Scotch. Scotch isn't really a digestif in the traditional sense; rather it is a jack of all trades, a renaissance drink that can fill all roles with verve.

There also is a world of difference between a Glenfiddich 12 and a Glenmorangie 18, despite the similar ring to the names. On the recommendation of the bartender, they ordered a couple of shots of a mid-range Scotch, Caol-something or other. It tasted like a bitter Bourbon to them, and they decided that Scotch was overrated. They'd stick with good old Jack.

After dinner, they decided to take a walk around town. Oban was a small village, even if an important tourist staging point. It consisted of little more than some ferry terminals, a few pubs, and a supermarket. There also was a scenic vantage point atop a nearby hill, which the guidebook had raved about. But after two weeks of real hiking, a local hangout for teens didn't really beckon. They decided to return to their room to plan the next day's activities, but ended up having an argument over whether to rent a car.

There are very few relationships which can survive travel, and fewer still that can survive an active outdoor vacation. It is easy enough to be on best behavior during a day trip or a weekend getaway. But when stuck with a person nonstop for weeks, subject to the stress of travel and possibly the physical strain and attendant setbacks of hiking, all the warts are visible. That smooth and perfect image, taken through a long lens and retouched by desire, yields to the grainy imperfections and blemishes of an unforgiving closeup. There is nothing that can be hidden, nowhere to hide it.

Snappiness, pettiness, selfishness, bitchiness, and all sorts of other 'nesses burst forth without warning, unable to endure their confinement a moment longer. Without the luxury of absence, small quibbles grow into resentments, arguments, fights. Problems can only fester, there is no room to maneuver, no convenient moment for an apology, for forgiveness. Traveling is an emotional prism of your future together. A wise couple takes this test early and often. If their bond endures, it may be love or a close enough approximation to suffice. Otherwise, it is best to tear off the scab, cauterize the wound, and heal before convenience and complacency and the fear of loneliness take two lives.

It had become clear to Louise and Rodney by the third day that their relationship would not survive the trial. It probably had been apparent before they even left New York, but after the first week abroad there could be no doubt. Still, the trip was booked, money spent. There is a short period when a relationship has failed the test, but traveling together still is better than traveling alone, and they were in it.

Even when visiting London, their interests had differed too much. This alone wasn't an issue, of course. Far more telling was that neither respected the other's interests, was willing to explore them, or patiently encourage them while quietly pursuing their own. Louise wanted to tour Parliament, Rodney was interested in the outdoor markets. He liked to have a nice dinner, she wanted to grab a bite here and there between activities. After several failed attempts at compromise, they settled on a few boring commonalities.

As a result, neither got to do what they wanted. They walked around a bit (though even *that* led to arguments about where to go), stopped in random places, and missed most of the grand attractions that London had to offer. All told, it was a very American vacation.

By the time their two weeks there drew to a close, they had exhausted conversation, and what promised to be a very romantic adventure had devolved into a platonic retreat. Privately, neither believed they even would manage to remain friends. Whenever Rodney opened his mouth, Louise pointed out that he was repeating the same story, and whenever Louise grew quiet and sullen, Rodney complained she was, "being that way again." The only hope that remained was the hiking part of the trip.

There are reasons to believe that, despite its inherent challenges, hiking briefly can revive a floundering relationship. Or at least redeem a dull vacation. Of course, that's only true when both wish it. When two people are placed in proximal stress or peril, they can bond. They can show their worst side, but also their best. It is quite the gamble, to be sure. But if the stakes are high, it is worth the attempt. To Rodney the stakes felt high. Louise just wanted to go home.

Nonetheless, they both found that the hiking part of the trip had a great deal to offer. They could spend large stretches of time lost in their own thoughts, while enjoying the spectacular scenery. There is a phenomenon in city life where a man and woman happen to walk side by side for a time en route to their respective destinations, often unaware of their apparent companion, while to observers they seem a couple. There also is its counterpart, where two who *are* a couple walk side by side, and each imagines themselves to be alone, wishes they were.

Louise and Rodney first had met two years earlier at a friend's party. Rodney had noticed her; Louise had noticed three guys, none of whom were Rodney. None of those three had returned her interest, and after several awkward attempts by Rodney, she agreed to date him.

It would not do to be without male companionship, and Rodney was male. Louise had expected to replace him with a more suitable boyfriend, and eventually work her way up to husband material. Instead, she found herself too busy and lazy to do so. He was there, a warm body next to her when she needed it, and he didn't demand too much. The actions of a city woman in her late 30s are driven by forces older and stronger than attraction or love.

At some point she probably would realize that time was running out, and end up in a tepid relationship with a man she didn't respect, let alone love, but who could give her children.

This was the pattern of most marriages she knew of, though she never had thought it would happen to her. *She* wasn't going to make the mistakes of her friends and settle. But, for all the pride and vanity and ambition, sooner or later everybody settles. Time sees to that. And she always could cheat on him if she found somebody better. Rodney was the type of spineless wimp who probably would blame himself. So far she hadn't cheated, though whether from lack of opportunity or for some other reason was unclear.

Rodney was not an outgoing man by nature. He had his fair share of relationships over the years, at least if one considers 3 or 4 fair. They all were ones he had stumbled into, and the woman usually took the lead in both initiating the relationship and terminating it. While he liked to believe that he was an enlightened man who appreciated emancipated women, at times he felt a marked lack of masculinity. He was passive. Perhaps not passive enough to get co-opted into marriage (not that anybody had offered), but certainly too passive to find somebody he really wanted.

At least until Louise. Her initial rejection had hurt, but there was something fulfilling about pursuing and "winning" her — if that's what lots of begging and wheedling that bordered on harassment could be termed. But she finally had agreed to go out with him, and now was his girlfriend. Yes, he had wooed and won her. She was the first girlfriend that actually caused his heart to pound, made him realize the basis for all those romantic cliches, that "love at first sight" was possible, even if a really bad idea.

The relationship had lasted as long as it had mainly because neither party required too much of the other. Neither insisted on living together, neither mentioned marriage, and neither made real demands on the other's time. Rodney never pressed for sex or acted resentful when denied it. He seemed grateful for whatever Louise acquiesced to.

Why it was the woman's decision when and how and where to have sex he never questioned, it was one of the many tenets of being a modern man. Besides, he had the vague sense that he did not rank amongst the great lovers. No, he was grateful for what he got and wouldn't risk driving her away by demanding more. And so things went, until he had the bright idea to take things to the "next level." To take a vacation together. Now, here they were.

On their third day in Oban, Rodney and Louise got up early. Last night's sex had been good. Not great, but good enough to rekindle a glimmer of hope. More important, it was unexpected; they hadn't made love in over a week. Rodney credited the hiking with sparking their passion, while Louise took a more pragmatic view.

Maybe he could be taught, she wondered. He never would be a real man, never would be attractive to her, but he *could* function as a passable vibrator. If the batteries weren't too expensive, that was. To him, last night meant they were capable of recapturing some small intimacy. Rodney was hopeful, Louise optimistic. She had settled to begin with, and was no longer convinced that her settlement wouldn't work. She conveniently forgot the feelings of the past three weeks and focused solely on her minor present content.

The couple made it downstairs around eight, in time for the complimentary breakfast. With another hike ahead of them, they decided to indulge in the full cooked offering.

"Full Cooked" means different things in different places. In Ireland, it technically includes eggs, toast, beans, cooked tomato, cooked mushrooms, bacon (actually a thick ham), breakfast sausages, and both black and white puddings. The Scottish variety dispenses with the white pudding and adds an oatcake, perfect for absorbing the grease. This was what they had, though Louise barely touched hers. She wasn't squeamish about the blood puddings, as are many Americans;

in fact, she had an adventurous palate and quite enjoyed even the oft-maligned haggis. However, filling up this early in the morning wasn't her habit. Rodney seemed to be enjoying himself, though, and she quietly sipped her coffee and ate a little yogurt.

Shortly after 8:30, a young couple came in and occupied a nearby table. From their accent, Louise could tell they were Scottish. Nonetheless, they probably were tourists if they were staying at the inn. The man was wearing jeans, a T-shirt, and a hoodie with the hood down. He was tall and wiry, almost handsome. The woman was a nondescript blonde, with a puffy face and bored look.

The man asked the waitress for a full cooked breakfast. She explained that they only served it until 8:30, pointing to a nearby clock for corroboration. It read 8:35. The waitress suggested that he still could have a continental breakfast, however. The guy started arguing with her, but she remained firm: no cooked breakfast after 8:30. The man grew louder and more plaintive, and the conversation concluded with the waitress walking off while he told her to go fuck herself.

That's not very polite, Louise thought. It's wrong for a man to treat a woman like that, even if she was being an inflexible jerk. The man had spread his legs out, slumped back into his seat with his arms crossed, and contented himself with staring menacingly at the walls. Louise avoided eye contact. Why didn't Rodney say something? She knew there was no point and that it wasn't his business, but resented him for not having sprung to the waitress's defense.

A man should have walked over and explained, "Hey Pal, that's no way to talk to a woman," backing this up physically if necessary. Instead, Rodney remained completely oblivious as he dug into his food. Louise gave a disgusted sigh, and looked at the disgruntled man. He was rubbing his legs restlessly and looking at the entrance to the kitchen, obviously waiting for the waitress to return so he could elaborate on just how she could fuck herself, in case she needed tips.

The girlfriend rolled her eyes. She seemed the eye-rolling type. Louise surmised that she had been doing so continuously the whole time, maybe even during her whole relationship with the man. He looked like the type of guy who inspired eye rolling. When the waitress didn't make an appearance, the man started muttering to himself. All Louise could make out were bits:

"... fucking shits ... "

"... time is so important ... "

"... paid my money ... "

"... fucking want my money ... "

"... show you time ... "

He made a V with his index and middle finger and thrust it up a couple of times in the direction of the kitchen, a distinctly British counterpart to the ever-elegant American middle finger. Then he stood up. "C'mon, let's go." His girlfriend, unwavering in her look of utter boredom, followed him out.

Louise wondered whether she really was bored, whether always wearing such a mask could make her boring. Perhaps the girl was filled with curiosity and life and excitement, but had feigned boredom for so long that it infected her, imprisoned her, became her. It didn't really matter, she decided. Time to hike.

"Are you ready?" she asked, looking up at Rodney. She suddenly had the disconcerting realization that he had been staring at her quietly for some time.

"What?" she demanded testily.

"Oh, nothing." He smiled and stood up. Something had flickered across his face, but she didn't know how to read it.

When they were packed and ready, Rodney and Louise loaded their rental car and took out the map. As always, Rodney was the driver. This had been one of their sources of contention. He insisted that he was qualified to drive on the left side of the road, just because he had a few days experience in the Virgin Islands. He refused to let Louise drive, even after she pointed out that she lived in Australia for six months.

Apparently, he felt it was the man's duty to drive. Or maybe it was a control thing. Who knew, with these wimpy, passive-aggressive sorts. Having seen him drive quite a bit, she knew herself to be much better. But he hadn't gotten into an accident, and she just put up with it.

The trailhead was just far enough from town that walking to it in addition to the hike itself would have proved untenable. Hence the car. It turned out to be quite straightforward to find the parking lot. One thing that could be said for trails in the UK: they were much more frequently used than those in the US. The start always was well marked, though the trail itself could be challenging to follow.

And with the rambling laws, there often *was* no trail for long stretches. It wasn't unusual to find oneself carefully hugging the edge of a field with a bull in it, or wondering if you would end up in a bog. Today's trail was neither dangerous nor difficult to follow, however. It started by a small road near a town named Druimnavuic, and quickly emerged from a wooded area onto the sort of expansive and eerily solitary landscape which characterizes the highlands of Scotland. From afar the terrain seemed to consist of gently sloping lawn, promising an easy and carefree stroll. Only up close did that quiet cover reveal itself to be a combination of tall grass and scrub, hiding an improbably marshy underbelly in places. An unwary walker who veered off-track easily could find himself knee deep in mud.

The notable mountains and hills of Scotland are divided into classes based on their Ordnance Survey heights. The 282 Munros are summits over 3000 feet (with an additional 227 non-peak "tops" that qualify), the 221 Corbetts are between

2500 and 3000 feet high (with at least a 500 foot "prominence" as their peak), and the 221 Grahams are between 2000 and 2499 feet (and with a drop of 492 feet on all sides).

The Corbet in question was Creach Bheinn, one of the easier climbs. They made the 4.3 mile journey in a little under 3 hours, the outer edge of the guidebook's estimated time. The view of Loch Creran from the top was spectacular, but they decided not to tarry. There was a steady wind up there, and they were sweaty from the climb. Even in August, a highland wind could chill. Besides, it was too early to stop for lunch. The hike was not a loop, and they could pick a spot from among the many beautiful vantage points they had passed along the path.

The way back was even more scenic than the way in, primarily because they no longer needed to turn to see the Loch and coast. There are few sights more entrancing than the crystal blue lakes nestled in the hills of Scotland. On this particular hike, they only had encountered a single small one of these, and were unsure whether it was a deep pond or merely a glorified puddle from the recent rain. Either way, Rodney had remarked it as an ideal spot for lunch.

Unfortunately, the wind had kicked up by that point, and a mist threatened. They had read about the deadly mists, descending without warning, enveloping, and freezing or misleading travelers. Rodney suspected that this was sensationalist hype, intended to sell books and scare tourists. There really was nothing dangerous in Scotland. How could there be? But Louise was adamant. She also had a tendency to chill faster, and was eager to get back to the car quickly even at the cost of lunch.

They had a minor spat over this. After some argument, Rodney told her just to continue on her own; he would eat and catch up. Louise gave him a withering look, and he quickly abandoned the notion. Meanwhile, it had grown even mistier and colder. Fortunately, this *wasn't* one of the deadly mists for which Scotland is notorious and which really *do* exist. It didn't blanket them in an opaque freezing cloud, but rather resembled a thick drizzle.

Rodney no longer was of a mind to disagree, and the two continued hiking. Though Louise had gotten her way, they maintained a sullen silence for the next hour. However, when the path began to descend they both expressed relief, and a gradual thaw in conversation ensued. Over the next half hour, the wind died down and conditions grew much more pleasant. The wooded area from which they had originated seemed quite close now, though they had enough experience to understand that appearances can be deceptive.

Now that they were warm again, Rodney insisted on stopping to eat. He made such a fuss that Louise finally agreed. Truth be told, she was hungry as well and rather glad that they had stopped. But she found it irritating that her companion was such a child. Either he should just stop and do what he wanted without her permission or he should be a gentleman and acquiesce without argument. She could respect either, but not the petulant whining. Was he going to convince her that she wanted to do something she didn't? How stupid.

It was a less scenic stretch or trail, and would not have been anybody's first choice for a lunch spot. They found a suitable nearby rock to sit on, and ate in stony irritation. Or at least *she* ate in stony irritation, he probably was oblivious and just thinking about whatever silly things he thought about when he wasn't annoying her.

After finishing his sandwich, Rodney walked a few dozen feet off-trail and behind a boulder to relieve himself. Louise still was upset, and decided to ignore him for the rest of the hike. Or maybe she should ignore him for the rest of her life. She was debating whether to endure the remainder of the trip or just cut her losses and head back to the States. If she didn't have to sleep with him or talk to him or deal with him, she still could enjoy the food and scenery, she supposed. But then, those conditions hardly were realistic. Louise hoisted her backpack on, and wiggled it to balance the load. As she adjusted the waist strap, Rodney startled her from behind.

"Hey, take a look."

Utterly oblivious, she sighed. Instinctively, Louise turned around. He was pointing toward something in the distance. She didn't really want to engage with him, but looked anyway. At first she couldn't see anything, and decided it probably was something stupid anyway. She was about to grace Rodney with a contemptuous eye roll, when she noticed it in the distance.

"That's odd," she observed.

The End

ACKNOWLEDGMENTS

This novel would not have come into being without the encouragement and inspiration of Meia G. She, more than anyone, convinced me to move beyond short works.

I'd also like to thank the beta readers who offered invaluable feedback and suffered through various iterations of this book. In addition to Meia, these include Ken O, Brian S, Patrick O, and Noel M, as well as my father and sister-in-law. My thanks also to the many others who helped with advice, encouragement, and understanding.

No acknowledgment would be complete without speaking to the substantial influence Naturi T has had on my writing over the years. She played a formative role in my growth as a writer, and I thank her for this.

Finally, I thank Scotland for sparing me some tiresome edits by not seceding from the UK before the publication of this novel.

Please do so soon, though.

ABOUT THE AUTHOR

K.M. Halpern was born in New York and, after spending far too much time there, finally returned to the Cambridge, MA he knew and loved from graduate school. Unfortunately, all that remained was a large Starbucks, several thousand bank branches, and two small universities whose names he forgets.

He divides his time between various ill-considered technical endeavors and various ill-considered literary ones. His current projects include a forthcoming book of very short works (*The Way Around*), a fantasy thriller series centered around a seemingly indestructible woman, and a book of pretentious and largely dystopian short stories (tentatively titled *Sjow*).

Ken holds a PhD in theoretical physics from MIT, more commonly known as 'that odd cluster of concrete buildings on the Charles River.' He may be found at www.kmhalpern.com (writing-related), www.aplaceofsand.com (general), and generating very small gravitational waves around town.

OTHER WORKS BY K.M. HALPERN

THE MAN WHO STANDS IN LINE

Killer flies, amorous dinosaurs, angry buildings, and one very large fish — all in a single volume. This quirky collection of flash fiction, vignettes, and poetry is variously absurd, dark, and comic. A monstrous blister, the secret to immortality, and a lost piece of brain are just a few other oddities one will encounter in this one-of-a-kind book.

"...the lasting impression of the writing within is without question. Don't let their brevity fool you; these works are tenacious, earnest, and overflowing with gloom."

— *Kirkus Review*

Available through Amazon, B&N, and bookstores everywhere.

THE WAY AROUND

More absurd, horrifying, and downright inexplicable shorts. These include such soon-to-be classics as Buzz-Saw Bob, the sport of pendulum watching, yet another secret to ultimate success, how to tend a garden with extreme prejudice, and Buddha's morning commute. We can't promise this book will make you excel in every possible way, but we can't promise it won't either.

COMING SOON

Visit www.kmhalpern.com
Subscribe for updates, special offers, and bonus short stories!